medical Good Thriller E. E. MD

INTENSIVE FEAR

"And there are other things . . ."

Somewhere inside Stephanie's brain a small light went on—Mike was talking about things that reflected some of her own anxieties at work—*I don't know everything that goes on here . . . And quite frankly, I don't want to.*

Then, as if he were pulling it all together for the first time, Mike told her about Pauline Minsky. At first Mike hadn't even considered that her death was anything more than a sad and unexpected misfortune, but now he wasn't so sure.

"It's very confusing," he said. "Everything feels off balance—I don't know what's really happening here. I don't even know who I can trust and who I can't, and who's being truthful and who isn't. All I know is that something very strange is going on, and I have to find out what it is."

Stephanie reached over again and gently took Mike's hand. He leaned forward a little, and she did the same, until their faces were only a few inches apart.

"I'm getting scared," she said.

store

D1472404

3081

Ⓞ SIGNET

COMPELLING MEDICAL DRAMAS
BY FRANCIS ROE

☐ **SECOND OPINION** When Dr. Simeon Halstead meets with teenage Andy Markle and his mom, Fiona, the diagnosis he has for young Andy is grim: a deadly brain tumor. While ignoring his private life and his wife's shocking betrayals, Simeon is racing against time to find a cure for Andy.   (185064—$5.99)

☐ **THE SURGEON** Dr. Paula Cairns is on the verge of making her dreams come true when she wins a fierce competition for a post at New Coventry Medical Center. But what Paula does not count on is a sophisticated scam in a medical center where base desires often come before dedication and duty.   (180240—$5.99)

☐ **DANGEROUS PRACTICES** Doctors and lawyers—in a scorching novel of passion and power, where their medical secrets and legal manipulations will keep you turning pages until its last shocking revelations.
(177908—$5.99)

☐ **INTENSIVE CARE** A beautiful woman and her doctor—a novel of love and scandal. . . . "Fascinating!"—Tony Hillerman.   (172825—$5.99)

☐ **DOCTORS AND DOCTORS' WIVES** Greg Hopkins and Willie Stringer, two powerful and dedicated doctors, find their friendship shattered by personal and professional rivalries. A masterful medical drama, this novel vividly portrays the lives and loves of doctors and their fascinating, high-pressure world.
(169107—$5.99)

*Prices slightly higher in Canada

Buy them at your local bookstore or use this convenient coupon for ordering.

PENGUIN USA
P.O. Box 999 — Dept. #17109
Bergenfield, New Jersey 07621

Please send me the books I have checked above.
I am enclosing $_____ (please add $2.00 to cover postage and handling). Send check or money order (no cash or C.O.D.'s) or charge by Mastercard or VISA (with a $15.00 minimum). Prices and numbers are subject to change without notice.

Card #_____ Exp. Date _____
Signature_____
Name_____
Address_____
City _____ State _____ Zip Code _____

For faster service when ordering by credit card call **1-800-253-6476**

Allow a minimum of 4-6 weeks for delivery. This offer is subject to change without notice.

UNDER THE KNIFE

Francis Roe

AN ONYX BOOK

ONYX
Published by the Penguin Group
Penguin Putnam Inc., 375 Hudson Street,
New York, New York 10014, U.S.A.
Penguin Books Ltd, 27 Wrights Lane,
London W8 5TZ, England
Penguin Books Australia Ltd, Ringwood,
Victoria, Australia
Penguin Books Canada Ltd, 10 Alcorn Avenue,
Toronto, Ontario, Canada M4V 3B2
Penguin Books (N.Z.) Ltd, 182–190 Wairau Road,
Auckland 10, New Zealand

Penguin Books Ltd, Registered Offices:
Harmondsworth, Middlesex, England

First published by Onyx, an imprint of Dutton NAL,
a member of Penguin Putnam Inc.

First Printing, May, 1998
10 9 8 7 6 5 4 3 2 1

Copyright © Francis Roe, 1998
All rights reserved

 REGISTERED TRADEMARK—MARCA REGISTRADA

Printed in the United States of America

Without limiting the rights under copyright reserved above, no part of this publication may be reproduced, stored in or introduced into a retrieval system, or transmitted, in any form, or by any means (electronic, mechanical, photocopying, recording, or otherwise), without the prior written permission of both the copyright owner and the above publisher of this book.

PUBLISHER'S NOTE
This is a work of fiction. Names, characters, places, and incidents either are the product of the author's imagination or are used fictitiously, and any resemblance to actual persons, living or dead, events, or locales is entirely coincidental.

BOOKS ARE AVAILABLE AT QUANTITY DISCOUNTS WHEN USED TO PROMOTE PRODUCTS OR SERVICES. FOR INFORMATION PLEASE WRITE TO PREMIUM MARKETING DIVISION, PENGUIN PUTNAM INC., 375 HUDSON STREET, NEW YORK, NEW YORK 10014.

If you purchased this book without a cover you should be aware that this book is stolen property. It was reported as "unsold and destroyed" to the publisher and neither the author nor the publisher has received any payment for this "stripped book."

Prologue

Altimeter to gyro compass—Dr. Fred Newsome glanced at the instruments, as he had done every few minutes since taking off from New Coventry airport a half hour earlier. Altitude was steady at 4,500 feet, on course at 348 degrees. For a second Fred looked out through the rain-spattered Plexiglas. The weather was overcast and deteriorating, and an inversion haze cut the visibility down to between two and three miles, not enough for accurate visual navigation. Overall, though, Fred wasn't too worried. He knew the terrain, and he'd done this trip to Bennington, Vermont, before.

Not for this reason, though. Before, it had just been a matter of old friends getting together for a couple of drinks and reminiscences, but this time he was going to get Paul's advice. He needed it. Badly.

A puff of thin white cloud whipped past, then another. The weather forecast had predicted increasingly thick stratocumulus topping out at eighteen thousand feet, too high to fly above in his unpressur-

ized Cessna 177B. A cluster of raindrops hit the
windshield and slid off to the sides under the pressure of the outside wind.

Altitude—a downdraft dropped the plane to 4,200
feet, so Fred eased gently back on the yoke. The nose
came up a little; there was no visible horizon, and
he made the adjustment more by feel and experience
than from what the instruments were telling him.
Back at 4,500 feet within a minute, he settled back,
trying to enjoy the flight. Usually flying was a relax-
ation for Fred. By instinct and training he was careful
to the point of obsessiveness, and much of his enjoy-
ment came from the meticulous attention he devoted
to what he was doing and the care he took in doing
it exactly right.

He glanced at the fuel gauges. Time to switch
tanks in about ten minutes, he figured, to keep the
plane balanced. On a light plane like this, weight
distribution had to be kept well in mind.

Below him and to his right, he caught a dull flash
of gray water surrounded by dark green trees and
patches of snow. That would be the Cobble Mountain
reservoir, he figured, peering down. Man, it looked
cold down there. Snow-covered ice stretched out for
about fifty feet from the banks, making a wavy rim
along the edge of the reservoir, which was shrouded
in mist.

The lines in Fred's craggy face deepened. Would
Paul be able to help him? Paul was a surgeon, too,
and, like Fred, was the head of his group practice.
Bennington wasn't a big medical center like New

Coventry, but jealousies and back-stabbings occurred everywhere, and Fred knew that Paul had had his share.

But Fred's group was in open revolt, led, it seemed by Dermott Spencer, Fred's friend and long-time partner. What Spencer and the others were proposing was nothing less than caving in to the pressures exerted by the medical center, the other hospitals such as Lovejoy, the insurance companies, and the big local corporations. All of these wanted to trap the doctors into HMOs, involve them in contract medicine and managed care, all things that Fred abhorred.

"You're wanting us to give up our independence," Fred had told his rebellious group at their last meeting. "Do you realize what you're suggesting? If we go along with this, we'll be nothing more than a bunch of employees at the whim of the insurance companies, gratefully taking whatever pittance they throw our way. Is that what you guys want? You want some utilization reviewer with a high school education telling you who you can operate on and who you can't? No, thank you. And what's more, I'm not going to allow you to wreck this practice, not while I'm still around, no sir."

The problem, as Dermott Spencer had carefully pointed out, was that all the other medical and surgical groups in New Coventry had been forced to toe the line, just as they had elsewhere across the country. Fred had refused to join any major medical plan, and now they were out of the loop. Not so long ago his group had been one of the busiest and most powerful in New Coventry, but now they were in deep financial trouble, and it was getting worse.

Paul had dealt with a similar revolt within his own group, and Fred wanted the details of how he'd done it.

Fuel—time to switch tanks. Fred checked the gauges. The left tank was about one-third full now, and the right one was full. There was plenty of fuel on board, even if Bennington was closed in and he had to turn back. He reached over to the floor-mounted selector valve and turned it clockwise so that the arrow pointed to the right-hand tank.

Trouble came without any warning a few moments later. The engine suddenly coughed, causing the whole plane to shudder, then caught again, but only for a moment, making the tachometer needle jerk violently from side to side. Startled, Fred checked the fuel gauge, made sure that the engine primer was fully in and locked, and that the ignition switch hadn't somehow turned off. He pushed the throttle fully forward to try to clear the fuel channel, but after a few more jolting coughs, the engine stopped. The sudden silence was deafening—the propeller slowed and was now windmilling in front of him, pushed around by the force of the wind, not by the motor. Thinking there must be a malfunction in the fuel-delivery system from the right tank, Fred rotated the selector valve back to the left tank and hit the ignition switch. The starter motor whined, but the engine didn't restart. It was either an electrical failure or fuel wasn't getting into the carburetor, but whichever it was, Fred realized that within a very short time he was going to have to make an emergency landing. Peering out, all he could see now were tree-covered hills some 3,000 feet below him, a wooden lookout tower on a high point, a few straight forest roads, not nearly wide enough to land on. Fred could feel panic rising in his chest. He'd often practiced forced landings, but he had never had to do a real one.

He checked his airspeed. He was now down to seventy knots, below his maximum-range speed, and too close to the stalling speed. He put the nose down, and the hissing wind picked up again. Desperately, he went through the procedures to restart the engine, but the prop just spun passively around. He turned his transmitter to the emergency frequency and pressed the call button on the control column. He made the mayday call, giving his location as close as he could. His altitude was now only a couple of thousand feet above the ground, and the needle was working its way counterclockwise faster than he liked. Down below, through the mist, he saw what looked like a clearing in the forest. Maybe he could land there . . . keeping his eyes on the spot because he knew that in a few seconds it would vanish behind him into the mist, he banked sharply, hoping to get into a position from which he could make some sort of landing at the slowest possible speed. Intent on his maneuver, and deep into the turn, Fred didn't see the airspeed indicator needle sliding into the stall zone until suddenly the warning horn

sounded in his ear. At the same moment the controls
went floppy and the left wing dropped suddenly, at
which point Fred realized that he was about to go
into a spin. Sweating with fear, he fought the controls, applied the proper corrective maneuvers, nose
down, hard right rudder, but he didn't have enough
altitude. For twelve long seconds he fought the controls and screamed while the ground rushed up at
him, twisting and spiraling around and around as
the plane spun faster.

About a half mile away, Doran Koslowsky, a forestry worker who was standing at the outside controls of his truck, tipping gravel for a new logging
road, heard the engine splutter and saw the plane
bank sharply before it went behind some trees. The
next thing he saw was a fireball suddenly erupting
on the side of the next hill, and a few moments later
heard the sound of the explosion, a deep *thump*
above the whine of his hydraulic lift. A small flock
of starlings, alarmed, rose from the nearby trees and
flew off over his head.

Doran's instinct was to get in the cab and drive to
the scene, but the road ended where he was standing,
and the truck wouldn't go ten yards into the snowy
underbrush before getting hopelessly stuck.

It took twenty minutes to drive back down to the
forestry office, by which time only a small black
plume of smoke rising through the trees indicated
the site of the disaster, and another hour and a half
elapsed before the state police arrived. By then it was
dark and the rain was beating down, and they

weren't able to reach the crash site until almost ten o'clock that night. Once they established that there were no survivors, they left one trooper on guard, reported their findings to the State Aviation Department and the NTSB, the National Transportation Safety Board, and went home.

Chapter 1

Mike Richmond sat on the narrow wooden bench between the two rows of white-painted lockers, still in his O.R. greens. He'd just finished a case, and part of his mind was thinking about possible postoperative complications and whether he should keep the patient in the I.C.U. for a while, which would temporarily free up a surgical bed.

He pulled off his paper mask, hood, and bootees, dropped them in the basket, then walked out of the locker room back to the O.R. desk.

Darla Finsten, the operating room supervisor, looked up. God, he's big, she thought, and wondered what he'd be like in bed.

"I'm looking for Terry Catlin," she said. "Have you seen him?"

"No. He's probably sleeping in the on-call room." Mike leaned forward on the counter.

"Dermott Spencer needs an assistant. He's doing an emergency gallbladder and Catlin's on call," she replied, reaching for the phone.

"I'll take care of it," said Mike, before she had time to dial. "Catlin was up most of the night. Let him sleep."

Darla glanced up at Mike, and her hand hovered uncertainly over the phone. She knew there was no love lost between Terry Catlin and Mike Richmond, and Mike was not likely to be doing Catlin a favor.

At that moment the door to the main corridor opened, and Dermott Spencer came into the operating suite, already in his greens. Good-looking, cheerful, in his early fifties, he had thick, carefully styled white hair that shone like a halo in the fluorescent light above the desk. Spencer was the senior partner of one of the busiest and most lucrative medical-surgical practices in the city. He didn't often operate here at the New Coventry Medical Center; most of his group's patients went to the neighboring Lovejoy Hospital.

"I'll be helping you with your case, Dr. Spencer," said Mike before Darla could say anything.

"Good." He gave Mike a quizzical glance, looked momentarily at the residents' on-call schedule taped to the wall. He grinned, then turned to Darla. "Are we ready to go?"

"In about five minutes, Dr. Spencer. The patient's in the room already, and Dr. Pinero's putting her to sleep."

A few minutes later, Mike was standing next to Dermott Spencer at the sinks in the scrub room. The noise of water was loud, and he had to raise his normally quiet voice over it.

"Who's the patient?" he asked.

"Florence DiGiovanni."

"The governor's wife?" Mike stopped scrubbing

for a moment and looked through the window into the operating room. There was nothing much to be seen; the patient was already on the table, anesthetized and being draped by the techs. Even for Dermott Spencer, surgeon to the Connecticut upper crust, this was an important patient.

"Yes. I could hardly refuse *her*." Spencer grinned a bit self-consciously, holding his hand under the Betadine dispenser. He turned the water faucet on with his knee. "We're going to use the 'scope," he said.

Mike nodded, and sighed quietly to himself. Spencer usually did only breast surgery and was probably not up to date in the changing techniques of laparoscopic surgery. Teaching junior residents was one thing, but having to nurse an attending through an unfamiliar procedure was going to be a chore. But he didn't mind the challenge—it might even work out to his advantage.

Mike finished scrubbing, turned off the faucet, and headed for the door, hands raised, wondering if Spencer knew how much trouble he could get into if he wasn't thoroughly familiar with laparoscopic technique.

A moment later Spencer followed him into the O.R. "I haven't done many of these," he confided to Mike. Now they were gowned and gloved and had taken up their positions on each side of the patient. "I did the laparoscopy training session, of course," Spencer went on, "but that was about a year ago, and I guess the technology's changed a bit."

Spencer turned his head to look over the instruments on the sterile tray. "I don't see the laser probe," he said after a moment.

The scrub tech said nothing but looked over at Mike, embarrassed.

"We don't use the laser probe much now," Mike said carefully, choosing his words. "It cuts nicely, but we mostly use the electrocautery because it gives better hemostasis."

"Good," said Spencer. "That darn laser inside the belly—it always made me nervous."

Not much had been said, but already a strange atmosphere of insecurity was developing in the O.R., always a sensitive place for collective feelings. When the patient was a prominent person, as in this case, there was a heightened awareness of the dangers involved in surgery, and everyone from the anesthesiologist to the circulating nurse was affected. But today it was clear that Spencer, a respected and highly competent surgeon in his own field, was not fully in charge of the situation.

Dr. Pinero, the senior anesthetist, looked out of his pouchy old eyes over the ether screen at Spencer, and was relieved that Mike Richmond would be assisting him.

After checking the light source and making sure that the tiny video camera was working, Spencer took the scalpel and made a small incision on the left side of the umbilicus, then reached for the sharp, foot-long Verris needle, preparatory to injecting carbon dioxide gas into the abdominal cavity, which would then inflate like a balloon. Just in time Mike grabbed the loose skin of the patient's belly and pulled it up, a precautionary measure to make sure that Spencer wouldn't damage the internal organs when he pushed into the abdomen with the sharp needle.

"Yeah, right, thanks, Michael," said Spencer, glancing over his mask at his assistant. "We don't want to run into any trouble with this particular patient."

Mike attached the carbon-dioxide line, turned it on, and they watched the patient's abdomen swell up, making a gas-filled cavern above the internal organs. Then Spencer replaced the needle with a wider, pointed trocar inside a metal tube and removed the sharp trocar, leaving the tube as a conduit into the abdominal cavity, now distended with gas. The scrub tech handed him the long scope, which he pushed through the tube. The monitor screen lit up, and they watched the image as the tiny TV camera on the end of the scope scanned the inside of the patient's belly. Spencer was concerned that he might have done some damage with the super-sharp Verris needle or the trocar, but everything looked intact.

Mike watched the big TV monitor set up to the right of the anesthesiologist's station.

"Does it look okay to you?" Spencer's voice was muffled by his mask, but it sounded hesitant, unsure.

"Just fine," said Mike.

Spencer was nervous enough so that his faint tremor made the magnified image on the screen shake slightly. He made three more small incisions, two below the breastbone for long forceps to hold each end of the gallbladder, the other for the cautery, used to cut the gallbladder's tight attachments to the liver before dissecting it out.

By the time all the instruments were in position, Spencer had settled down, and for a while the operation progressed smoothly enough.

"Did you hear the story about the construction guy who was hired to frame a house?" asked Spencer after they had been working in silence for some minutes.

Mike shook his head. At this point he didn't particularly want to hear one of Spencer's stories, although they were usually funny enough.

"Well, the guy was taking nails out of his bag and hammering them into the frame, and the foreman was watching him," said Spencer, still working, his eyes on the monitor. "Every so often the guy would take a nail out of his bag, look at it, and throw it away."

As he talked, Spencer clipped and cut the artery to the gallbladder, and was clearing off the cystic duct, the communication between the gallbladder and the main bile-carrying system that passed from the liver into the intestine.

"After a while the foreman comes over and asks why he's throwing away perfectly good nails. 'Some of them have the head on the wrong end,' the guy told him. The foreman takes a deep breath, and says, "You idiot! Those are for the other side of the house!' "

Mike grinned, but his eyes were fixed on the monitor. One of the problems with this particular video system was that the color definition wasn't good enough to distinguish between bile and blood, both of which had the same reddish color on the screen. And he knew already that something was wrong. The suction apparatus was going almost continually to keep the operative field clear, while Spencer went on dissecting the gallbladder off the liver with the cautery. Every few moments there would be a small puff of smoke inside the abdomen when he cauterized a blood vessel. The normal procedure was to pause occasionally to check the area for bleeding or other problems, but Spencer just went on with his dissection. Mike said nothing, did his job, pulled on the gallbladder with the long forceps, moving it from side to side so that Spencer could get at the sides with the cautery to cut and coagulate the small arteries and veins between the gallbladder and the liver.

Finally Mike said, in a neutral tone, "The suction's been on a lot, Dr. Spencer."

"That's okay," said Spencer. "The gallbladder's very inflamed, and there's a lot of tissue fluid. That's why I scheduled Florence as an emergency."

Mike's impression was that the gallbladder was only moderately inflamed, and they would have seen any excess of tissue fluid when first examining the inside of the abdomen through the scope. He could feel the scrub tech's eyes boring into him. The tech knew that something wasn't right, but it wasn't his place to say anything.

"Her blood pressure's falling," said Gabe Pinero, getting up suddenly from his stool on the other side of the ether screen. "Started at a hundred and thirty over eighty; now it's ninety over fifty. Just in the last minute." He muttered something to his assistant, who hung up a second bag of saline.

The tension in the room took a quantum jump, and although Spencer kept on dissecting the gallbladder, his own anxiety was visibly increasing.

"There's a lot of blood coming up through the suction," said the circulating nurse, looking up from the twin bottles of the suction system. She spoke to Mike, instinctively realizing that he was the one who understood best what was going on, although Spencer was far senior to him.

Spencer paused. Sweat was forming on his forehead and soaking the edge of his paper cap. "What do you think?" he asked Mike. His voice was almost unrecognizable.

"Maybe we should take a look at the stump of the artery," murmured Mike. "Maybe that let go, or one of the veins."

"Good thought," said Spencer. He moved the scope to search for the artery to the gallbladder, which he had previously clipped and cut, but now the entire area was awash in blood and no anatomical structures were visible. The suction apparatus was pumping at full capacity, but it wasn't coping with the amount of blood collecting inside the patient's belly.

"You might want to hang up a couple of units of blood, Dr. Pinero," said Mike very quietly over the screen. "It may take a little while to fix this."

"Maybe we should abort the laparoscopy and open her up the normal way," said Spencer. "I don't feel comfortable taking out a gallbladder without being able to see and touch the damn thing."

"Let's get a second suction apparatus," suggested Mike. "I'm sure we can take care of this." He nodded at the circulator, who pulled the plastic cover off a new suction apparatus and hooked it up. It took a little while, but the suction was now strong enough to cope with the bleeding, and the structures of the abdomen were beginning to appear like islands in a sea of blood.

"It's like watching the tide going out," said Spencer, looking at the monitor, trying to reestablish control over himself and the situation.

"There." A small fountain appeared in the depth of the field, like a miniature geyser under the surface. Mike had gently taken over the scope, and now he trained it on the jet of blood. "Suction, right there," he said. "Yes, it's the cystic artery. The clips must have come off." Without waiting for Spencer, Mike took the long forceps and grabbed the open, bleeding end of the artery. After that temporary maneuver, it took only a few moments for the two suction machines to clear the field.

"Clips," said Mike, and the scrub tech handed the instrument to him. Mike passed it through the metal cannula and applied two clips across the end of the artery in such a way that they couldn't possibly be dislodged. "Bleeding's stopped," he told Gabe Pinero, who was already pumping blood from a transfusion bag into the patient's veins.

"Good. Her pressure's going back up. She's okay

at this end." Gabe Pinero sounded tired but confident. He had a reputation for being unflappable even in the most hair-raising situations.

"We're almost done," Mike said cheerfully. "We just need to get that gallbladder out." He passed the scope back to Spencer as if he'd simply been doing a minor chore for his boss.

It took only a few minutes more to finish the operation, but Spencer looked shaken and said very little until after the dressings had been applied and the patient was being wheeled to the recovery room. Together they walked behind the stretcher.

"Thanks for your help," he said to Mike very quietly. "And I won't be doing gallbladder surgery again, not even if it's the president's wife begging me on bended knee."

A couple of minutes later, after Spencer had gone and Mike was writing post-op orders in the chart, the recovery room door opened and Terry Catlin strode in. He came up to Mike, his face white with rage. He was tall but not as big, and was usually careful about what he said to Mike. But this time he was too furious to care. "You goddamned sonofabitch," he said, spatters of saliva coming out with his words, "you stole that case from me. You knew I was on call and I'd want to do it."

Unperturbed, Mike looked up at him and grinned. "Take it easy, Catlin," he said. "It was a tough case, and you couldn't have handled it anyway."

Chapter 2

Dermott Spencer left the O.R. suite through the automatic doors and headed for the waiting room, making an effort to pull himself together. He certainly hadn't distinguished himself back there, he reflected. His palms were still wet from tension, and he wiped them down the sides of his green scrub pants. It was bad enough getting himself in trouble in the operating room, something that hadn't happened to him in years, but to have to be extricated by one of the residents . . . He blushed with annoyance and embarrassment. He was just lucky that it was Mike Richmond who'd been helping him.

Mike Richmond. Spencer knew of Richmond's rivalry with Terry Catlin—in fact, Spencer and his partners had in some sense encouraged it. Richmond and Catlin were both due to finish the residency program in a few weeks, and they both knew that Spencer's group was looking for a new partner. Catlin was no mean contender for the job—he was as smart and as hardworking although technically not as adept as Mike Richmond, and he tended to be a bit high-handed with his patients. But unlike Richmond,

Catlin had a powerful father, a state senator, and some of the partners felt that weighed strongly in Catlin's favor. Spencer quickly reviewed what he knew about Mike. He was a good surgeon, technically very capable, usually easy to get along with although occasionally stubborn. He was generally well liked, and physically he certainly stood out in the crowd. And he had endurance. All surgical residents had to have endurance, but like the drummer in the battery ads, Richmond just kept going, and that was a huge point in his favor.

Best of all, he was hungry. Mike's father had owned a successful precision-tool shop near Boston, but lost everything at the tables in Atlantic City and Las Vegas. Then he got sick, and although his mother went back to work as a part-time accountant, they didn't have enough to get the best care, and not nearly enough to pay for the care he did get. Spencer knew that Mike's father was dead, but he didn't know how. Late one night, sick and emaciated, Robert Weston Richmond had climbed painfully out of bed, got into his car, and drove that old familiar route to Atlantic City, then at break of light crashed through a fence on to the boardwalk, drove along a pier, accelerating all the way, and with a spectacular dive into the water, he symbolically waved a single digit at the city that had destroyed him and at the same time ended his pain, frustration, and misery. What Spencer did know was that Mike's dad had left him an awesome load of debt, and Mike, who had just started med school, worked as a bouncer in a bar on Tremont Street in Boston's war zone, and spent his summers installing X-ray equipment in hospitals. Spencer recalled once asking Mike about a round white scar on the back of his hand. "Somebody accidentally hit the on switch," Mike replied, "while I was attaching a high-tension cable on an MRI unit."

Desperate for money, Mike also sold his AB-group blood to the blood bank, and eventually got a part-time job there. He wasn't married, but he liked women, and they certainly liked him. Now Mike's passion was old cars, an expensive pastime. Yes, thought Spencer, Mike Richmond would do nicely, but he'd have to discuss it with his colleagues and win over the ones who would be rooting for Catlin.

In the waiting room Spencer found Judy Powell, Florence's personal secretary, talking in a low voice with one of Governor Jack DiGiovanni's aides. They both stood up when Spencer came in.

"Florence is just fine," he told them. "Everything went very nicely. I expect she'll be able to go home tonight or tomorrow at the latest."

"That's wonderful," said Judy, her large brown eyes gazing at Spencer with great respect. "My mother had gallbladder surgery a few years ago, and she was in the hospital for over a week."

"Things have changed quite a bit since then," replied Spencer, smiling confidently but thinking that maybe some things had changed a bit too fast. "With our new laparoscopic techniques, we can get our patients home quicker, and the surgery's a lot easier on them, too."

Before going back to his office, Spencer stopped in the recovery room. Mike was there, writing a brief operation note in the chart. Strictly speaking, it was Spencer's job to do that, and he appreciated that Mike was taking the time to do it.

"I've dictated the operation report," Mike told him, looking up over the chart. Spencer nodded, knowing that Mike would have worded it carefully.

"And she's stable," Mike went on, glancing over at the sleeping patient.

"She lost quite a bit of blood," said Spencer.

"We just did a 'crit,'" replied Mike. "And the lab called back a minute ago. It was thirty-nine, no sweat."

Spencer went over to check Florence's pulse. The overhead monitor showed that her heartbeat was regular and her pressure was satisfactory. Florence woke up at his touch, stared at him for a second, then smiled.

"It feels better already," she said. Her voice was hoarse, and she licked her dry lips before repeating what she'd said. "Thanks, Spencer. You're the greatest." Then she went back to sleep.

Spencer's confidence started to come back as he walked back toward the changing room. He had three breast cases scheduled for the afternoon over at Lovejoy Hospital, where he did most of his operations. With these cases he would be in familiar surgical territory, and he knew he wouldn't run into any problems.

That had been a very satisfactory move, he reflected, transferring the practice to Lovejoy Hospital. For many years Lovejoy had been a private institution that served the wealthier citizens of New Coventry, but a couple of years previously it had run into severe financial problems, failed to meet the Joint Commission and State accreditation standards, and lost its federal and state funding. Spencer grinned wryly to himself. It hadn't been the best of times for his own group practice, either. Anyway, on the brink of bankruptcy, Lovejoy had been sold and totally overhauled. All the administrators and most of the department heads had been fired and replaced, and it now rivaled its neighbor, the world-famous New Coventry Medical Center. Lovejoy's new administration had wooed the big medical groups in town, offering substantial incentives to join it, and for a variety of reasons it had targeted Spencer's group first. After they joined, others had followed. Now Lovejoy was making money hand over fist, and, Spencer reflected, that was good for everyone except the medical center.

At five o'clock that afternoon, Spencer met with the members of his group's executive committee in the conference room of their penthouse suite, on the twenty-second floor of the Hartmann Building, a luxurious addition to the skyline of New Coventry. Only a few of the most successful medical groups could afford the rents there, and most of the space was rented to major stockbrokers, a few big corporate law firms, and the offices of prestigious local corporations.

"There's one other thing," said Spencer after they had taken care of their other business. He told them about his experience with Mrs. DiGiovanni's gallbladder operation. "As you know," he said, "we've been short a general surgeon since Fred Newsome died. We've talked about getting a replacement, and narrowed it down to a couple of candidates. I think it's time to make a decision, and after seeing the way he handled things this morning, I think we should hire Mike Richmond."

"What about Terry Catlin?" asked Lou Gardner, one of the internists. "He's as good as Richmond, and his father is Bruce Catlin, the state senator. Now, that's a man who wields a lot of clout, and he could be very useful to us."

"It's not about his dad," replied Spencer, smiling. He knew that Gardner was committed to Catlin, and he didn't want to antagonize him. "And we all like Terry a lot, but my strong feeling is that Mike's the better surgeon of the two, and that feeling is shared by the other surgeons here." He glanced at Derek Provost and Chas Miller. "But we may have an opening for another surgeon in the near future," he went on to placate Lou. "Our work is building up faster than we can handle it."

"Mike Richmond would be fine with me," said Derek Provost. "He's good, and . . . well, I'd trust him in this group sooner than Catlin." He looked around. Everybody knew what he meant. Derek had been chief resident when Mike was an intern, and knew him better than the others.

"I don't agree. Several of us on the medical side feel that Catlin would fit in better with us," said Lou Gardner stubbornly. He obviously wasn't happy, but he knew that the surgeons would be making the final decision, and they seemed to be solidly behind Richmond, so there wasn't much he could do about it.

Spencer had anticipated this problem.

"Nothing's engraved in marble, Lou," he said. "For one thing, Mike wouldn't come in as a full partner, and if he didn't work out, we could simply get rid of him."

Lou shrugged. He knew that once the candidate was in the group, he would be there permanently unless something catastrophic happened.

"We can put him on probation for six months," Spencer went on. "Then on salary for a year, and after that, if he turns out to be as good as I think he will, he can start buying into the group, so it could be several years before he became a full partner."

"Do you think he'll fit in?" Dan Bentley, one of the internists, sounded doubtful. "After all, we're not exactly just any medical group."

"He'll fit in," replied Spencer confidently. "Remember, he's been our resident, and we've been working with him for four years now. We know what he's made of."

Derek turned to Spencer. "I agree with you that Mike's the outstanding candidate, but I heard he might be going to work in Caleb Winter's research lab for a year."

"Mike wants this job so bad he'd kill for it," replied Spencer very deliberately. "Sure, Cal Winter would like to have him, and we all know Mike talked to him. Mike also made sure we heard about it. He's pulling out every stop to get on board, including stealing my case from Catlin this morning. So let's keep it under advisement right now and see how he handles the fallout from this case. Because for sure there'll be some."

"Fine with me," said Derek. "That should be a good test of character."

Spencer glanced around, satisfied. "Good. We'll get Carl's people to do a security check on him, then, assuming he's cleared, all of us should have a chance to interview him. Is that agreeable to everyone?"

"Okay," said Lou, obviously still far from convinced. "But you all know how careful we need to be."

Chapter 3

Florence DiGiovanni was still asleep in the recovery room when Evie Gaskell, one of the O.R. nurses who'd been on the case, came by to see how she was doing.

"Florence okay?" she asked Susanne Hecht, the recovery-room nurse assigned to Florence. At that moment Susanne was changing an I.V. bag, and the slight movement woke Florence up although she didn't open her eyes.

"Yeah. She's asleep but doing good. How did it go in the O.R.?"

"Okay. Eventually."

"Eventually?"

"Well, you know, Spencer doesn't really know a laparoscope from a proctoscope," said Evie. "Luckily Mike Richmond was there."

"What happened?"

"Nothing much. Just a major hemorrhage from the cystic artery. If Mike hadn't been there, by now she'd have had a tag with her name on it tied to her big toe."

"Jesus! Spencer? I can't believe it. Everybody says he's one of the best—"

"For breasts, yes. If you ever need a boob off, he's the guy to do it. Anything else, he's not so hot."

"So Mike got him out of trouble?"

"He sure did."

There was a silence for a moment while Susanne made a notation on her clipboard. Then she sighed. "I'd love it if Mike Richmond would get me *in* trouble," she said.

Florence moved a little, and Susanne gave Evie a warning look. Evie grinned and went back to the O.R. She looked at the clock—it was lunchtime, and most of the schedule was done. She called her friend Stephanie Hopkins to invite her over to the hospital for lunch, and went into the changing room for a quick shower.

She thought a little enviously about Stephanie, who'd been her best friend in nursing school. Stephanie, who turned heads wherever she went, had worked for a couple of years in the I.C.U. at New Coventry Medical Center, then got a job in utilization review with a local medical insurance company, and had recently been made supervisor of the U.R. department.

And so it was that Stephanie Hopkins and Mike Richmond first saw each other in the hospital elevator, Stephanie going up to the O.R. floor to pick up her friend Evie, and Mike talking with Ed Moran, his junior resident, coming back up from the X-ray department. Stephanie saw a large, athletic-looking man wearing greens, who seemed full of energy and sparkle, with lots of curly brown hair and surprisingly gentle gray eyes, talking to a junior doctor who was listening attentively. The big man seemed to radiate such enthusiasm and energy that Stephanie smiled to herself when she got off at the fourth floor.

Ed looked after her receding figure as the elevator doors closed. "Who was that?" he asked.

"No idea," replied Mike, who had barely noticed her beyond the fact that she was well dressed and attractive looking. He had other things on his mind.

From the point of view of getting in with Spencer's group, the events in the O.R. had worked out beyond his wildest expectations—getting Dermott Spencer out of trouble was a coup he couldn't have anticipated.

But that wouldn't be the end of it, he knew. It had been a near miss, and it had happened to an important person, so the case would surely be reviewed by the quality-control people and questions would be asked. As they started rounds, he instinctively started to think about damage control.

Rounds proceeded in a familiar routine. Mrs. Gomez, a round little apple-cheeked woman who owned a small restaurant, had been operated on for diverticulitis three days before and this morning had developed a fever.

"Take a look at the incision," Mike told Ed, who removed the bulky dressing. Sure enough, the incision was puffy and red, the skin tight and bulging between the sutures.

"You have a little abscess there, Mrs. Gomez— *pequeño abscesso*—" Mike told her, "and we'll need to drain it. *Necessitamo abrirlo.*" There was something reassuring about him, she thought, even though his Spanish was so bad. Maybe it was his smile, or his size, or the friendly way he put a hand on her arm . . .

"*Adelante, Señor Richmond,*" she said, with a sigh. She reached for the silver crucifix on the chain around her neck and held tightly on to it. "Go ahead."

Ed fetched a sterile dressing set, pulled on a pair of gloves, cut out a couple of stitches with scissors and gently opened up the outer layers of the incision. Mike watched Mrs. Gomez's face to see if it was hurting, but he'd trained Ed well, and he pushed the skin edges apart with the utmost gentleness. A moment later, a small fountain of yellowish pus welled up. Ed irrigated the cavity with hydrogen peroxide and put in a latex rubber drain before applying a fresh dressing.

While this was going on, Mike was thinking about the end of his four-year residency. His best friend from college, Jack Mills, also a football player, who now worked as a trader for a big Wall Street firm, couldn't believe Mike's schedule or his resident's pay. "For Christ's sake, Mike," he said. "That's not a salary—it's barely a tip. I got twice that much last year as a year-end bonus."

"Just wait," Mike had told him, smiling. "When the market crashes, come on over—I'll buy you a meal." But Mike was tired of having no money, scraping by. He'd figured how long it would take to pay off his debts, and even making the kind of money he could expect after finishing his residency, it would take years.

When Dr. Caleb Winter, chairman of the surgery department and one of the research stars of NCMC, had asked him if he'd like to spend a year working in his transplant lab, Mike had given it some thought.

"You'll be on the cutting edge, so to speak," Dr. Winter had told him with that calm, ironic grin of his, "and of course you won't have to worry about malpractice suits or any of the other problems that can nowadays turn the lives of surgeons into nightmares."

It was an honor to get an invitation from such a distinguished source, but Mike was interested mostly because it might give him a little more clout with Spencer's group; they had to be impressed, because Caleb Winter was known to be very picky about whom he invited to work for him. Spencer had stopped him one afternoon in the corridor on his way to the O.R. and over a cup of coffee had mentioned that his group considered Mike a top candidate.

"Thank you, Dr. Spencer," he said, "I certainly appreciate the compliment."

"Good. Can you come over to my office one afternoon next week to meet with some of my group, maybe Monday, after grand rounds? Then we can talk about this in some more detail."

"Yes, sir."

"Great." Spencer grinned, then stood up. "I suspect the next grand rounds will be of particular interest," he said rather pointedly. "That's why I decided we'd meet with you afterwards. Meanwhile, stay out of trouble, huh?"

As Mike left the cafeteria he remembered that the records department had complained about his huge pile of discharge summaries waiting to be dictated. Spencer's group wouldn't like that. There and then he resolved to start working on them as soon as he had a free half hour.

The pager on his belt went off just as he came through the double doors of the O.R. The nurse behind the desk was holding the phone and called to him. "Mike, it's the E.R. Dr. Catlin's on call, but he's operating, and they need someone down there right away."

Luke Spier couldn't remember when he'd been an accountant. If someone sitting next to him in the emergency room had held up a balance sheet, he couldn't have read it any better than the Dead Sea Scrolls. Luke was not drunk, although he couldn't stand straight without stumbling, and his tremor was so bad that the only thing he could do dexterously was open a bottle.

The police had picked him up that morning and brought him directly to the E.R., before even booking him, when they saw the infection on his arm. It was a big red swelling on his elbow that was leaking pus and should have hurt, but because his nerve endings had been burned out by alcohol, he felt it only when he bumped it against something. The cop was standing a few feet away, waiting for him to be taken care of, chatting with one of the nurses at the desk. Every few moments he'd turn to look at Luke, who was known to be unpredictable, but he seemed quiet enough right now.

Luke wasn't paying any attention to him. He could feel the fever in his bones, the anxiety. He was waiting, his red-rimmed eyes watching the door. He knew exactly what was going to happen. He was scheduled to die, and the messenger bringing in the final instructions to the doctors would be appearing any moment and would come right through the door. He fingered the big old bone-handled knife in his pocket, and when the cop wasn't looking he opened it, still inside his pocket, and felt the edge of the blade. He didn't know what the messenger would look like, but he'd know instantly when he saw him. He had to get that messenger before he could reach the doctors, or that would be the end of him. He sat on the edge of the seat, ignoring the patients on either side of him. He leaned forward and waited.

Pauline Minsky was at her desk in the medical office when Dermott Spencer poked his head in. "Pauline, do you have a few minutes?"

"Yes, Dr. Spencer, of course." Pauline's fingers stopped, poised over the keyboard.

"Good. I'd like you to take some papers over to the medical center," he said. "You know where the administrative offices are?"

"Ground floor," responded Pauline promptly. "At the end of the main corridor."

"They have to be there before noon," said Spencer, glancing at the clock above her head.

"I'll take them over right now." Pauline stood up. She was in her mid-forties, a little overweight, with a pleasant, open manner, and she was wearing a neat dark blue dress with a brightly colored scarf around the collar.

A few minutes later, Pauline was walking briskly along Elm Street, the folder under her arm. If she went along to the main entrance, she'd have to come back along the central corridor to the administrative offices, but it was a direct shot if one walked through the emergency room.

Pauline went in through the E.R. doors, past the security guard, and headed for the main corridor, the crowded waiting area on her right. She never even saw the man until he jumped up and his unshaven face and crazy red eyes were a couple of inches from hers. She saw a flash of metal, screamed, and jumped back, suddenly aware that he had a knife in his hand. Although she could see blood on it, Pauline didn't realize that she'd been attacked, that he'd slashed her, until she felt the blood running down her shoulder. She heard a shout nearby, then another, and she watched with horror as the man raised his knife again, but she couldn't move or speak, and stood frozen helplessly to the spot. Then a white-jacketed aide burst into her field of vision, grabbed her assailant by the wrist, followed by a guard and a cop who leapt on him and pulled him to the other side of the corridor, away from her. Luke tried to fight them off and kept staring and shouting incoherently at Pauline. The waiting area was pandemonium, with everybody yelling and screaming. When the cop twisted the man's arms behind his back, she heard an agonized yelping noise, the knife dropped with a clatter, and a second later the cuffs clicked on him. A Hispanic woman who had been sitting next to Luke started to sob and scream. Pauline, suddenly weak, sat down on a chair. Her papers had scattered all over the floor and one of the secretaries came around and bent down to pick them up. A nurse saw Pauline's neck, gasped, then pulled her dripping scarf off and slapped a big gauze pad on the cut, temporarily stemming the flow of blood.

By the time Mike arrived a couple of minutes later, Pauline had been escorted into one of the booths, and the top of her dress had been unbuttoned and pulled down over her shoulders to expose the slashed area. The nurse was still holding the pressure dressing when he came in.

"Tell me what happened," he said to the nurse.

While she recounted the incident, he smiled quickly at Pauline, then lifted the dressing. The blood welled up instantly from the ragged three-inch cut. He replaced the dressing quickly.

"Keep the pressure on," he said to the nurse, and reached over and opened a packet of sterile gloves.

"I'm going to put in a local anesthetic," he told

Pauline. "It'll be just a little sting, then it'll be numb. Just so you won't feel me poking around in here."

Within a few moments Mike found the cut ends of the vein that had been doing most of the bleeding. "A branch of the external jugular," he explained to Pauline, who was watching and thinking how delicate his hands were for such a big man. "Just a little one." He kept up a steady, gentle flow of conversation with her as he quickly tied off the ends of the cut vein, and by the time he'd finished, she was feeling almost relaxed.

"I work with Dr. Spencer's group," she said, sitting up after he'd taken off the towels and taped on a dressing. "I heard you might be joining them. I certainly hope so."

Mike barely heard her, because he'd pulled back the curtain, and saw Terry Catlin come down the corridor into the E.R. Now he was talking to the nurse at the desk and looking over in his direction. Terry's face darkened, but he waited until Pauline had gathered her papers and rather shakily went to the desk to check out. Then he strode the few steps towards Mike, the light of fury in his eyes.

"You did it again, you fucking bastard," he hissed, his face almost in Mike's. "I was in the O.R., and I told them I'd be down in a few minutes."

Mike shrugged, keeping his eyes warily on his colleague. Catlin seemed to be losing it—not an unknown phenomenon after four years of the continuous stress of a surgical residency. There was nothing to say—it was part of the system. You cov-

ered for a co-worker if he wasn't available. As Caleb
Winter had tried to instill in their minds, *The patient
comes first.*

"You knew she works for Spencer's group, didn't
you?" he said, raising his voice. Someone looked up
from the desk, and the patients on the row of seats
nearby stopped talking.

"No, I didn't . . ."

Without warning, Catlin swung at Mike's head, a
blow that could have done some damage, but Mike's
training in the war zone had prepared him for rowdy
encounters. He leaned quickly back, and Catlin
missed. In what could have been taken for a friendly
gesture, Mike put out his hand and grasped Catlin's
wrist. Catlin caught his breath and winced with pain
at the pressure. It felt as if his wrist joint were being
crushed in a vise.

"Let's go into the lounge," said Mike quietly, and
a moment later Catlin found himself being propelled
into the small doctors' lounge across the hallway.
Mike pushed the door closed behind them and
slammed Catlin down into one of the chairs with
a jolt.

"Don't ever do that again, Catlin," said Mike. "Not
in front of the staff or patients. It gives a bad impression. Now what was it you wanted to say?"

Catlin held on to his wrist, scared. There was no
sensation in the hand. His face twisted. "I've said
everything I ever want to say to you."

"You're acting like an asshole, Catlin," said Mike.

"The only reason I saw that patient was because you weren't available and I was."

After Catlin left, Mike wrote a quick note in Pauline Minsky's chart, then went back along the corridor toward the main part of the hospital, watched by the vindictive eyes of Terry Catlin, who was at the desk, filling in an emergency X-ray request form for his wrist.

Chapter 4

Ten days after the operation on Florence DiGiovanni, Mike got to his apartment to find a large FedEx package waiting for him. Inside, there was a matched set of expensive Mark Cross leather luggage, and an envelope stuck on the outer bag with a piece of tape. With increasing puzzlement, he opened the envelope and found two open-date airline tickets to Cancun, and with them a handwritten note. "Dear Dr. Richmond," he read, "This is to thank you for the wonderful care you took of me in the operating room. You need a vacation—enjoy it! With very best wishes, Florence DiGiovanni."

Mike took a can of Bud out of the refrigerator and popped it open. It was a real luxury to have a drink—it meant that he wasn't on call, that he had a few hours for himself.

Feeling vaguely unsettled, he wandered into the bathroom. His last girlfriend, Monica, used to spend the first part of her visits tidying up his apartment, vacuuming, cleaning the sink, putting his toothbrush and toothpaste tube in a glass, cleaning the mirror. He noticed the difference, although it had seemed okay to him before. Monica, a nurse practitioner, had eventually got tired of his unavailability and gone to Seattle. They still talked on the phone from time to time, but less and less frequently. He walked back into the living room took a green leather toolcase from the bookshelf and went down to the garage. His car was an Aston-Martin coupe, 1961 vintage, gleaming in British racing green, which he and his father had found in a wrecker's yard when Mike was in college. They had spent a summer rebuilding it from the chassis up. That was their last happy summer, reflected Mike. Although they knew about his father's frequent trips to the Plains, as he called Las Vegas, and more often to Atlantic City, at that time neither Mike nor his mother had any idea that his father's gambling losses were already beyond any hope of recovery.

Mike unlocked the door and sat in the vehicle, enjoying the feel of the leather bucket seat and the unmistakable aroma of this classy old car, painstakingly build by hand, piece by loving piece. He ran his hand over the polished wood trim on the instrument panel; when they found the car, most of the damage had been to the engine and the front suspension. The cockpit had luckily escaped.

Restless by nature, Mike didn't sit there very long. He spent the next hour on his back, working on the front off-side shock absorber mounting, thinking about how much money it would take to really fix this car up and get it into shape for racing again.

*   *   *

In the old days at New Coventry Medical Center, the university surgeons and their "town" counterparts got along reasonably well. The academics were paid by the university, taught students and residents, did their research, and brought fame to the institution. They also took care of the indigent population, while the town docs took care of the patients who paid cash or had insurance. When the university discovered that all this money was passing it by, it started to lean on the academics to bring in more money from clinical work. This caused much grumbling; the professors begrudged the time taken from their research, and because many of them had only mediocre surgical skills, their clinical results weren't particularly good. The town surgeons were furious because the professors—*amateur surgeons*, as they called them—were starting to cut seriously into their business.

Now there was little love lost between the two groups, and when they met to discuss problem patients at the monthly grand rounds, the tension was palpable, sparks usually flew, and the residents often took the brunt of the conflict. The residency program was under the control of the academics, so an attack on their residents was an attack on them. And when the academics got into trouble, they usually managed to put the blame on the residents.

The key individual who kept the situation from breaking out into open warfare was Dr. Caleb Winter, chairman of the department. An outstanding transplant surgeon and researcher, he was strict, fair,

and possessed of an unshakable integrity that sometimes seemed out of place in the present commercial-
ized medical scene.

This Monday there was a bigger than usual turn-
out for grand rounds. On one side was Dr. Winter's
team. And on the other side of the old sloping amphitheater, the town doctors were coming in, sitting
protectively together. Mike saw Spencer come in and
sit down with his surgical partners, Derek Provost
and Chas Miller.

As chief residents, Mike and Terry Catlin were
with their own teams down at the front, close to the
podium where they would present their cases. Mike
could feel a tension in the air; there was something
about the attitude of the academics that put him on
guard, and he wondered what they were up to.

Catlin had a couple of cases that aroused little
comment, and after Mike presented his cases without
more criticism than usual from his seniors, he
thought that maybe after all he was home free, when
Dr. Caleb Winter stood up.

"Thank you, Dr. Richmond," he said with his
usual courtliness. "Those were most informative
cases. However, there's another case that came to my
attention within the last couple of days, and I would
like to discuss it now."

Mike, who had been thinking ahead to the next
day's operating schedule, suddenly became alert.

"I'm referring to a laparoscopic cholecystectomy performed on a female patient, unit number 8435/3/96,"

said Dr. Winter. It was an unspoken grand rounds rule never to refer to patients by their names.

"Yes, sir, just a moment," said Mike. Of course he knew whom Dr. Winter was referring to, but he went through the motions of checking his notebook, mostly to give himself a little extra time. He glanced over to where Catlin was sitting, staring fixedly at Mike.

"I don't have the chart, Dr. Winter," he said. "I'll be happy to schedule the case for next month—"

"I have the chart right here," said Dr. Winter. He gave it to the person sitting in front of him, who passed it down to Mike. By this time a kind of stillness had fallen over the amphitheater; it was clear that a confrontation was about to take place.

A voice was heard from the private surgeons' sector, and Mike looked around to see Walt Eagleton. "Dr. Winter," he said in his relaxed drawl, "we've been sitting here for the last hour being educated by you and your academic colleagues. We've enjoyed it a lot, but there's only so much education me and my friends here can handle at any one time. Could we not discuss this case next month?"

A faint ripple of laughter went around the amphitheater; Walt Eagleton, an extremely intelligent and cultured man, always took any opportunity to poke fun at his academic colleagues, and he was one of the few who would risk taking on Caleb Winter.

"This won't take long, Dr. Eagleton," replied Dr. Winter calmly. "I'm sure your stockbroker can wait another ten minutes."

This time the laughter came from the academic benches, and Mike was on full alert. Clearly he was going to be on trial, and a lot more depended on the outcome than he wanted to think about right now. Someone had brought Florence DiGiovanni's case to Dr. Winter's notice, knowing how furious he would be that such a screw-up had happened in his department. And if he decided that it was Mike's fault, Dr. Winter was quite capable of throwing him off the program and ending his surgical career there and then, even though he only had a couple of weeks to go.

"Well, are you going to present the case, Dr. Richmond, or would you like me to do it?" There was something about Dr. Winter's tone that told Mike to get on with it or face some unpleasant consequences.

"Yes, sir." Mike stood up. "Patient 8435/3/96 is a forty-six-year-old female," he started. "She came to the hospital complaining of severe right upper quadrant pain and was seen by her private physician . . ."

"And who was that?" asked Dr. Winter, who knew perfectly well.

Spencer, sitting near the back of the auditorium, spared Mike the trouble of answering. "If you are talking about Mrs. DiGiovanni," he said in his loud, cheerful voice, "she's my patient."

"Thank you, Dr. Spencer." Dr. Winter nodded at Mike to go on.

"The patient had complained of right upper quadrant pain and fatty food intolerance for several months," Mike went on. "A cholecystogram done two weeks before admission showed the presence of several medium-sized gallstones, and this was confirmed with a CAT scan. The admission was okayed by the patient's insurance carrier, and since her symptoms were increasing, her attending made a diagnosis of cholecystitis with impending rupture, so she was scheduled for—"

"Did you agree with that diagnosis?" interrupted Dr. Winter.

"I didn't see the patient preoperatively," replied Mike.

"Did anyone? Aside from Dr. Spencer?"

Mike glanced up at Spencer.

"The E.R. doc saw her when she first came in," he said. "Dr. Win Phu. He wrote a note in the chart."

"Which is almost illegible," said Dr. Winter. "But his admitting diagnosis was acute cholecystitis. He said nothing about an impending rupture." He looked back at Mike. "Please go on."

"She was scheduled for an emergency lap choly," said Mike, using the usual abbreviation for a laparoscopic cholecystectomy. "And that was carried out later on the morning of admission. An inflamed gallbladder was found, with several gallstones. A cholangiogram taken during the procedure showed no stones present in the common duct. Her postoperative recovery was uneventful, and she was discharged the next morning in good condition."

"Actually, her discharge time was two p.m. the next afternoon," said Dr. Winter. He paused, looking thoughtfully at Mike. "Dr. Richmond," he said, "how long do most of your patients stay in the hospital after a lap choly?''

Mike's mind was racing, trying to figure out what Dr. Winter was getting at. It was essential not to say anything that would put Spencer on the spot, but on the other hand his own career was at stake.

''We try to get them out the same day,'' he said. ''But that's not always possible. And this case was only started around noon, so we felt that an overnight stay was in the patient's best interests.''

''According to the O.R. report, the case was started at exactly eleven a.m., said Dr. Winter. ''Dr. Richmond, you seem to be having difficulty remembering times today. Are you feeling all right?''

There was a faint giggle from the audience, and Mike replied calmly. ''Yes, sir,'' Like any surgical resident, he'd had to put up with repeated criticisms and sarcasm in the last four years, but this was very different. He *had* to stay cool.

''Was there any other reason why the patient couldn't be discharged on the day of her operation?''

Now Mike was really in a predicament. Winter would jump on whatever he truthfully replied, and would then force him to recount every problem that had arisen during the entire sorry episode—the hemorrhage, the blood transfusions, everything. Mike was resolved not to do this, although he wasn't going to lie, either.

''I don't recall any right now, sir.''

Dr. Winter's lips tightened. ''I see on the chart here that the patient's temperature rose to 102.5 degrees at five p.m. on the day of her operation," he said. "Do you think that might have had something to do with the delay in her discharge?"

"Yes, sir, I suppose so."

"That's what you wrote in the progress notes, if you'd like to check the chart."

Mike took a deep breath. "Dr. Winter, if I'd been told that you intended to review this case, I'd have been better prepared," he said.

"The chart is right there in front of you," said Dr. Winter coldly. "What more do you want?"

Mike didn't reply. The auditorium was so quiet one could have heard a gallstone drop. Occasionally grand rounds gave rise to confrontations of this kind, and the audience watched, fascinated. Most of the doctors there had at some point in their careers been on the receiving end of this kind of interrogation, and they were just glad that it was Mike Richmond sweating it and not they. Spencer sat impassively in his seat, watching Mike.

"To come back to this bout of fever that this patient was unfortunate enough to suffer," went on Dr. Winter relentlessly. "Dr. Richmond, what do think might have caused it?"

"We checked her lungs," said Mike. "We thought it could be postoperative atelectasis."

"And your findings?"

"Her lungs were clear, sir."

"So there was no postoperative partial collapse of her lungs to explain the fever?"

"Not that we could find, sir."

"So?"

"Well, her temperature came down to normal within a couple of hours and stayed normal until the time of her discharge, so we didn't worry too much about it."

Dr. Winter seemed to be having trouble controlling his annoyance, and Mike watched with increasing apprehension, but there was nothing he could say without implicating Dr. Spencer.

Finally Dr. Winter said, in a voice of thunder, "Dr. Richmond, I'm coming to the conclusion that either you're shell-shocked from too many nights on call, or else you're trying to cover up mistakes in this case—mistakes made by you or by others. The reason for this patient's fever, as you know very well, was that she had a reaction to a blood transfusion. And my next question to you is, why was she given a blood transfusion of two pints during a simple cholecystectomy?"

"We ran into some bleeding during the procedure," said Mike, holding his ground. "A clip came off the cystic artery. That's not unknown, as you know, Dr. Winter. In fact, at this hospital a bleeding complication occurs in about ten percent of all lap cholys. That's why the patient was given blood." He paused, aware of the tension that gripped the audience. "In about thirty percent of cases nationwide, Dr. Winter, attempts at lap cholys are unsuccessful and the patient has to undergo open surgery. That didn't happen in this case. The patient was in the hospital less than two days, and her postop recovery has been excellent."

Mike paused. "And I'm not trying to cover up anything, Dr. Winter, nor is anyone else. Everything that happened to this patient before, during, and after the procedure is written clearly in the chart. As I said, if you'd given me the opportunity to review the entire case, if you hadn't sprung it on us like this, I'd have been able to give you better answers."

The atmosphere in the amphitheater was electric. It was unheard of for a chief resident to talk back to Dr. Caleb Winter like this, and the audience waited, holding its breath, to see the manner in which Dr. Winter would choose to destroy this impertinent resident.

To Mike, the silence lasted an eternity.

Finally Dr. Winter spoke in a quite different tone of voice. "Yes, thank you, Dr. Richmond. You make a very valid point, that the final result on this patient was satisfactory. That, of course, is the most important issue, and I may have lost sight of that. However, Dr. Richmond"—he stared coldly at Mike, but his anger seemed to have evaporated—"I would like to remind you that grand rounds were instituted to discuss problem cases, and this patient should have been on the schedule for today. By not doing so, you put yourself in a dubious position to start with."

He looked up into the seats opposite. "Dr. Spencer," he said, "I wonder if you'd stop by my office some time next week, please."

Chapter 5

"That was pretty damn good the way you handled that, Michael," said Spencer, smiling. After grand rounds, Mike had walked down the street with him to his office and was now enjoying the spectacular view from the twenty-second floor. "It's not often that anyone gets the better of Caleb Winter."

"I'll be glad when I'm finished with the program," replied Mike simply. He turned and sat down in the comfortable visitor's chair.

"I bet you will. Well, this interview won't take long. By the way, I took the liberty of getting your transcript from the human resources people over at the university. I hope you don't mind."

"No problem. You're welcome to it."

"You should be proud of it. And of course I've been talking to the other surgeons you've worked with here. You have a pretty outstanding rep, I must tell you, or else they're all lying to me."

"They're not lying."

Spencer grinned. "I assume you decided not to work with Caleb Winter?"

"Yes. I turned the job down."

Spencer raised his eyebrows, watching Mike with a quizzical, half-humorous look. "I sort of figured that this morning . . . but Winter has a hot team, Mike, with an international rep, and it isn't every day he invites people to work with him."

"Two reasons," replied Mike. "I want to work with patients, and I need more money than he was offering. A lot more."

"Of course." Spencer nodded, pleased. "Let me tell you a bit about our practice," he went on. "Then you can ask all the questions you want. Would you like some coffee?"

"Yes, please."

Spencer pressed the button on the intercom and spoke into it, and a couple of minutes later Pauline Minsky came in with two cups. She was wearing a scarf that partly hid the dressing on her neck, and she gave Mike a big smile but didn't say anything. Spencer was just starting to tell Mike about how their practice had started, about twelve years before, but when Pauline had closed the door behind her, he grinned, and said, "Pauline's the latest member of your fan club," he said. "Thanks for taking care of her cut." Then his face became serious and he returned to his previous topic. "Fred Newsome had started the group and was our guiding light, and we built up a pretty good business, and brought in a bunch of internists and other specialists. But when HMOs and managed care and all that stuff started to come in, Fred couldn't quite cope with it."

Spencer stood up and went over to a framed photo on the wall. "That's us," he said, "two years ago, a couple of months before he died." Mike came over to look. The group photograph had been taken in bright winter sunlight and wasn't very good. "That's Fred there, sitting in the middle . . ." Mike remembered Dr. Newsome's portly figure and bald head, and the way he used to rub it when he got upset.

"About the time Fred died, our whole practice was on the brink of going under. Poor old Fred. He got very depressed, and some of us think he may have committed suicide. You know he flew his own plane, and crashed in a forest up in northern Connecticut."

Mike nodded. He remembered reading about it and seeing the aerial pictures on the TV report. There hadn't been much left of the plane.

The door opened, and Derek Provost came in. He was quite a bit younger than Spencer, in his early forties. Derek was lean, dark, and quick—a very capable and occasionally flamboyant surgeon. Mike knew him from way back when he was chief resident, and liked him.

"Hi, Mike." Derek grinned. "We all enjoyed your presentation back there. Spencer tells me you may be joining us."

"I'd certainly like to."

"I was over in the record room at the hospital just now," said Derek. "You have a whole bunch of unfinished charts to complete. They're not too happy with you down there."

"I know. I'll get to them."

"We're very fussy about records in the practice," said Spencer, taking the cue from Derek. "In this climate, with all the malpractice suits that are flying around, we have to document everything. Otherwise they can tear us to pieces in court."

"You'll find that being in practice is a whole new deal," said Derek, sitting down in one of the white leather and chrome chairs. "After you come out of your residency, you wouldn't believe you're still in the same business. Nowadays, it's a case of protect your ass first, then take care of the patients. Right, Spencer?"

Spencer nodded, then turned back to Mike. "I was telling you about our practice. As you know, we have three general surgeons in the group, that's Derek and me and Chas Miller. We also have several internists, an ENT doc, a couple of neurologists, for a total of twelve physicians. They've been with us for years and they're the best. We're all very close, partly, I suppose, because we've all gone through a lot together. Also we have a staff of about forty techs, nurses, and administrative types. We all work very hard, as I'm sure you know, and if you join us we'll expect you to work just as hard."

"Harder," said Derek.

"We work mainly out of Lovejoy Hospital," went on Spencer. "They have a big managed-care plan with almost two hundred thousand members. Since we were there first, we get the cream of their surgical problems."

"Most of the big New Coventry employers joined

the Lovejoy Plan," added Derek. "Raytech, United Electronics, Millway, a couple of the major insurance companies."

"We also see a lot of private patients, of course," went on Spencer. "But that's gravy. The main course is Lovejoy. That's what pays the bills."

There was a perfunctory knock on the door, which opened to let Lou Gardner in. He looked very businesslike but not unfriendly, although Mike knew that he was one of Terry Catlin's backers. Mike stood up, shook hands, and Lou sat down heavily, keeping his eyes on Mike.

Spencer took a few moments to tell Lou what had happened at grand rounds, and Lou seemed to be impressed. He sat back in his chair, still with his eyes on Mike.

"Yes, we believe very strongly in loyalty, Dr. Richmond," he said slowly. "That's how our group stays in business, by backing each other up. Now, just supposing . . ." Lou sat even farther back in his seat. His eyes were small, bright, and seemed to bore right into Mike's. "Suppose a situation where I refer a patient to you with say, a malignant colon tumor. X-rays, biopsy, everything is positive. But during surgery you can't see or feel the tumor where the X-rays show it. What would you do then?"

Mike could feel a sudden stillness come over the group. Each one of them had his eyes fixed on him, and he could sense that a lot depended on his answer.

"I'd get on with the resection," he replied, without

hesitation. "Sometimes you can't always feel a tumor even if it's there, and a biopsy can remove the visible part of a small tumor, although of course there's microscopic invasion still present."

Lou nodded slowly, with some reluctance, and Spencer beamed as if his protegé had just won the Daily Double on *Jeopardy.*

But Lou wasn't done. "I'm told you're pretty competent," he went on, "and that's good. We all are." He waved a hand as if that were of minor importance. "But we're very efficient, too." He glanced at Spencer. "We think of ourselves primarily as a business, and everything we do is directly related to the bottom line. We don't do Medicaid because it doesn't pay enough, and outside of the Lovejoy plan, everything is on a cash or insurance basis. And we hit the insurance companies as hard as we can. Part of our office manager's job is to see that no stone is left unturned in that direction. Do you have any problem with that?"

"No," said Mike. "I don't. That side isn't pushed too hard in the residency program, but I'm as hungry as any of you and I learn fast."

After a few more questions, Lou stood up. "Okay with me," he said to Spencer in a rather flat tone of voice.

"Good. I'm glad you agree Mike's the right guy for us. Thanks for coming in, Lou."

After Lou had gone, Spencer, looking relieved, said, "Now, let's get down to brass tacks, as Fred Newsome used to say." Spencer put his hands flat on the desk. "If you join us, we'll pay you a salary of $200,000 for the first year, plus the usual benefits, health and malpractice insurance and so on. You'll get two weeks' vacation, a generous allowance for travel and continuing education, and we'll lease a car for you. Then after six months, if all goes well, as we expect it will, you'll be allowed to start buying into the group, a certain amount each year for five years, at which time you'll have an equal share with the rest of us."

Mike was stunned. He'd been expecting to make money, but this was better than he could have possibly expected. "Sounds pretty good to me," he said. "But I won't need the car, thank you. I like to tool around in my old Aston-Martin."

"Did you know that Mike's a famous car racer?" Derek asked Spencer, then turned back to Mike. "Didn't you once win a race at Brands Hatch?"

"That was a long time ago," replied Mike. "For the last couple of years I've hardly had time to check the tires."

Let alone have the money for gas, thought Spencer. "We want you to be absolutely sure before you make a decision about this, Mike," he said, with steady emphasis. "Getting a new associate is a very big deal for us, and we don't want you changing your mind after a couple of months."

"This is the only job I'm interested in," replied Mike, just as steadily. "And I'll give it everything I've got."

They talked for a half hour longer, and then Mike had to get back to the hospital. By that time they had a tentative agreement; the group would make a few more inquiries, and if these came out okay they would make a formal offer. Mike would then give a firm decision within the next week, and if he decided to join the group, he would start as soon as he finished his residency program. Spencer was inflexible about that, so Mike's vacation, courtesy of Florence DiGiovanni, would have to be postponed.

After Mike left, Derek said, "Well, that seems to have worked out all right. I was a bit worried about what Lou might ask him and what he would say." He paused. "You're sure we shouldn't have given Mike a probation period? Supposing he doesn't work out?"

"We've already discussed that," replied Spencer. "It's partly psychological. It makes us more careful about who we choose, and obviously we don't want even the possibility of him leaving once he's joined." He hesitated for a moment. "I know what you're saying, Derek. We can't tell him the whole story now, but once he's been with us for a while, he'll be committed, whether he realizes it or not, and then we can gradually let him know how things work." Spencer's natural optimism took over. "Mike's the man for us, Derek, I'm convinced of it. Everything will work out just fine."

There was a brief silence, then Derek asked quietly, "What about Carl? Is it okay with him?"

Spencer hesitated for just a second. "Well, I can't say he's totally delighted about bringing in a new guy, but I told him we didn't have the option. There's just too much work for the three of us. So, yes, it's okay with him."

Chapter 6

It was raining hard when Stephanie Hopkins came to work in downtown New Coventry, a continuous stinging April rain that reminded her of a weekend she'd once spent with her parents on Block Island. They'd hardly been able to get out of their hotel, let alone go sailing, but the excitement of the howling, tree-bending, blow-you-off-your-feet three-day nor'easter had almost made up for it.

A powerful gust of wind swept along Haven Street, caught her raincoat, and blew her along the sidewalk, making her feel almost weightless. She stretched out her arms and ran with it, enjoying the wildness of the weather all the way from the parking lot to the big glass doors of her building. She pushed the revolving door and, once she was inside, took off her hooded raincoat and shook it.

"Nice morning, Miss Hopkins," said Oscar, the security guard. He grinned over at her from behind his podium. "You could almost have sailed in here in your little boat."

Stephanie looked down; her shoes were soaked, and her dark blue stockings were wet up to her shapely knees. "Right," she said, smiling back. "I feel as if I'd fallen out of it and swam." She pulled off her bright red and gold scarf and shook out her hair—shoulder-length, so dark brown it was almost black. Normally straight, it became curly and hard to manage in this weather. There was something healthily sexy about Stephanie, and Oscar couldn't decide if it was her shape, the look in her big dark eyes, or just the way she walked.

"Mr. Hartmann's the only one up in your place so far, Miss Hopkins." Oscar stepped over to the elevators and pressed the button for her.

Stephanie was surprised. Carl Hartmann, the CEO and owner of the Hartmann Insurance Company, traveled a lot and didn't spend much time in the office.

The elevator door opened, and Stephanie stepped in, looking forward to her day. Five years ago, she thought, she wouldn't have dreamed that she'd be working here, certainly not as the head of utilization review. Five years ago . . . at the time she was an I.C.U. nurse at New Coventry Medical Center, loving it but going crazy with the emotional strain. "You mustn't get so involved, Stephanie." Claire Dalton, the head nurse, had found her weeping in the corridor after the death of a young patient. But Stephanie couldn't help getting involved. She liked her patients, made an effort to get to know them and their families, and took it very badly when things went wrong. After a year the strain was showing. She couldn't sleep at nights, was having nightmares; she was losing weight, and her friends were getting anxious. One day the head nurse gave her the job of categorizing all the I.C.U. admissions, required for an accreditation visit by the Joint Commission. Stephanie found she had a talent for turning data into usable and easily understood information, and learned to improve on her skills using computer graphics. Other departments started to use her expertise, which led to a job analyzing data for the hospital. Then the cutbacks came. For the first time in its long history, New Coventry Medical Center started to lay off personnel—middle managers, nurses, and secretarial help. Stephanie was lucky to get a job in the utilization-review department of Hartmann Insurance, and had recently been promoted to supervisor.

She stepped out of the elevator on the eighth floor, pressed the entry code numbers and slid her access card in the slot. When the tiny red light turned to green, she turned the brass handle and went in. It was exactly seven-thirty by the clock on the wall in front of her, and as usual there was nobody in the outer office. She walked past the empty life-insurance booths, then past the corridor that led to the suite of executive offices. As she went by, the end door opened and Carl Hartmann came out. He was in his mid-forties, big, robust, in shirtsleeves, with thick, curly reddish hair that came down in a bristly V, leaving only about a couple of inches of aggressive forehead. Carl gave the impression of bluff, uncompromising strength, and nobody doubted that he had a very smart business mind.

Stephanie said, "Good morning, Mr. Hartmann," and kept walking, wondering if he had recognized her.

A moment later she heard a quick step. Mr. Hartmann was right behind her, moving faster than she'd expected. "Excuse me, miss . . . ?"

Stephanie stopped and turned.

He stared at her for a moment. He had shale gray eyes, the kind of all-seeing eyes that one would not even think of lying to. "Yes," he said. "That's you. Same woman. Why didn't you tell me you worked here?" He had an aggressive, direct way of talking— Stephanie knew that Carl Hartmann was a man who made a lot of people nervous, especially those who worked for him.

"You didn't ask, Mr. Hartmann," replied Stephanie. "Did you catch your plane all right?"

About a month earlier, Stephanie had left work and was walking along Haven Street toward the parking lot with Jean Forrest, one of her fellow workers. It was a cold, blustery evening, and the sidewalks were crowded with office workers on their way home.

"What's that?" Stephanie stopped in her tracks and looked around. Somebody was shouting a little distance behind her. A second later, she saw a movement in the crowd, then a tall man burst through, running in her direction, just a few yards away, zigzagging through the crowd like a basketball player, a black wool cap on his head. He was holding on to an expensive-looking briefcase that swung wildly as he ran. In the second before he came up to her, Stephanie heard someone shout, 'Stop . . . thief!' As the man came abreast of her, she saw his fixed expression and heard him grunting, concentrating on getting away through the crowd. Without even thinking, Stephanie stuck out a foot as he passed, and he went up in the air, then down with a thud, spread-eagled, the wind knocked out of him, but still holding onto the briefcase. There was a second's pause before a couple of young men jumped on him and twisted his arms behind his back. By this time a crowd had gathered, and for once there was a policeman at the pedestrian crossing a few yards away, and he came up and took over.

A big, burly man pushed his way through the small crowd. He wore a beige camel-hair overcoat and had a commanding presence. "That's my briefcase," he said to the officer, "and I need it. I'm in a hurry; I have to catch a plane in forty minutes."

The officer went on putting cuffs on the still prone prisoner. "Sorry, sir, but right now it's evidence. You can pick it up at the station tomorrow."

"Here," said the man, pulling a driver's license from his wallet. "That's my name." He picked up the briefcase and opened it. Inside was his business card. "Look," he said, "same name. Carl Hartmann," and showed it to the cop. He gave the handcuffed man a chilling look. "I'll come to the station and press charges when I come back, in two days."

The policeman recognized the name and nodded. "That'll be just fine, Mr. Hartmann, sir," he said.

Stephanie noticed that something had caught her hose, probably the man's shoe, and had made a run all the way to her ankle. She grabbed Jean's arm and was starting to leave, but the officer called after her. "Don't you go yet, miss," he said. "I need your statement first."

For the first time Hartmann turned and looked at her. "Did you stop this man?" he asked.

Stephanie nodded. He thanked her briefly, hesitated, then shook her hand. At that moment a taxi pulled up next to them, and he picked up his briefcase and climbed heavily into it.

"Yes, I caught the plane. Sorry I didn't thank you adequately at the time," he said, "but I was already late." His face changed. "By the way, I'm making sure that guy'll be off the streets for a long time." Hartmann's eyes glittered momentarily, and Stephanie felt that she had glimpsed something of the inner man.

"How?" asked Stephanie curiously. "He hasn't been tried yet."

Hartmann grinned with faint amusement. "You can count on it, Miss . . ." He looked at the name on her I.D. tag. "Hopkins. Stephanie Hopkins." He nodded. "You're the new utilization-review supervisor. Dr. Sammons speaks highly of you."

"He'd better," replied Stephanie, smiling. "I take very good care of Dr. Sammons."

Hartmann didn't smile, and Stephanie remembered that he wasn't known for his sense of humor.

He nodded and turned back toward his office, saying, "Good. And thanks again, Miss Hopkins."

"You're welcome," she replied, and then, feeling that she was pushing it, added, "By the way, you owe me for one pair of wrecked pantyhose."

Stephanie could feel his glance following her as she walked on to the utilization-review department. Her office, at the end of the row of booths, wasn't very big, but it did have a door she could close and a window through which she could see, in the distance, over the New Coventry rooftops, a thin blue strip of Long Island Sound.

For the next half hour she busied herself with paperwork. Her company administered the Lovejoy Health Plan, a cooperative venture with Lovejoy Hospital, and right now she was reviewing a problem they were having with one of their participating doctors, a problem she had inherited from her predecessor, Karen Paige, who had been oddly reluctant to deal with it.

A few minutes before eight, her crew started to come in to the office, greeted her, complained about the weather, and soon the phones started ringing and the office was in full swing.

Jean Forrest came into the office holding some papers. As usual she looked anxious and fluttery. "I got the information that you wanted on that doctor," she said, glancing around as if she'd been on a secret mission. "It wasn't easy, I can tell you."

They went over the data. Stephanie showed her where it was incomplete, and together they made phone calls and a number of calculations to get the full picture. At about ten-thirty, Stephanie made a phone call to her boss, Dr. Bill Sammons, the company's medical director.

"Sure, come on over," he said.

Dr. Sammons had a corner office on the floor above, with two windows. He could see a little more of the sound than Stephanie could from her office, and he also had a partial view of the university campus and the central green with its three churches.

Dr. Sammons was jovial and balding, a cheerfully overweight middle-aged man who had spent most of his career as a general practitioner. After years of struggling with the system, he'd finally tired of arguing with the insurance companies and decided that if he couldn't fight them, the only way to keep his sanity was to join them.

"Come on in, Stephanie," he said. "Have a seat. What's the problem?" He leaned back in his chair, watching her. He liked Stephanie because since she'd become supervisor, his own work load had diminished substantially, for she took care of many of the problems that had previously landed on his desk. He also recognized that she was a very attractive woman, but that didn't interest him nearly as much.

"I don't know how much of a problem this is," said Stephanie, putting her papers on his desk. "It's a Dr. Gardner. In the last three months he's admitted two hundred and thirty four private patients to Lovejoy Hospital, and the admitting and discharge diagnoses were the same in only forty-eight percent of these cases, compared with our standard value of eight-five percent. The admitting diagnosis in a lot of these was pneumonia, but most times the patients turned out to have bronchitis or asthma, or just a cold."

Dr. Sammons said nothing for a few moments, and thoughtfully scratched the back of one liver-spotted hand.

"You did say they were private, not plan patients, right?" He waited for Stephanie's nod before going on. "Well, that's an easy enough mistake to make, actually," he said. "You know, those patients come in coughing and wheezing to the E.R., and often it's difficult to tell what's what."

"The other doctors have a much higher accuracy rate, usually about ninety percent," Stephanie reminded him, although he must have known that anyway.

He moved on his chair, looking uncomfortable. "If you'll leave the papers with me, Stephanie, I'll take care of it."

"Thanks," replied Stephanie. She stood up.

"How's everything else going?" he asked. "Any other problems?"

"No. We can take care of most of them," she replied, thinking that he was dealing a bit strangely with the case she had brought him. She had expected him to go over the situation in detail, to find out if the doctor had any problems in other areas, or if he needed to take a refresher course in a particular disease or condition.

"I got a call from Mr. Hartmann about a half hour ago," said Dr. Sammons, giving Stephanie a curious look. "He wanted to know all about you . . ." He hesitated for a second. "He told me about how you'd stopped a man who stole his briefcase in the street and got him arrested. He also said that he's going to get you one of those New Coventry civic awards, the one the mayor started last year. Good for you, Stephanie."

"A civic award?" said Stephanie, laughing. "Wonderful. Now the guy'll know who to come after when he gets out of jail."

"They thought of that already," replied Dr. Sammons. "They don't tell the media what you did to get the award. They just have a ceremony and you get the check and your photograph in the paper. It's not much money, mostly just the kudos. Actually, it'll be good publicity for Hartmann Insurance." He stood up. "Thanks, Stephanie," he said. "And congratulations. Keep up the good work."

"Thank you," said Stephanie. "Will you let me know what you decide about Dr. Gardner?"

"Sure." Dr. Sammons watched her leave, then picked up the papers she'd left. He read them, sighed, then lifted the phone.

Back in her office, Stephanie was kept very busy until five o'clock, when her team left for home. A half hour later, she picked up the phone and called her friend Evie Gaskell, her old buddy from nursing school, who now worked in the O.R. at New Coventry Medical Center. Evie was home; she was on the day shift and finished at three in the afternoon. Stephanie told her about her day. Evie sighed. "It sounds like you have a fun job," she said. "Here, all I've been doing today is going through inventory lists and checking instruments. Remember how glamorous we thought it would be, working in an operating room with surgeons?"

"*You* thought it would be glamorous," replied Stephanie, "Most of us wanted to take care of our patients while they were awake."

"You want to go to the movies tonight?" asked Evie. "There's a rerun of *Forrest Gump* at the Bijou."

"No, thanks. I meet enough people every day with I.Q.'s of eighty without paying extra for the privilege," said Stephanie, laughing. "Actually, I've seen it twice already. Why don't you come over to my place? I'll make dinner."

"Okay," said Evie promptly. Stephanie was a great cook and Evie wasn't, although she liked eating. "Seven?"

"Seven-thirty. See you then."

Ten minutes later, Stephanie straightened up her desk and headed out and started to walk up Haven Street toward the car park. There was an intermittent rain, and the wind was coming in hard gusts. The rain, rolling off the Atlantic, felt cleansing and wild.

Home for Stephanie was in Waterford, a pleasant bedroom community on the west side of town. She parked in her assigned space and let herself into the lobby, a bright area with a big flower arrangement near the entrance. Her two-bedroom condo had been sadly decrepit when she'd bought it, with peeling flowery wallpaper and worn brown carpeting. That summer she painted the interior walls and doors in ivory white, put in a new carpet, a brightly covered sofa and easy chairs, a roll-top desk she found at an auction, and colorful Paris street scenes on the walls. Now the apartment was cheerful and welcoming, a happy place to come home to.

Stephanie went into the kitchen, thought for a moment, then put the salmon fillet she'd bought in a bowl to marinate in sherry and lemon juice. By the time Evie arrived, Stephanie had taken the fish out, wrapped it in foil and put it in the oven. Evie, shapely as ever, came into the kitchen, wearing a white T-shirt tucked into her Calvin Kleins.

"You're looking good," said Stephanie.

"Thanks. You're not looking bad yourself, for an older woman." Evie was a year younger than Stephanie and never let her forget it.

Stephanie opened a bottle of chardonnay and filled their glasses.

"We have two minutes before the salmon's ready," she said. "So what's happening up at the hospital?"

Evie took a sip. "Oh, the usual. Except worse. They're cutting staff to the bone—I don't know from one week to the next if I even have a job. Lovejoy is killing us—half the private surgeons have gone to work over there, and a lot of our staff people have jumped ship too. I guess everybody in town has joined the Lovejoy plan, so Lovejoy Hospital is where the action is now."

"Lovejoy's where the money is, for sure," said Stephanie. "Patients do notice things like new equipment and fresh paint."

"I was talking to one of the girls in the Lovejoy O.R.," said Evie through a mouthful of salmon. "They can't believe the number of patients going through the system. It's as if everybody who goes near the place is getting operated on."

"I'd heard something like that too," said Stephanie, fishing some capers out of a jar. "You make it sound like an epidemic."

"Except it's an epidemic of everything," went on Evie. "From gallbladders to breast cancer to hemorrhoids."

Stephanie passed the asparagus to Evie. "I suppose that's good for everybody," she said. "It certainly keeps the hospital full and making money, which means it won't have to go through that awful reorganization again. Here, try these capers."

Evie looked doubtfully at the jar, then extracted a single caper with a spoon. "Yeah, well, all that business is good for the docs too, for sure. Look at Spencer and his group. A couple of years ago, those guys were hanging around the emergency rooms and nursing homes, hoping to pick up a few cases. Now they're so busy they don't even have time to go out in their yachts."

Stephanie and Evie had strawberries for dessert.

"If NCMC's falling apart," asked Stephanie, "why don't you get a job over at Lovejoy?"

"I already applied," replied Evie. "I'm going for an interview next week."

"Great. I hope you get it."

"So what else is new in your life, Stephanie?" asked Evie, sprinkling her strawberries with sugar. "Are you still seeing that big, gorgeous pediatric resident? I can't remember his name."

"Bobby Marks? He's still around, I guess, but I'm not seeing him," replied Stephanie. She grinned. "He was sweet, but he really preferred his teddy bear to me. I don't mind a bit of competition now and then, but I couldn't deal with ole teddy."

"Was it a male teddy?"

"I never got close enough to it to know. And how does Evan like being here? It was nice that he was transferred."

"I wish he'd stayed in Montana. He does the big brother routine with me all the time, checks out who I go out with." Evie took a deep breath. "I told him, Evan, do your FBI stuff at work, leave me alone. Finally I told him if he didn't lay off, I'd call his boss and tell them he's secretly a militiaman."

Stephanie laughed.

"Don't laugh," said Evie. "You know he has no sense of humor. He thought I was serious."

They chatted for a while longer, then Evie looked at her watch. "Have to go," she said, getting up. "I have an early start tomorrow."

After Evie left, Stephanie puttered around for a little while, tidying up, thinking about their conversation. When the Lovejoy Plan was first started by the hospital's new management and Hartmann Insurance, everybody had expected it to fail. It would be so expensive to run, informed opinion confidently predicted, that it would drive both the hospital and the insurance company into bankruptcy. Not so. On the contrary, the plan was not only flourishing, it had cleaned up on the competition.

Feeling a little uneasy, Stephanie went to fill the dishwasher. Maybe it was what Evie had been saying about the unusual numbers of patients who were being operated on there, together with her recent problem with Dr. Gardner, but there seemed to be something that wasn't quite right about the now thriving Lovejoy Hospital. And Spencer's group, going so quickly from near disaster to the heights of prosperity . . .

Stephanie decided to take a shower before going to bed, so after getting her papers ready for the next day, she went into the bathroom, took her clothes off, turned the shower on, and stepped in. There was something close and luxurious about the heat and the steam, and she could feel her whole body relaxing. She shampooed her hair and enjoyed the feel of her smooth skin, the firmness of her breasts. And then, with her hand flat on the side of her right breast, she stopped. There was a lump there, in the deep tissue on the outer part of the breast. Not big, she thought, smaller than a peanut. She checked again, then compared how the other side felt. The left side seemed quite normal, no lumps aside from the normal slightly bumpy feel of the breast tissue. Hardly able to breathe, her hand went back to the right side. The lump wasn't tender or painful, but it was still there, no question about it.

Chapter 7

Mike Richmond started work with Spencer's group the day after finishing his residency, and one week later, he was in operating room five at Lovejoy Hospital, assisting Spencer in a breast case. Spencer was enjoying himself. He was on his home turf, so to speak, and here his expertise was unquestioned. Also he had a small self-esteem problem to rectify with Mike, and he was taking care of it right now.

"There's a plane between the tissues, right there," he showed Mike, pointing with his laser probe at the center of the half-inch layer of fat between the skin and the breast tissue. All Mike could see was the yellowish nodules of the fatty subcutaneous layer. Spencer started dissecting. "I never use skin hooks for a mastectomy," he went on. "They leave marks and cause scar-tissue build up. Here, hold the edge of the skin with a moist towel and apply some tension. Gently. Good." Spencer found the tissue plane and started dividing the tissues. "You see?" he said. "No bleeding. Well, not much. Here, you try it." He passed the laser probe to Mike and took over the retraction of the tissues. After a few moments, Mike got the hang of it and was carefully removing the skin, with its attached thin layer of fat, from the underlying breast tissue.

The patient's arm had been extended at right angles to her body, and they were working toward the armpit, where the lymph nodes draining the breast were located. These would be removed together with the breast tissue, since they provided one of the common routes of spread of cancer.

"That plane runs out before you get to the lymph nodes," warned Spencer. "The skin gets thin, and you have to be careful not to buttonhole it. That's a big no-no."

Although Mike was competent enough in this area of surgery, Spencer's mastery was apparent, and Mike was glad to be learning from such an expert.

The operation proceeded efficiently; Spencer held out his hand, and instantly the scrub tech passed him the correct instrument. Very little was said—a rhythm had developed between the two surgeons and the scrub tech, a good tight rhythm that they all joined in and appreciated. When the breast tissue together with all the accessible lymph nodes from the axilla had been removed, the only thing that remained to be done was to close the long incision over the bare chest wall, and since this was a relatively simple matter, they both felt able to relax.

"Make sure you label that specimen correctly," said Spencer to the circulating nurse. He glanced at Mike. "You probably know this already," he said, "but we send all our pathology specimens to Conn-Path Laboratories. It's a private outfit, and they're quick and accurate, not like the medical center path lab."

He stopped operating briefly and watched the circulator carefully while she filled in the forms and attached them to the specimen container. Mike kept on putting in the skin clips, wondering why Spencer was paying so much attention to a routine function. He figured that maybe in the past they'd lost one of his specimens or sent it to the wrong lab.

"We used to send our stuff to the med center labs, like everybody else," went on Spencer, still watching the circulator, who was getting uncomfortable under the scrutiny. "But they'd been known to lose our specimens, and they were too slow with their reports. The ConnPath people are very efficient, and we send them *everything*." He emphasized the last word, and turned to glance at Mike, then back at the incision. "Good, we're just about done. Now we check for any residual bleeding, especially up in the axilla . . ." Spencer spoke with an easy confidence, backed up by the huge number of similar operations he'd performed.

Now that the difficult part of the procedure was done, the atmosphere in the O.R. relaxed. They all knew they'd done a good job, the case had gone well, and there was a kind of mild euphoria in the air.

"Put another rubber drain up in the axilla, Mike," said Spencer, after critically examining the area. While Mike put the drain in, Spencer pulled off his gloves but stayed at the table. "Did you hear the story about the two old ladies sitting out on their porch?" he asked Mike, grinning over his mask. The anesthesiologist, who had heard it before, rolled her eyes, and the scrub tech grinned in anticipation.

Mike hadn't heard the story.

"Well, these two old girls were out there on the porch, rocking in their rocking chairs, and through the door they could hear the sweet strains of old-time music coming from the radio. One of the old ladies stopped rocking and said, 'Mildred, do you remember the minuet?' The other old lady sighed and said, 'Honey, I don't even remember the men I *slept* with!'"

They laughed. Even the circulating nurse, who didn't always appreciate Spencer's occasionally sexist humor, laughed too, then clicked her tongue in mock disapproval.

"You're in a pretty good mood today, Dr. Spencer," observed Naomi Price, the anesthesiologist, as she put away her equipment.

"I'm on vacation," he replied. "Starting tomorrow. Well, it isn't really a vacation, I'm going on one of those continuing-education cruises."

"Where?" asked Mike.

"The Greek islands. Have you been there?"

Mike grinned and shook his head. "No sir," he said. The farthest he'd been from New Coventry was Indianapolis, where he'd taken part in a vintage-car race.

"You'd like it," said Spencer. "Just prescribe

enough Verafamil or whatever, and the drug companies'll send you there for free. Even better, if you publish a paper that pushes their product, they'll set up all-expenses-paid seminars for you in Tahiti or wherever you want. Now let me show you how we apply the patented Dermott Spencer mastectomy dressing . . ."

Mike had been given the vacant office next to Derek Provost's. Derek's wife, Evelyn, was an interior decorator, and Derek, Evelyn, and Mike had put their heads together to decide how the office would be furnished. Mike liked things plain and simple and would have been perfectly happy with the existing furnishings—an old wooden desk, chairs, and metal bookcase—but he was firmly overruled on that. They finished up by ordering a big walnut table that he would use as a desk, two big ivory-colored leather armchairs, and a computer work-station that would go next to the window. When Mike suggested filing cabinets, Derek shook his head. When they reorganized the practice after Fred Newsome's death, he explained, they decided to keep all patient files on the computer. Actually, Tony, the office manager, had made that decision. When it was essential to have hard copies, these were kept in a central filing area.

"All the old paper files have been transcribed," said Derek. "We don't have a single one left in the office."

"So how do you access records of somebody else's

patients? What if I'm covering for you and need to
see a chart?"

"No problem," said Derek. "We have an IWS that
connects all the computers in the office."

"What's that?" asked Mike.

"Internal web server," replied Derek. "That way
we can exchange patient files from one computer to
the other. I can write into your files and you can do
the same into mine, although you can't take anything
out. So the clerks can do the billing from one central
terminal, input lab data, stuff like that. It's really
cool. The system also ties into the Radiology Associates downstairs, and ConnPath . . . and a couple of
other places. We use them exclusively for our refer-
rals. Did Spencer tell you about that?"

Mike nodded, looking at the terminal on the desk.
He was used to computer systems and had of course
used the one at NCMC, but it wasn't nearly as sophisticated as this one.

"Here . . ." Derek was enjoying himself. He
pressed a few keys, and the screen lit up with a
blotchy purple image. "What do you think this is,
Mike?" Derek grinned at him.

Mike came around to Derek's side of the desk, and
stared at the screen. "Looks like colon . . ." A moment later he pointed at a clump of dark blue nucle-
ated cells in the upper left-hand corner. "That looks
like a cancer up there, an adenocarcinoma. Lots of
mitotic figures . . . It's clearly invaded the
muscularis . . ." Mike used the mouse to scroll the

entire slide. "I don't see any lymph node metastases. So that would make it a Duke's B lesion, right?"

"You should have been a pathologist," grinned Derek. "You're entirely correct."

Mike was about to say something when he noticed the patient's name in small letters at the top of the screen. "Darla Finsten? Our Darla in the O.R.?"

"Yes. I'm operating on her tomorrow. She's in Room 1204, if you want to stop by and say hi. She'd be glad to see you."

"Sure will." Mike pointed at the computer. "Can somebody show me how to use this?" he asked Derek.

"Yes, Tony will. Tony Danzig. He's the office manager. I don't think you've met him yet, have you? Derek grinned, and looked at Mike, hesitating for a moment. "You'd remember him if you had, because he's into body building . . . Tony's very competent, but . . . well, he's originally from Germany or Austria or somewhere like that. He's one of those hyperefficient types, and I'm warning you right now that he's a bit arrogant and doesn't have much sense of humor."

"Sounds like one of us, all right," said Mike. "How come I haven't seen him?"

"He's been away," replied Derek vaguely. "He's due back on Monday. Tony takes care of just about everything that isn't strictly medical. That includes keeping track of billing, cash flow, insurance, stuff like that. He also put in our computer system, so he'll give you the official computer tutorial."

"Great." Mike stared at Derek for a moment. "You don't sound entirely enthused about the guy."

Derek grinned, and looked unexpectedly embarrassed. "No, actually, Tony's okay. It was tough at first, I admit. He came on board about a couple of years ago—after Fred Newsome died and we reorganized the practice. He . . . well, actually, the good folk who put up the financing for us found him, and we really needed somebody to run the office, somebody with the right kind of experience, so we were glad to get him." Derek gave Mike a sidelong look. "Actually, there was a fair amount of tension in the practice for a while after he came, but we're pretty well settled down now." Derek was obviously anxious to change the subject, and glanced at the door. "Is Pauline taking good care of you?"

"She's great. I'm very glad she was assigned to me."

"She insisted. I think she'd have left if we'd given you one of the other secretaries." Derek grinned. "You certainly have quite an effect on women." He paused for a second, looking at Mike. "I think Evelyn dreams about you."

"Nightmares, more likely."

Derek went to the door, opened it and said, "Pauline, when Mr. Danzig comes back on Monday, will you ask him to give Dr. Richmond the computer orientation course?"

Derek came back and looked at his watch. "Let's pack it in for the day. Evelyn and I are taking you out to dinner tonight, in case you'd forgotten."

"I hadn't forgotten."

Mike walked back to the hospital, still feeling disoriented after the ending of his residency. In a way he missed the moment-to-moment excitement and responsibility of being a chief resident, the leader of a team. Although now he slept every night, he still occasionally jumped awake in the early hours, thinking his alarm hadn't gone off and that he was late for the O.R.

He went up to the twelfth floor and looked into Darla's room, but she was asleep and he didn't want to wake her. Coming out of the elevator on the ground floor, he saw Terry Catlin and Lou Gardner walking past, deep in conversation. They didn't see him, but Mike had a feeling that they weren't talking about patients. Terry was presently working in the emergency room, a traditional in-between job, which was surprising, because the New Coventry surgical program had a good reputation and graduates didn't usually have much difficulty finding jobs. Maybe he was just treading water, waiting for something.

Derek had made dinner reservations at the Moti Mahal, a small Indian restaurant on Park Street, which he said was particularly good. Mike didn't know anything about Indian food, but he was enthusiastic and ready to learn. The Provosts were already there when Mike arrived. Evelyn was tall, attractive in a rather flamboyant way, with an impressive figure, and her smooth, shoulder-length blond hair shone in the candlelight. She wasn't looking too happy, and Mike wondered if she and Derek were having problems. She seemed to brighten up when he appeared.

"The chef makes a really delicious tandoori chicken," said Derek, glancing over his menu after Mike had sat down. The restaurant was rather dark, with candles in glass containers on the table, and Mike had to peer to read the menu. Not that it told him much; words like *dahl*, *biriyani*, and *chapati* meant nothing to him.

"Tandoori means that it was cooked in a tandoor," explained Evelyn, watching Mike. "That's a clay oven with a live coal or wood fire. Before it's cooked, the chicken's marinated for twenty-four hours, then it's roasted and served with pickled onions and vegetables."

"Why don't you guys order?" suggested Mike. "I'll eat whatever you select."

The waiter appeared and Derek ordered the tandoori chicken for Mike, sindhi gosht for himself, and Evelyn wanted to try the eggplant bharta. It all appeared a few minutes later on a laden trolley, with accompanying poppadums, naan bread, shredded coconut, sliced bananas, and various chutneys and relishes.

"This is a great time in your life, Mike," said Derek, sitting back, looking very relaxed. "You're getting really busy, and by the end of the year you should be more financially secure, and you'll be starting to make some real money."

"The only problem is that you won't have any time to spend it," said Evelyn, glancing at her husband.

Mike nodded. "I'm having a good time. I even did some work on my car yesterday and took it out for a ride on the Monoxide Highway."

"What's that?" asked Evelyn.

"I–95. You notice the air quality more when you don't have air conditioning."

"Mike has this fantastic old car," Derek told Evelyn. "It's an Aston-Martin, the kind James Bond used in the 007 movies."

"I love old cars," said Evelyn, watching Mike. "Would you take me out in it some time?"

"Sure. It's a bit cramped, though."

Evelyn didn't look as if that would present a major problem.

"Don't you have a girlfriend right now, Mike?" asked Derek.

"Nothing serious," said Mike, glancing at the tandoori chicken. He picked up his fork. "I'm glad Indians don't use chopsticks."

Out of the corner of his eye, Mike saw a heavyset, well-dressed man get up from a table at the far end of the restaurant and come toward them.

"Hi, Derek," said the newcomer, smiling, his hand outstretched. "Nice to see you without a tape recorder between us."

"Yeah, hello, Haiman," said Derek. "Evelyn, this is attorney Haiman Gold. I may have mentioned him to you."

"Whatever he said is probably unprintable, Mrs.

Provost," smiled Haiman, looking very much at ease. "But I'm sure he told you that outside the courtroom we're good friends."

"This is Mike Richmond," said Derek, looking unaccountably flustered. He nodded in Mike's direction. "He's just joined our group."

Haiman turned to face him and gazed at Mike with interest. "Nice to meet you, Dr. Richmond," he said, looking as if he were filing the name away for future reference. "I'm sure our paths will cross sooner or later."

Haiman stayed and chatted a few moments longer, apparently not aware that as far as Derek was concerned, he wasn't welcome.

"So that was Haiman Gold," said Evelyn thoughtfully after he'd gone. "He seems a lot nicer than what you said."

"You've probably heard of Haiman," said Derek to Mike, who got the impression that Derek was choosing his words carefully. "Haiman Gold was a nothing attorney just a few years ago, and now he does most of the medical-malpractice business in New Coventry county."

"He sounded pretty sure of himself," said Mike, breaking off another piece of naan bread. It tasted good—something between regular bread and pizza crust, with a slight herbal flavor.

"When he said your paths would cross at some point?" Derek sighed, and looked over Mike's shoulder at where Haiman Gold had returned to his table and was sitting down. "Well, you know, in our group we've all had malpractice suits against us. Of course, we're not alone—I don't know of any surgeon in New Coventry who hasn't been sued a few times. Hey . . ." Derek lifted one shoulder in a deprecating way. "The way we look at it nowadays, it's just part of the cost of doing business. The cases take up a lot of time, what with depositions and everything, and you have to deal with people like Haiman Gold, but after you've been hit with a few suits you just shrug and keep going. Unless you've really screwed up, they all get settled anyway."

"Is that why Spencer is so obsessive about documentation?"

"Right. Now let's talk about something else, for God's sake. You can't even go out for a goddamned meal these days without bumping into a malpractice attorney." He turned to his wife. "Evelyn, what's on at the Long Wharf Theater this month?"

"Waiting for Godot." She smiled at Mike. "We saw it a couple of years ago, and it was just boring. I'd have more fun waiting for a bus, and the hell with Godot."

As she spoke, she moved slightly in her chair and Mike felt her leg come up against his and stay there. Thinking it was an accidental motion, he moved away a little, but within moments her leg was back firmly against his, and this time there was no mistaking its pressure.

"I see your friend Terry Catlin's working in the E.R.," Derek mentioned casually.

Mike bent to pick up his napkin and moved his

legs out of range. "Yes," he replied noncommittally. "I saw him."

"He still seems to think he can join our group." Derek's voice was casual, but his eyes weren't. "Just thought I'd mention it."

"Thanks. That thought had crossed my mind."

Derek nodded. "He's got some friends in the group. They're watching you already, I'm sure you know. They're waiting for you to make a mistake or two."

They finished their meal and went their separate ways, Derek and Evelyn to their exclusive home in Rocky Point, and Mike to the same apartment he'd lived in as a resident. He wasn't going to stay there much longer—Evelyn had already found what she called *a suitable place* for him. A mile from their home some very nice condos were going up next to the golf course, with a pool, a private beach, and a health club. Mike thought it would be better to live somewhere a little farther from the Provosts.

Chapter 8

For several days Stephanie simply ignored the lump in her breast. She knew it was still there, and that awareness was at the back of her mind all the time, but she figured that if she waited long enough, it would eventually go away. She'd probably had several that had come and gone, she rationalized, bumps that she'd never even known about. And then there had been the civic award announcement, the presentation by the mayor, the media coverage, all of it done in what seemed a great hurry. Stephanie wondered about the level of Carl Hartmann's influence in the town—he certainly had a lot of irons in the fire, she reflected, and knew how to use them.

The next morning Stephanie got in to work a little later than usual, and the phone on her desk was ringing.

"Oh, good, Stephanie, I'm glad you're here," said the voice of Dr. Sammons. "Can you come over to my office, please?"

"Give me ten minutes," said Stephanie, wondering about this unusual summons. She had a scheduled meeting with Dr. Sammons once a week, and rarely saw him otherwise.

"Okay, ten minutes."

She replaced the phone, and looked up to see Jean Forrest, who was making signs at her through the window. Stephanie waved to her to come in.

Jean sat on the corner of the desk, one long leg swinging. "You remember that doc we had a problem with? Dr. Gardner? Well, I wanted to see what his recent admissions were like, if he'd straightened out—you know." Jean's big eyes were fixed intently on Stephanie. "Well," she went on, standing up, "you're not going to believe this."

Stephanie waited, smiling. Jean had the ability to turn the simplest event into a drama.

"He's off the computer!" said Jean, her long hands coming up as if she were pulling a rabbit out of a hat. "I tried five different ways to access his file, but each time it came up with 'This area cannot be accessed without Class One clearance.'"

Stephanie pressed a few buttons on her computer terminal but came up with the same message. "I don't know," she answered. "I don't have a Class One, so I can't help you. Why do you want to access his file, anyway?"

Jean said, "No real reason. Actually, I wanted to see if he was still, you know, having the same problems with his admissions that he was before."

"Good thought," replied Stephanie. "I'm going up to see Dr. Sammons in a few minutes, and I'll ask him. I did mention it last week, and he said he'd take care of it."

Jean looked at her boss with her big, questioning eyes, hesitated, then went back to her booth.

Stephanie picked up her folder and took the stairs up to Dr. Sammons' office. He was on the phone, looking preoccupied, and waved her to a chair, then half turned away from her, the receiver pressed to his ear. Finally he said, "Yes, she's here now, sir. I'll send her along in a few minutes."

Dr. Sammons put the phone down. "That was Mr. Hartmann." He looked at Stephanie for what seemed a long time. "You seem to have made quite an impression on him," he said, putting his hands together on his desk. He had a way of arching one thick eyebrow when he was puzzled or annoyed, and right now it was up. "Mr. Hartmann wants to talk to you," he went on. "I believe he wants you to do some kind of research project for him, something involving numbers." He pulled on the distal joint of his left index until it clicked, then, satisfied, he dropped his hands under the desk. "Not permanent, probably just for three or four weeks." He paused.

"Why me?"

"I have no idea." Dr. Sammons sighed. "At his level, I'd expect him to be more interested in financing and acquiring new companies, that kind of thing." He shook his head. "That's what I would have thought, anyway." He glanced curiously at Stephanie. "How well do you know Mr. Hartmann?" he asked.

"Not at all. I'd never even talked to him until that time he had his briefcase stolen."

"I suppose that's where he's coming from, then."
He sat back in his padded chair, looking more relaxed. "He's been asking how things were going with
you, if you were doing a good job, that kind of thing,
and wanted to see your CV and your personnel file.
And then he arranged that civic award . . . He seems
to have taken a real shine to you."

"When am I supposed to start?"

"He'll tell you. Soon, I think."

"Dr. Sammons," said Stephanie, "can you tell me
a bit about him? Mr. Hartmann?"

Dr. Sammons hesitated, staring up at the ceiling.
"I suppose if you boiled it all down, what he wants
most is loyalty," he said. "Unswerving loyalty from
the people who work for him. Unless you're quite
sure you can give him that, Stephanie, and that you
can keep whatever you learn to yourself, don't take
the job." Dr. Sammons shook his head, as if he'd
maybe spoken too frankly. "Now, to get back to U.R.
I decided to try Jean Forrest out as your replacement—until you come back, that is. What do you
think?"

Stephanie nodded. "She'll do a good job. And that
reminds me," she went on, "What happened with
that Dr. Gardner? One of the reviewers told me that
he's off the computer."

Two small spots of red appeared on Dr. Sammons's cheeks. "Actually, he still is on the computer," he said carefully. "But apparently he's
getting some kind of special handling. I suppose

they're just keeping a very close eye on what he's doing."

"Isn't that our job?" asked Stephanie. "We've kept an eye on different doctors before, flagging them so we can check on their admissions and take corrective action if we need to."

"Stephanie," said Dr. Sammons, standing up. "I don't make the rules here. And I don't know everything that goes on in this company—and quite frankly I don't want to. I just do my job and figure that if they want me to know something, they'll tell me, so I don't ask questions. It's just . . ." Dr. Sammons suddenly looked old and tired, and his smile didn't come as easily. He stood up. "I guess I've learned the hard way how to be a survivor in this business, Stephanie, and I hope you can do the same." He paused. "And now you'd better go along to see Mr. Hartmann." He stood up, smiling his close-to-retirement smile. "If you have any more questions, you can ask him."

Ann Boyd, Carl Hartmann's secretary, ushered Stephanie into his office. It was big, or rather, long—the walls between two adjacent offices had been knocked down and the second office was now used as a conference area, judging by the big table with ten high-backed chairs around it. On a huge wooden desk were a computer terminal and a phone console, and the rest of the space was taken up with little piles of papers, each with a paperweight perched on it.

Carl was behind his desk, facing the door, shirtsleeves rolled up over his thick arms. He looked even bulkier sitting down. Every button doing its duty, Stephanie thought, looking at his big belly bulging under his shirt. His dark jacket hung off the back of his chair. He looked up when Stephanie came in, and grinned at her. "You looked good on TV last night," he said. "Congratulations on the award."

"Thank you," replied Stephanie. "I don't feel I did much to earn it."

"Not your decision," replied Carl. "I thought it was a pity to waste someone with such abilities on running utilization review. Have you ever used spreadsheets?" he asked.

"Yes, sir."

"Well, don't just stand there, sit down," he said, amicably enough, indicating one of the two upholstered chairs facing the desk.

Stephanie sat down.

"Do you know statistics? Can you apply standard tests, like chi-squared? Have you used any statistical software packs, like Lotus? Or Microsoft?"

"Yes, I have, but I'm not really—"

"Good." Carl swung around on his chair. "Now, this is what I want you to do," he said. "You may know that Hartmann Insurance is at the center of a group of interrelated corporations and other entities. Each member of the group is independent within certain parameters and designated as a profit center. But each corporation is owned by a single entity, a nominal offshore holding company." He stopped, and gazed at Stephanie for a moment. "Is your accounting background keeping up with this?"

Stephanie nodded, wondering if he was being sarcastic. "Yes," she replied. "So far."

"For a number of tax reasons that don't concern you, each of these entities is a legally independent corporation, and the books reflect this. What I need is an integrated system that will reflect the overall financial status of each unit and also the entire organization. The people from Iber Corporation recently put in identical accounting systems in each of the companies, so your work shouldn't be too difficult."

"Couldn't Iber have set up integrating software programs when you put in the new accounting systems?" asked Stephanie. "Then they could give you all the data you need automatically."

"Yes, of course we could have done that." Carl sounded as if he were talking to a bright but painfully naïve child. "But I specifically didn't want to get the information that way. This is to be a purely internal project," he went on, his voice barely patient. Stephanie got the feeling that he couldn't wait to finish this interview so he could go back to talking to adults. "The information's going to be for my use only, and I don't want it to be accessed by anyone but me. And that's also why I wanted somebody outside the accounting system to do this research."

Stephanie was about to comment but decided not to. Carl Hartmann was telling her what he wanted, not asking for her opinion.

"Could you tell me something before we get started?" she asked.

"Sure."

"How long do you think this job will take? Will I be going back to utilization review when it's done?"

"I'm not sure," he replied. "I've been considering getting a personal assistant to help me coordinate the different aspects of this business. As you can see, I'm not the best-organized person in the world." He waved a fat hand at his desk. "So depending on how things go in the next couple of weeks, we'll see. If it works out, fine. If it doesn't work out, then, yes, you'll go back to U.R. if that's what you wish."

"Okay," she said. "Thanks. That's all I wanted to know."

"I'm putting you in one of the offices down the hall," he said. "And I've authorized Security to give you a Level Two clearance. You'll get a new password and I.D. number, and that'll give you access to the data you'll need, but with Level Two, all corporate identifiers are removed. Which means you'll be dealing with Corporation One, Corporation Two, and so on. You'll soon get the hang of it."

Stephanie knew that Carl Hartmann had a reputation for being close-mouthed about business matters, but it seemed that this level of corporate secrecy didn't make too much sense. For instance, his businesses would have to be registered with the Connecticut Insurance Commission, so if anyone wanted to know the corporate structure of Hartmann Insurance and its affiliated companies, it wouldn't be too difficult to find out.

Carl gave her some more details about the format he wanted. Then he said, "I'm sure you understand that this project is totally confidential. You are not to discuss this material with anyone, whether you stay on with me or go back to U.R. I want that to be absolutely clear." He stared at Stephanie.

"Yes, sir. When do you want me to start?"

"Monday. That'll give you time to finish up any projects you're on, and familiarize whoever will be replacing you in U.R. Oh, and by the way, you'll be getting a raise, starting next week . . . let's see, right now you're making $42,250, right? We'll bump that up to $50,000," he said, then stood up. He was massive, friendly, and intimidating at the same time. "It's not just a gift," he said, still smiling. "I expect a great deal from people who work with me. You become part of the family, with all the privileges and the responsibilities that go with that. I hope Dr. Sammons explained that to you."

Getting her new I.D. number and password from Security took longer than she'd expected. The office was located on the ninth floor, the floor above Stephanie's utilization-review area, and along the corridor from Dr. Sammons's suite. She stopped at the reception desk. The man behind it was talking on the phone, but he looked at her steadily in a way apparently designed to make her feel uncomfortable, until he put the phone down.

"Yes?"

"I've come for a new security clearance," she said.

"Okay . . ." The man was small, agile-looking, with a pointed face and a gravelly voice that was deeper than she expected from his appearance. A plastic I.D.

with an unflattering photo bore the name Sam Scheiffer. "You need to see Mr. Rankin." He stood up. "Come with me."

Stephanie followed him down the corridor, past an open door on the left. She got a glimpse of a large room with several men inside, a bank of black-and-white surveillance monitors, and a high stack of electronic gear with little colored lights on a console.

George Rankin looked what he was, a former military policeman. He had humorless, aggressive blue eyes, a fleshy nose with little veins on it over a reddish mustache, and the ruddy features and rounded gut of a man who liked beer in spite of what it did to his blood pressure.

"Have a seat, Miss Hopkins." Rankin stared at her with the same kind of predatory inquisitiveness as Sam Scheiffer. From the all-male feel about the place, Stephanie was willing to bet that no women worked in that department.

"We're going to give you what we call a security interview," said Rankin. "Now it's purely voluntary, you don't have to do it if you don't want to, and you'll sign a statement that I've told you so."

"How about if I don't want to do it?" asked Stephanie, smiling.

"No problem. You just don't get your clearance, and Mr. Hartmann will be informed."

In the next fifteen minutes, Rankin asked her about every detail of her life, her parents, friends—both men and women—past and present, any clubs and organizations she belonged to, the name of her bank, credit cards, whether she paid off her account each month, and whether she owned stocks and had a broker. By the time he finished, Stephanie felt as if she'd been stripped naked.

He then took her into another room where a young man with short, bristly hair fingerprinted her and took a photo of her that he laminated into a special plastic I.D. card with an electronic strip, marked Level 2. Then he brought her back to Rankin's office and handed him the I.D.

Back in her department, she thought that if this was what she had to go through to get a Level 2 clearance, she never wanted a Level 1. Why was Carl Hartmann so obsessed with security? And it must cost a lot to maintain such a bunch of people and all that equipment. A strange man. He seemed so disarmingly large and earthy. He had been completely professional with her, but why all the secrecy with Corporation 1, 2, 3, and all that? And Dr. Sammons had warned her to be careful.

As she came through the doorway to her office, she must have jarred something, because she became aware of her breast again. It wasn't painful, but it didn't let her forget about it for more than a few hours at a time. She knew she had to do something about it. Whom should she see? She decided to ask Evie. She would know whom to recommend. But she put it off, and by the time she thought of it again, it was time to go home.

Chapter 9

Mike's introduction to the office manager, Tony Danzig, occurred the next Monday, and not under the best circumstances. They had arranged to meet for the computer tutorial at eleven that morning, but Mike got tied up at the hospital and didn't get to the office until twenty minutes after the hour.

He found Tony sitting at his desk, with the computer on. When Tony looked up at him over the monitor, he was obviously not pleased.

Tony was five foot ten, Mike guessed, built like a welterweight, all bone and muscle. He was about the same age as Mike, light-complected, with very pale blue eyes whose small black pupils gave them a staring quality. He had blond hair, so blond that it was almost white, with almost invisible albino eyebrows of the same color. Mike glanced at his hands. They were businesslike, bigger than one would expect from the rest of him, thick-fingered, strong, with thick fine hair on the back that caught the light from the monitor.

"Come in," said Tony, glancing at the clock. "I'm Tony Danzig, the office manager. Welcome to the practice." Tony spoke in precisely enunciated English, and although it was almost accentless, it was obviously not his native language.

"Sorry I'm late," said Mike cheerfully. "Chalk it up to Dr. Miller. I was helping him over at the hospital."

Tony nodded. "Next time, please let me know if you're going to be held up," he said, then smiled over the desk at Mike.

Watching him, Mike almost caught his breath. There was something about Tony's white-toothed smile that was so cold-blooded, it took Mike by surprise.

Then Tony's face was watchful and bland again, and Mike thought he'd imagined it.

"Please pull up a chair," said Tony. "I assume you're familiar with the Windows 95 operating system?"

Mike sat down. "I wouldn't say I'm familiar, but I can find my way around it."

"Good. First I want to show you how we have set up our different office forms. Once you're in the Medform program, each of those icons . . ."—Tony indicated the top of the screen—"represents a template. For instance, if you're doing an initial history and physical exam, you would select this icon." Tony moved the mouse a little until the arrow was over the icon, then he pressed the left button, and instantly a blank form appeared on the screen. "Now your secretary will already have typed in the patient's name, address, insurance information, and so forth." Tony went on very methodically; he showed Mike how to enter data, and explained how it would be used for coding, billing, and information retrieval. His big fingers wandered quickly across the keyboard as he demonstrated the functions. Mike watched him; there was no question that the man was an expert. But Mike found all of it rather boring.

"Are there games?" he asked. "Like Solitaire or Seventh Guest? I hope they're included in the package."

There was a pause, and Tony's fingers froze over the keyboard. "Games? I have no idea, Dr. Richmond," he replied slowly. "But in any case I don't suppose that Dr. Spencer hired you to sit here in your office and play games."

"No. I'm sorry, I was joking. Please go on."

Tony nodded, watching Mike carefully. "Yes," he said, then took a deep breath. "The office computers are connected by an internal web server," he went on. "That way the work you do here on this terminal can be picked up on the main office computer for billing, or by a colleague who needs to see the data on one of your patients."

"It sounds like a pretty powerful system," said Mike, concerned by the palpable tension between Tony and himself. There was no point making an enemy of the office manager, and he made an effort to placate Tony. "Dr. Provost said you're quite an expert. Did you set this system up?"

Tony nodded, apparently unmoved by Mike's conciliatory tone. "I did," he replied, "with some professional assistance. We designed it to have plenty of room for expansion, for instance, if at some point we need to add more work stations."

"How about security?" asked Mike. "How about if the cleaning lady wants to take a peek at my files?"

"You'll be assigned a code name and an eight-digit number that only you will know," replied Tony, in his impassive, careful voice. "Security is one of our highest priorities here, and you can be sure we're on top of it."

For the next half hour, Tony went over the various functions of the computer. "Of course there are certain additional functions you won't be concerned with," Tony mentioned. "So there's no point in my going over them with you."

Mike looked at his watch. "Are we about done? I'm sorry, but I have to go back to the hospital."

"Yes, we're finished, Dr. Richmond. And if you have any questions or run into any difficulties, please contact me. As you know, I'm here to help." Tony nodded briskly, as if his last words had cost him some effort. He stood up and left the office, walking like an athlete, on the balls of his feet, leaving Mike with the feeling that Tony Danzig was one very tough character, and a very strange person to be office manager of a medical practice, although he certainly seemed to know his stuff. He decided to ask Derek about Tony's background, and how they had come to employ him.

On his way out, Mike stopped at Pauline's desk. She had turned out to be a capable and pleasant woman, and of course she had a soft spot for Mike.

Today she was in a formal, dark blue business suit with pinstripes, and she looked good.

"How did it go?" she asked, looking up from her papers. She had a nice smile, open, with little wrinkles at the corners of her eyes that suggested laughter even when she was at her most serious.

"With Tony? Great. Didn't you hear us joking and carrying on in there? I hope we didn't make too much noise."

Pauline's eyes smiled, and she glanced at the door, but she didn't laugh.

"To change the topic, Dr. Richmond," she said, "did you ever come across a Dr. Newsome? I occasionally get papers with his name on them, and I know he doesn't work here."

"He used to," replied Mike. "In fact, he was the head of this group before Dr. Spencer."

"Oh, yes, I remember now," said Pauline, in what seemed to Mike to be an over-casual tone. "I saw it in the papers a couple of years ago. Didn't he die in a plane crash?"

"Yes, he did." Mike headed for the door. Pauline seemed to want to carry on with the conversation, but he had to go back to the hospital.

She smiled at him in a motherly way. "Did you remember you're seeing new patients this afternoon?"

"Yes. I'll be back in a little while. I still have some charts to finish up over at NCMC."

"You also have Dr. Spencer's follow-ups to see."

"Right. When does he come back?"

"This coming Monday."

"Okay . . . I should be back in about an hour."

After Mike left, Pauline took a little walk along the corridor to see what everyone was doing, then, finding that all was quiet, she came back into her office and closed the door. She shut down her computer terminal and switched it on again. Then she took a folded piece of paper out of her purse, smoothed it out, and placed it next to the monitor so she could read the columns of letters and numbers. She started to copy them into the computer after the C: prompt, one after the other, but none of them allowed her to enter the system. After about a half hour, she got scared and put the paper back in her purse, entered her normal password that gave access to the part of the system she was authorized to enter, and went back to inputting billing data for the accounting department.

Stephanie put it off for another couple of days, then finally got around to calling Evie. The operator tracked her down in the break room.

"What's up?" she asked.

Stephanie explained.

"Go see Spencer," replied Evie immediately. "He's the best breast man around here," she said. "You want his number?"

"No, thanks," replied Stephanie. "I have it here. That group's in the Lovejoy Plan, no problem."

"Oh," said Evie. "I just remembered. He's away. I mean Spencer—he's out of town." She paused. "Hey, listen, go see Mike Richmond. He's in the same group. I'd take my boobs to him any time, whether there was something the matter with them or not."

"Evie," said Stephanie, "I'm sure you like this guy, but I want to have this checked by somebody who knows what he's doing."

"I was just kidding, I'm sorry," replied Evie. "Mike's really good. He's careful, and he takes very good care of his patients. He has a great rep around the hospital; ask anybody. You'll like him—Spencer's group took him on, and that's enough of a reference in itself. Anyway, you know I wouldn't suggest him just because he makes my heart beat faster."

"Okay, thanks, Evie. I'll think about it."

"Will you call him?"

"Yeah. Maybe."

"Do it. Don't mess around with this, Stephanie. The sooner you take care of it the better. You know that."

"Okay, okay. Listen, I'm going down to the mall after work. You want to come?"

"Sure. At six?"

"Right. I'll meet you there."

Stephanie put the phone down and stared at it. Without thinking, she put her hand on her right breast, then looked up Dr. Spencer's phone number in the list of Lovejoy Hospital's affiliated doctors, and, after confirming that Spencer was indeed on vacation, she asked the receptionist for an appointment to see Dr. Richmond.

"Just hold on, I'll put you through to his secretary. Her name is Pauline."

A moment later, Pauline Minsky was on the line. She had a friendly and reassuring voice, thought Stephanie, whose anxiety was making her unusually sensitive to vibrations from other people.

"Did you say you work for Hartmann Insurance?" asked Pauline.

"Yes. I'm in utilization review."

"Oh, sorry, I didn't recognize the name, but I know we talk to you people all the time." Pauline had a pleasant, friendly laugh. "Anybody who works for Hartmann Insurance gets special treatment here, you can be sure of that."

"Just the ordinary treatment should do nicely, thanks," replied Stephanie, smiling, but feeling reassured all the same. If Dr. Richmond was anything as nice as Pauline, the whole experience might not be too bad.

"You want to come in this afternoon?" Dr. Richmond has a slot open at four-fifteen."

"Wonderful. Four-fifteen. I'll see you then," said Stephanie, relieved. She knew that except for emergencies, the usual wait to see a surgeon in New Coventry was at least several days, and she was glad she wouldn't have the wait and the anxiety.

"Would you mind coming about twenty minutes earlier? That would be five minutes to four? Since you're a new patient, we'll need to get some details. I'm sure you know the routine."

"Sure, no problem. Five to four—I'll see you then. And thanks for getting me in so quickly, Pauline. I really appreciate it."

Stephanie put the phone down, her heart beating fast, but feeling that she had just done something rather virtuous. She also felt that she might just be wasting everybody's time, and imagined this Dr. Mike Richmond looking at her, examining her, laughing, and saying "You're worried about *this*?" Stephanie, who didn't blush easily, blushed at the mere thought. It was just as well her appointment was for today, she realized; otherwise she knew she would have canceled it.

Her mind went back to her interview with Carl Hartmann. Mr. Hartmann, with his big belly, rolled-up shirtsleeves, his friendly expression and a gaze that went right through you . . . Still, it sounded like an interesting project, and something she could do well. The security aspect had stopped bothering her—they probably did the same thing in the other insurance companies.

Thinking about secrecy made her think of the errant Dr. Gardner, so out of curiosity, she tried again to pull up his file on the computer. She got the same message as before—*This area cannot be accessed without a Level 1 security clearance.* Dr. Sammons had said that there were things that went on in the company that he didn't want to know about, but that didn't really mean anything—he was close to retirement and more interested in improving his golf score than worrying about the inner workings of the company. Stephanie sat down in her office chair and got back to work, but she couldn't shake the persistent notion that there was something not quite kosher going on.

Chapter 10

At a quarter to four that afternoon, Stephanie put away her papers, locked her desk, then closed her office door and went over to Jean Forrest's booth.

"Jean," said Stephanie, looking over the partition. "I have a doctor's appointment in a few minutes. I'm taking my pager, so you can call me if anything comes up."

Jean looked up. "Are you all right, boss?" she asked. "I mean, healthwise?"

"Sure. This is just a checkup, routine stuff. You know how it goes."

"Okay. I'll page you if there's a problem."

When Stephanie came through the door of the twenty-second-floor medical offices, she was astonished by the luxury she saw everywhere. A penthouse location, lots of space, elegant lighting, costly wood and chrome furnishings, ivory-colored leather chairs, and smoky glass tables, with two huge arrangements of fresh exotic flowers in the reception area.

There were none of the usual long desks or counters. A young woman sat at a glass-topped table on the right and Stephanie came up to her. The discreet tag on her dress said, Imogene, and she invited Stephanie to sit in one of the easy chairs. On the coffee table were current copies of *Vogue*, *Architectural Digest*, and *Paris Match*, with a rack of other magazines next to the table.

Stephanie tried to control the anxiety that had taken hold of her when she came through the door, and she looked around. Behind her were two big glass-walled booths, each with comfortable chairs and a computer terminal on a glass-topped table. One of the booths was occupied, and Stephanie watched unobtrusively. An attractive, white-uniformed nurse was asking questions of an elderly gentleman and his wife and typing the answers directly into the terminal. Stephanie thought that was a good idea, getting rid of the forms that most doctors' offices required. She tried not to think about why she was there, but her anxiety was rising. Come on, she told herself, most women develop little lumps there from time to time, and it's no big deal.

A door opened, and a young woman wearing a white uniform came over to her. "Miss Hopkins? Stephanie?" she said, smiling. She led the way to the unoccupied booth. "Hi, my name's Michelle. Let's sit down over here so I can get your details. Can I get you a cup of coffee? Or juice?"

Michelle brought up a new-patient form on the screen and started to go through a comprehensive list of questions about Stephanie's health, asking about any previous illnesses, her family history, and a host of other matters. Michelle typed the answers directly into the computer. As she answered the questionnaire, Stephanie noticed that there was a fair amount of traffic in the area; doors opened, white-coated doctors and technicians walked in and out, patients came and went, but the carpeting muffled any noise they might have made. Without seeming to be, the office was obviously very busy.

At exactly fourteen minutes after four, one minute before she was due to see Dr. Richmond, Michelle pressed some keys on the terminal and smiled at Stephanie. "That's it," she said. "Now you can see Dr. Richmond. All the information I've input is now available to him. His office is right down that corridor, third on the left."

Stephanie went down the corridor, her feet sinking into the luxurious ivory-colored carpet. But in her nervousness she knocked on the second door on the left, and went in. It was clearly a business office, and the blond man who looked around from his computer terminal was obviously startled by the interruption. He stood up quickly. "Can I help you?"

"I'm sorry," said Stephanie, flustered. "I was looking for Dr. Richmond's office."

"It's the next door down." The man accompanied her to the door. Unsmiling but polite, he pointed out the door of Mike's office. Stephanie heard the door close and lock behind her.

Mike Richmond's office seemed out of keeping with the rest of the office area, but Stephanie didn't know that his new furniture hadn't arrived yet, and he was still using the old desk and chairs. A small metal bookcase stood against the wall opposite the window, and a couple of diplomas hung rather haphazardly on the wall behind him.

And Dr. Richmond himself didn't look particularly sophisticated or elegant, unlike what she'd expected from a member of the elite Spencer group. He was big, sure—Evie had gone on about that. But he grinned at her with such a wide, good-natured expression that she smiled back at him. His face had a few deep lines, she saw; his years of residency had left their permanent mark on him. Stephanie noticed that the ones around his mouth deepened when he smiled, making him look older.

"Come on in," he said reassuringly. "Have a seat." He pointed at the chair.

He watched Stephanie advance into the room and sit down. She had a nice way of walking, was carefully dressed in a businesslike outfit—what looked to Mike like a dark blue gabardine skirt, with a pleated white cotton dress blouse with more pearly buttons down the middle than seemed strictly necessary to hold it together, long, slim legs in dark stockings and shoes with a little stripe of white across the top. She certainly looks in sparkling good health, he thought, observing her with the steady gaze that physicians are permitted to level at men and women alike under professional circumstances.

"So what's the matter?" he asked after she sat down and arranged her skirt.

Stephanie told him.

"When did you notice it?"

"Oh . . . just a few days ago. Last week."

He asked a number of other questions, then Stephanie, not wanting to waste his time, said, "Your nurse, Michelle, already took a history, Dr. Richmond. She put the answers on the computer."

Mike grinned. "I know. But I can't tell much about you by looking at the computer. I can tell a lot more from looking directly at you and listening to your answers."

For no reason, Stephanie felt herself blush. Not enough, she hoped, for him to notice.

He finished with the questions a few minutes later and pressed the intercom button. Michelle came in and took her through to the exam room, where she instructed Stephanie to take her clothes off. She gave her a gray hospital-type gown to put on.

"I was thinking about you," said Michelle, "and I'm sure I've seen you before. Didn't you use to work at NCMC? I seem to remember your face."

"Sure did," replied Stephanie. "Mostly in the I.C.U., but that was a few years ago."

"I did my I.C.U. rotation there when I was a junior. We all thought you guys were something between Mother Teresa and God Almighty."

They found they had friends and acquaintances in common, so Michelle stayed and chatted while Stephanie changed.

"How do you like it here?" asked Stephanie, then couldn't help adding, "And how about Dr. Richmond?"

Michelle grinned. "Dr. Richmond's great. You know, this is a different kind of practice. They're very—well, I don't know quite how to say it—competitive, success-oriented, maybe. But Dr. Richmond's different—he's a lot more interested in taking care of his patients." Michelle dropped her voice and glanced at the door. "Between you and me, he's the one I would personally want to go to."

There was a knock on the door, and Michelle opened it.

"You guys ready?" asked Mike.

"Come on in."

In the office, Mike had been friendly with Stephanie, but now he was unsmiling and professional. He examined her breasts with a complete detachment that she found reassuring. And he was so gentle; she watched his face while he checked her, and his eyes were elsewhere, as if all his attention were focused on the sensors in his fingertips. He examined her very carefully, and Stephanie was starting to feel panicky when he finally closed the open front of her gown.

"I don't think there's anything there you need to worry about," he said.

Stephanie could feel herself exhaling as if she'd been holding her breath in ever since she first discovered the problem.

"Great," she said, getting off the examining table. She wanted to hug him. "Thank you. Oh my, what a relief!"

"Now, just hold on a minute," said Mike, smiling.

"We're not quite through yet. Just for safety's sake, I want you to have some blood tests and a mammogram. That is, unless you've had one done recently."

"Sure." At this point Stephanie was feeling euphoric enough to agree to just about anything. "No, I haven't had one. Ever."

"We'll set it up, then," he said. "Radiology Associates does our X-ray work, and they're very conveniently located right here in this building, on the floor below this one." Mike picked up the intercom and asked Pauline to set up the test. While they were waiting, Mike asked casually what Stephanie did for fun.

"I sail," she replied. "Small stuff, just out in the sound. I have a sixteen-foot centerboard O'Day. It's small, but it keeps you on your toes when the weather's rough."

"Hey, that's cool," said Mike, his eyes lighting up. "My cousin and I used to crew on Stars at weekend races, up near Marblehead. We never had one of our own, though."

There was a silence for a moment, then Stephanie asked, "Do you still sail?"

"Not for ages. Not because I didn't want to, there just hasn't been time."

The intercom buzzed. Pauline had set up Stephanie's appointment with Radiology Associates for Thursday at one p.m. And, Pauline told him, Mike's next patient was waiting.

Stephanie was walking on air when she left the office, holding the appointment slip in her hand.

She'd always thought that she appreciated her own health, and her job constantly reminded her of other people's illnesses, but now she promised herself never to take anything good in her life for granted anymore.

It was too late to go back to the office, so she walked along to the parking lot, thinking how beautiful life was and what a wonderful day was coming to an end.

Dr. Richmond had said he wanted to see her after the tests . . . as she drove, she had a very clear picture in her mind of him, with his thick, untidy dark hair and boyish good looks. And his hands—there was something about the touch of his hands . . . maybe he'd like to go sailing with her . . . come on, girl, she said to herself. You've just seen a surgeon who told you that there's nothing wrong with you. That's all. Don't get carried away.

She was almost home by the time she realized that she was supposed to have met Evie Gaskell at the mall twenty minutes before, and Evie would be seriously pissed off.

Chapter 11

A half hour after Stephanie left, Mike was completing the chart work on the computer when Derek Provost appeared at his door. He seemed a bit preoccupied, but he grinned at Mike, sat down in the visitor's chair, stretched out his legs, and tried to look his usual cool self.

"What's on your mind?" asked Mike.

"Mr. Danzig came in to see me earlier this afternoon," replied Derek, looking everywhere except at Mike. "He was a bit . . . concerned. He said he gave you the introductory course in our computer system . . ."

"Mr. Danzig? You mean Tony?" Mike grinned at Derek.

"Right," said Derek, glancing at the door in the same way that Pauline had when Mike had mentioned Tony's name. He took a deep breath. "Anyway, a little while ago, he came into my office, and he was upset. He said that you were almost a half hour late for your appointment, and that your only interest in the computer system was to know if you could play arcade games on it."

"Right, I was late." Mike was surprised that Derek was taking the time to discuss Tony's complaints, let alone take them seriously. "I was held up at the hospital, I couldn't do anything about that. Sure, I asked him if Solitaire was included in the software, but I was just kidding."

"Well," said Derek, avoiding Mike's eye, "I told you Mr. Danzig doesn't have much sense of humor." He sighed. "Look, Mike, the office manager in this kind of practice has a very important function. Tony does a good job here, and we all try to get along with him. Sure, he can be a bit dictatorial and humorless, maybe, but he wasn't hired to keep us amused."

"Okay. I really didn't mean to offend him."

"Of course not. It's just . . . well, Tony keeps the practice running smoothly, from a business standpoint, and what I'm saying is, just go along with him and try not to get him all bent out of shape. If that happens, it's—well, it's disruptive for the group, and none of us like that." Derek looked hard at Mike, hesitated, then stood up. "I have a bunch of reports to do," he said. "I'll see you later."

Mike sat still for a few moments, digesting what Derek had told him. Something changed on his computer screen, and a little red light went on at the side of the monitor. A message appeared. *Laboratory results have just come in for you. Press ENTER to view.* Mike pressed ENTER, thinking that all this new technology was a big improvement on having to go down to the lab and cajoling a secretary to type up the results. On the screen now was an upper G.I. report, originating from the Radiology Associates, on one of Mike's patients, a Walter Sorrell, an anxious man Mike had seen a week before, complaining of indigestion. Sorrell had an Aetna policy, and right from the beginning had made it clear to Mike that he intended to take full advantage of his extensive coverage. Mike took a medical history and examined him carefully, and came to the conclusion that his indigestion was due to his dietary habits, which included a daily lunchtime double cheeseburger with a large portion of fries.

"You've got McDonalditis," Mike told him cheerfully, and was suggesting some dietary remedies when Sorrell interrupted him, shaking his head. "How about those Lovejoy ads?" he asked, referring to the huge posters that Lovejoy Hospital had recently put up, visible from the expressway. ABDOMINAL PAIN? screamed the billboards in red letters, illuminated at night for the edification of weary travelers, SURE, IT COULD BE INDIGESTION, BUT IT COULD ALSO BE CANCER. SEE YOUR LOVEJOY DOCTOR NOW.

Sorrell didn't want to hear Mike's suggestions about adjusting his eating habits in favor of a more balanced diet supplemented by antacids. "I could figure that out by myself," he said in a stubborn voice. "But my company pays a lot of money for medical insurance, and I want to be sure that I don't have stomach cancer or anything like that. Actually, I think the whole problem's centered in my sarcophagus."

Keeping a straight face, Mike had sent Sorrell for an upper G.I. series, which consisted of swallowing an unpalatable barium solution that showed up on X-rays while the radiologists took pictures at regular intervals. It was an uncomfortable and tedious procedure, and Mike hoped that when that came back negative, Sorrell would see the light, ease off on the burgers, buy himself a packet of Tums, and get himself a life.

Now Mike read the radiologist's report with growing astonishment. *Irregularity is noted in the lower esophageal segment, with some mild spasm at the esophago-gastric junction. Moderate esophageal regurgitation is noted, and the gastric mucosa is roughened, with rapid passage of contrast material into the duodenum. Further studies concerning the esophageal sphincter mechanism are suggested, together with gastroscopy.*

"Whew." Mike sat back, exhaling through pursed lips. This was a surprise, and it started to come home to him that maybe he wasn't as capable a diagnostician as he'd thought. But he would have sworn there was nothing serious the matter with Sorrell—and Mike had certainly seem plenty of patients with similar problems. Well, he thought, I guess I'm still learning. Maybe God sent him to keep me humble. He sat looking at the screen for a few moments, then decided to go talk the radiologists in their office on the floor below, and go over Sorrell's films with them. He glanced at the signature on the report. *Marty Rosenfeld, MD, Radiologist.*

*   *   *

Down one flight of stairs, the offices of Radiology Associates were quite different from the Spencer group's. Severe and functional, the outer office had a long counter covered with a light wood laminate. The large waiting room was full of patients and humming with activity.

"Yes, sir, can I help you?" One of the women behind the counter spoke to him.

"I'm Dr. Richmond, from upstairs," he said. "I want to talk to Dr. Rosenfeld about a report."

"Did you say Dr. Richmond?" asked the woman, her hand on the phone.

"Mike Richmond."

"Oh, yes," she said, her face lighting up. "We've heard about you. Sorry. I didn't recognize your face."

A moment later, a rather surprised-looking Dr. Rosenfeld poked his head through the doorway and glanced around. "Dr. Richmond? Come on through."

Mike stuck out his hand, and Rosenfeld shook it in a perfunctory way.

"Yeah," said Rosenfeld. "You're the new guy with Spencer's group, right? Welcome to private practice." He grinned at Mike in the semidarkness. "So what can I do for you?" Rosenfeld led the way through the corridor toward their reading room. As in many radiology departments, the light intensity was kept at a minimum so that the doctors, who spent a good part of their day in the darkened X-ray reading rooms, didn't have to keep on readapting their eyes to the dark.

"You did an upper G.I. on a patient of mine," said

Mike, following him. "A guy by the name of Sorrell. You did it Tuesday, I guess."

"Didn't you get the report?" asked Rosenfeld. He stopped and turned around. "Or was there a problem with it?"

"Yes, I got it," replied Mike. "No problem, I don't think. I just wanted to go over the films with you, if you have a minute." At the medical center, Mike had been used to a fairly close relationship with the radiologists, who usually were happy enough to go over cases with the residents.

Rosenfeld hesitated. "Yeah," he said, "I suppose so." He was obviously not used to outside doctors doing any more than just reading his reports. "Didn't you get the films? We always send a couple of representative films with the report."

"I didn't know that," said Mike. "They came with the report?"

"Yes. I guess you're new at this. You press ENTER twice after the typed report, and the films come up on the screen."

"Good, thanks, I'll do that. But since I'm here, do you have a minute to go over the original films?"

Rosenfeld hesitated again. "Listen," he said, "right now I'm in the middle of a brain scan. Could we do this later?"

"Sure," said Mike, thinking he should have called in advance. "When will you be done?"

"In about an hour, I guess," said Rosenfeld, after a slight, uncomfortable pause.

"I'll come back then, if that's okay."

"Okay," said Rosenfeld, but the reluctance was evident in his voice. "In about an hour. You remember the way out?"

Mike went back upstairs and let himself into the office. The security system was fairly complicated, and the week before he'd triggered a call from the security system, and within minutes two men from the security company had arrived to see what the problem was. Mike looked at his watch. It was after five-thirty already; those radiology guys are really busy and work late, he thought.

In his office, he sat down and switched on the computer, accessed Sorrell's X-ray report, and found the films. Unfortunately, they were fuzzy and had obviously lost something in the transmission, because he couldn't be certain that he'd actually seen the reflux and other problems that Dr. Rosenfeld had reported. Mike went back over Sorrell's computerized records, hoping to find some indication or symptom that agreed with the X-ray diagnosis, but it was pretty much as he remembered it. Sorrell's abdominal pain was central, came on a half hour after his hamburgers and fries, sometimes accompanied by heartburn. He hadn't reported any weight loss, vomiting, bleeding, or pain unrelated to the food. There was nothing to indicate that he had anything more serious than indigestion. And now Mike would have to do a gastroscopy and a bunch of other expensive tests on Sorrell that he felt would be just a waste of time and money. An hour later, after doing some more work on his computer and leafing through the current *Annals of Surgery*, Mike looked at his watch, remembered his meeting with Dr. Rosenfeld down at Radiology Associates, and ran out. He took the fire-escape stairway down one flight, but although he was only about five minutes late, the offices of the Radiology Associates were locked up, the lights were out and the place was shut up tight for the night.

Chapter 12

The next day was a busy one for Mike. He had a couple of small cases to do at Lovejoy, a hernia and a wrist ganglion. Lovejoy was very different from the staid New Coventry Medical Center. At Lovejoy, the walls were painted pastel colors, the lighting was bright and modern, and the staff seemed more cheerful and relaxed. But behind all the client-friendly approach, Lovejoy was strictly a for-profit hospital. And it didn't take long for Mike to find that he too was there strictly for profit. Everything he did, every moment he spent had to be accounted for and had to finish up on somebody's bill.

Mike finished his cases and was walking along the main corridor from the operating suites when his pocket pager buzzed.

Mike went to the nearest phone and called the number. It was Dr. Lou Gardner, Terry Catlin's principal ally in the group, on his cellphone.

"Mike? I guess you have the surgical call today, right?" Lou's voice was friendly enough, as if he'd got used to the idea that Mike was now a member of the group. "Well, I have this patient up on B Four

I'd like a surgical opinion on," he said. "Della Marcus. I admitted her yesterday because of pain and severe swelling in both legs, and I'm not sure what's going on with her. I figured she was maybe in congestive heart failure, but her EKG's okay and there's nothing much abnormal with her blood work."

"Sure," said Mike, writing the patient's name in his notebook. "I'm in the hospital, so I can see her now."

"She's in Room 448," said Lou. "Let me know what you find. Oh, and by the way," he said after a brief pause, "She's a Lovejoy Plan patient."

Mike hung up and retraced his footsteps toward the elevators, wondering vaguely why Lou had mentioned that she was on the plan—it wouldn't have any bearing on whatever problem she was suffering from. On the fourth floor, he stopped at the desk and read the chart, but it didn't tell him much that Lou hadn't already told him.

The head nurse, Linda Alpert, came with him to the patient's room.

Della Marcus was a large woman with a round face, round tortoise-shell glasses, and a round body. She was lying back in bed, a single sheet covering her domelike belly. She seemed in pain, but she smiled when he came in and introduced himself.

He pulled up a chair, and glanced down at her legs for a moment. They were uncovered below the knees and looked swollen with bluish, distended veins.

"What happened?" he asked her, putting his hand

on her arm. He had a direct but sympathetic way of talking to people, and she smiled at him again. She had a face that was obviously used to smiling a lot.

"My legs," she said. "They've been swelling up for the last few weeks. I didn't pay much attention . . . I figured they just had too much to do, carrying my weight around."

Mike nodded, then looked carefully at her. Swelling of the legs was certainly one of the signs of congestive heart failure, as Lou Gardner had suggested, but if that had been the problem, she would have been very breathless lying back as she was, and her neck veins would have been distended as well. Mike asked her to turn her head away from him to expose the external jugular vein, but it seemed normal enough and certainly wasn't distended like her leg veins.

"The swelling's been getting worse?"

"Yes. Last night my legs got suddenly quite a lot more swollen, and they felt so weak I couldn't stand up. And then they started to get more and more painful, and my husband wasn't home, so I called the plan's hotline and they told me to go to the emergency room."

"Do you normally have a lot of trouble from your varicose veins?" he asked.

"A bit. Not that much. I suppose everybody my age and size gets them." She smiled. "They got a lot bigger since last night, though."

"Okay, let's take a look. May I pull back the sheet?"

"Sure. My goodness, we have a polite doctor!" Della smiled at the nurse. "He's the first, right, Linda?"

Embarrassed, Linda Alpert muttered something Mike didn't hear, and he pulled back the sheet. The veins of both legs were distended, even though she was lying down, and raising them didn't reduce the venous congestion. He felt for pulses in the groin and the ankles; these seemed to be quite normal on both sides. There was no evident inflammation in the legs, no rashes or abscesses, and Mike was beginning to feel puzzled. He checked her heart, although Lou Gardner had already told him it was okay. Her breathing was all right too, as far as he could tell with his stethoscope. Della's arms and neck were large and rather flabby, but certainly there was no venous congestion there.

What could possibly cause slowing of venous return in the legs but not in the upper part of her body?

He scanned his memory and recalled a patient he'd had about a year ago. He even remembered his name, Bobbie Fitzgerald, an unrepentant but entertaining alcoholic well known to the E.R. staff. It turned out that a clot had blocked Bobbie's inferior vena cava, the main vein that drained blood from the lower part of the body, and he almost died before they'd figured out the correct diagnosis. Della's symptoms and signs were almost identical.

Mike finished his examination and put his stethoscope back in his pocket.

"It looks as if one of the big veins in your tummy's blocked," Mike told Della. "We'll have to do a special X-ray called a venogram, but I'm pretty sure that's what it is."

"Can you unblock the vein?" Della's deep voice was unconcerned. "I had Charlie the Roto-Rooter man in last week for my drains at home. Do you want his phone number?"

Mike grinned. "I hope we won't need Charlie," he said. "But we can bring him in as a consultant, if you like."

Della laughed, a deep rolling laugh. "He's cute, isn't he?" she said to Linda.

"That's what all the women around here think, anyway," Linda replied.

"We'll arrange that venogram," Mike told Della. "Then we'll start you on treatment to dissolve that clot."

When he got back to the desk, he took Della's chart and was just starting to write when Lou Gardner came up, wearing a spotless, tailored white coat over a pink-striped Sulka shirt, and a red silk tie with a horse pattern. Lou made little effort to hide that he was one of the most successful internists in New Coventry. He drove a maroon Bentley, and even the way he walked reflected his self-assurance.

"Ah, yes, Mike," he said, in his slightly pompous tone. "I was hoping to find you here. So what did you find on our friend Della?"

"I think she's got a clot in her inferior vena cava," replied Mike. "I ordered a venogram, and I was just going to start her on a course of streptokinase, if that's okay with you."

Lou sucked in his breath and looked thoughtfully at Mike. "The diagnosis sounds right," he said. "That was very smart of you; quite frankly, I hadn't considered that possibility." He paused for a moment, watching Mike. "However, I think that heparin would be the drug of choice, Mike, in this particular case."

Mike looked around, surprised. "Heparin?" He hesitated. This was an area in which he had more expertise than Lou Gardner, but he didn't want to sound arrogant. "We used heparin before streptokinase became available, Lou, but streptokinase is way more effective, there's really no question about that. If you're interested, there's a good review article about streptokinase in this months' *Journal of Vascular Surgery* . . ."

Lou's face seemed to solidify, like ice propagating across a lake. "Mike, I know all I want to know about streptokinase," he said, interrupting abruptly. "And I certainly don't need to hear a lecture on it."

He took a deep breath, obviously collecting himself, and even managed a smile. "Look, Mike," he said, "I told you that Della is on the Lovejoy Plan. That means that in return for her tiny premium, the plan pays all of her medical expenses, hospitalization, tests, and all medications. Which means that we can't ring every diagnostic bell and blow every therapeutic whistle on each individual patient—it would simply be too expensive. In practical terms, if we did that, the plan would go bust inside a year."

Mike opened his mouth to reply, but Lou kept on talking.

"To bring it down to dollars and cents for you," he said, trying to mask his condescension with a cheerful and informative tone, "Streptokinase costs over a thousand dollars per dose. Whereas heparin costs just a few dollars for the entire course. Now do you see where we're coming from?"

"I know that, Lou," said Mike, alarmed that he was about to antagonize one of the most powerful internists in town, and one who was already not well disposed toward him. "But to me, the big difference is that streptokinase is effective, because it dissolves and breaks up the clot, and heparin just prevents more clots from forming, and won't clear her blockage. So in this case, Dr. Gardner, I'm sorry, but it seems to me that streptokinase is the drug of choice for Della. And we should give it soon, because it won't be effective if we wait much longer."

Lou took a small step back and smiled, a chilly, disapproving, superior smile. "Mike, I appreciate your idealism," he said. "I suppose I used to feel the same way myself. But the realities of the situation have to take precedence. I'm sorry, but I have to remind you that I asked you to see this patient only in consultation, not to take over her treatment. In my opinion, you have correctly established the diagnosis, so we won't need to subject her to a venogram, which quite incidentally would cost the plan approximately eight hundred dollars. And I'm sure she'll respond very favorably to heparin." Lou stretched out his hand and picked up the chart from in front of Mike. "I thank you for your most capable assistance on this case, Dr. Richmond," he said formally, then took the chart over to the other side of the desk and started to write in it.

Mike watched him for a moment, then shrugged. He'd done what he was supposed to do, but he felt the beginnings of a great anger starting to rumble, like the first hints of a major storm in the distance.

Lou Gardner stood up, put Della Marcus's file back in the rack, and went off without another glance at Mike. Nor did he go in to see Della; Lou was very busy, and his time was taken up with private patients who had insurance policies that covered everything, or who paid cash.

Linda came back along the corridor from one of the patients' rooms. She was pretty, with a dark, pert look and a beautiful, smooth complexion. "So did Dr. Gardner let you use the streptokinase on Della?" she asked, smiling amusedly at him.

"He decided to use heparin," replied Mike.

Linda stood close enough so he could feel the warmth of her body. "I could have told you that in advance," she said. "He'll probably send her home tomorrow and treat her as an outpatient." She smiled brightly. "She'll probably do just as well on the heparin, don't you think?"

"I certainly hope so," replied Mike.

He didn't have any patients of his own in the hospital, so he walked back to the office. When he came in, Pauline looked up from her console. "You remember earlier when I asked you about Dr. Newsome?" she asked.

Mike nodded.

"Well, I was talking with a friend of mine who knew him. She was saying how much the practice had changed since he left."

Mike was only half paying attention to Pauline.

"I guess it has."

Pauline glanced through the open door down the corridor. "They seem a lot more . . . well, I suppose *prosperous*, than in Dr. Newsome's time. That's what she said, anyway."

"Right." Mike grinned at Pauline. "That's how they could afford to bring in a high-priced expert like me."

Mike went into his office and sat down. He could already feel the pressure building against him. Lou Gardner had almost as much clout in internal medicine as Spencer had in the surgical field, and he would probably make as big a deal as possible about the Della Marcus business. A little germ of self-doubt crept into Mike's mind and grew. Maybe Lou was right—maybe this was the way that medicine was practiced out in the real world beyond the residency program. Certainly if he wanted to survive in this group, he would have to make some major changes in the way he practiced medicine and, even more, how he really felt about it.

Chapter 13

That Monday, Stephanie started on her project for Carl Hartmann, and after a few days of collecting data, she began to get the hang of it. He wanted figures for his different corporations so that he could compare sales, overhead costs, which included personnel, salaries, development, equipment, rent, and all other expenses, and then calculate the overall profitability of each unit.

She leaned down and pulled a data tape from the box at her feet, and glanced at it before putting it into the tape reader. The tape had a neat, handwritten label, marked *Corp. 2, Mar. 1996*. All the tapes were color-coded, had a similar label, each with the same careful script, and, she noticed, each had the same initials, *A.D.*, written in the lower right hand corner. She wondered briefly who A.D. was, and assumed he or she would be someone in the accounts department. Yes. The nice young woman with short, boy-cut black hair and big earrings who had brought her the box was named Alice, so it was probably her. Stephanie pressed a key, the tape reader whirred for a couple of minutes, transferring the data onto her hard disk. Meanwhile, she reviewed what she had already done, and it was becoming clear that the structure and function of the corporations were so different that comparisons would be hard to establish, even be ultimately misleading.

There was a knock on the door, and Carl came in. "How's the work going?"

"I'm having a problem with the numbers on Corporation Two," Stephanie replied, pointing at the computer screen. "Maybe I just don't have all the input data I need."

Carl stood behind her, looking at the different-colored columns of figures on the screen.

"That's very good for a start," he said. "The trick was to find a format that all the corporations can fit into, and this looks as if it might work."

"I don't have any real sales figures," Stephanie went on. "Corporation Two gets big payments on an irregular basis, but I can't find any sales expenses. In fact, there don't seem to be any sales, and no kind of pattern in the payments. There are what look like executive salaries and usual office expenses, but no sales force, no warehousing costs, no shipping."

"Corporation Two is . . . well, I guess you could call it a service company," said Carl, who was still gazing at the multicolored histogram display. "It doesn't sell any actual goods. What it sells is its expertise."

"Oh, okay," said Stephanie, relieved. "That explains it." She paused; actually, she had thought of that possibility, but the sums coming in were huge.

"It must be some kind of expertise those guys have," she said, glancing around at him. "Some of the checks coming in are in the millions."

"Right." Carl straightened up. "Don't worry about it. Right now all I need you to do is put the totals together. All the corporations have substantial income, but most of them are in much smaller amounts."

Carl lumbered across the room; he liked to move around when he was thinking, and Stephanie watched him, noting the decisiveness in his steps, their quickness in spite of his size. He wasn't somebody to get in the way of, she thought.

"Okay," he said. "I have one additional thing for you to do. Put in the cost of processing the income, including bad debts, collection, and accounting personnel as a separate function," he said, coming back to the desk. "It costs a lot more to process thousands of hundred-dollar accounts than a dozen million-dollar ones. I'd like to know how much more."

Stephanie made a note on the pad beside her keyboard.

Carl went back to his pacing. "The accrued capital expenditures for each corporation are on separate files, so when you get the income figures, you can work out the annual and overall returns, and the income/expenditure ratios of each of the units and compare them."

Stephanie nodded, knowing that it would take some serious data-bending to get the numbers into a form that would give Carl the information he wanted.

For the next several minutes they talked about the statistical techniques that Stephanie would use to analyze the data, then he glanced at his watch.

"I'm going to be out of town over the weekend," he said. "I hope you can have a preliminary report together by Monday."

"I'll try," she said as he headed for the door. "Have a good trip."

As the afternoon wore on, Stephanie took a break from the data analysis to go over her old job description as U.R. supervisor, and added explanatory marginal notes for Jean's use. A little later Stephanie looked at the clock and saw she was due to have her mammogram in fifteen minutes. She tidied her desk and headed over to Radiology Associates, which, as Mike had told her, was on the floor below his. The R.A. offices were busy and obviously efficient. They took some information from her, but her clinical records had already been transmitted from Mike's to their database. The X-ray itself didn't take long—it was finished a half hour after she got there.

"We'll send the report to your doctor," the tech told her when Stephanie asked about the results. And that made her think about Mike again, and she visualized him opening the envelope, reading the contents, smiling, then forgetting about it. And about her. Spencer's was a very busy group, she knew that. To Mike, all these patients coming one after the other would be like items on an assembly line—not really distinguishable one from the next. And women must have a very different impact on a surgeon, she reflected. To them, bodies would be like car engines to a mechanic. She thought of that silly joke someone had told her back in high school, of the doctor to a female patient—"Take off your clothes, quick! My wife's coming!"

But as she waited for the elevator, one floor below the penthouse level, she had a strong awareness of his presence directly above her, as if she were within the range of his aura. The feeling diminished as the elevator went down, and by the time she got back to her office, it had gone.

Chapter 14

By mid-afternoon, Mike had finished office hours. He turned on his computer, pressed some keys, and watched as the screen first went black, then, starting at the top, a name and I.D. number showed up, then below that, a white and gray pattern developed that after a few moments became recognizable as an X-ray. This is really amazing, he thought, watching the picture as it developed. It saved time-wasting trips to the X-ray department, avoided the usual problems of finding the right films and having to sort through a thick envelope to find the one film you needed. Mike thought about the countless hours he'd spent looking for X-rays when he was a junior resident.

The X-ray was Stephanie Hopkins's. Mike peered at it—although at first it seemed an excellent reproduction, the fine details were slightly blurred. Of course, thought Mike. The resolution on even a top-of-the-line computer screen couldn't be as close as on film, because the screen image was composed of a bunch of pixels, unlike the smooth and much more detailed photographic silver emulsion on the originals. Mike stared at the films for a few minutes before reading the report, a habit he'd developed years ago while training himself to pick up abnormalities he might have otherwise missed.

As far as he could see, both breasts were entirely normal. He concentrated his attention on the upper outer quadrant of the right breast. Maybe there was a slight increase in density . . . it was really hard to tell. There was a magnifying feature on this computer program, and Mike used it, but it just made the pixels look bigger.

"Okay," he said to himself, "I don't see anything very serious there. Now let's take a look at the report." He pressed Page Up and the films disappeared, replaced by a typewritten report, signed with the initials *MR*. The name under the scrawl was Marty Rosenfeld, the same radiologist who'd done the upper G.I. on Walter Sorrell, the suspected malingerer.

The report started in the usual way, describing the radiological technique used, then *a minor degree of nodularity and scattered densities are noted in the left breast, but these are all within normal limits. On the right, similar findings are noted, together with a small number of tiny, ill-defined microcalcifications in the region of the reported mass. Due to the malignant potential of this finding, biopsy is recommended.* Mike's mouth opened slightly. He had totally missed the microcalcifications, which usually showed up as tiny white streaks, often almost invisible except to the trained eye. Microcalcifications were important, because they were often the first sign of serious trouble. Well, that's what radiologists are for, thought Mike. To pick up what people like me miss. He went back to the films and stared at them until he persuaded himself that he'd seen the little flecks of calcium. But he knew that if he were presented with the same films, he still wouldn't be able to identify the lesions.

Then he understood. Of course. These little white specks were hard enough to spot even on the regular films, and they would get lost when the data was digitized for copying and transmission over the computer system. He'd find them when he saw the original films.

Mike reached for the phone and speed-dialed Radiology Associates. Dr. Rosenfeld was scanning, he was told, and couldn't come to the phone; they weren't sure how long he would be. Mike left a message asking for him to return the call.

Pauline came in with some papers. "By the way, Mike," she said, "my husband's coming here later this afternoon . . ."

The phone rang, and Pauline picked it up, and quickly passed it to Mike. It was Linda Alpert, the head nurse on the Lovejoy medical floor, and she sounded breathless and panicky. "It's Mrs. Marcus," she said. "Remember Della Marcus?" She went on without waiting for a reply. "Please come over right away," she said. "She's in a lot of trouble—"

"Della's Dr. Gardner's patient," said Mike. "Call him."

"He said to call you," said Linda. "He's tied up

and he'll be over as soon as he can. Anyway, Della's having some kind of hemorrhage and you'd better come over right now."

"I'm on my way," replied Mike. He grabbed his pager and ran. A familiar shot of adrenaline hit him—this was like the old days, when as a resident he responded to emergencies a half dozen times a day.

He raced the four blocks through the busy streets, hoping that Linda had called a code, or found someone from the E.R. or the I.C.U. who could get to Della sooner. He thought about what could have caused her hemorrhage. Probably the heparin, if Lou Gardner had started her on it as he'd said . . . He'd just have to play it by ear when he got there.

By the time he arrived at Della's door, there was pandemonium inside. The patient was lying on the bed—all the top bedclothes had been stripped off, and her legs looked more swollen than the last time he'd seen her. A resident, a Korean doctor whom Mike knew only by sight, had the heels of both his hands on Della's chest and was giving external cardiac massage, and at the same time was shouting medication orders in almost incomprehensible English. Linda Alpert was hanging up an I.V. A young respiratory therapist was trying to get Della to breathe oxygen, but blood was bubbling out around the black rubber face mask. Three medical students stood immobile, backed up against the wall near the door, watching, big-eyed and scared, intent on staying out of everyone's way.

Mike glanced up at the EKG monitor. There was only an occasional small blip on the screen.

"Does she have a blood pressure?" he asked Linda.

"Not for the last five minutes," she answered.

"Hold it a second," Mike told the resident, who had drops of sweat running down his face. "Let's see if we can get a pulse."

The resident stopped pumping on Della's chest and looked at Mike, who listened to her chest with his stethoscope. What he heard agreed with the EKG monitor—her heart had stopped.

He looked at her eyes. Both were wide open, sightless, and the pupils were dilated. He looked at the respiratory therapist and shook his head slightly, telling her to hold off for a few moments.

"Do you have an ophthalmoscope?" he asked Linda quietly. Without a word she handed the instrument to him. Total silence fell on the room, and they all watched as he adjusted the lens wheel. He leaned forward, put the 'scope up to his eye, and shone the beam into the back of Della's retina. There was no question; there was beading in the blood vessels of the retina, which indicated that the flow of blood had stopped.

He straightened up. "She's dead," he said. "Now could somebody tell me what happened?"

Automatically, Linda looked at the clock, then noted the time on her flow chart. The Asian resident went over to wash his hands at the sink, then walked to the door and left without a word. The medical students headed in the same direction, after giving a scared glance at Della's huge, unclothed body, which already had the pallor of death on it.

"One of the nurses just happened to look into her room," said Linda, her voice shaking. "There was blood all over her face, the sheets, everywhere, and she was unconscious. I called a code, then called you. I guess we just got to her too late."

"Dr. Gardner had put her on heparin?"

"Yes. She was getting one thousand units per hour, I.V."

Mike looked at Della's body.

"Does she have relatives?" he asked Linda.

"There's a husband. He came in the room just after this started. The poor guy was in shock."

The door opened, and Lou Gardner came in. He glanced for a moment at Della, taking in the situation. "What happened?" he asked Mike.

"She bled out," replied Mike. "I was just going to ask Linda if she had any history of stomach ulcers, or anything that the heparin could have lit up."

"Absolutely not," said Lou, shaking his head emphatically. "If she had, of course I wouldn't have put her on heparin."

"Her husband just brought in her bottle of Tagamet," said Linda very quietly, indicating a paper container on the bedside table. "He said she'd been on it for her ulcer for two years, but hadn't been taking it since she came into the hospital."

There was a long silence. Then Lou smacked his fist into the palm of his other hand and said, "God damn that woman! She never told me!" His face suddenly red, he glared at the body on the bed. "Those fucking fat imbecile patients, they're all the same, not a fucking brain in their heads."

Linda looked away, embarrassed, and Mike stared at his shoes. Lou, realizing he'd gone too far, took a deep breath and pulled himself together. "I'm sorry," he said in a conciliatory tone. "But it's infuriating when patients cause such problems for themselves, especially when they could have been avoided."

"Mr. Marcus is in the waiting room, Dr. Gardner," said Linda. She didn't look at him. "I suppose you'll want to talk to him."

"Yes, of course." Lou was realizing that he'd just made a major faux pas and wanted to defuse the situation. "And I'm sorry for what I just said. It came out in the heat of the moment. I'm sorry, okay?"

"Of course," said Linda. "No problem."

The door opened, and Mr. Marcus came in, a small, scared-looking man with dark hair and a dark suit. Before anyone could stop him, he ran up to the bed, shouting something incomprehensible, then he caught her naked white shoulder, and said, "Della, Della, look at me! Oh, please, God . . ." He turned to Lou, his face desperate. "What happened? Will she be all right?"

Lou went up to Mr. Marcus, his face full of instant sympathy. "Let's go outside, please, Mr. Marcus," he said, taking the man's unresisting arm and leading him back to the door. Mike came out with them, and closed the door behind him.

"I'm afraid there's been a tragedy here, Mr. Mar-

cus," said Lou in a quiet voice. "Why don't we sit
down on this bench?" He guided Mr. Marcus, who
seemed in shock, and sat him down. "You knew that
Della had a potentially fatal condition," went on Lou.
"The biggest vein in her body, the inferior vena cava,
had become blocked . . ." He watched Marcus carefully, trying to match what he said to the man's attitude and responses. "As a last-ditch effort, we had
to put her on an anticoagulant . . ."

Mr. Marcus moved restlessly on the bench and was
about to say something, but Lou raised a hand. "I
know," he went on, "when there's a stomach ulcer
or certain other conditions, it makes that form of
treatment more risky, but there was nothing else we
could do. We all thought about it very hard. I even
got Dr. Richmond here to come and give us the benefit of his expertise in this kind of case . . ."

Thank you, Dr. Gardner, for sharing this fiasco
with me, thought Mike, but he composed his features
and said nothing.

"Dr. Richmond and I agreed that we had to give
her every chance, which of course meant giving her
the heparin, although we knew the risks." Lou
locked his hands together in a priestly gesture. "The
alternative was just to do nothing and watch her
die."

Mr. Marcus was staring at the door of his wife's
room and didn't seem to be fully aware of what Lou
had told him. "I was out of town," he said. "I only
got back last night."

Lou sensed the man's feelings of guilt and got ready to take advantage of them.

"I work for the phone company," went on Marcus, "and I have to travel all over the state. Sometimes I'm away for a week at a time. Oh, God . . ." He buried his face in his hands.

Sympathetically, Lou patted him on the shoulder. "She knew, of course."

Marcus looked up. Tears were running down both sides of his face. "She knew what?"

"She knew the risks of the heparin treatment," said Lou gently. "I talked to her for a long time about the pros and cons, whether we should go ahead with it." He took a big, saddened breath. "And I'm just sorry you didn't have a chance to discuss it with her and give her the support she needed." He paused long enough for the knife to sink in and turn. "Yes, Della was a very courageous woman," he went on. "She knew that the heparin could kill her, and it must have been very difficult for her to make that decision alone, but she said to me, 'Dr. Gardner, I can't go on like this. Let's go ahead with the heparin.' "

Mike, feeling nauseated, said, "Excuse me, I have to go."

Lou nodded without looking at him.

As he turned the corner, Mike glanced back. Lou Gardner still had his hand on Mr. Marcus's despairing shoulder, and was still talking to him in the same gentle, regretful tones. Mike wondered how many times Lou had performed this kind of circus with grieving relatives.

Again a strange feeling of isolation started to get to him as he walked along the corridor toward the hospital exit. What would he have done in Lou's shoes? If he'd prescribed streptokinase or any other super-expensive drugs on Della, he'd have run into the plan's cost-control system, and he'd have been warned and told that his prescribing habits would be carefully watched in future. So what would *he* have done?

Mike nodded at the security guard and stepped out of the hospital into the street, still wrestling with the question. It was clear how Lou Gardner had answered it—how about the others? He decided to ask Derek. But a small voice inside him reminded him that he couldn't answer his own ethical questions simply by finding out what other people did.

The weather was humid, spatters of rain were polka-dotting the sidewalk, and he was feeling uptight and anxious. In his mind he went through the list of what he had to do back at the office. One of the jobs waiting for him was to call Stephanie Hopkins and ask her to come in to talk about doing a biopsy.

Pauline was working at her computer when he came in. She looked up, seeming a little flustered, pressed a couple of keys and the screen went blank. "I didn't expect you back quite so soon," she said. "Was everything all right? You ran out of here as if the place was on fire."

Mike told her that one of their patients had died, and Pauline made sympathetic noises. Mike was about to go into his office when she said, "You remember I told you my husband, Andy, was coming here in a little while? I want you to know that he can't talk properly because he had a stroke just over a year ago."

"Oh, I'm sorry," said Mike. "How did it happen?"

"He's a smoker with a bad family history," replied Pauline. "He's having some tests done across the street, and he wants to meet you." She smiled. "I guess I've spoken about you often enough, so he's curious."

At that moment the door opened and a large, flabby man walked in, slowly and deliberately, as though he should be using a cane but had forgotten to bring it. He was escorted by Imogene, the receptionist.

"And here he is," said Pauline. She came around the desk and kissed him on the cheek. "Andy, I'd like you to meet my boss, Dr. Richmond."

The two men shook hands, and a rather curious three-way conversation ensued. It was clear that Andy understood everything that was said to him, and Pauline interpreted his grunts and strange whistling noises for Mike. Pauline told Andy about Mike's Aston-Martin. Andy had done some stock-car racing in the past, and Pauline proudly told Mike about the trophies he'd won. Mike was astonished by how well Pauline knew what Andy was saying—all he could hear was noise. "Luckily we always talked a lot," she explained. "Most of the time I know what Andy's thinking even when he doesn't make a sound."

After Andy went off, Mike's concerns about Stephanie came back at him like a tidal wave. "Pauline," he said, "would you try to reach Stephanie Hopkins for me?"

Chapter 15

Stephanie was coming out of her office when her pager beeped, and she pulled it off her waistband to read the display. *Dr. Richmond at 265–1445.* She went back to her office, closed the door, and picked up the phone, feeling a now familiar tightening in her chest.

"Dr. Richmond?"

"Well, you certainly answer promptly," he said. Mike liked her voice—it was no-nonsense but had some kind of a lilt in it, and he wondered if she had a Scottish background. "Listen, Stephanie, I'd like you to come over so we can talk about your test results," he said, thinking that he'd have time to go downstairs and go over the original films with Marty Rosenfeld.

"Why?" she asked, suddenly alarmed. "Is there a problem?"

"Not exactly," replied Mike gently. "But I do need to discuss it with you. Otherwise I wouldn't waste your time getting you back over here."

"I'll be there in ten minutes," Stephanie said and put the phone down before Mike had a chance to suggest a later time.

Damn, thought Mike, replacing the phone. The chances of getting Rosenfeld at this time would not be good. He picked up the phone, and to his surprise, the receptionist put him through, and in a few moments Marty Rosenfeld was on the line.

When Mike asked if he could go over the films with him, Marty was not happy. "Jesus Christ, Dr. Richmond, if I get called out from doing a procedure, I expect it to be some kind of emergency. Is this really urgent?"

When Mike explained, Rosenfeld, obviously in a foul humor, took an audibly deep breath and said, "Look, Dr. Richmond, a year ago we all spent a lot of money putting in a system that would transmit images across the telephone lines. The reason we did that was to avoid all this time-wasting shit of conferences and discussions. We don't have the time. When I'm not in there doing procedures or reading films, I'm not making money. If you'd just go back and examine the films we sent you with the report, I'm sure you'll be able to pick out the microcalcifications. Okay?" Rosenfeld hung up with a bang.

"My God," thought Mike, unnerved by the radiologist's reaction, and looking at the phone in his hand. "What in the hell is going on around here?" Then he wondered, in a couple of years, would he be like that too? Too busy to talk to colleagues about a patient they'd referred to him? He went back to his computer, flipped up Stephanie's report on the screen, went to the films, and was still studying them when Stephanie walked in. She was wearing a pale green business suit with a dark green silk shirt and was managing to appear quite calm and confident.

"Hi," said Mike. "Come in. Here, take a look at these. I was just looking at your films."

Stephanie came around the desk and looked. The two X-rays side by side on the screen looked like blurry relief maps of two black-and-white islands.

"Here," said Mike, not happy to be explaining something he wasn't too sure about himself. "The left breast is fine . . ."

"It seems to have a lot of those dark areas," said Stephanie, pointing. She had nice hands, Mike noted. Small, with slender fingers, but she moved them in a decisive way.

"That's normal," said Mike. "It just shows the different densities in normal tissue. Now over here . . ." He pointed at the film on the right of the screen. "There are some very tiny dense areas called microcalcifications, and that's what we're concerned about."

Stephanie peered at the screen, then stepped back. She could feel her heart pounding. "I'm no good at reading X-rays," she said. "When I was in training, I could hardly tell when there was a bone fracture. I'm just going to take your word for it."

"In that case, you'd better read the report, then," said Mike. He pressed *PgUp* a couple of times, and when the report appeared on the screen, Stephanie read the words. "A biopsy?" she asked, beginning to feel seriously alarmed. "Why?"

"Because as the report says, the microcalcifications indicate there might be a more serious problem in there," said Mike. "It certainly would be the safest way to go at this point." He hesitated for a moment, watching her expression. "Listen, in cases like this it's never a bad idea to get a second opinion," he said. "Dr. Spencer is back, and—"

"No," said Stephanie, to her own surprise. "I've checked you out," she went on. "And I trust you. I'm sure you wouldn't suggest a biopsy if it wasn't the proper way of dealing with it."

"No, I wouldn't," said Mike. "And the biopsy isn't a big deal; we'll just do a needle biopsy, so there won't be an incision and it won't leave any scar or anything like that."

"Couldn't we go ahead and do it now?"

Mike hesitated and looked at his schedule. "Let me check." He picked up the phone. The minor surgery room would be free in a few minutes, he was told, and a tech was available to assist him.

"Okay," he said to Stephanie, standing up. "Let me take you out to the waiting room. The room's being used right now, but it shouldn't be long."

He took her to the minor surgery room, where he carried out the needle biopsy. When he was done, he labeled the tiny specimen himself and put it in the special container, ready for shipment to ConnPath for microscopic examination.

"When will you get the results?" Stephanie asked after she had dressed. Mike already had his hand on the phone. "I'm about to find out."

He spoke to Dennis Cowlie, the chief technician at ConnPath, who'd worked previously at NCMH.

Mike remembered when Dennis left the medical center—there had been a big upheaval, with lawsuits threatened by both sides, although neither followed through. Mike didn't know what the disagreement was about and had always found Dennis friendly and helpful.

"Sure, Mike," said Dennis cheerfully. "We'll be happy to take care of it. We'll have the report back to you inside twenty-four hours."

Chapter 16

Next morning at eight-thirty, Mike came into the office. Imogene, the receptionist, was sitting as usual at her table, but this morning Mike didn't get his usual brilliant smile, and she was looking pale and upset.

"Dr. Provost was looking for you," she said, her voice shaky. "He wants to see you as soon as you come in." She pressed a button on the console in front of her.

Before Mike could ask what it was about, the door to the doctor's corridor opened and Derek hurried across the carpet toward him.

"Come with me, please, Mike," he said in a low voice. Close up, Mike could see that Derek too was looking shaken. He took Mike's arm, led him back into his office, and shut the door, then went behind his desk and sat down. "I don't suppose you heard about Pauline?" he asked.

"Pauline? My secretary?"

"Yes. Something bad happened to her here this morning. She's in a coma over at the hospital."

For a moment Mike could only stare, open-

mouthed, at Derek. "A coma? She was here yesterday. There wasn't anything the matter with her
then."

"Well, apparently she came in to the office early
this morning and must have had a heart attack or
a stroke or something, because when Tony Danzig
showed up she was slumped over her desk and he
couldn't rouse her. He did all the right things, called
911, tried to resuscitate her—unfortunately, none of
the docs were here that early, so he was on his own.
Anyway, they got an ambulance pretty fast and took
her off to Lovejoy."

"Do they know what happened?" Mike shook his
head, still adjusting. Pauline had seemed the picture
of good health only the day before, and it was difficult to visualize her in a coma.

"Probably a heart attack or maybe a stroke, from
the sound of it, but I don't know. Of course, she is
a bit overweight, and that would be an additional
risk factor for her."

"What time did this happen?" Mike glanced at his
watch. Pauline usually got to work about eight, when
everybody else came in.

"I don't know exactly. It must have been early,
around seven, maybe, or a little later. Apparently
today she came in before everybody else and was
working at her computer." Derek glanced casually at
Mike. "Did she often come in early?"

"I don't think so. As far as I know, she usually
came in around eight, but I'm not certain. Don't the
secretaries check in?"

Derek hesitated for a second, and kept his eyes on Mike. "Well, not exactly. If someone uses their card key to get in outside normal hours, the time's automatically recorded. Tony would know . . ."

"So if I come in during the night for any reason, that's recorded somewhere? Also, if Pauline *did* come in early, wouldn't you know that too?"

Derek pulled on the crease of his pants, looking slightly uncomfortable. "Well, *I* wouldn't, but the security people would, yes. Didn't Tony mention that to you? The card keys are identified electronically, so Security knows who comes in at odd hours."

"Did anyone tell her husband?" Mike had an image of Andy—his life would suddenly get very much tougher if Pauline wasn't able to take care of him.

"Tony called him after she'd gone off to the hospital and told him what happened, but apparently the guy can't talk, had a stroke or something, so I don't know if he understood what he was saying, let alone whether he made it there."

"I have to go over to the hospital anyway, so I'll look in on her. Do you know what room she's in?"

"Lou Gardner's taking care of her." Derek's momentary discomfort had passed. "So I guess she'll be on the medical floor. I can find out for you . . ." His hand reached for the phone.

"Don't bother," said Mike. "I'll find out at the admissions desk."

On the way over, Mike thought about Pauline. That was really a shock, even though dealing with sudden illness was part and parcel of his daily life, just as Pauline had been since he joined the group. She'd really taken care of him and helped him settle in, more than the average secretary would.

"Room Five-oh-two-oh," the blue-haired volunteer at the desk told him, after checking the computer file. She had a bad Parkinsonian tremor, and Mike wondered how much longer she'd be able to work. He took the elevator up to the fifth floor.

Room 5020 had a sign on the door, No visitors. He knocked softly on the door and opened it. He just caught a glimpse of Pauline, with I.V.s hanging by her bedside, before a private duty nurse he didn't recognize jumped up from the chair beside the bed and came toward the door to intercept him. She was big, with a square, uncompromising face. "I'm sorry, sir," she said, in a loud voice. "Didn't you see the sign? No visitors. Dr. Gardner's orders." Mike looked at her I.D. Riva Zorek. He'd never seen her before.

"Mrs. Minsky works for me, Ms. Zorek, and I just wanted—" he started, but the nurse wasn't listening.

She put her hand on the phone. "Doctor, you have to leave *immediately*. Dr. Gardner said absolutely *nobody* was to come in here."

Mike didn't want to get into an argument and backed off. "That's okay, nurse," he said. "I'll check with Dr. Gardner myself."

Out in the corridor, Mike paused. It wasn't uncommon for a No Visitors sign to be up when a staff member was ill, but that didn't usually apply to doctors. He walked back to the desk to look at Pauline's chart, but the secretary told him it was being kept in the patient's room. "Dr. Gardner's orders."

"Has Mr. Minsky come?" he asked.

"The husband? I haven't seen him."

Mike paged Lou Gardner, but Debbie, his secretary, picked up. "He's in a meeting right now, Mike," she told him. "I'll have him call you when he's through."

Mike went down to dictate some charts in the record room, and didn't hear the "Code Blue, Room 5020" when it was broadcast over the public address system a few minutes later.

Lou Gardner was sitting in the conference room, and the other members of the group—the full partners—were coming in one after the other, all looking very serious. Spencer came in with Derek and nodded at Lou before sitting down.

When they were all assembled, Tony Danzig, dressed in a dark suit that made his pale blond hair look even paler, came in and walked to the projector that had been set up in the middle of the room. He switched off the main lights and turned on the projector.

"Gentlemen, I'm sure you remember that we installed a new surveillance system last year," he said. "Yesterday there were indications that our computer system was being tampered with," he said. "It happened before the office opened, and the other security systems were not activated. That means, of course, that it was someone who had authorized access to the premises." Tony looked around the group, his face highlighted by the glow of the projector lantern. "I checked with security, and it turned out that Mrs. Pauline Minsky had come in about seven a.m. on the last two mornings. So this morning I came in at six a.m. I would now like to show you a film from the surveillance camera in Dr. Richmond's office covering a period of several minutes around seven o'clock this morning."

The film was black-and-white but of high resolution. For about a minute the image didn't change, and the only way they knew it was running was from the digital time indicator in the top right-hand corner of the screen, below the date: 0705, it read, and the seconds flicked away. Almost filling the screen was the image of a computer with its monitor and keyboard. After a minute the image panned out to show the entire empty office and stayed that way for about ten seconds before panning in again.

At 0708 the image was blocked momentarily, and when it reappeared, a pair of hands were on the keyboard. Female hands, plump, with a wedding ring on the fourth finger of the left hand.

Tony turned a knob that slowed the projection until the fingers were moving at about a tenth of their normal speed. "These hands belong to our employee Pauline Minsky," he said. "Do any of you gentlemen recognize what she is doing?"

No one spoke, but all eyes were glued to the screen.

"If you watch the fingers carefully," he said, "she

is keying in the first part of our Level One systems access code."

"How in the hell did she get hold of that?" exploded Spencer.

Tony didn't answer. On the screen, the right hand was slowly placing a floppy disk into the A-drive slot in front of her.

"That disk," said Tony, "is a part of what we call a code-busting program. Every second it puts in and checks thousands of different coded combinations. Sooner or later she would have found Part-Two of the code and would have had complete access to our system."

"Why? What's it to her?" Spencer was angry and pounded the arms of the chair.

The film kept running, and a moment later the hands slowly slid off the keyboard, one to each side. The back of a female head with curly dark hair came into the picture, and slid slowly forward and face down on to the keyboard. The viewers could just see the side of her face as it flattened gradually on contact with the keyboard, bounced slowly back once, and after that the head didn't move. A few moments later, the screen went dark, and Tony switched the lights on again.

"It turns out that this woman is a private investigator," said Tony. "These people are licensed by the state, and I found her I.D. tucked away in a concealed pocket of her purse. I made some further inquiries and found that she was part owner of a small agency based here in New Coventry, started some years ago by her husband and herself. But fortunately for us, the husband's had a stroke and can't function. She was working essentially on her own."

"Who hired her?" Derek voiced the concern they all felt.

"I don't know," replied Tony. His face was lined and grim. "I went through everything in her clothes, her purse, her desk. There was nothing to indicate who her employer is."

There was a long silence while they digested the information.

"I assume that what we saw just now . . ." Spencer's voice was suddenly quiet, almost shaky.

"She was struck on the back of the head," replied Tony, calmly. "She never saw it coming."

"Was that all?" asked Spencer, sounding relieved. "Just a tap on the head?"

"No. That would have given her only a temporary concussion," replied Tony, "But it lasted long enough for me to call Mr. Hartmann. We had previously agreed what to do if a situation like this arose. I injected her with a large dose of Nembutal and insulin."

This time the silence was almost palpable, and although everyone there tried to look impassive, the shock was obvious in their faces.

Again Spencer broke the silence. "Tony, we had Mr. Hartmann's word that after Dr. Newsome's death, no other . . . incidents would take place."

Tony, who had switched off the projector, swung around quickly to face Spencer, and the audience froze. But Tony's voice was calm and respectful. "Of course, Dr. Spencer," he replied. "But nobody could have foreseen this. And it was clearly a potentially hazardous situation. I'm sure you agree that we had to take appropriate steps."

"Well, I'm still concerned," said Spencer. He got to his feet and stood behind the tall chair, one hand tapping on its rosewood back. "Whoever hired her is going to wonder what happened to her. This could set off a whole train of very nasty investigations."

"We considered that, Dr. Spencer," replied Tony. "I informed Dr. Gardner here of the situation, and he came immediately to the hospital and took charge of the patient. His clinical diagnosis was that she had a heart attack, and she was treated as such. And of course I took other precautions. I called Dr. Eric Tarvel, who as the owner of ConnPath, with his partner Dr. Marilyn Fox, is part of our group. You also know that Lovejoy Hospital contracts out all its lab work to ConnPath, together with the pathology function."

Spencer nodded slowly. Tony had certainly not acted hastily or without thought for the consequences. "I told Dr. Tarvel that Mrs. Minsky was being admitted and would have routine blood tests, including the usual toxicology tests. I told him that all of these were to be reported as negative."

"How can he do that?" asked Spencer. "Their system's fully automated, and all the technician does is put the labeled sample into the machine. The analyzer prints out the report with a time and date stamp. He can't just change a couple of the values—the techs or the secretaries would query it immediately.''

"Correct," said Tony. "Which is why I suggested to Dr. Tarvel that he take a blood sample he already knows is normal, relabel it with Pauline Minsky's name, and put it through the analyzer a second time."

The group members sat very still, listening.

"I also told him that when the woman dies, probably some time this morning, an autopsy will be requested, according to Connecticut law, and of course it will be performed by him or Dr. Fox. The report will be that she died of heart disease, confirming the clinical diagnosis."

"That's all very well," said Spencer, "but it doesn't tell us who's so interested in our affairs, or whether they'll send somebody else in to pick up where she left off."

"I suggest that we don't replace Mrs. Minsky, at least for a while," said Tony. "We've never had any problems of this kind until she came along, and there's been no indication that she was working with anyone here, although we considered Dr. Richmond. We employed Mrs. Minsky through an agency, and maybe that was a mistake. Meanwhile, if everyone agrees, Dr. Richmond's clerical work can be shared between the other secretaries."

"Okay," said Spencer slowly. "Does anyone have a problem with that?"

No one did.

Everybody stood up. There was no conversation.

Tony looked at them with a speculative eye; they all seemed seriously concerned. A couple of them, Derek included, looked gray—and there was no doubt that they were shaken by this disturbing turn of events. Tony smiled grimly to himself. *No pain, no gain*, as the athletes used to say. Those men were all happy enough to rake in the vast amounts of money they made from being part of the group, but when things became tough, their attitude changed. Well, that was just too bad. Carl hadn't been sure if they should tell the group about the Minsky woman, but Tony's argument was persuasive. "It makes them accessories," he said.

"While you're all here, gentlemen," said Tony, from the doorway. "Please remember to turn in your lists of complicated discharges from the hospital. I need them by tomorrow."

Chapter 17

Lou Gardner called Mike back after the meeting was over. "Yes, very sad,"; he said. "I suppose you heard Pauline died about an hour ago. Cardiac arrest, couldn't get her restarted. . . . Yes, I'm sorry too. Nice lady, worked for me a couple of times when Debbie was on vacation." He paused. "You paged me?"

"Yes. It's too late now, I guess. I wanted to ask you about Pauline, what had happened. I went to see her, but there was a private duty nurse in her room, a real tiger. She threw me out."

"Riva Zorek? Yeah, she takes her work seriously." Mike heard the satisfaction in Lou's voice. "There's not much else I can tell you," he added. "She had a major anterior M.I., documented by EKG, not much we could do. Sorry."

"One other thing, Lou," Mike gulped. "About Della Marcus and the streptokinase. I'm going to write a letter to the pharmacy committee to ask for it to be made an approved drug. I know you're on that committee—would you back the request?"

"Sure, of course, Mike," replied Lou. "We'll approve it just as soon as it costs the plan less than five bucks a dose."

Mike's phone went dead. He looked at it for a moment, shrugged, then went back over to his office. The small red light was blinking on the monitor. He pressed the appropriate keys, and brought up a stack of X-ray and lab reports. The last one was from ConnPath, a report on Stephanie's biopsy done the day before. Pretty fast, he thought, contrasting it with the medical center labs, which routinely took four or five days to come up with a pathology report. Maybe that was the difference between public and private enterprise . . . Suddenly his whole body became rigid. *Small areas of well-differentiated infiltrating adeno-carcinoma are noted in the specimen*, he read. *. . . Invasion of the duct walls are seen in a number of areas, with marked desmoplastic reaction in the surrounding tissues.* The report was accompanied by high-magnification color photographs of the tissue sections. And unlike the X-rays, there was no question about these, even with the slight lessening of details resulting from the computer imaging. It was cancer.

Mike pushed his chair back, feeling shocked and breathless.

There was a knock on the door, and Derek came in. "You look sick," he said. "You must be still upset about Pauline."

Mike jolted his mind away from Stephanie's biopsy report. "Yes. You know she died?"

Derek nodded somberly. "Well, at least it was

quick. Better that way than dying of something slow and painful," he said philosophically, and sat down in the visitor's chair. "On an entirely different topic," he said, looking at Mike with a curious expression. "Have you had much dealings with our radiology friends downstairs?"

"The usual," replied Mike. "An upper G.I. series here, a CAT scan there, you know. Why?"

"Well, apparently Marty Rosenfeld called Spencer this morning. Marty's pissed because you've been calling him about various patients and wanting to go over films with him."

"Yeah, right," said Mike, "I was going to ask you about those guys. A couple of times I wanted to review films with them, and they kept putting me off. The last time I wanted to go over a mammogram Marty Rosenfeld reported on, and he got mad and chewed me out. What's their problem?"

Derek shrugged a shoulder. "Well, it goes back to when they first joined us," he said, stretching his legs out in front of him. Mike got the impression that he was making an effort to look relaxed. "We'd be in and out of their office looking at films, asking questions—you know how it goes. Then they started to get real busy and didn't want to be interrupted, so we set up a weekly session when we'd go over films with them. That didn't work too well, because we were getting busy too, and we never knew for sure when we'd all be free, so the meetings sort of petered out."

Mike watched Derek as he spoke. What Derek was

really telling him was that communication had to take second place to economics. That basically was what Marty Rosenfeld had told Mike—"If we're talking, we're not working, and if we're not working, we're not making money."

"So what do you do now?" asked Mike. "What if you have a film or a study you're not sure about?"

"Well, we've learned to take their word for it," said Derek. He shrugged again. "You have to remember, reading X-ray studies is their job, just like operating is ours. They work with their images day in and day out, and you have to admit that they are good. So it's not smart on our part to try and second-guess them. Which means we accept their findings and get on with our part of the job." He smiled tolerantly at Mike. "And of course," he went on, seeing that Mike was about to say something, "the same goes for ConnPath. They tell us what they find in their microscope slides, and we take it from there. They're legally responsible for the accuracy of their findings, and of course they stand behind their reports and can back them up if need be. The system works very well and saves a lot of time, too. Ours as well as theirs. It's a waste of time and money to try and second-guess them."

Mike nodded and kept his reservations to himself. "Okay. Thanks, Derek. I just wondered."

The door opened and Spencer came in, looking very fit, his tan contrasting with his thick white hair.

"I was just telling Mike here about the radiology

lab," said Derek, getting up and heading for the door.

"They can be prickly," said Spencer cheerfully. He sat down in the chair Derek had vacated and his expression became somber. "Mike, I was really sorry to hear about Pauline. We'll all miss her."

"Right. Me too. I still can't quite believe it . . ." Mike glanced at his monitor. "I'm glad you're back, because I've got a case I'd like your opinion on." He gave Spencer a brief outline of Stephanie Hopkins's case. "Here's the path report on the biopsy," he said, pointing at the images which were still up on the screen.

Spencer came around the desk, and his lips pursed as he examined the biopsy slides. "Not much doubt about that," he said. "Give me her unit number and I'll go over the X-rays and lab data. From the sounds of it, you've gone about it right so far. What definitive treatment are you going to recommend?"

Mike hesitated. "I thought I'd discuss it with her," he said. "Tell her what the options are, go over the different procedures that are available, and let her decide what she wants."

Almost before Mike had finished speaking, Spencer was shaking his head. "Well, of course," he said, "you're at liberty to go about it whichever way you want, Mike, but I've found that patients much prefer to be *told* what's best for them. You go over the possibilities with them, of course, but you should be the one to tell them what needs to be done. After all, you're getting paid for your expertise, not just to give them a bunch of choices."

"Most women I've dealt with who have this problem prefer a lumpectomy plus radiation," said Mike. "They know that the results are almost as good as with mastectomy."

"Right. *Almost*, but not *as* good. And that's what we have to impress on these women. They can usually get away with it for a year or two, but ultimately it catches up with them and they come back with metastases in their lungs and bones and brain." Spencer sat back in his chair, his eyes fixed on Mike. By then it's too late. What I tell them," he went on, "is that it's better to be alive with one breast than dead with two. That usually gets their attention."

"So you think I should do a mastectomy on this woman?" Mike's reluctance was evident—for a moment, he had a flashback of how Stephanie looked, then how she *would* look . . .

Spencer had no such qualms. "From what you've told me about the case," he said, "yes, a radical mastectomy would be the procedure of choice, without question. Of course, I still have to go over all the clinical and other data on her, but I don't imagine my opinion will change." Spencer looked at Mike sympathetically. "This is a classical case of where we have to put our . . . sensibilities aside in the interests of curing the patient," he said.

"Do you think that lumpectomy is ever the best choice?" asked Mike, curious to find where Spencer stood in this field, where clinical fashions changed from one year to the next.

"*Ever?* Possibly," replied Spencer in a dismissive tone, "And of course I'm occasionally forced to do one, but personally I think it's a fad, and it'll pass when all these lumpectomized patients start coming back in droves with their metastatic cancers."

Spencer left shortly after, and Mike sat back in his chair and felt his heart sink at the thought of telling all this to Stephanie Hopkins. And what made his heart sink even further was the prospect of actually performing the operation.

Then it occurred to him that, from the little he'd already seen of Stephanie Hopkins, she would certainly not just say, "Go ahead, you're the doctor, do what needs to be done." She would have substantial input into whatever final decision was made.

He reached slowly for the phone. Stephanie was not in her office, so he left a message with her voice mail, asking her to come to his office at five to discuss her biopsy results.

Chapter 18

Carl Hartmann sat at his desk, thinking hard. Tony had just called to tell him that Pauline Minsky was dead and that the autopsy and other arrangements had been taken care of. In a way, thought Carl, it had shown that they were well prepared to deal with problems—even one as unexpected as this. The main question, though, still hung in the air—who had hired the woman?

He sat still for a few moments, then reached for the phone. There was no point in having a dog and doing the barking too. "Tony? Meet me up in Security in ten minutes," he said. "We need to get Rankin working on this."

Carl headed for the stairs. He was a little out of breath when he reached the top and decided that in future he'd use the elevator. That's what the damned things were there for, after all.

He glanced into the surveillance room. One man was sitting in front of a double stack of monitors, each numbered on the frame with black marker, and another was listening to a crackling short-wave message, microphone in hand. Carl nodded to them, then went on along the corridor and found George Rankin in his office, talking to Sam Scheiffer, his second-in-command. George stood up smartly when Carl came in, followed by Scheiffer. Carl took the chair Sam had been using.

"So what the hell's been going on over at Spencer's office?" Carl asked George. "Why didn't you know what this woman was doing? How come she got employed there? Have you guys stopped doing security checks on new employees, or what?"

As Carl bombarded Rankin with his questions, Sam Scheiffer sidled toward the door and was about to slip out when Carl pointed a finger at him and peremptorily signaled him to come back.

"We're reviewing our procedures, sir," said George, still standing at attention. "Mrs. Minsky was just a clerical Level Four, and we don't normally do an in-depth on them."

"Sam, go get a chair. Sit down, George. Now, what have you come up with? Who hired her to spy on Spencer's group?"

George sat down. "We don't know." He put his hands flat on the desk. "We do know that it isn't any of the professional societies, although they're not above using investigators if they're checking out a medical facility." He glanced at Scheiffer, who had brought in a chair and was doing his best to look inconspicuous. "Sam here checked with his contacts in Hartford, and it's not the state, and if it had been the feds, they'd have been all over us by now."

"That's what I figured. Who else?"

"I called the temp agency that sent her and asked

how they signed on their personnel. They faxed me copies of Mrs. Minsky's references, and they're here. Sam checked them."

Carl shifted his gaze to Sam.

"They're all okay, sir," said Sam, moving on his chair. "Solid references. They're old, though. She worked in a doctor's office here in town, and before that in New Haven as a legal secretary. She and her husband both got private investigators' licenses five years ago, and since then they've done mostly small stuff, tracking down skips, debtors, lost husbands—stuff like that."

"What about the husband?"

"Oh, he's had a stroke or something and he's out of the picture. I called her office number and there's no answer."

The door opened and Tony walked in. He nodded to Rankin and Scheiffer.

"We're talking about the Minsky woman," Carl said. "Do you have anything new on her?"

"Not really. I've been wondering if she was working with Dr. Richmond, Spencer's new doc. She was his secretary, and there's no indication that anybody else is involved, inside or outside the office."

Carl looked skeptical. "Richmond? What would he have to gain?"

Tony bounced lightly on his feet a couple of times. "He could have been planted." His cold blue eyes traveled over to George.

"We did a thorough background check on Dr. Richmond before he joined Spencer's group," said George, a hint of defensiveness in his voice. "We didn't find anything to suggest any kind of involvement with law enforcement or anything else suspicious."

"And as you know very well, these background checks don't mean shit," said Tony.

George bristled and started to say something, but Carl interrupted. "Tony, you took care of the hospital records and the autopsy?"

"Yes, sir. Dr. Tarvel has an arrangement with one of the pathologists at the state medical examiner's office, and the autopsy's been scheduled for next Wednesday."

"Wednesday?" Carl stared at Tony. "Why can't they do it sooner?"

"That's the earliest Dr. Li can attend," replied Tony. "And obviously we don't want any of the other state pathologists involved."

Carl stood up, intimidating the others with his size and presence. "I want to know who hired Mrs. Minsky and why," he said with deliberate emphasis. "And I want to know by the end of this week." He turned and stared at George Rankin. "You guys have been sitting on your fat asses watching those surveillance monitors long enough. It's time to get out there and earn your pay."

Back in his office, Carl thought about calling Jack DiGiovanni, but since becoming governor, Jack had distanced himself, understandably enough. He moved the piles of paper on his desk around, trying not to overbalance the various paperweights, looking for DiGiovanni's phone number. Carl's money had put him in office. Now it was time to repay a favor.

Chapter 19

The afternoon went by agonizingly slowly for Stephanie, and by the time the clock showed a quarter of five, she was shaking inside. She tidied her desk and locked it with a sense of finality that scared her, and she still had that sense when she appeared at Mike's office.

"Come on in." He sounded cheerful enough, but as she walked into the room, Stephanie watched him closely, trying to anticipate his words by watching his body language and the tone of his voice.

"Have a seat."

Just like the last time, Mike had his computer terminal on, and she could see a pinkish-colored image with small dark blue blobs on the screen, but she couldn't tell what it was.

"Well, it seems the radiologists were right after all, Stephanie," he said. His face was looking a little drawn, and indeed he was feeling the strain of having his clinical impressions proved wrong again. "Unfortunately, the pathologists found some malignant cells in the biopsy."

Stephanie felt as if her heart had stopped. She

heard herself say, "Are you telling me that I have cancer?"

"I'm sure you know that the term *cancer* covers a wide variety of conditions," replied Mike, but Stephanie was getting more and more alarmed, partly because of what he was saying, but also because he wouldn't look her in the eye. "But to answer your question, yes," he went on. "The biopsy showed a reasonably well differentiated adenocarcinoma. Because it was only a biopsy, we can't tell for sure, but there was no indication that it has spread anywhere else." Mike finally was able to look at Stephanie. He was feeling shaken and stupid because it seemed that all he'd learned about clinical surgery in his eight years of medical school and residency was either inadequate or totally wrong.

"Would you like to see the slides?" he asked, nodding at the computer screen. He pointed at one of the darker areas.

"No, thanks," said Stephanie. Her voice was steady, but slightly higher pitched than usual. A thought struck her. "Does Dr. Spencer review this kind of case? I mean, last time you said something about getting a second opinion from him."

Mike moved in his chair. "As a matter of fact, I've already asked him to review the case," he told her. "He hasn't gone over all the data yet, but we've talked about it and he agrees with what I've told you."

Stephanie could feel her shoulders starting to shake, and she gripped her hands together. "So what do we do now?"

Mike was feeling almost as tense as she was. "Well," he said, as he had dozens of times before in similar situations, "there are several ways of dealing with this . . ." Then he remembered Spencer's words: *Tell them what needs to be done—you're getting paid for your expertise, not to give them a list of choices.* "But of all of these," he went on, "the safest and the best way of dealing with this is to remove the breast tissue and the lymph nodes in the axilla."

Stephanie looked down, feeling tears prickling in the back of her eyes. A mastectomy . . . when she was in nursing school, she'd seen women who'd had mastectomies, sometimes young women, and felt so bad for them. But the thought had never crossed her mind that it could ever happen to her.

"What about lumpectomies?" she asked. "I know a lot of women are having that done, and of course it's . . . a lot more aesthetic."

Mike hesitated for a second. "Yes, and I've done many lumpectomies," he replied. "The problem is that although aesthetics are certainly very important, it's even more important to get rid of the cancer." Watching Stephanie, he took a deep breath. "I'm sure you know many surgeons are developing major doubts about the long-term effectiveness of lumpectomies," he went on. Mike put his hands on the table. "To put it bluntly, Stephanie, we may be dealing with a situation where it's more important to be alive and healthy with one breast . . ." He swallowed, and Stephanie filled in the words for him.

"Than dead with two, is that what you were going to say?"

He nodded glumly.

"How about radiation?" asked Stephanie, feeling a scream starting to rise somewhere inside her. She'd seen women who'd had radiation, with those stiff, shiny pink scars and brown pigmentation on their skin.

"Yes. That's something we'll need to discuss . . ."

"Chemotherapy?"

"No, not unless there are signs that metastases have already occurred. We'll put you on tamoxifen after surgery, because that's been proven to reduce the chances of recurrence. Of course, before the surgery you'll need a CAT scan, and we'll need to check for metastases in various places, although at this time there's no indication that you have any."

"What places?" Stephanie's mouth was dry, and she licked her lips.

"Bones, lungs, brain," replied Mike. "But since we caught this so early, I really don't think we'll find any problems there."

"Just as there was little chance of my getting this in the first place." Stephanie tried to smile, and so did he. He was trying not to show how insecure he felt, how shaken he was that his clinical diagnosis had been so wrong.

"So we'll set up the tests for tomorrow, that's Saturday, and do the surgery on Monday. As you know, Stephanie, in this kind of situation, the sooner the better."

"Okay . . ." Stephanie hesitated. "It all seems in

such a rush.'' She stood up and almost fell, and leaned against the glass-topped table.

Mike came around quickly and put a supporting hand on her arm.

She looked at him. "I still can't believe this is happening to me." Her voice was shaky, and she couldn't think straight.

Stephanie didn't remember the drive home; she didn't see the distant flash of blue water on the sound between the trees as she turned into Spring Street, or the banner across the street advertising Abrahamian's carpet store's going-out-of-business sale. A hundred yards from her apartment, she didn't see the black-and-white soccer ball until it hit her car, and she slammed on her brakes and came to a screeching halt in the middle of the road, watched by two round-eyed kids on the sidewalk.

That did it. She made it home, but her hands were shaking so much she had trouble opening her door, then she ran in and fell down on the bed and wept.

After a few minutes, she sat up, and then took her clothes off and went into the bathroom and looked carefully at herself in the full-length mirror.

She looked good; Stephanie had never been one to spend a lot of time in front of the mirror, but she could see that her skin was smooth, her hips were okay, and she had a good shape. She remembered reading that some ninety percent of American females were unhappy about the way they looked. She'd wondered if she'd be happier if her eyebrows were a bit thicker, her nose a bit smaller, and her hair lighter. For a second she saw herself as a strawberry blond, with her hair up . . . no. No way. She stretched out her arms and forced herself to stare at her right breast. There was a slight bruising on the outside from the needle biopsy, but it was barely noticeable. She tried to visualize what was happening inside—the malignant cells already growing out of control, ready to course into her veins and arteries, using these convenient channels for their lethal migrations to other parts of her body.

Still in front of the mirror, she turned slightly to the left and, in her mind, removed the right breast. How would it look? How would it feel? Just asking herself those questions made her feel strangely disembodied, as if the reflection in the mirror had no real relation to her. Would she forever feel out of balance when she walked or ran? And what man would ever want to have anything to do with a woman with such a deformity, a woman who was also carrying the potential for an early death?

"Why me?" she asked the mirror, but it just stared back at her.

She turned away and walked blindly into the living room. The worst part of it all was the awful feeling of helplessness. Until now, Stephanie had been able to solve her problems by hard work or by using her intelligence, or sometimes just by waiting a situation out. But with this, it seemed that nothing she could do would make any difference.

Chapter 20

Stephanie's mother, Emily, lived with her second husband, Len, in Stonington, in a nice little house that had once belonged to a sea captain. Emily wasn't home when Stephanie called, and, feeling desperate and shaky, Stephanie just kept on pressing the redial button. After about ten minutes, by which time she was so up-tight she didn't know what to do, her mother picked up.

"Oh, Mom . . ." Stephanie was ready to weep.

"What's the matter?" Emily's voice was loud with concern. Stephanie was the eldest of her three children, and usually the most sensible and calm.

Stephanie told her what was happening, and Emily caught her breath. "I can't believe it," she said finally. "At your age? Who's your doctor? Did you get another opinion?"

"They're supposed to be the best," Stephanie told her, deriving a slight comfort from her own words. "And you know Lovejoy's a big center for . . . well, for this kind of thing."

"Who's there with you?" asked Emily. "Is Evie there? I can't come down, you know, what with Len and everything."

"How's he doing?" Len, whom she loved dearly, suffered from severe emphysema.

"He's on oxygen almost all the time now, and I can hardly leave him long enough to do the shopping."

"I'll be fine," said Stephanie. "Evie's around, and that'll be a comfort."

"When are they planning to do the surgery?"

"Monday."

"Oh, my." Emily's voice was shaking. "I feel so terrible that I won't be there."

"Don't worry, Mom. I've taken care of people who've had that kind of surgery, and it's not really a big deal." Stephanie swallowed. "They're usually out of the hospital in a couple of days."

"Will you be doing rehab?" A thought struck Emily. "I read where they're doing breast reconstructions—plastic surgery. Did your doctor talk to you about that?"

"Yes. But they'll probably do it later." Stephanie heard her own voice, but it felt as if she were talking about someone else, some woman she knew only slightly. Reconstructions . . . she'd seen a few of those too. Maybe they made it easier to wear clothes, but in fact reconstructed breasts never looked or felt like the real thing, and in fact were just a different kind of mutilation.

Stephanie thought about calling her two sisters but decided not to. Barbara lived in Seattle and Margaret with her banker husband in Hong Kong, and in any case both had small children they wouldn't be able to leave. And the news would just upset them, so

Stephanie decided to tell them about it afterward, if her mother didn't tell them first.

She did manage to reach Evie, who wanted to come over immediately, but right now Stephanie needed to be alone. She had a lot of stuff to do, she truthfully told Evie, and work was the best way of not thinking about Monday.

Stephanie decided to go and do some work on her boat. It had been parked for the winter in a corner of the Milford boatyard. Grass was growing around the wheels of the trailer as she walked around, checking the hull. As she took the tarpaulin off, her fear took hold again. Something inside her head was screaming, *This can't be happening to me! They're all wrong! I'm perfectly healthy!* Denial, she knew, was the first part of the process of dealing with this problem, but that knowledge didn't make it any easier.

Even her body wasn't doing what it was supposed to do—her knees were weak, she couldn't grip things properly with her hands, and there was a kind of motionless trembling throughout her body that she could neither identify nor control. It crossed her mind that maybe the tumor had spread to her brain, and that was causing her weakness. The mere thought made her sit down on the metal bar at the back of the trailer. It could happen. She'd taken care of women it had happened to.

There was no way she could concentrate on the boat, and after mechanically noting that the trailer tires needed air, she got back into her car and sat there for a while before driving to the hospital for her first CAT scan.

When she finally got home. Stephanie spent the rest of the day scrubbing, cleaning her apartment, sorting out clothes, trying to exhaust herself physically to the point where she couldn't think about anything else. At six-thirty on Monday morning she found herself, breakfastless, at the admissions office at Lovejoy Hospital, holding tightly onto her small overnight bag. Evie met her there and went up to her room with her. The nurse, after taking a quick admission history, brought in a mock-up of an I.V. with a narcotic demand device. "You'll have this on your arm when you come out of the O.R.," she said. "You just press on this button if you're hurting and you feel you need pain medication. Actually, you probably won't have that much pain," she went on, "But at least you'll know the system's there if you need it."

A few minutes later, Stephanie, clad in a shapeless white hospital gown, climbed into the thin-sheeted bed. Evie had to go back to work, and went off after giving Stephanie a gentle hug and a big, tearful kiss on the cheek. Stephanie lay there alone, very afraid, staring at the sound-absorbing ceiling panels and feeling her heart beating in her chest, thump, thump, thump.

She didn't have to wait long. A half hour later, a nurse came in with her pre-op medication, and after that she felt warm and sleepy and didn't really care what they did to her.

Carl had returned to the office early that morning, coming straight from the airport, anxious to get to work. When he came in, Ann Boyd, his secretary, mentioned that Stephanie had left a message on the voice-mail saying that she was taking a few days of sick time and wouldn't be in this week.

"Sick time?" he asked. He stopped and stared at her. "She's sick? What's the matter with her?"

"I've no idea, sir," replied Ann. Sometimes the intensity of his manner made her uncomfortable. "That was all she said."

"Find out. Now." Carl went into his office, feeling annoyed—he'd set time aside to go over the data with Stephanie and didn't appreciate the delay.

Ann tried Stephanie's home number, then thought for a moment before calling Jean Forrest.

"I'm looking for Stephanie, Jean," she said. "My boss is all bent out of shape because she isn't here."

"She's in the hospital," replied Jean, surprised. "Didn't she tell you?"

"Oh, my. No, she didn't. What's the matter with her?"

Jean hesitated. "Well, I shouldn't be the one . . . okay, Mr. Hartmann'll know about it soon enough. Stephanie had a breast biopsy last week, and it was positive. They're doing the mastectomy right now."

"Oh, my goodness . . ." Ann looked up to see the door open. Carl came back into her office. "Thanks,

Jean . . . hold on a second." She put a hand over the phone and told Carl what Jean had said.

Carl looked astonished, and then a curious expression came over his face. "Who's her doctor?" he asked. Anne repeated the question to Jean.

"Dr. Richmond," replied Jean promptly. "He's with the Spencer group."

Carl, who could hear Jean's voice, muttered, "God-damn!" He almost ran back into his office, slamming the door behind him, picked up his phone, and quickly dialed a number, his fingers tripping over each other.

Stephanie didn't even hear the clatter of the stretcher as it came down the corridor, but she could feel a kind of haze of general goodwill and help-fulness from the people around her. Later she did remember the ceiling lights flicking past at a great speed, and they made her feel dizzy so she closed her eyes. She was so sleepy that she'd have closed them anyhow, and kept them closed while they put her in the holding area off the operating suite. She dozed, and brightly colored dreams went through her mind. She was with her mother on a roller coaster that was going too fast, and at each turn it seemed they were going to fly off into space, and on the last turn they did. The feeling of weightlessness, of falling, startled her, and she wakened for a moment, and clung to the sides of the stretcher. Every-thing she could see was white, brightly lit; even the people were too bright for her eyes. She closed them again. The stretcher started to move and bumped into something. It felt like her little boat docking a bit roughly. Then the sheet under her was picked up by a lot of hands and deposited gently on the operating table. It felt cold on her back and her bottom, and she shivered for a second.

The anesthesiologist, a woman, started to speak, telling her about what she was going to do, but to Stephanie it was all a soft, meaningless blur of words.

". . . Mask . . ." She heard the word, and felt the edges of it on her cheeks, then they must have injected something into her veins because that was the last thing she remembered.

Mike finished his morning rounds at Lovejoy Hospital before coming to the operating suite, where he found Sophie Petersen, the new O.R. supervisor who had replaced Darla Finsten, waiting for him. Sophie had worked at NCMC when Mike was in training and liked him, but rules were rules and applied to everybody.

"There's hardly anything in your patient's chart," she said, tapping the aluminum chart cover. "There's a consent form, and she's signed that, and we have her admission lab slips, but there's none of her X-ray or biopsy reports, and I can't let you operate without a copy of the history and physical or lab reports in the chart."

"Damn," said Mike, taking the chart and glancing through it. "I'm sorry, Sophie . . . you know what kind of a weekend we had. Look, I'll write a detailed pre-op note, and I'll get somebody to bring the rest of the stuff over from the office right now, okay?"

"If I didn't know you, and if it was anybody else," said Sophie sternly, "your patient would go back to the recovery area until all reports and everything else were physically present in the chart."

Mike picked up the phone and dialed his office. Luckily, one of the secretaries was there, and he asked her to drop whatever she was doing and bring the printouts on Stephanie Hopkins's file over to the Lovejoy operating suite immediately. Then he sat down and wrote a detailed preoperative note in the chart under the supervisor's watchful gaze.

"Okay this time, Dr. Richmond," Sophie said, taking the chart back. "Next time your patient goes back to her room, and you can do the explaining to her." She poked her head into the operating room where Stephanie was, and nodded to the anesthesiologist. "You can go ahead," she said.

"Good," replied the anesthesiologist, her voice muffled by her mask. She leaned forward, keeping the face mask in position with one hand, and with the other pressed on the plunger of a syringe attached with tape to Stephanie's wrist, injecting the rest of the pentothal into her veins.

Mike walked into the room a few moments later. Stephanie was already asleep.

"It's really sad, isn't it?" said the anesthesiologist over the ether screen as he pulled down the sheet to expose her breasts.

Mike nodded. He didn't want to think about that.

Instead he forced himself to see through the skin, estimating the thickness of that layer of tissue that Spencer had demonstrated to him, figuring how much skin he'd need to remove and how it would all come together after the breast tissue and axillary lymph nodes had been taken out. He took a pen off the tray, a special skin pen with violet ink, made specifically for marking out incision lines. Taking off the cap, he drew two S-shaped lines, starting at the front of the axilla, parting around the main part of the breast, and rejoining near the midline, a little above the rib margin.

"Okay," he said to the waiting circulator, "you can prep her now. Don't wash out my incision lines."

He didn't wait to see the circulator prep Stephanie's chest with Betadine, a brown antiseptic solution, but went into the scrub room, forcing his mind to focus on the technical details of the operation. This wasn't a person he was dealing with, he told himself, this was a technical problem, to be taken care of as skillfully as he possibly could. But there was a deep sense of reluctance inside him, trying to paralyze his actions, making it difficult for him even to take the small steps into the scrub room, because these were taking him inexorably closer to the operating table. A strange feeling, which he recognized as a close relative of panic, came over him. Would he be able to ask the scrub tech for the knife, and if he could, would he be able to use it on her? He felt sick, and leaned against the wall for a few moments, forcing reason to come back to him. He was there to save her life from cancer, in a way that had proved successful for countless thousands of women. He'd discussed the pros and cons with her, and she'd agreed that losing a breast was a reasonable sacrifice, considering the alternative.

John Henly, the junior resident scheduled to assist him, was already scrubbing. Mike told him about Stephanie's problem, and made the case, maybe a shade too emphatically, for radical mastectomy versus lumpectomy and radiation.

A few minutes later, Mike shut off the faucet with his knee and went to the door, turning and pushing it open with his back, holding his dripping hands out in front of him. The scrub tech gave him a sterile towel, and he dried his hands. They had already draped Stephanie's chest, which looked orange brown and glistened with unreal highlights from the high-intensity O.R. lamps. It didn't look like a part of a human body, and that was good, he thought, putting his arms into the sleeves of the gown that Ken Willis, the scrub tech, was holding out for him. He kept his mind busy by running through all the different steps of the operation, the instruments and sutures he would need. The last thing he wanted to do at this point was to think of Stephanie as the living, breathing young woman who had made such an impression on him.

Gloves . . .

Finally, he went over to the right side of the table, forcing himself to move. His assistant was already positioned on the other side, busily arranging the various electrical cords and suction tubes so they would be out of the way but readily available when needed.

Mike took a deep breath. "Skin knife," he said quietly, and the tech passed it to him. He looked over at the anesthesiologist, who nodded.

"Go ahead," she said.

Mike started the incision and had cut through a millimeter or two of skin when there was a commotion outside, and the door swung open.

"Mike, stop!" It was Spencer, red in the face and out of breath, not even wearing a mask.

Mike stopped, scalpel in midair. "What's the matter?" he asked.

"Have you started already?" Spencer's voice was higher than normal.

"We were just starting the incision," replied Mike. "What's the problem?"

"We'll talk about that outside," he said, but his tone showed anger as well as relief. "Meanwhile," he said, addressing the anesthesiologist in a commanding tone, "Wake her up and get her back to recovery."

The anesthesiologist glanced at Mike, who, after all, was in charge of the case.

Mike was angry and startled. "Can you tell me why?" he asked Spencer. "What happened?"

Whatever reason Spencer had for doing this, it was going to cause serious trouble, with both the patient and the hospital authorities. "Not now," he replied. "As soon as she's awake and you feel it's safe to leave her, please meet me in the small conference room on B-Two, and we can discuss the matter then. Just make sure she's okay before you come over."

Mike flushed under his mask. He didn't like Spencer's tone, which sounded accusatory and unpleasant.

"Okay," he said slowly. "I am terminating this operation on your orders, Dr. Spencer, and not for any medical reason that I'm aware of. You're taking full responsibility for this action?"

"Yes, I am." Spencer's voice was less grim, and now that he knew the operation hadn't been carried out, he sounded almost relieved. Suddenly realizing that he'd barged into the O.R. without proper clothing, he turned and left without another word.

In total silence, Mike put subcutaneous stitches into the incision, then a couple of Steristrips to keep the skin edges together before applying a dressing to the wound. The anesthesiologist, confused by this extraordinary turn of events, had turned off the anesthetic and was giving Stephanie pure oxygen to breathe, injecting medication to counteract the muscle relaxants she had already administered. Stephanie was beginning to stir.

She woke up soon after they reached the recovery room, and looked around, trying to get her bearings and figure out where she was. She looked up and saw Mike, and misinterpreted his grim expression. Her lips were dry, and her mouth felt like the bottom of a vulture's nest.

Mike saw that she was awake, but his expression

didn't change. "We didn't do the operation," he said. "I'll explain to you later. It's . . . look, I can't really tell you now . . ."

He turned away in his anger and frustration.

"Just tell me one thing," said Stephanie, feeling desperate and, if anything, even more frightened than before. "Was it inoperable? Was the cancer too far gone?"

Mike came back, took her hand, and smiled at her. "No," he said. "It wasn't that, Stephanie. I'll come back just as soon as I can, in maybe ten minutes, and I'll tell you exactly what happened, okay? I promise."

He walked with long, fast strides to the conference room, feeling his anger and resentment soaring. What reason could Spencer possibly have to terminate the operation in that way? It had made him look like a fool, and there would surely be major repercussions at every level.

Spencer was sitting at the end of the table, with a manila folder open in front of him. He looked up when Mike came in. "Is she all right?" he asked. "Miss Hopkins?"

"Yes, she's all right," Mike answered, trying to keep the anger out of his voice, then added, "Except for her breast cancer, of course."

"Well, that's one of the things we have to discuss," said Spencer. He seemed relaxed now, in contrast to his alarm of a few minutes ago in the operating room. "Come and sit down."

Mike hesitated for a second, then came and sat at

the table, leaving one chair between Spencer and himself.

Spencer tapped the folder in front of him. "Mike, a few days ago you asked me to take a look at the data on your patient Stephanie Hopkins, and I said I would." He glanced at the folder. "That was just after I'd come back from my vacation. As you can imagine, I've been very busy catching up with my own work, and I only got around to your case this morning, not realizing that you'd scheduled her for today." He paused, looking at Mike with an expression Mike couldn't fathom. "In fact, it wasn't till I saw the O.R. schedule on the computer that I realized I hadn't gone over her chart." He shook his head. "Anyway, when I did review the data, I couldn't see any reason to be doing any kind of surgery on her, let alone a mastectomy, and that's why I came over and stopped you."

Mike stood up. "What the hell are you talking about?" he asked. "She had a positive mammogram and a positive biopsy. What more do you want?"

Spencer let his breath out with a long sigh. "I don't think you saw the corrected report." He took a print-out from the folder and passed it over to Mike.

" 'Corrected pathology report,' " he read out slowly, feeling as if a huge hand were starting to squeeze down on his chest. "I've never seen this," he said after reading on for a moment. He put the paper face-down on the table, denying its existence.

"Just read it, please," said Spencer, watching him. "Starting with the date."

Reluctantly, Mike picked up the paper again. "It's dated the tenth—that's last Friday."

"Right. Two days after the original report."

Mike took a deep breath. "Okay . . . *This report corrects and supersedes report number 5X55496/97,'* " he read. *"The breast biopsy on patient Stephanie Hopkins, Unit #ABS44245, was examined by our Histology Review Committee, and there was disagreement about the presence of malignant tissue in the right breast, as reported earlier. Only one member of the committee felt that such tissue was present. Our revised diagnosis is that minor inflammatory changes, probably fibrocystic in nature, are noted in this specimen, and no malignant tissue is present. Our recommendation at this time is to repeat the mammogram in three months if clinical indications are still present."*

Mike stared at the paper, and then at Spencer. His hand was shaking. "As I said, I've never seen this before."

"It was on your computer," said Spencer.

Mike felt the sweat wet on his palms. "I never saw it," he repeated. "Anyway, with a major change in diagnosis like this, shouldn't the pathologist have called to tell me about it?"

"No," said Spencer. "By filing a modified report, they did what they were required to do. They don't have time to hold our hands and explain everything to us."

"Doesn't the computer light blink when an unread report is in the system?" asked Mike. The whole room seemed to be closing in on him, and he heard his own voice speaking in a metallic tone, as if it came from some other person.

"The light was blinking this morning when I came into your office."

"Oh, my God . . ." Mike stood up. "Dr. Spencer, would you like me to quit? I mean, resign from the group? I can't believe I did anything so careless."

"No, of course not," said Spencer easily, but there was a coldness in his voice, and Mike wondered whether he wanted to discuss the matter with the other members of the group before firing him. "You're young, Mike, and you're inexperienced, but you'll be all right," Spencer went on. "Show me a surgeon who never makes mistakes, and I'll show you a surgeon who never operates." He stood up, and although his expression remained chilly, there was more relief than anger in his face. "And now," he said, standing up and putting the papers together, "you'd better start thinking about what you're going to tell Miss Hopkins."

Chapter 21

Mike went slowly back along the corridor, appalled by what he had almost done. At the door of the recovery room, he stopped and thought for a moment, trying to decide exactly what he would tell Stephanie. All kinds of self-preserving notions flashed through his mind, but finally he decided that he would just tell the truth. He pushed the door open and walked in.

Stephanie was still groggy but awake, and a nurse was taking out her I.V.

"What happened?" she asked Mike.

"Well, it's nearly all good news," he said, smiling at her. "We got a last-minute report that the lump was benign, so we terminated."

Stephanie hesitated. Her dark hair was falling over the left side of her face, and she pushed it away, watching him. "So now what do we do?"

"Well, you have a small incision . . ." He pointed to the dressing. "And we'll need to take the Steri-strips off in about five days."

"A small incision," repeated Stephanie slowly. "My head isn't very clear right now, and I don't understand. Will you explain it all to me at some point?"

"Sure. You'll be ready to leave soon. Is somebody coming to pick you up?"

"Well, no." Stephanie smiled at him. "I was supposed to stay here in the hospital for at least a couple of days, remember?"

Mike shook his head. "You said *your* head wasn't too clear . . . ." He thought for a moment. "You'll be ready to go in about half an hour, I'd guess. I'll take you home. After all, I'm the one who put you through all this."

"Oh, no, thanks, really . . . I can get someone, or get a cab."

"I'll see you in half an hour," he said firmly, and was walking out of the recovery room just as Evie Gaskell came in.

She stopped at the door. "How's she doing?"

"Just fine." Mike didn't stop to elaborate. "She's going home," he said over his shoulder.

"She's what?"

But Mike was already around the corner, thinking that he'd gotten away very lightly so far, but he knew full well that there would be a serious reckoning somewhere in the future. And the thought kept hammering at him, how could he possibly have made that mistake? Never in his career had he done anything like that, not even when he was a junior resident, half trained, exhausted and swamped with cases. Sure, his paperwork wasn't always in the best of shape, but he gave his patients the best possible care, he was convinced of that. Again, the germ of self-doubt kept creeping into his mind, growing fast, and it scared him. Maybe he was in the wrong profession. Maybe he wasn't temperamentally suited for the practice of surgery. Maybe he really was too careless to be trusted with the lives of patients.

But at the back of his mind, some other questions were beginning to form. How come he hadn't seen that indicator light flashing on the computer? Sure, two of those days were over the weekend, and he had been so busy at the hospital that he'd barely stopped over at the office, but still, it must have been blinking from Friday to Monday, as it was still blinking when Spencer saw it. And hadn't he downloaded other incoming reports on Friday afternoon? At this point his memory was not entirely reliable because he'd been so busy, but it just didn't seem credible that he would miss a crucial report like that. Yet he had. He went back to the recovery room desk to check the hospital chart. There it was, the incriminating second pathology report was there, right on the top, above the stapled reports that the secretary had brought over earlier that morning.

A half hour later, he brought his car around to the E.R. entrance, and called up to the recovery room. Stephanie was ready, and although she felt well enough to walk, they insisted on taking her down in a wheelchair.

In the car, Mike said, "How are you feeling?"

"Fine," she replied, "considering. No headache, no

dizziness. But I'm still confused about what happened up there.''

"Would you like to stop for a cup of coffee?" he asked. "I need one, and I really have to talk to you."

"You can talk in the car," said Stephanie, but either he didn't hear or didn't want to hear, because a couple of minutes later he pulled into the parking lot of the Hot Tomato Cafe on Gladstone Street and he got out and came around to open her door.

"You're pale, Stephanie," he said contritely. "I'm really not being very considerate," he went on, thinking that everything he was doing today was wrong. "Listen, if you'd rather just go straight home, that's okay. As you said, we can talk in the car."

He seemed so agitated and concerned that she smiled.

"Now we're here, we might as well go in."

The restaurant was only about a quarter full, and Mike took her arm and headed for a table where they would be alone. He pulled back a chair for her and they sat down. When he passed her the menu, she said, "I'll just have a cappuccino, please."

Their coffee arrived, and Mike leaned forward, holding his mug with both hands. "Stephanie," he said in a tone of voice she'd not heard before, "something terrible almost happened this morning, and I have to tell you about it." He told her exactly what had happened, and just in the telling, it made him sweat all over again.

Stephanie listened in astonished silence.

"How come you didn't see the second pathology report?" she asked when he had finished.

"That's what I can't figure," he said. "I was in the office yesterday, and I just can't remember if the light was blinking or not. It's quite a small light, but I can't believe that I'd have missed it if it was on."

Now Stephanie was starting to feel very shaken. If Spencer hadn't come over to the hospital and stopped the operation, right now she'd have already lost her breast.

"I'd like to go home now," she said.

They drove to her apartment building in silence. He accompanied her up to her second-floor apartment and said, "Please call me if you have any problems, Stephanie. Do you think you'll need any pain medication?"

"No, thanks," she said, taking out her keys. "And thanks for driving me home." She hesitated, then opened the door and went in, closing it softly behind her. Mike looked at the closed door for a long moment, then turned and went downstairs to his car.

Stephanie leaned against the inside of the door, feeling more tired than she ever remembered. The incision was starting to hurt, too, and she went and lay down on her bed for a little while. She had to call her mother, and thought about how she would tell her what had happened. She'd be relieved, of course, but Emily was very much into women's rights, and would get on the warpath immediately.

She got up and went into the living room, sat down at her work table, and picked up the phone.

"Mom?"

"Oh, thank God," said Emily. "I've been so worried, I can't think straight. How are you? How do you feel? Oh, dear, I feel so bad you had to go through all that by yourself." Emily was in tears.

"Everything's fine, Mom. Actually, it's more than fine. It turned out not to be cancerous after all. What a relief, huh?"

"Thank God," said Emily again. "So they didn't operate? Where are you? At the hospital?"

"No. I just got home a minute ago, but I'm still a bit shaky. From the anesthetic, I suppose."

"Anesthetic? I thought you just told me they didn't operate on you."

"No, Mom, that's what *you* said. Actually, it's a complicated story, and I'll tell you all about it, but not now. I just wanted to let you know everything's okay. I'm going to go and lie down for a while. I'm pooped."

"It sounds all a bit strange to me," said Emily in a worried voice. "First you have tests and a biopsy that turns out positive and you need surgery, then you don't . . ."

"I'll explain it all to you later," said Stephanie. "How's Len doing?"

"Well, he's been worried about you too," replied Emily. "Otherwise, he's okay. His breathing isn't great, and he keeps on smoking those disgusting cigars and I'm tired of nagging at him."

Stephanie went back to the bedroom, but the phone rang, and she went back to answer it. It was

Jean Forrest, who'd called the hospital and been told she'd gone home. Jean wanted to come over and take care of her, but Stephanie told her no, thanks, she was fine, and anyway she was tired and just wanted to rest for a while. After hanging up, Stephanie took the phone off the hook and lay down on the bed. She went to sleep for a couple of hours, but the incision at the front of her right armpit started to throb and hurt, and after she got up to get an aspirin she didn't feel sleepy anymore.

Chapter 22

Mike returned to the hospital, did rounds, then went back to his office. In his mind, every moment, he was going over the details of the morning's events, trying to figure out how he could have made such a basic and inexcusable error.

When he came in through the outer office, he thought about Pauline and wondered how her husband was faring. He had tried a couple of times to call his home over the weekend, but there had been no answer.

Derek Provost was sitting at Mike's desk, grinning over the monitor at him, and Mike felt a bit better just seeing his cheerful face. But, Mike thought miserably, he would have a different expression once he heard what Mike had done. His anxieties were soon put to rest.

"I've been hearing about your adventures this morning," said Derek. "That must have been quite a sight, Spencer storming into the O.R., all red-faced and out of breath, screaming 'Stop the operation!' "

"I wish he'd been in better shape—he might have gotten there before I started," replied Mike, trying to smile. "That would have saved us all a lot of aggravation."

"Well, from what I heard, you didn't get very far."

"Luckily." Mike was surprised at the matter-of-fact way Derek was talking about this; Spencer also had seemed relaxed once he knew that the operation hadn't already taken place.

Mike's feeling of reassurance was short-lived.

"You know there'll be a lawsuit," said Derek.

"God, I hope not," said Mike. "I explained the whole thing to the patient, and she seemed to understand pretty well. I drove her home."

Derek was shaking his head. "Sure. Right now she's still in shock over the whole thing, and she's feeling happy she got away with both her tits intact. Then her boyfriend, her dad, whoever, everybody she knows, they'll all start in on her. 'See an attorney!' they'll tell her. Everybody knows somebody who made five million dollars from a malpractice suit. It's become the American way to get rich quick. And all those people know a malpractice attorney. I'll bet you a set of new tires for your Aston-Martin that you'll be hearing from one of these guys, and soon."

"I don't think so," said Mike. "Not this woman."

"So what?" said Derek, smiling at Mike's expression. "It's not the end of the world, even if she does sue you. You know we've all got cases pending, and none of us loses any sleep over them because they nearly always get settled and the public never hears about them. Anyway, it's time you joined the group—you're a full member only when you have a lawsuit on the books." Mike sat down in front of his terminal, and glanced at the tiny red light. It was off. "Have you had any problems with the system?" he asked Derek. "The reason I got into this jam was because I missed a revised path report they sent over on Friday."

Derek thought for a moment. "It usually works okay," he said. "It took us all a while to get used to it. I guess you're still in the shakedown part of the cruise."

"Maybe I'll get Tony to put a bloody big alarm bell on the top of the monitor instead of that dumb little light," said Mike.

"Yeah, that should do it," said Derek, but there was a warning in his tone.

"I mean Mr. Danzig," said Mike.

Derek laughed. "You're learning," he said.

"I guess there'll be a hospital inquiry," said Mike, glum again. "I mean about today's fiasco."

"Don't worry about that," said Derek confidently. "Spencer'll take care of it. He's an expert on this kind of stuff. He's also chairman of the surgical quality-assurance committee at Lovejoy, so there shouldn't be any problem. He's taken care of a lot worse situations than this."

The door opened, and the secretary who was working for Mike poked her head in. "Your first patient's here, Dr. Richmond," she said. "Mrs. Donaldson. The chart's on the computer."

Derek stood up and headed for the door. "I'll leave

you to it," he said to Mike. "Have fun." He went off down the corridor, past his office, and into the conference room, where Spencer was reporting to the other members of the group on the events of the morning. He came in and softly closed the door behind him.

"What got into Carl?" Chas Miller was asking. "He's never interfered before, not in the details of how we run our operation."

"The woman works for him," replied Spencer. He shrugged. "I suppose he was worried that she'd be taking time off." He turned to Derek. "Well, how's our boy taking it?"

"Mike's okay," replied Derek. "He's a bit shaken, as you might expect."

"I hope we can get him fully on board soon," said Chas Miller, who didn't usually say much. "I for one do not like this present situation."

"I'm working on it, Chas," said Spencer. "And this whole business with the mastectomy will help to put him firmly in with us."

"Why?" asked Chas.

"Mike is a smart young man," replied Spencer. "And two things are going to happen. First, he's going to figure out more or less what happened this morning, and just to make sure, Tony'll help him. Then, after he gets over being pissed off, he'll do a bit of soul-searching. At that point he'll realize that once he's a full member and accepts the way we do things, he'll be protected. Without us behind him, he's vulnerable, and this case would land him in such deep professional trouble that he could lose his license.''

"You didn't plan this whole mastectomy case with that in mind, by any chance?'' Derek grinned at Spencer.

"No way. You should have heard Carl on the phone. He was *not* amused. We should keep employees strictly out of the system, he said.'' Spencer looked thoughtful. "But Carl wants to handle the case in the usual way, and he said he'd personally make sure Miss Hopkins talked with Haiman Gold.''

"Cold-blooded bastard,'' muttered Derek.

"No.'' Spencer's voice was sharp. "He's just a good businessman, taking advantage of opportunities as they arise.''

Derek looked at him with mild surprise. Spencer's usually unshakable good humor had been shaken— as with the others, the events of the last few days were taking their toll, and it was showing.

"What about Mike?'' asked Chas Miller. "I'd like to bring him on board faster. The sooner he's committed, the safer we'll all be. I know that originally we said he'd be fully on board after six months, but I think we'd all be happier if it happened sooner.'' He looked around at the others for support.

"I agree,'' said Spencer, nodding. "I'm working on a way to do that so that there'll be no going back for him. I would hope that'll happen within the next week or two.''

"Did you see all the cases that are coming in

now?" asked Derek. "We actually have enough work for another surgeon, over and above Mike."

Lou had been waiting for something like that. "And I just happen to have the right guy for you," he said. "Terry Catlin's ready, willing, and able, and I can assure you that with him we won't have the kind of problems we've been having with Mike Richmond."

Spencer thought for a moment. "Actually, that might not be a bad idea," he said. "Let me think about it. And now," he said, standing up, "time's a-wasting, and we're not making any money sitting here talking."

Chapter 23

A couple of hours later, after seeing his office patients, Mike sat back and stared at his computer monitor. It seemed to loom over him like a great, hostile eye—a presence, something Tony Danzig had put there to watch and betray him when possible.

Finally he pulled up last Friday's work schedule. He'd operated most of that morning, and he'd seen a couple of patients after Stephanie—a nice old gentleman with a hernia who bred hybrid roses, and Mrs. Nelligan, who complained nonstop about her alcoholic husband and refused to talk about her own diverticulitis.

Mike stopped in his tracks. He'd used the computer to bring up the images and report of Mrs. Nelligan's barium enema from the week before. Why hadn't the amended report on Stephanie Hopkins shown up then? In retrospect, he was certain that the red light hadn't been blinking at that time. Maybe it only stayed on for a certain time, then switched itself off . . . No, Tony had told him clearly that when there was material out there, the light stayed on until it was downloaded. So what did that mean? Maybe he'd just been too upset about Pauline's death and had simply missed it. Another case of human error in a world of computers.

Mike started to feel a throbbing between his temples. None of this was making any sense.

The hospital called; one of his patients in the I.C.U. was having breathing difficulties. The respiratory-therapy tech was there and seemed to have the situation under control, but the nurse wanted him to know. With a sense of relief, Mike picked up his coat and went off to the hospital, happy to be dealing with matters over which he had some control.

It was just as well that he came over; the patient had developed pneumonia, her blood gases were off the scale, she'd developed respiratory acidosis, and it took him over an hour to stabilize her. After the emergency was over, he didn't want to go far, because he knew she could go sour again quickly. Instead he went down to the records department and started to work on his pile of unfinished charts.

A half hour later, he had dictated discharge summaries on eight charts and was already feeling restless. He hated this part of his work, and found himself thinking about all the other things he should be doing. Looking around, he saw Marianne Russo, the assistant head of medical records, at the same moment she saw him. She had been a junior record clerk at NCMC, and had spent a lot of time chasing after him to complete records on his patients. She smiled at him, astonished, and came over.

"I can't believe it, Mike," she said in the quiet,

almost whispery voice used by librarians and hospital-records personnel the world over. "Did somebody drag you down here in chains?"

"Just about," he grinned. "Actually, I've learned the error of my ways. What are you doing here so late, Marianne?" he asked. "I thought all you guys picked up and went home at five."

Marianne grinned. "Yeah, sure. Actually I have a meeting in a little while. I'm very glad you're here. I was going to send you another little note about your charts."

"I've totally reformed," he answered. "From now on, my records will be up to date. I promise."

"Right. And I'm the Queen of Sheba, and I'll dance for you until I drop, I promise. Anyway, starting next week, with the new system, there'll be no more dictating. You'll be typing your summaries into the computer, and they'll go directly into the record."

"What's the advantage of that?" asked Mike. "Won't it just slow everything down? I don't know about you, but my talking's faster than my typing."

"No, it'll actually speed the system up a whole lot. For one thing, you'll be able to see on the screen what you're writing, and make your corrections there and then, without having to play it back. Also you won't have to come back and sign the summaries. You get a private code number, you key that in, and that does away with signing."

"And also you'll be able to let go a bunch of transcriptionists."

"Right. Got to get those costs down."

"What else does your new system do?" Mike asked.

"God, there's so much . . . you want to come and see it?"

"Sure." Mike stood up, glad to get away from his summaries, and followed her into the well-lit central records office. She stopped at one of the several terminals. "We've had eight people working for six months to put all our data into this system," she said. "Now we can analyze cases by age, sex, occupation, disease group, symptoms—you name it."

"How far back does it go?" asked Mike. An idea was forming inside his head.

"Five years," replied Marianne. "Back to the last big change in the system."

"Can you look at, say, one particular doc's cases?"

Marianne looked sideways at him. "We could. I don't think most of the docs would like that idea, though."

Mike was getting quietly excited. "Right, of course not. But could you tell me, for instance, how many breast biopsies the surgeons in Spencer's group did in a certain time frame? Like in the last two years?"

"Sure." Marianne, pleased to show off her system, sat down at the terminal. "Let's see, there's Spencer himself, Derek Provost . . ." Marianne listed them by name, pressed a few keys, and within a second, a row of numbers appeared on the screen.

"Nearly all of these are Spencer's cases," she said. "Wow, has that guy ever been busy."

"Okay," said Mike, a gleam appearing in his eyes.

"Now comes the test of your system. How many of these went on to have surgery? I mean for cancer, local mastectomies, lumpectomies, modified radicals, and so on."

"Hold on while I get the codes . . ." She checked the list. "Does axillary node dissection go into that category?"

Mike thought for a second. "Yeah, I guess so, if it follows a breast biopsy."

This time it took a little longer, but in less than a half minute the numbers were there, categorized by procedure.

"Can you give me a percentage?" asked Mike. "I mean, what percent of the biopsies went on to have major breast surgery?"

In a few moments, Marianne had the answer for him. "Ninety-three percent," she said proudly. How about that? What do you think of our system now?"

"It's fantastic, Marianne," said Mike slowly. "Absolutely fantastic." He looked at her smiling face, flushed with pleasure at having been able to summon up all those numbers for him. "Can we do the same thing with all the other surgeons here, excluding Spencer's group?"

"Sure. But after that I don't have time for any more, okay? My meeting starts in five minutes."

A few moments later, Mike had his answer, and Marianne switched the terminal to standby and stood up. "Gotta go, Mike," she said. "And I don't want to keep you from your charts."

Mike thanked her, then walked slowly back to his

booth, where the almost undiminished pile of charts was still waiting. The new system was fantastic, there was no doubt about it, and Marianne was extraordinarily skilled at turning raw data into usable information. But of course, Marianne didn't know what those numbers meant. He sat down in the cramped booth, overwhelmed by what she'd quite innocently found for him. Almost all of Spencer's patients, ninety-three percent of them, who underwent breast biopsies had gone on to have cancer surgery. From his reading of surgical journals, he knew that the national average was in the region of ten percent.

What did it all mean? Mike stood up and walked slowly toward the door. These numbers meant that either Spencer was the best clinical diagnostician in the entire history of medicine and surgery, able to spot breast cancer with near-infallible accuracy, or else there was something very strange going on. The problem of Stephanie Hopkins came back to him, and Mike wondered if it was related in some way.

Walking back upstairs to the ICU it struck him. Neither Spencer nor any other surgeon could ever do a major operation of that kind without the presence of a positive biopsy report in the chart. For one thing, it wouldn't get past the O.R. supervisor, just as Mike had been nailed on Stephanie's case, and even if it did, the hospital's quality-assurance people would be onto it in no time. He might get away with it once, but no more. And anyway, Spencer wouldn't risk his reputation in such a foolish way. No, *it meant that all, or almost all, of Spencer's biopsies were being reported*

*as positive for cancer by the pathology lab, even if they
were benign.*

"Jesus Christ!" he muttered to himself. If this was
a scam, it was almost undetectable. Nobody would
question a report from the pathology lab. If they said
it was cancer, to all intents and purposes it *was* cancer, and there was no other independent way of
checking. But what possible benefit could there be
for the pathology lab to do this? Why would they
take such a risk, let alone compromise their professional integrity and reputation? Wasn't there some
kind of oversight system that monitored their work?
Mike didn't know the answers to those questions,
but he could find out. ConnPath was a commercial,
for-profit lab that did contract work for hospitals and
private practices in New Coventry, unlike the big
university-based labs at NCMC, and he couldn't just
march into the ConnPath and demand to check their
records and go over their slides.

When he reached the I.C.U., Mike remembered
that Pauline's autopsy had been scheduled for that
afternoon, so after checking his patient, he walked
down the fire escape stairway to the pathology department, located in the basement floor. At the far
end of the pathology corridor was a door marked
AUTHORIZED PERSONNEL ONLY. He pushed the bar. It
opened and he found himself in the autopsy suite.
At the end of another short corridor was a double
door with a red light above it. Outside the door was
a table with four charts, presumably of the patients
whose autopsies had been completed, and Mike

walked up to the table. Pauline's chart was there, much thinner than the others. He picked it up and was leafing through the contents when an alarmed voice behind him said, "Hey, you! Put that chart down!"

"That's okay," said Mike, turning to face the tech. "I'm Dr. Richmond. I work here in the surgery department, and I'd like to talk to the pathologist who did the autopsy on Mrs. Minsky." He tapped the chart.

"I'm very sorry, Dr. Richmond," said the tech, taking the chart out of Mike's hand and putting it back on the table. "But this is a restricted area, and you're not supposed to be in here without written authorization . . ."

At that moment the autopsy room door opened, and a tall, rubber-booted and gowned man came out, pulling off a pair of thick red rubber gloves. The tech looked relieved. "Dr. Tarvel, this gentleman was inquiring about the autopsy on Mrs. Minsky."

For a second Tarvel looked startled, then, to Mike's surprise, afraid. He took a half step back and sucked in his breath. "Who are you?" he asked in a harsh, tense voice.

Mike introduced himself. "Mrs. Minsky was my secretary," he said. "I was wondering what you found at the autopsy."

There was a long pause, during which Tarvel stared at Mike over his mask, obviously pulling himself together and deciding what to say to this uninvited visitor. Finally he said, "All I can tell you, Dr.

Richmond, is that the proximate cause of Mrs. Minsky's death was an acute coronary occlusion, as her physician had suspected from her clinical findings. The official autopsy report will be issued tomorrow or the next day, and if you have the proper authorization, you can get a copy from the pathology office." Tarvel took a deep breath. "In future, Dr. Richmond, please call us in advance if you feel that it's really necessary to come here. This is a restricted area, clearly posted, and you shouldn't have come in without permission."

He turned to the tech. "Brian, would you show Dr. Richmond out, please?" With that, Dr. Tarvel turned about and went back into the autopsy room, unable to hide the fact that he'd been severely jolted by Mike's appearance. The tech silently escorted Mike to the door and closed it behind him. Mike heard the lock click on the inside, and shrugged. He was beginning to get used to this kind of treatment, he thought, and headed back up the stairs. But as he walked up, a couple of things he had noted in Pauline's chart made him slow down and stop very thoughtfully at the top of the stairs. And why had Tarvel acted so strangely?

Chapter 24

It was twenty minutes after six when Mike walked back to his office, and although the place was well lit, it seemed empty. He checked the operating schedule for the next day, then sat back in his new leather chair, thought for a minute, then pulled his little address book out of his pocket and searched for Pauline Minsky's home phone number. He found it and dialed the number. It rang for a long time before it was answered.

"Wha' . . . ?"

Mike recognized Andy's slurred voice and told him how sorry he was about Pauline's death. The reply was so jumbled that Mike didn't understand any of it.

"Who's taking care of you?" he asked. "Do you have any family, or anyone?"

"Sitta," replied Andy after a long pause.

"Your sister?"

The reply was an affirmative grunt, followed by a kind of wheezing noise, then "Annaseeya."

It took a moment for Mike to understand that Andy was saying he wanted to see him.

He replied, "Sure . . ." Then Andy must have given the phone to his sister, because a woman's voice came on. "Hi, I'm Annabelle, Andy's sister. You're Dr. Richmond, right? Well, Andy would like to see you—that is, if you have time." Her voice dropped a little. "Please."

"Sure, of course. When?"

"As soon as possible," she replied. "It's . . . well, Andy says it's sort of important."

Mike looked at his watch. It was six-thirty. "I can come over right now," he said. "Tell me where you live."

Fifteen minutes later, he knocked on the door of the Minsky's sixth-floor apartment on the outskirts of New Coventry. Annabelle opened the door; her eyes teared up when she saw him. Andy was right behind her, his big face sad and gray-looking.

"Come in," said Annabelle. Andy stepped back so that Mike could come in.

The apartment was cheerful and well kept, not very large, with colorful Van Gogh prints on the wall and bright flowery covers over the sofa and chairs. A television was on in the corner next to a small fireplace, and its light flickered on the shiny brass fire tools.

"I know you don't have much time," said Annabelle. She went over and switched off the TV, then sat down next to Andy. She glanced at Mike, and patted her hair nervously. "Pauline always told Andy how nice you were, and that you weren't one of the . . ."

She hesitated, and Andy said "Egng," with bitter emphasis. A few drops of saliva shot out of his mouth with the word.

"The gang," she explained, although Mike was beginning to understand the sounds Andy was making.

"That's what she called them," explained Annabelle. "She didn't know exactly what, but they were involved in something illegal. That's what she said, anyway." She glanced apologetically at Mike, then at the floor.

Mike's gaze went from Annabelle to Andy. "You mean my group? The Spencer group?"

Andy nodded.

"You see, Dr. Richmond," said Annabelle, "Pauline wasn't just a secretary. She and Andy are private investigators, and she was hired to investigate them."

Mike was remembering Pauline's questions to him about the group. "Who hired her?"

Annabelle hesitated, and glanced at her brother, who nodded. "When you said you were coming," she said, "I called the person who hired her. She should be here in just a few minutes." After a moment she added, "She's very upset about what happened to Pauline."

Mike was feeling increasingly anxious. Although what he'd found in the record room about Spencer's biopsies was very troubling, it hadn't occurred to him that the others might be implicated, or that there might be other questionable activities going on. *The gang . . .*

Common sense returned. "You don't think they

had anything to do with Pauline's death, do you?"
Mike's gaze went from Annabelle to Andy and back.

"At first Andy thought they'd done something to
her," answered Annabelle, "but Pauline did have
some trouble with her heart a few months ago—an
arrhythmia, they called it. They told her to lose
weight, but Pauline always agreed with everybody
and then did whatever she wanted to do."

"She died of a heart attack."

Annabelle looked at him questioningly. "You
know that for sure?" she asked.

"They did the autopsy today," said Mike. "I spoke
personally to the pathologist, and that's what he told
me. The official report should be out tomorrow or
the next day."

Andy grunted something and nodded, obviously
relieved.

The doorbell rang, and Annabelle went to answer
it. The person in the doorway was a woman in her
mid-sixties, Mike guessed, not very tall, immacu-
lately and expensively dressed in a light gray suit
with a large gold pin on the left lapel. Her hair, a
bluish white, was as immaculate as the rest of her.
She seemed vaguely familiar to him, but he couldn't
remember where he'd seen her.

Annabelle brought her in, and Mike stood up.

"This is Mrs. Laura Newsome," said Annabelle.
"Dr. Michael Richmond."

They shook hands. Mrs. Newsome was looking
very carefully at him, and when he heard the name,

Mike remembered who she was. Dr. Fred New-some's wife.

"I remember your husband very well, Mrs. New-some," said Mike. "He helped me do my first gall-bladder."

"You came to the Christmas party at our house three years ago," said Mrs. Newsome. "You were the biggest person there."

"Yes, I did," replied Mike. "The residents' Christ-mas party. You have a very good memory."

"Yes, I do." She turned to Annabelle. "What did you tell him?"

"Nothing much. We were waiting for you."

"Good." Laura Newsome sat down on a chair, her back very straight, and smoothed her skirt. "Well, as you probably know," she said, addressing Mike, "my husband was killed when his plane went down. The investigators found that it was an accident, and I have no quarrel with that. He may even have com-mitted suicide . . ." She looked squarely at Mike. "He was terribly depressed about what was happening with his group, although it was partly his own fault."

The three of them listened. To Mike, Mrs. New-some seemed an intelligent and determined woman, although there was a kind of unemotional chilliness about her.

"You see," Laura went on, "Fred had started the group in the sixties, and everything was very differ-ent then. He developed a big practice and was doing well. Very well. Then came Medicare and Medicaid and all kinds of insurance programs, and he didn't want to have anything to do with them. 'When people get their car fixed,' he used to say, 'they pay for it. When they get themselves fixed, they should pay for that, too.' He managed to convince his group—Spencer and Derek Provost, who'd recently joined, and the others—that they shouldn't give in to the insurance groups, but they kept losing patients, and were going broke. It was too late for them to get into the insurance plans, because all the other docs in town had already joined them, and Fred's group had nowhere to go."

Laura paused. Her eyes were fixed on Mike—Andy and Annabelle already knew the story.

"Fred was so depressed, it was awful. He wasn't eating, and couldn't sleep . . . anyway, the way I understood it, Spencer came up with some kind of proposal that made Fred really mad. He never told me the details—I probably wouldn't have understood them anyway—but it started a big fight in the group. Fred didn't want anything to do with what Spencer was suggesting, but the others seemed to side with Spencer. Fred was always a real straight-shooter, the most honest person I ever met."

Laura took a small handkerchief out of her pocket and dabbed at her eyes, although Mike didn't see any tears. Annabelle got up quietly and went off to make coffee. Andy sat there in his chair, his face impassive. Mike wondered how he felt, unable to talk properly but obviously very aware of everything that was going on.

"Then Fred died. He'd been flying planes for years;

it was his only hobby, and he loved it. He was going up to Vermont to visit Paul Ness, an old buddy of his, who was also a pilot."

Laura was holding on to her handkerchief, twisting it in her hands. "It wasn't the accident itself that bothered me," she went on. "In a way it was a blessing for Fred. It was what happened after that." A hard look came into her face—it was clear that when Laura Newsome took on something, she didn't abandon it easily.

Annabelle came back with a tray and put it on the table. "There's milk and sugar there," she said. "Help yourselves." She had a mug already poured for Andy, and helped him drink it.

But nobody was really paying attention to the coffee—they were all listening to Laura.

"Well, when Fred died, I must say Spencer and the others were very nice to me. They made all the arrangements, sent flowers to the funeral, and made sure that I was properly provided for. Luckily for me, Fred had taken out a big life-insurance policy a few years before." Laura's lips tightened, and a lot of little radial lines appeared around her mouth, making her look older. "But then all of a sudden their luck seemed to change," she said. "I mean Fred's group. Spencer took over everything, and they completely refurbished and decorated their offices, bought a lot of expensive equipment, got that foreign office manager working for them . . ." She turned to Mike. "They must have spent a fortune. And then all of a sudden they were all busy again, very busy, mostly with that prepaid health plan at Lovejoy Hospital, a place Fred despised and refused to work in. And then within weeks Derek Provost bought this gorgeous house, and before you know it, here they were all driving around in BMWs and Lexuses, and spending money like water."

"I think I can tell you how that came about, Mrs. Newsome," said Mike gently. "They got a contract with the Lovejoy Plan, which gave them instant access to a whole new group of patients. I suppose that's why things started to go better for them."

Laura snorted. "Rubbish," she said. "All the other groups in town had contracts with various insurance and hospital plans. And none of them were doing as well as Spencer and his boys." She shook her head decisively. "No, they must have got a big infusion of money from somewhere, enough to put them back on their feet. But how? Who would put up that kind of money, and what would they want in return?"

Mike looked at his watch. "I'm sorry, Mrs. Newsome, but that idea doesn't make much sense to me," he said. "They could have taken out a big bank loan or obtained financing in some other perfectly legal way. I think we may just be looking for problems that don't exist. The fact that they've been very successful doesn't mean that they're doing anything wrong."

Laura stood up, her eyes flashing. "Fred told me," she said, emphasizing every word, "that what Spencer had proposed to him, and what they were planning to do was not only totally unethical but criminal. And Fred didn't use words like that lightly." She took a deep breath. "So the reason I employed Pauline was because Spencer and his cronies caused Fred months of misery and depression, and that ultimately caused his death. And now, here they all are, strutting around like pigs in clover . . . and poor old Fred . . ."

Laura's handkerchief came up again, and she sat down on the chair. She looked at Mike. "I know you feel obligated to defend them, Dr. Richmond," she said, "but Pauline was finding things that seemed to confirm my suspicions." She stopped for a sip of coffee. "The last thing she told me was that she was getting close. There seemed to be some network the group was involved in, and it was run by that office manager, Tony Damn Pig, or something like that."

"Danzig," said Mike.

"That's right. They hired him soon after Fred's death. Anyway, Pauline thought that this network was linked up through their computer system, but of course, now . . ." Laura's shoulders sagged. She sighed, then turned to Mike. "Pauline once put some kind of device—a bug, she called it—under the table in their conference room when they were having a meeting." She paused for a moment. "Pauline said that they talked about getting you on board but they didn't like your not being a full member because they couldn't discuss things freely when you were around."

Mike listened, not at all convinced. "So what are

you going to do now, Mrs. Newsome? Are you going to get another investigator?"

Laura's lip quivered. "I don't know," she said. "I'll have to think about it."

"If you think something criminal is going on, wouldn't it be a good idea to give your information to the police?"

Laura smiled. "The New Coventry police? Are you joking? Spencer would know about it before I got out of the headquarters building. No, I do not think that's a good idea."

"Well, I'll be quite honest with you, Mrs. Newsome," said Mike. "There's been a few things going on at the hospital that have bothered me and that I don't fully understand yet," said Mike. "And what you've told me is troublesome, sure, but I honestly don't think there's anything criminal going on in the group."

Driving home in his Aston-Martin, Mike tried to reconcile what he'd just heard with what he knew. He wasn't sure quite what to make of Laura Newsome. Maybe she was just a disgruntled widow with too much imagination and too much money to throw around. He grinned at the thought of his colleagues, Spencer, Derek, Lou, and the others, all reputable physicians, banding together in some kind of medical Mafia. But his smile faded when he thought of the unexplained statistics he'd uncovered in the record room, and his head started to throb when he thought about all the things that had gone wrong in his life recently, the near-disaster with Stephanie Hopkins, and the likelihood that he'd be hit with a lawsuit over that. And of course, he didn't know what action, if any, the hospital would take over Stephanie's aborted operation. As Derek had told him, Spencer was in charge of the quality-assurance committee and ran it with an iron hand. If Spencer got seriously pissed at Mike, he could have the QAC blow the whistle on him, and if that ever happened, for sure he'd lose his hospital privileges—maybe his medical license.

Chapter 25

The next day, Tuesday, Stephanie showed up for work as if nothing had happened, but she was still feeling shaky and weak, as if recovering from a bout of flu. There was a message on her voice mail from Carl Hartmann to call him as soon as she came in. She dialed his number, not expecting him to be in yet, but he answered it immediately.

"Oh, yes, Stephanie," he said, "Do you have a moment?" he asked. "Come to my office, please."

He was sitting at his desk with his sleeves rolled up. "How are you feeling?" he asked.

"Okay," she said, wondering at his tone. That morning she had chosen a light, loose cardigan to hide the surgical dressing.

"I might as well tell you," he said, "I heard about what happened to you yesterday in the hospital."

"You did?" Stephanie knew that Carl had an effective information system, but she wondered how he'd heard so quickly about yesterday's fiasco.

"Yes. Miss Boyd found out, then I made a few phone calls." Carl put both hands on his desk, and his heavy, square face became grim. "I think that what happened to you is one of the most outrageous things I've ever heard of," he said. "The thought of you undergoing surgery because of sheer incompetence and carelessness . . ."

"Well, in the end it turned out all right," said Stephanie reasonably.

"Yes, it turned out all right, in spite of your surgeon," he said. "Why on earth did you pick this guy, just out of his residency? There are plenty of highly experienced surgeons around."

"Dr. Richmond's very well thought of," said Stephanie, feeling defensive. "I checked him out before making any decision."

"Obviously," said Carl, his tone tinged with sarcasm. "Stephanie, I want you to see a malpractice lawyer, and as soon as possible."

Stephanie looked at him with surprise. "Why? I think he made an honest mistake, and he was very up front about it afterward . . ."

"An honest mistake that could easily have left you mutilated," said Carl, standing up. "How many times do you think that kind of honest mistake has happened before? How many times will it happen again?" Carl glowered at her. "Stephanie, I absolutely insist that you see an attorney who specializes in this kind of situation. In fact, I've already contacted one, the best in town. His name is Haiman Gold. He's very experienced, I know him well, and unlike your surgeon, he'll take very good care of you."

Carl picked up a piece of paper from his desk and

held it out to her. "Here. This is the number of Gold's private line. He's expecting your call." Carl's expression softened for a moment, and he smiled. "Judging from the recent medical-malpractice settlements in this town, Stephanie, you should get enough out of this to retire on," he said. "Not that I would want you to do that—not until I get my data, anyway." He grinned at her. His teeth were rather small and irregular, and they reminded Stephanie of an alligator poster that her dentist kept on the ceiling of his office.

"Thanks," she said, taking the paper. "I'll think about it."

"Don't *think* about it," said Carl. "Do it. Talk to him. If he doesn't think you have a case, he'll tell you. And remember, it's not just for you. It's for all the other people who could get into this kind of trouble."

As Stephanie went to the door, he said after her, "You want to take the rest of the day off? After what you've been through, you deserve it."

"No, thanks," she replied. "I'm fine. Really. Anyway, I'm better off working than sitting at home." Her natural bounciness came to the surface again. "But I'll take a rain check, if you insist."

"No rain checks," he said. "Have you got that data together yet?"

"No. The financials on those corporations are very difficult to compare. I'll try to have them to you by the end of the week, unless I run into more problems."

Carl nodded, then started to pull together some of the papers that littered his desk. "Don't forget to call Haiman Gold," he said as Stephanie left.

Back in her office, Stephanie couldn't concentrate on what she was doing. All kinds of loose ends seemed to be floating around inside her head. Finally she switched off her computer, stood up, and went down to her old office to talk to Jean Forrest.

Jean seemed to have been waiting for her, with problems of her own. "God, Stephanie, I wish you were back here." Jean looked tired and anxious—she was finding her job tougher than she'd expected. "Yesterday I went to ask Dr. Sammons for an update on Dr. Lou Gardner, because he suddenly reappeared on the computer. Stephanie, you won't believe this, but all Dr. Gardner's admissions statistics are okay now, and I couldn't understand it."

"What did Dr. Sammons say?"

"Well, he was angry, and he told me that the subject was closed, and he more or less said that if I liked my job I'd better just forget about that particular problem and concentrate on other, more important work." Jean shook her head as if it had been just a bad dream. "How about you?" she asked, suddenly embarrassed by her own self-absorption. "How are you feeling?"

"Okay." Stephanie told her briefly what had happened. Then she asked, casually, "Jean, what happened here yesterday? Did you tell Mr. Hartmann I was in the hospital?"

Jean's expression turned anxious, and her big eyes fixed on Stephanie. "I'm sorry," she said, "but Ann Boyd called, and said Mr. Hartmann was looking for you, and that you'd called in sick, so I had to tell her. And he asked who the doctor was who was taking care of you." Jean kept watching Stephanie's face, then pushed the door closed with her foot, and her voice dropped. "I had lunch with Ann," she said, "and she told me that Mr. Hartmann had called Dr. Spencer, then came back and said that you weren't going to have the surgery after all." Jean's big eyes were fixed curiously on Stephanie. "She said he wasn't very nice to Dr. Spencer. He talked to him like . . . like he'd talk to the elevator operator or somebody like that. Ann told me what he actually said. Well, you know Mr. Hartmann isn't exactly polite to everybody, but Ann couldn't believe the way he talked to him."

"What did he say?"

"Well, Ann told me he said 'God damn it, Spencer, she got caught in the system. Get yourself over to Lovejoy and take care of it right now!' "

"He really talked to Dr. Spencer like that?" asked Stephanie, astonished. "You're not exaggerating just a bit, are you?"

"Honest to God. I'm telling you exactly what Ann told me."

Stephanie didn't let Jean off the hook. "What do you think he meant about being 'caught in the system'?"

Jean rolled her eyes. "I don't know. Ann said that

he closed his office door about then because he thought she was listening, so maybe she didn't hear it right in the first place."

Stephanie was beginning to feel a sense of panic in her chest. She considered Jean for a moment. "Okay," she said rather absently. "Thanks, Jean." As she walked back to her own office, Stephanie recalled Dr. Sammons's words: *I don't know everything that goes on in this company—and quite frankly I don't want to. If they want me to know something, they'll tell me, so I don't ask questions. I guess I've learned the hard way how to be a survivor in this business.*

Of course, Jean Forrest could have been exaggerating, or misinterpreted what Anne had told her. In any case, there was nothing she could do about it right now, so she decided to file her impressions away, and get on with her job.

Chapter 26

"They've dug a hole for Mike," said Lou. He and Terry Catlin were sitting at the long brass-rimmed bar of the Marriott in downtown New Coventry. Behind them, a small band was playing sixties music behind a fence of potted palms. A couple sat at the other end of the bar, staring into space. "They don't want him to fall into the hole, of course," Lou went on. "They just want him to know it's there if he does something stupid."

Terry took a sip of his vodka martini. He knew he had to control himself and give the impression that there was nothing more than normal professional rivalry between him and Richmond. If Lou or the others knew the extent of the hatred he bore for Mike Richmond, it wouldn't work in his favor; the group didn't insist that everyone like each other, but they all had to be able to work well together. Right now his hope was that Mike would not last with the group and that he would replace him when Mike left. And he was working on an idea that might accelerate that process.

"Everybody's talking about that breast case he

screwed up," said Catlin after a pause. "I don't know how Spencer and the others are going to react to that. It doesn't put them in a specially good light."

Lou glanced at him. Catlin obviously hadn't understood what he'd said about digging a hole, and he wasn't about to enlighten him. He shrugged. "Mike's okay. Everybody makes mistakes from time to time."

Catlin nodded. He could feel that something had gone by him, and decided to change the subject. "By the way," he said, "my dad wanted to tell you that he has a real good opportunity for you right now." He leaned forward on his elbows, looking along the bar at Lou. "There's this little California company called Electron Biotics he's taken a position in. They're scheduled for an IPO in a couple of weeks and it's already sold out. If you'd like to take a piece of his private placement now, you could make a few bucks."

"Sounds good," replied Lou. "How much?"

"He suggested twenty thou, which should come back at about seventy if you want to sell it immediately. And of course, your name won't show up in the corporate transaction records, so the IRS won't be aware of it."

"Sure, Terry, that'll be fine. Sign me up. And say hi and thanks to your dad."

For the next few days, Stephanie kept busy with her project, but at the back of her mind was a growing anger at what had happened to her, and it took her breath away when she thought of what had *al-*

most happened. At first she'd just felt relieved that she didn't have cancer, that she wasn't going to lose her breast, but after she'd heard how it happened, it gradually became clear that it had been too close, a matter of luck rather than of proper medical care, and that was *wrong*. As a result, her whole feeling about Mike Richmond was changing to one of anger and hostility.

At work, she tried to guess what the different corporations actually did. The biggest one was easy: although the data she had was limited—big payroll, heavy professional salaries, large equipment and supply expenditures, major utility usage—that was surely Lovejoy Hospital. To Stephanie, the most interesting thing in the entire project was the bottom line—the smallest corporation, from the point of overall expenditure, made the most money, although it was only a tiny fraction of the size of the largest. The others were a mystery, which was no doubt what Carl intended, although they all seemed to be providing services of some kind, and for sure they were all making a lot of money too.

Mike had called her a couple of times to see how she was, but the second time she cut him off. "I'm very upset by what happened, Dr. Richmond," she told him. "So please don't call me anymore."

Finally, after some more prodding by Carl Hartmann and also from her mother, Stephanie called Haiman Gold's office, using the direct-line number that Carl had given her.

Haiman sounded assured and confident. "Mr. Hart-

mann told me you would be calling, Miss Hopkins,"
he said. "I can see you at two this afternoon."

"I haven't made any decisions yet," she said.

"Of course not," he replied. "Nor have I."

Haiman Gold's office was modern, with flashy
silver-and-gold furniture and fittings, big easy chairs
and a wall-mounted closed-circuit television in the
waiting room. On the screen was Haiman himself,
big, rather florid-faced in a dark business suit, three
little corners of a white handkerchief poking up from
his breast pocket, explaining to his unseen audience
what medical malpractice consisted of. He had a rich
baritone voice that Stephanie thought would sound
terrific in a courtroom. Just getting a bad result didn't
mean that malpractice had occurred, he was saying,
but every doctor was obligated to tell his patients
what they could expect from a treatment or operation, the chances of success, and the types of complications that could be encountered. He was just
starting to tell his audience the terms under which
he accepted cases, when Marie, the receptionist, a
shapely, tough-looking blonde, came to fetch her.
After getting details of who Stephanie was, her age,
occupation, income, and other information, she led
the way along the corridor to Haiman's office. It had
the same kind of decor as the rest of the suite: bright,
loud, metallic, with a few flashy paintings on the
walls.

Haiman was in his mid-forties, Stephanie figured.
He stepped forward, a sturdily built, square-faced
man with a thick, almost bull-like neck, tanned,

good-looking in a rather red-faced, heavyset way, wearing a dark blue suit with a thin pinstripe, a white shirt, and an expensive-looking silk tie, dark blue with thin diagonal red stripes. The thing that struck Stephanie the most was how confident he seemed. He looked her straight in the eye with a concerned, sincere look that reminded her of the guy who had sold her the old Plymouth she still drove. He stretched out his hand to shake hers. His grip was firm, manly, and dry.

"Carl has told me a little bit about you," he said, looking at her with some curiosity. "Please have a seat." He pulled a chair out for her, then went back behind his desk and sat down, straight-backed, putting his hands together as if he were still on camera.

Stephanie sat down and rearranged her skirt in front of her. Quite unexpectedly, an image of Mike Richmond came to her, standing all disheveled-looking at the top of the stairs after he'd taken her home, obviously so contrite and concerned, and she angrily put the thought away. She'd really believed in him, trusted his integrity and competence.

"I want this guy put out of business," she said, surprised at her own vehemence. "He's a public danger and shouldn't be allowed to operate on people."

Haiman nodded understandingly. "Of course," he said. "Many of my clients feel the same way. Now, let's start at the beginning. Tell me why you decided to consult a physician in the first place." Haiman pulled a yellow legal pad in front of him and poised a thick black-and-gold fountain pen over it.

She told him about the little lump, how she'd talked with Evie. "She's a nurse, and the first doctor she suggested was Dr. Spencer," she said. "Unfortunately, he was out of town at the time."

Haiman nodded, obviously in full agreement.

"Then she recommended Dr. Richmond, who had recently joined Dr. Spencer's group. I didn't want to wait any longer, so I made an appointment to see him." Stephanie took a deep breath. "She said he was very good and generally highly thought of." She went on to review all the steps of the case, as she knew them, up to the point Dr. Richmond had driven her home.

Finally, Haiman said, "I think we may have a case here, Miss Hopkins. So far it looks quite promising. Of course, I can't make a firm decision until we've checked a few facts—I'm sure you understand that." He pushed his chair back from his desk. "Now, I'd like to tell you about our terms. When we undertake a case, we guarantee that it won't cost you anything. Not a penny. By that I mean that the time we use to research your case, to get depositions from doctors, nurses, anyone else even remotely involved—all that time is paid for by us. The cost of obtaining expert witnesses, travel, and other expenses are also borne by us. If we lose the case, we swallow the loss."

"And if you win?"

"Our policy is to pay the plaintiff thirty-three percent of the amount collected, minus certain of the costs," replied Haiman, watching her.

Stephanie's eyebrows went up. "I thought most

law firms more or less split it down the middle with their clients," she said, trying to sound more businesslike than she felt.

"On the surface, that's true," he said, leaning back, holding his Mont Blanc pen with both hands. "But there are two factors you have to consider. First, in cases handled by other firms, a good part of the client's half is eaten up by expenses, and we keep these expenses to the client at a minimum. Also . . ." Haiman pulled his chair forward again, "and more importantly, we have the best record of success in this type of litigation in the entire state of Connecticut. Not only that, but we win, on average, substantially the highest awards for our clients." He smiled in a friendly but assured way at her. "So you see, with us there's a proven high chance of success. And, of course, thirty-three percent of a substantial sum is a whole lot better than fifty percent of nothing."

"Okay . . . so what do we do now?"

There must have been something in her tone or her expression that made him think she was backing off, because he fixed Stephanie with a steely judicial gaze and said, "You needn't waste any sympathy on the doctor, Miss Hopkins, or worry about his reputation. To them, this kind of lawsuit is just part of the cost of doing business." Haiman put his hands together, the thick pen sticking up between his fingers, and leaned forward, elbows on his desk. "It may turn out that the worst injury you suffer, although you may not have thought of it, is psychological. I've seen many cases like this where the victim couldn't sleep, suffered recurrent nightmares, couldn't do her job . . ." He looked intently at Stephanie, as if he were telling her that those were the kinds of symptoms she *should* be having.

"I understand," said Stephanie. "And don't get me wrong. I want you to go after him as if . . ." she hesitated for a second. "As if he *had* cut my breast off. Otherwise, it'll happen to someone else."

"Good." Haiman nodded. "In the next few days I'll be sending subpoenas and getting some more facts." He stood up and escorted Stephanie out to the elevator. "We'll do a good job for you, Miss Hopkins, you can be assured of that."

Coming out of the elevator on the ground level, Stephanie walked across the marble floor to the doorway and turned left onto Milton Street to where she had left her car. The sky was dark and smelled of rain, but she didn't notice. As she hurried along, all kinds of disjointed thoughts crowded into her mind. She thought about Haiman Gold and what Carl had said about him. Then she thought about the corporations she had been working on. Corporation Two, the one Carl said was a service company, with its irregular income and huge checks . . . that fitted the general picture of a law firm that got big settlements. Then she thought about what Jean had told her, the phone call to Dr. Spencer, and the way Carl had apparently talked to him. Could Carl *own* those corporations? She decided to call the office of the insurance commissioner and find out—not that she thought it was illegal, but more out of curiosity. The first fat raindrops started to fall, hitting the sidewalk and exploding.

When Mike came out of Lovejoy Hospital's front entrance, the rain had momentarily stopped and he ran down the ramp and walked over toward his office, jumping over puddles and thinking about Stephanie. The rain started to come down again, and he sprinted along the street, wondering if she was still upset with him.

He had intended only to get his car and go home, but as he turned into his building he decided to go up to the office. He had a thyroidectomy scheduled for the next day, and since he hadn't done one for a while, he wanted to review the technique in his surgical atlas. The lights were on when he let himself in; all the office doors were open, except those of the conference room, and he walked down the corridor past the business office, glanced in, and saw Tony Danzig working at his computer.

Mike stopped and came back.

"Hi, Tony. You're working late."

"Ah, yes," said Tony, glancing up. "Dr. Richmond. I'm glad you're here." He pressed a couple of keys and the screen went blank. "Do you have a minute?"

"Sure," replied Mike. "Come on down to my office. I'm only stopping in to pick up a book."

Tony followed Mike into his office.

"What's on your mind, Tony?" Mike's voice was friendlier than he felt.

"A couple of things, Dr. Richmond." Tony put his

hands primly together on his lap. "First, your records. As you know, we do an audit every four weeks . . ."

"Tony, I'll have them up to date by Thursday," said Mike. "I have that day off, and after I do hospital rounds, that's how I'm going to spend it."

"Excellent. There is one other thing . . ." Tony moved slightly in his chair. "Dr. Spencer told me about the unfortunate incident involving your patient, Stephanie Hopkins," he went on in his smooth voice. "And I'm sure you've been wondering how you could possibly have missed the second pathology report."

Mike, on sudden alert, nodded slightly but didn't say anything.

"Well, I went over the systems program and found that under certain circumstances, new lab reports were being kept on hold for twelve hours only and were then transferred directly into the patient file without further notifying the physicians concerned, and at that point the warning light goes out. I think that must be what happened in this particular case." Tony shrugged slightly. "Actually, that's what I was doing in the office just now, correcting that software problem. From now on, the light on the monitor will remain on until the physician has called up the report and signed off on it."

"Good, thank you," replied Mike. "I don't want any more incidents like that."

"Indeed," agreed Tony. "We can only hope that other problems don't arise."

Mike glanced at him, but Tony's eyes held no more expression than two holes in a wall.

After Tony left, Mike pulled the big atlas of head and neck surgery from the bookshelf and read the article on thyroidectomy, but his mind kept going back to what Tony had said. The problem with Tony's explanation was that when the secretary had downloaded Stephanie's chart on the morning of her operation, stapled it, and brought the paperwork over to the hospital, the second pathology report was loose and separate from it. Which meant that it hadn't been automatically downloaded into the patient's file. And Spencer had said that he'd pulled the report *off the computer* that morning. So why was Tony lying so obviously? If he'd really wanted to mislead him, he could certainly have put together a more credible story. This way, he was pushing Mike's face in it, saying, yes, we deliberately put you in a bad position, and what are you going to do about it?

Mike felt a sense of apprehension growing inside him. Why were they messing around with him like this? Until Tony came up with his explanation, there had still been a possibility that he'd made a careless error, but not now. So from that point of view, he felt better. Was that what they wanted?

Mike put the atlas back on the shelf and was heading down the corridor when the conference room door opened and Spencer came out, chatting with two or three of the other doctors in the group. And inside, sitting at the table and talking with Lou Gardner, was a person he had not expected to see.

"Oh, Mike," Spencer said, catching Mike's glance, and smiling broadly, "I'm glad you're here." He took Mike's arm in a friendly grip. "I want you to be the first to know that Terry Catlin's going to be joining the group as of next week."

"It shouldn't be so difficult," said George Rankin. It was seven o'clock in the evening, and he was talking to Sam Scheiffer in the ninth-floor surveillance room. Behind them, images on the black-and-white monitors moved from time to time. In the Spencer group's outer office, a cleaner with a broom crossed the field of view, getting disproportionately larger as she approached the camera. On the second bank, the only movement was when a lab assistant placed a stack of labeled test tubes in front of her and started to enter data into a computer. The third bank, which monitored Haiman Gold's offices, was still, as was the fourth, Radiology Associates, also closed for the night.

Rankin moved his feet. "Richmond does some long cases in the operating room, right?" he went on. "He puts his outdoor clothes in his locker, right? He leaves his keys in the pocket . . . what more do you want?"

Sam nodded. "Okay. I'll get Tony to send up copies of the O.R. schedule," he said. "It takes ten minutes from the hospital to his apartment, five minutes to put the bug in his phone, ten minutes to get back to the hospital and return the keys. No sweat."

"What about his cellphone?"

"We've already taken care of that. We're monitoring his calls, and they're being automatically recorded. He doesn't use it much, though."

"Let me know if anything comes up. Carl's been on my back again this morning."

"Sure." Sam paused, his eyes on Rankin. "By the way, I did the security interview on the new guy, Dr. Catlin, yesterday."

Rankin grinned. "Yeah. He should fit in good with this bunch. I know a couple of the guys up in Hartford who work for his dad."

"I did the usual checks on his education background, and it sounds as if he maybe cheated on his college entrance exam."

"Tut, tut," said Rankin, clicking his tongue. "I wonder how much that cost his dad."

"I dunno. But the guy I spoke to told me the college now has a Catlin Prize in political ethics."

Rankin nodded approvingly. "I guess at that level they know how to deal with that kind of problem," he said.

Sam shrugged. None of that really concerned him—his job was to get the facts, not comment on them. "How about Richmond?" he asked. "What happens if he was working with the Minsky woman?"

"I dunno. I don't make that kind of decision. But

what worked for her should work for him too, right?''

It was early afternoon by the time Mike got over to his office. On his desk he found a small pile of neatly stacked mail. On the top was a large envelope with the green sticker of registered mail. Curious, Mike picked it up, then felt a sudden chill descend on him. Whatever it was, he thought, it wasn't good. He ripped the envelope open and pulled out a long document of a half-dozen pages. It was official notification that legal proceedings had been started against him on behalf of Stephanie Hopkins. He skimmed through the document, which outlined the case. He saw words and phrases that he never thought would be applied to him—carelessness, lack of proper preoperative evaluation, cynical disregard for the welfare of the patient . . . The document was signed by Haiman Gold, J.D., whom Mike remembered meeting at the Moti Mahal restaurant with Derek. Gold had predicted then that their paths would cross . . . well, so they had. Mike sat down and dropped the document on his desk as if it were burning his fingers. He was not totally surprised, but still, he felt heartsick that Stephanie had gone ahead and taken this step. On the other hand, he thought, supposing he'd been the patient? Wouldn't he be furious, knowing what had happened, and wouldn't he feel that he'd been mistreated? He had to admit it—yes, he would.

He sat back. What now? He'd have to tell Spencer

and call his malpractice insurance carrier. Presumably they would contact whatever defense attorney they used. Derek had told him that every member of the group had lawsuits against them—now, thought Mike wryly, maybe he would be accepted as one of the boys.

Terry Catlin had been given the office two doors down on the opposite side of the corridor, and when Mike passed it on his way to the front desk, Catlin's door was ajar and he could hear the sounds of conversation. He recognized the voices of Lou Gardner and Tony Danzig, and although Mike couldn't hear what they were talking about, there was something about the confidential buzz of their voices that made Mike feel uncomfortable. Knock it off, he told himself, annoyed at how fast his paranoia was growing. You've got more important things to think about than them. His stomach churned again as he thought of the document sitting on his desk, and when he came back to his office, he picked up the phone and called the insurance agent, a brisk and reassuring man who somehow managed to make Mike feel a little better and a little less alone.

Chapter 27

Evie Gaskell had got the job she'd applied for in the Lovejoy O.R. a few weeks earlier, and since she hadn't been home for a while, she took the Friday afternoon off and drove up to Portland, Maine, to spend a weekend with her mother. Her brother Evan had hoped to come up with her, but he was on duty for the weekend and couldn't make it.

On Saturday afternoon, Evie noticed some cramping pain in her belly but didn't pay much attention, thinking it was probably her period coming early.

Her mother knew better. "You're constipated," she told Evie, who sighed, said, "Yes, Mother," and decided to say no more about it.

The pain was still there and actually worse on Sunday afternoon when Evie was setting off back to New Coventry. Evie had trouble carrying her suitcase into her car.

"Evie, it's your stomach again, isn't it? Just you wait here one minute." Her mother went back into the house and reappeared holding a blue bottle and a big spoon in her hands. Evie sighed and rolled her eyes. Her mother had always been obsessed by the

state of her family's bowels, and the standard cure
was milk of magnesia.

"Oh, Mom . . ." said Evie. "Come on, I'm a nurse,
a grown woman. I don't need—"

"Don't argue, dear," said her mother. She opened
the bottle and filled the spoon until it was brimming.
"Just because you're a nurse doesn't mean you know
everything. Here, open your mouth. . . . Okay, and a
second one . . . it'll work by the time you get home.
You'll thank me then."

By the time Evie reached Route 128, the pain was
coming in waves and was almost unbearable. Several
times she stopped at the side of the road until it
diminished. Then, a half hour later, she barely had
time to pull over and wind the window down before
she threw up. But she was determined to get home
and drove grimly on. Not far from Providence, she
felt something odd happen inside her belly, and the
pain got better suddenly, but just for a short time.
Then it got really bad, not a colicky pain this time,
but a steady, worsening pain that seemed to invade
her whole body. By the time she crossed the Gold
Star Bridge over the Thames at New London, she
was starting to have shaking chills, so bad her teeth
rattled. She couldn't figure what was the matter with
her, probably some kind of intestinal flu, she thought.

She just made it to New Coventry, parked her car
outside her apartment building, left her suitcases
where they were, and managed to get up to her
apartment. She got into bed without even un-
dressing, pulled her legs up, and wrapped herself in

blankets in an effort to get warm. She didn't know it, but her temperature at that time was 103 degrees and climbing.

She tried to sleep, but the pain in her abdomen wouldn't let her rest. She had some pain pills somewhere, she remembered, strong ones, from about a year ago when she had a tooth abscess. Getting out of bed was a problem. She rolled over slowly, moaning with the pain, put one leg out, put her foot on the floor, and pushed herself into an upright position, then struggled into the bathroom. The pills were there, half a dozen of them. She took two, gagged, but got them down. She went back to bed, hoping that she'd feel better by the time she woke up.

Around seven the next morning, Evie became aware that she was sweating, but she didn't feel any pain in her belly until she tried to turn over in bed. And then it hit her so hard she couldn't hold back a scream. She couldn't move, couldn't get out of bed, and felt a weird kind of fear invade her. Her breathing was shallow, she could feel her heart pounding fast, and she had never felt so sick in her life. Her belly felt full, and after a moment she felt she was going to vomit, so she dragged herself out of bed into the bathroom and threw up into the toilet, a huge amount of dark, mostly liquid material.

At this point she panicked. She knew she wouldn't be able to drive herself to the hospital. Stephanie would be on her way to work, and she didn't want Evan to see her like this, so she called 911 for the first time in her life. The bedside clock showed fifteen minutes after seven, but even though it was light outside, Evie couldn't figure out if it was a.m. or p.m. She felt a bit better as long as she wasn't moving, and it almost killed her to get out and open the door to the ambulance medics who arrived about twenty minutes later. Ten minutes after that she was being wheeled into the emergency room of the Lovejoy Hospital.

"Who's your doctor, Evie?" asked Jill Booth, the E.R. physician, after examining her. She looked very serious. "You're going to need a surgeon."

Until Mike Richmond's screw-up with Stephanie, Evie would have asked for him, but now . . . "Who's on call?" she asked.

Jill looked at the call schedule. "Terry Catlin," she said.

Evie hesitated, but only for a second. She felt that she was going to throw up again. "Fine," she said faintly, "Whoever," and a few moments later she heard Terry Catlin's name being called over the public address system.

While they waited for Catlin, the tech drew blood and started an I.V.

Evie heard Catlin's officious voice asking the nurse where she was, and when he appeared, she had a moment's unease, but he examined her competently enough. It didn't take Catlin long to figure out the problem. "You have appendicitis," he said. He talked at her without inflection, not looking her in the eye, as if he were addressing a tape recorder rather than a living person. "And I think it's burst. We'll do an ultrasound just to make quite certain it isn't an ovarian cyst or anything like that. Then we'll get you upstairs and into the O.R."

She could hear him talking to the O.R. supervisor through the thin green curtain around the booth.

"No," he was saying loudly. "We can*not* wait till the end of the schedule. If you have to bump a case, that's too bad. It's Evie Gaskell, she's very sick, she has peritonitis, and we're dealing here with an emergency."

Listening to him, Evie was scared. Was she really that sick? Her teeth started to rattle again, and she pulled the sheet up over her.

A nurse, a young Asian woman, hung up a small piggyback bottle on her I.V. "Antibiotic," she said.

"Could I have a blanket?" asked Evie. "I'm freezing."

The nurse hesitated. "I'll ask," she said. "But . . . Your temperature is over 104 degrees."

After that, everything was mostly a blur. She remembered the bearded ultrasound tech smearing her belly with cold jelly before sliding the probe over her. She remembered signing a permission form, being trundled along the corridor, getting pain medication, but it just made her feel more nauseated.

The last thing she remembered before going out was Catlin saying that her white count was over twenty-nine thousand, and the anesthesiologist's awed reply. "Jesus!"

As soon as Evie was asleep, Catlin, already in his

green O.R. garb, walked toward the scrub room, accompanied by the resident who was going to assist him.

"Usual appendix incision?" called out Bob Steel, the scrub tech.

Catlin half turned, his expression sarcastic. "Well, yes, of course." In the scrub room, he turned the faucet on with his knee.

"That's one sick lady," said Rick Chalmers, the resident, a cadaverous, tired-looking young man with a couple of days of dark stubble on his face. They could see Evie indistinctly through the window. The techs had started to prep her abdomen with Betadine. Then they draped her with big green sheets, leaving a rectangular opening for Mike to operate through.

Catlin shrugged. "Just another hot appendix," he replied shortly. Now that he was an attending, he didn't have much patience with the residents.

Rick finished scrubbing first and went into the O.R., leaving Catlin to his thoughts. Rick knew that appendicitis could occasionally be a really virulent condition, and it looked as if Evie had caught it in spades—less than a day had elapsed between her first symptoms and rupture. He glanced at Catlin. He didn't seem worried, which relieved Rick. He knew that if he'd been in Catlin's shoes, he'd have been very worried indeed.

Catlin came through, hands in the air, and once he was gowned and gloved took his place on the right side of the table. Luckily, Evie was slim, he thought.

He detested fat people, partly because they could be such a dangerous nightmare to operate on.

Normally, the attending would have given the case to the resident and helped him to do it, and Rick waited expectantly for Catlin to tell him to go ahead, but Catlin didn't, making the excuse that Evie was a staff member.

Rick was disappointed, but it didn't really bother him. He had a premonition that this was going to be one tough case, and he was happy to leave the responsibility to Catlin.

After getting the go-ahead from the anesthesiologist, Catlin took the scalpel from the scrub tech's hand and with one sweep made a standard McBurney's incision, an oblique cut on the right lower abdomen. They worked in silence; Rick retracted the tissues while Catlin cut through the different layers of muscle and tissues. The final layer he opened up with his fingers; Evie was slim, but she was strong, with good abdominal muscles.

"Right angles," he said to Rick, who put in two angled retractors to open up the incision. "And lean on them." Rick pulled hard, and at the bottom of the incision, they could see the gray membrane of the peritoneum, bulging ominously. Once they opened the peritoneum, they would be inside the cavity of the abdomen.

"Pick-ups. And give a pair to Dr. Chalmers."

The scrub tech took over one of the retractors, and Catlin and Rick each picked up the membrane with their forceps, tenting it up.

"Metz."

The scrub tech passed Catlin the Metzenbaum scissors, curved blades closed. Catlin's voice was impersonal, but he was thinking that it was his good luck to have been on call. Evie Gaskell was popular, and once she'd recovered, she'd be recommending him to her friends and relatives . . .

"Are we going to need the suction?" asked Rick.

"Yeah, I guess." Catlin was thinking that after this case, other staff members would start flocking to him, and he could imagine them stopping him in the corridors—"I've got this gallbladder problem, Dr. Catlin, and Evie says you're the only surgeon to see . . ." or "My mother has a stomach ulcer, Dr. Catlin, and since everyone says you're the best, I'd love for you to see her . . ."

A moment later, Catlin used the scissors to cut the peritoneal lining, but he wasn't fully prepared for what happened next. A sea of gray pus welled up inside the wound, and it took several minutes of continuous work with the suction apparatus before they could clear the operative field. And what they saw was not encouraging. Inside the peritoneal cavity, the bowel was an angry dull red color, unlike the healthy, shiny normal intestine. Catlin put a finger in and felt around. Everything seemed to be stuck together, and he couldn't identify the appendix, or, for that matter, any structures at all except the loops of bowel, which all seemed to be stuck together and not identifiable as large or small bowel.

Catlin suddenly realized that this case was a far

cry from the ordinary appendectomies he'd performed, and he felt sweat beading on his forehead. A kind of quiet had fallen over the O.R.—everyone there knew that Catlin was in trouble.

He kept trying to separate the loops of intestine, but they were so inflamed that he was afraid he might cause a tear, which would put him into still deeper trouble.

Rick started to say something, but Catlin interrupted brusquely. "Just shut up, Rick," he said. "We're having problems here and I can't think if you're talking."

The silence deepened.

Catlin turned to Bob Steel, the scrub tech. "Gimme a sponge on a stick," he said, his voice high and showing the strain. "And for Christ's sake, hurry up," he went on, raising his voice when the tech didn't instantly place the instrument in his hand. "When I ask for something, I want it *now*."

"Yes, sir." Bob, an experienced former military paramedic, stayed calm but braced himself for more trouble.

Catlin was immediately apologetic. "I need to get the intestines out of the way before I can reach the appendix," he explained. The last thing he needed at this point was to lose Bob's cooperation.

Bob folded a gauze square, placed it in the jaws of a long clamp and dipped it in saline before passing it, handle first, to Catlin.

As Rick watched Catlin, his anxiety soared. It was

clear that he was now out of his depth and didn't
know how to deal with this situation. Nor did Rick.

Using the sponge, Catlin tried ineffectually to separate the loops of bowel, but even the slight pressure
from the wet sponge made them bleed. And the
loops were all stuck together.

Maybe if he could lift some of the bowel out, Catlin
thought desperately, he could reach the appendix . . .
"Let's try a Babcock."

The tech passed him a grasping forceps with flat
tips, designed to minimize damage to the tissues.

That didn't work either. Catlin was starting to
shake and could feel panic rising in his chest. He
realized that everyone was waiting for him to figure
out a way to deal with this situation. Rick was looking at him with a concerned expression, and so was
Bob, the scrub tech. Dr. Anastopoulos, the anesthesiologist, glanced anxiously over the ether screen at
him. He didn't like working with patients who had
a fever, and Evie's temperature was still way up.
Anastopoulos already knew she was a setup for
major postoperative problems, and he was preparing
for them.

Catlin turned and spoke to the circulator, his voice
high and unsteady. "See if any of the other at-
tendings are around. I need some help here."

The circulator hurried silently out of the room, and
Rick blushed under his mask, feeling that this was a
slap at him. He could have helped Catlin perfectly
well if only Catlin had known what to do.

The silence while they waited was oppressive. The

only sounds were the rhythmic sighing of the anes-
thesia machine and the soft hiss from the air conditioning vents. The circulator came back several
minutes later. "They're all operating," she said. "Dr.
Provost just started a colectomy and Dr. Miller's
doing a gallbladder. He'll be finished in about forty
minutes . . ." She paused. "None of the other surgeons are in the hospital."

She glanced through the square window in the
door. "Oh," she said, "there's Dr. Richmond. I'll
get him."

Before Catlin could say anything, she went out
and, a moment later, came back with Mike.

Mike stood in the doorway. "What's up?" he
asked.

Catlin took a deep breath, hating him but power-
less to do anything about it. A rush of bile surged
up into his mouth and he swallowed.

"I'm having a problem here," he said, and in a few
sentences explained the situation. He tried to sound
casual. "If you're not busy, maybe you could give
me a hand."

Mike said nothing, but came into the room and
looked over Catlin's shoulder. "You couldn't get at
the appendix?"

"There's no way. Everything's stuck together, and
if I even touch that bowel, it bleeds."

"Okay . . ." Mike was thinking hard. He knew that
if he assisted Catlin and things went wrong, either
during or after the operation, Catlin would make
sure he got the blame. And right now things were

not looking good for Evie. And to be Catlin's fall guy, he decided suddenly, was not something he was going to accept.

"If you feel you can't deal with this," he said, "I'll be happy to take over the case."

He'd hardly finished speaking when Catlin answered.

"Oh, no," he said, speaking quickly, "It's not that. I just need a little assistance, just to get out of this tough spot."

"How are you going to do it? What do you want me to help you do?"

Catlin exploded with frustration and rage. "For Christ's sake, Mike, that's why I need you to help me." With a visible effort he forced himself to calm down. "I'm . . . I'm not sure quite how to proceed here."

Mike's voice hardened. "In that case, as I said, I'll be happy to take over. And by that I mean I'll also take care of the patient post-op."

The part of Catlin's face that Mike could see seemed to swell and go red, then suddenly his voice changed. "Okay, Mike. If you're refusing to assist me, I'll give up the case to you, in the patient's interest." He glanced at Bob, then over the ether screen at Dr. Anastopoulos, as if to make sure they would remember exactly what had been said. "I'll stay here until you scrub."

Mike turned and walked to the scrub room, trying to figure out the best way of dealing with this apparently hopeless surgical situation.

When he came back, Catlin said in a smooth voice, "I'll be happy to assist you in finishing the case, if you wish."

"No, thanks," replied Mike, catching his second latex glove by the cuff and pulling it on. "But maybe you should stick around for a little while and see how to deal with this kind of situation."

Catlin's face reddened again. He muttered something vicious under his breath, then turned and walked out, his fury evident in every step.

He stormed out of the O.R. suite. Sophie Petersen, the supervisor, called after him, but he ignored her. His face was hot with humiliation, and his mind teemed with violent ways of getting even with Mike Richmond. Catlin's father had lots of labor union contacts in Hartford, and it wouldn't be difficult to get a couple of guys to come down and break Richmond's legs . . . Catlin visualized the scene, the details made sharper by his fury, but by the time he reached the elevators he had calmed down. There were better and more permanent ways to destroy Richmond than that, and he remembered that he'd chosen his words carefully in the O.R. Unethical bastard . . . all Terry had needed, he told himself, was an extra pair of hands to assist him, and instead of helping, as any other surgeon would have done, that asshole had blackmailed him into giving up the case. Well, he'd have time to figure out how to deal with that. Meanwhile, he could spread the word about how Richmond had once again unethically stolen a case from him. He'd report the matter to Spencer, although he might not get a great deal of sympathy there. Lou would be a better bet—they talked the same language, and Lou would understand Terry's need for revenge, although that word would never be mentioned.

Catlin found himself outside the records department. He checked his watch. He had at least an hour free, long enough to dictate a half dozen discharge summaries. Unlike Richmond, Catlin always did his summaries promptly, and as a result was something of a favorite with Marianne Russo and the others on the records staff.

Mike took a deep breath. "Okay, guys," he said to Rick and Bob, "it's obvious that we can't get at this appendix in the usual way, so we're going to approach it through another incision," he said, unclipping the drapes and repositioning them. "We'll use a lower midline."

"Couldn't you just enlarge this one?" asked Rick in a low voice. The idea of making another incision hadn't even occurred to him.

"No. We'd have to cut through too many muscles, and even then we wouldn't get the exposure we need. Skin knife."

Bob was relieved that Mike had taken over and showed it by the way he slapped the scalpel handle into Mike's hand. Inside the peritoneal cavity, Mike encountered more pus, but to his relief the bowel in this location looked normal.

"Let's wash all this pus out," said Mike, and they

repeatedly flushed the peritoneal cavity with saline until it was clear in the plastic tubing.

"Tip the table, feet down, fifteen degrees." Mike instructed the circulator, and a moment later there was a whine from the electric motors and the table started to tilt.

"That'll do," said Mike, and the whining stopped.

"Why?" asked Rick as they worked. "I mean, why did you tilt the table?"

"If that pus gets up under her diaphragm she could get a subphrenic abscess," replied Mike, "and that is one bad complication. We'll keep her in a feet-down position for the next few days, too, for the same reason."

With better access, Mike was able to separate the loops of bowel so that finally he reached the appendix—or, rather, where it had been. There was only a stump now, opening directly into an abscess cavity formed between the adherent loops of intestine.

"Jesus," said Rick in an awed voice. "I never saw an appendix like this. I never even knew they could get like this."

"People still die from appendicitis," said Mike somberly. "Now you can see why."

Mike closed the open end of the appendix and sewed the bowel wall around it to form a seal. But the tissues were very fragile and the sutures kept tearing out. Finally Mike found some bowel wall that was less inflamed than the rest, and used a special looping stitch to reduce the tension and the chance of tearing.

They started to close the incisions in silence.

"How's she doing?" Mike asked Dr. Anastopoulos as the last stitch went in.

"Her blood pressure's down a bit, and her lungs seem to be getting a bit stiff," replied the anesthesiologist. "She's going to be hell on wheels post-op."

"I think we should put her straight into the I.C.U.," said Mike. "We'll bypass the recovery room."

"Okay with me," said Anastopoulos. "They're keeping a bed open for us. I think she's going to need to be on a ventilator for a while."

Mike and Rick looked at each other. That was not a promising turn of events.

"Okay . . . she's had her I.V. antibiotics?"

"Yes. And I had to give her two liters of Ringer's to keep her pressure up."

"What's her urine output?" Mike asked the circulator, who bent down to check the level on the bag hanging over the side of the table.

"Just over thirty cc's. Only five in the last half hour."

Mike looked at the clock and did a quick calculation. "That's not enough," he said. "Let's give her mannitol, 12.5 milligrams in a twenty percent solution."

Dr. Anastopoulos murmured something to the circulator, who went off to fetch a vial of mannitol, a powerful diuretic also known for its protective action on the kidneys.

Working as fast as they could, Mike and Rick finished closing the two incisions.

"I'm going to leave her endotracheal tube in for

now." Dr. Anastopoulos sounded concerned. He had shut down the halothane some minutes before and was now giving Evie pure oxygen through the face mask, but she still wasn't showing any signs of waking up. "I'll bag her till we get to the I.C.U."

A few minutes later, a small procession trundled through the corridor to the I.C.U., Anastopoulos holding the breathing bag and compressing it every few seconds to push air into Evie's lungs.

In the I.C.U., they quickly lifted her limp, unconscious body onto the bed, checked the I.V.'s, and reconnected the EKG leads to the overhead monitor.

Anastopoulos gave the respiratory therapist his instructions. "Set it at twelve respirations per minute at forty percent oxygen for now," he told him. "She's not making any kind of respiratory effort yet. When she does, set it on demand. But I'll be keeping a close eye on her anyway."

While Rick wrote up the post-op orders, Mike was on the phone checking with the lab for Evie's blood gases, and while he waited, he asked if any of Evie's relatives were around. There was no sign of Terry Catlin.

"There's somebody in the waiting room who's with her," answered the nurse.

When things had calmed down and Evie seemed stable, Mike, still in his O.R. greens, went through to the waiting room. There was only one person there, facing away from the door, watching the ceiling-mounted TV. She turned around, and Mike caught his breath. It was Stephanie Hopkins.

Chapter 28

Mike stared at Stephanie with astonishment, then his face became rigid and his voice chilled. "Are you here for Evie Gaskell?"

"Yes. She's my best friend." Stephanie hadn't expected to see him, and for a moment she couldn't hide her confusion.

"Doesn't she have any relatives here in town?"

Mike's tone made it clear that he didn't want to talk to her about Evie. Or about anything else.

"She has a brother here in New Coventry, and I've called him. He'll be here later. Her mother lives up in Maine." Stephanie took a deep breath and looked Mike straight in the eye. "The nurse at the desk told me that Dr. Catlin was operating on her."

"He was, but he had to leave, and I took over the case from him," replied Mike, who had no desire to discuss what had happened.

Stephanie stared. She'd never heard of a surgeon leaving in the middle of an operation. "Is she all right?"

Mike's voice didn't change. "No, she isn't. She had a burst appendix with generalized peritonitis, and she's very sick. She's in intensive care, and she'll probably be there for quite a while. Right now she's on a ventilator."

"A ventilator! My God . . ." Stephanie stared wide-eyed at him. "I didn't know you could get into that kind of trouble just from an appendix."

"Well, you can. I don't think we could have saved her if she'd come in a few hours later. As it is—"

"Can I see her?"

"Not now." He saw Stephanie's expression. She looked so upset that he paused, although his strong inclination was to finish the conversation and get away from her and back to his patient. "Okay . . . I'll go and see what's happening, and if there aren't too many techs and nurses swarming around her, I'll bring you in. But just for a minute, okay?" His voice sounded so stern that he thought she'd back off.

She didn't. "Thanks, Dr. Richmond. I'd really appreciate that."

She watched him leave the room. He looked very tired, and the lines on his face made him look a lot older than the first time she'd seen him, only a few weeks ago.

When he came back, he was wearing the same fixed, impersonal expression. "I'll let you see her," he told Stephanie, looking at a point a few inches above her head, "but as I said, just for a minute. She's not awake yet, and I'm warning you that the way she looks may be a shock to you."

It was. Evie, in a thin white cotton hospital johnny with a hem that came to mid-thigh, was lying flat on her back on the tilted bed. There was no pillow under her head, and what Stephanie could see of her face was shiny and waxy-pale. The visible part of an endotracheal tube emerged from her mouth and was taped to her face. The tube was connected to the ventilator, a washing-machine-sized cabinet on the right side of the bed. The machine hissed every few seconds, pushing air into Evie's lungs and making the connecting tubes move slightly. Above her head, the line on the cardiac monitor flickered its orange course across the screen. Evie's heart rate was regular but rapid; Stephanie figured it was running at about a hundred and fifteen beats per minute.

A nurse was reaching up to change the I.V. She glanced at Stephanie. Her expression wasn't hostile, it just said "Don't get in my way."

From the foot of the bed, Stephanie stared at her friend, shocked at her appearance. Even now she couldn't have sworn that it was Evie she was looking at.

"Okay?" Mike looked at her, telling her that her time was up.

"Okay." Stephanie's voice wasn't quite steady. "Thanks for letting me see her, Dr. Richmond. I'll call her mother, and it'll make her feel better that I've seen her."

Stephanie walked quickly out of the I.C.U. and along the corridor to the bank of elevators, where a couple of male residents in O.R. greens were already waiting. On the way down one of them, tall, thin, and unshaven, was telling the other about the appen-

dectomy he'd been assisting on. "I never saw anything like it," he said to his colleague in a shocked,
quiet voice. "It was ruptured, with pus everywhere.
If it had been my case, I'd still be in there trying to
figure out what to do."

Outside, Stephanie, still shaken by her encounter
with Mike, checked her watch. It was almost noon,
and by the time she got back to the office everybody
had left for lunch. There were a few people waiting
when the elevator arrived, and just as it was closing,
a very blond, athletic-looking man in a business suit
slipped in and stood in the corner, bouncing gently
on the balls of his feet. Stephanie glanced at him, and
it took her a second to recognize him. He was the
man whose office she'd walked into by mistake that
first time she came to see Mike Richmond, and he
didn't look any happier now that he had then. His
eyes flickered over the other people in the elevator,
including her, but he didn't recognize her. There was
no reason why he should.

To her surprise, he got off at the same floor as she
did and hurried ahead. She watched him turn into
the executive corridor, and saw him opening the
door to Carl Hartmann's office. But Stephanie's mind
was occupied thinking about Evie, and she didn't
think any more about Carl's visitor until much later.

Chapter 29

That afternoon an emergency meeting of the group was called by Lou Gardner.

"Is this something Mike should attend?" asked Derek Provost when Lou called him in his office.

"It emphatically is not," replied Lou in an ominous tone. "In fact, this meeting is going to be mainly about him. However, I have Spencer's permission for Terry Catlin to join us for part of the meeting, as he has some important information to give us."

When they were all assembled, Spencer, who evidently didn't know any more than the others, asked Lou to explain why he'd interrupted their busy day. "It'd better be good," he told him, smiling, but it was clear that he was put out.

Lou stood up. "I'm very concerned about the presence of Mike Richmond in our group," he started. "And I don't think we were adequately consulted before he was brought on board."

"Everybody was invited to meet him before he was hired," said Spencer curtly, "and if you didn't take that opportunity, it's a little late to be complaining about it now."

"I did meet him," admitted Lou, "but at that point it was already a done deal. You and Derek and Chas Miller had already decided to bring him in. We never had any real discussions about him."

The door opened, and Tony slipped in, nodded to Spencer, and sat down at the table.

"I thought we'd discussed it pretty well," replied Spencer. "And of course we checked with Carl"—he glanced at Tony—"and got the okay from him. What more do you think we should have done?"

"Come on, you guys, that's all water under the bridge," said Derek. He looked at Lou. "I'm sure you didn't call this meeting to tell us you're pissed off about something that happened three months ago."

"Lou, have you had an actual problem with Dr. Richmond?" asked Morgan Grant, one of the internists, a quiet, hardworking individual who usually didn't say anything at meetings. "I've worked with him, and he's always done a good, careful job. I'd even say he is outstanding."

"I certainly have, but that's not why I called this meeting," replied Lou.

"One of the problems is that Mike's with us but he's *not* with us," commented Chas Miller. "He's a member of the group, but he doesn't really know what's going on, and that makes it difficult to deal with him. But he's good. I think we should get on with it, make him a full member, tell him the facts of life, and the sooner the better."

Lou grunted, then said, "How about Terry Catlin? Does the same go for him?"

"Not yet, I don't think," said Spencer carefully. "He hasn't proved himself. In fact, what I hear about him on the clinical side isn't always good, I'm sorry to say."

"Well, I think you may change your mind when you hear what he has to tell us," replied Lou. "I've found Terry great to work with, very capable, and he also has the right attitude for our practice, which I can't say for Mike."

The surgeons listened to him in silence. They all knew that Catlin had been brought in to the group largely to appease Lou, and they were getting irritated at his continual bad-mouthing of Mike.

Spencer nodded impatiently and looked at his watch, then at Lou.

"Okay," said Lou, biting his lip. "Let's go over some of the things that have happened since Dr. Richmond came on board. First, he's antagonized the other groups, specifically ConnPath and Marty Rosenfeld at Radiology Associates—"

"That's because Mike wasn't totally aware of the ground rules," interrupted Spencer. "And that was my fault. And of course, he doesn't know of the precise relationship between the groups. And in any case, I've talked to both the radiology and the ConnPath people, and the problems are all straightened out."

"Yeah, right, but I talked to Marty Rosenfeld yesterday, and he's still bent out of shape, and like us, Radiology Associates is also concerned about security. They feel that Mike Richmond's a loose cannon, and it's making them very nervous."

"Have they mentioned this to anyone else? That they feel it's more than just a temporary problem?" Spencer addressed Tony.

"Not that I know of," replied Tony, "Nobody's said anything about that to Mr. Hartmann, I'm sure. For one thing, as you all know, the group members aren't allowed to talk directly to him except at our scheduled out-of-town meetings."

"Well, is that it, Lou?" asked Spencer.

"Not quite," said Lou. "And at this point I'd like Terry Catlin to join us. He can tell us what he found." Spencer pursed his lips, but nodded at Tony, who went to the door and opened it. Catlin came in, wearing a well-ironed white coat, looking brisk and matter-of-fact.

"Thanks for joining us, Terry," said Lou. "Now, would you kindly tell the group what you told me earlier?"

"Sure." Terry nodded self-confidently at the group and sat down. "Yesterday I was in the record room dictating charts and happened to talk to Marianne Russo, who I get along with very well, about the new records system. She mentioned that Mike Richmond had asked her to access certain information . . ." Catlin paused for effect, and glanced at the silent faces around him. "When I asked her what kind of information he was looking for, she told me Mike wanted to check all of Dr. Spencer's breast biopsies, and then he had her correlate them with the mastectomies that were carried out later." Catlin paused and looked at his audience. Now he had their full attention; Spencer's face had changed color, and the others were exchanging apprehensive glances.

Tony calmly crossed his legs, watching Catlin.

"He also checked the same data for other surgeons," went on Catlin, doing his best not to look complacent. "And I can think of only one possible reason he'd be doing that."

They all looked shaken, Spencer more than any of them. "Are you quite sure of your facts, Terry?" he asked. "After all, we all occasionally need to check statistics in the hospital computer."

"Yes, I'm sure," replied Catlin. "Marianne was very specific. Mike was looking at the statistics in a way that simply wouldn't occur to most people. First he checked the biopsies, then he got Marianne to trace each individual patient and find the ones who had mastectomies or whatever, and that of course is a very complicated and irregular way of using this data. Actually, she was proud that she'd been able to get the info he wanted."

"And why do you think he did that?" asked Dr. Spencer. "You said there was only one possible reason."

The others sat very still.

"Can I be totally frank with you guys?" asked Catlin, looking around.

"Of course," replied Spencer, after a quick glance at Tony.

Catlin leaned back in his chair, and adopted a confidential tone that grated on all of them except Lou. "Well, you know that my father is a very close personal friend of Governor DiGiovanni's," he started. "And when Jack knew I was going to be joining this group, he told me *in the strictest confidence* how the business side operated and explained the symbiotic relationship with the hospital, the malpractice attorneys, the path lab, and Radiology Associates."

The tension was now tight as a bowstring, and Derek, watching Tony and remembering Pauline Minsky, realized that whether he knew it or not, Catlin was putting himself at considerable risk.

"That wasn't very discreet of Governor DiGiovanni, now, was it?" said Spencer.

"I'm glad he did tell me," replied Catlin. "Now I know what's going on here, and I like it, partly because it's a brilliant idea, but mostly because I'll be able to make a lot more money than if I was just another surgeon trying to make it in private practice."

"To come back to Mike for a moment, Terry," said Spencer mildly, "why do you think he made these inquiries in the record department?"

"I've been thinking about that. My hunch is that he's working for someone else."

A long silence followed, broken finally by Spencer.

"Thank you for your time, Terry," he said. He sounded friendly enough, but there was a finality in his tone, and Terry stood up quickly, straightened his white coat and left.

"You see?" said Lou, when the door closed. He

was beaming with satisfaction. "Terry knows the score, and already he's found the bad apple in our group. I'm really glad he's on board."

"I'm not," said Derek bluntly. "I don't trust him, and I think this story about Mike pulling Spencer's mastectomy data is a bunch of bullshit. Everybody on the staff is entitled to look at the hospital stats. And he could have simply been curious about the cases Spencer does. If I'd thought of it, I might have done the same thing."

"I agree," said Chas Miller. "It's obvious that Mike didn't go down there with the idea of causing trouble. Marianne volunteered to show him the new system, and he thought of a way of seeing how powerful it was. Big deal."

"After the Pauline Minsky business, we all wondered it she might be working with someone in-house," said Lou doggedly. "How do we know that she wasn't working with Richmond?"

Tony moved in his chair. "That question did come up," he said in his quiet voice. "We've been keeping an eye on Dr. Richmond. We have his phones bugged, and so far there's no sign that he's doing anything besides his work."

"But now that he does know that all of Spencer's biopsy cases go on to have mastectomies," said Lou, annoyed at the show of support for Mike. "How do you know that he isn't going to take the information to the feds or whoever?"

"Why should he?" Spencer's irritation was getting more obvious. "He's a smart guy, he's going to get rich working with us, and now he's beginning to know how the system works."

"I suggest we bring him fully on board, and as soon as possible" added Derek. "Then there'll be no question about his loyalty."

Spencer nodded. "We've talked about this before," he said. "All we need to do at this point is give him a carefully selected case, one he can't turn down." He turned to Lou. "Lou, would you take care of that for us?"

Lou who had been glowering at the floor, looked up. "Sure," he said. "I can do that. But I want you to know that I'm still concerned about Richmond. I think he's a danger to us all."

Chapter 30

Evie's first major post-op emergency occurred at ten minutes to five on the afternoon of her operation. She was semiconscious and having problems with her breathing. The problem was that the ventilator was set at exactly sixteen breaths per minute, and Evie wasn't awake enough to adjust her breathing rate, with the result that she was trying to exhale when the machine was pushing air into her lungs, which made her cough and panic. Mike tried switching the ventilator off for a while, but her breathing muscles were too weak, and her breathing became shallow and ineffective.

"Evie, I have to put the ventilator on again," he said, his mouth near her ear. "I'll tell you when to breathe in and when to breathe out. Try to go along with it, okay?" He was holding her hand, which seemed to reassure her, and she squeezed weakly to show that she understood. At that moment Mike happened to look up at the monitor and saw that her heart had stopped. Just like that. Halfway across the screen, the EKG had turned into a straight orange line. A moment later, the asystole alarm went off, a penetrating, high-pitched sound that brought the nurse running.

Mike tried the simplest tactic first, without much hope of success. He gave a hard thump with his closed fist on her chest, then looked immediately up at the monitor. The straight line oscillated wildly when he struck her chest, then the normal heartbeats started again, flicking their way across the screen. Mike mopped his brow, then went back to getting Evie to work with the ventilator while he kept an eye on the monitor. Evie wasn't an easy patient. The ventilator panicked her, and she needed constant reassurance and attention. After her cardiac arrest, he spent the next two nights in the hospital, watching her like a hawk, checking her vital signs, her lab reports, trying to anticipate problems before they arose. Her fluid and electrolytes were a particular problem; her kidney function was marginal, and her blood urea levels kept climbing ominously, and by the evening of the third day, Mike was seriously thinking about starting her on dialysis.

He called in Dr. Abe Weiss, a nephrologist in charge of the dialysis unit, for consultation.

"No question," he told Mike after examining her. "Her kidneys are shot to hell. Her creatinine's going up now also. We should dialyze her, and the sooner the better."

"What's her chance of spontaneous improvement?" Mike asked. He knew that he was grabbing at straws—Abe Weiss was very competent and his opinion had to be taken seriously.

"Sometimes it does happen," agreed Dr. Weiss. He shrugged. "But if she doesn't improve and dies, how will you explain that in court?"

After Abe Weiss went off, Mike leaned back against the wall and thought about the situation. In spite of Abe's opinion, he was reluctant to go ahead with dialysis because of the risk. Evie was still considered an infected case, because she still had a fever and a high white-cell count, and dialysis in infected cases was a hazardous undertaking. He also knew that if spontaneous recovery of kidney function didn't occur within three days, the chances of its happening at all decreased rapidly as the hours went by. He took a deep breath and decided to wait a little longer.

By now Mike was unshaven, gaunt-looking, and exhausted. He'd hardly slept for three nights, although they'd put a cot up for him in the X-ray viewing room next to the I.C.U., and he was beginning to worry about his ability to make competent decisions.

Evie's brother, Evan, came in every day, and Mike talked to him a couple of times. Stephanie was spending every evening in the hospital, and most of that time at Evie's bedside. The I.C.U. rules, which allowed only short visits from relatives and close friends, had been bent at Mike's request. "She's a nurse," he told them, "and she's worked in the I.C.U., so she can free up the other nurses." Evie's mother had come down from Maine, but she wasn't well either, and Stephanie had finally persuaded her to go back to Evie's apartment and get some rest.

"What did Dr. Weiss say?" asked Stephanie when Mike came back in. She was sitting near the head of the bed, doing some work she'd brought with her. Evie was asleep, waking only infrequently, and even then her eyes were dull and she didn't seem totally aware of her surroundings, although her breathing had improved after Mike had taken her off the respirator.

"He wants to dialyze her," replied Mike wearily. He glanced at Evie's white face, then bent down to check the plastic urine bag hanging down from the bedframe. There were only a few milliliters of yellow fluid at the bottom. "I think I'll wait a bit longer. Hemodialysis in this kind of situation is a risky proposition."

"She's been very restless since you were last here," said Stephanie. She and Mike had developed a cautious rapport in the last few days, in spite of their adversarial situation. "And her temp's been fluctuating quite a bit, up to 102 this afternoon." The temperature chart was hanging off the bottom of the bed, and the tracing looked like a cross-section through the Colorado Rockies.

Mike did some calculations in his head. Then, not trusting his tired brain to function accurately, he took out his pocket calculator. Stephanie watched him. She had never seen a doctor so concerned about his patients or one who spent so much time with them. Then she thought about Haiman Gold and his subpoenas, and she found she was beginning to feel guilty.

"Ten o'clock," Mike was saying. "That's absolutely the last moment. I'll let her go until then. If things haven't improved a whole lot by then, we'll get the dialysis team in."

They both looked at Evie.

"At least she doesn't have to worry about it," he said to Stephanie, but his smile just reflected his anxiety.

Evie opened her eyes for a moment. They were puffy, as was the rest of her face. With a shock, Stephanie thought that if she'd just walked into the I.C.U., she would not have recognized the pretty, attractive Evie of a week ago.

Evie looked at Mike, standing at the foot of the bed, and smiled through cracked lips. "Thanks for everything, Dr. Richmond," she said, then closed her eyes again.

Stephanie felt tears coming up into her eyes, and took a tissue from the box on the bedside stand. She blew her nose.

Mike came around and put a hand on Evie's shoulder. "You're doing fine, Evie," he said. "Just hang in there." Looking at Stephanie, he nodded toward the door. She stood up, put her papers down on the chair, and followed him.

Outside, he said, "Let's go into the waiting room."

"You just want somewhere to sit down, right?" Stephanie was feeling nervous, and tried to smile.

"You're quite right," he replied without a change in tone. "But unless Evie's mother or brother are here . . ." He paused, looking at Stephanie, who shook her head. "I need to talk to you some more about her."

The door to the waiting room was about fifty feet away, on the opposite side of the corridor, and they walked there in silence, both suddenly uncomfortable with each other's proximity.

They sat down in the mauve plastic chairs, Mike straddling his so he was facing Stephanie. Then his face seemed to crumple. "I think we may lose her," he said.

Stephanie's eyes widened and she grasped the side of the chair. She couldn't believe it; even now she didn't realize that people could still die of a perforated appendix.

"The antibiotics don't seem to be getting to the infection," he went on, his voice dulled by exhaustion. "And her renal function isn't even borderline. Dr. Weiss says her kidneys are shot to hell . . ." Mike paused for a moment, and Stephanie could feel that he was working, trying to get his facts and figures straightened out in his numbed mind. "The thing is, Stephanie, that dialysis is particularly dangerous in this kind of patient. When there's a generalized infection, the cannulas tend to get infected. Then the infection spreads through the bloodstream into the entire body, causing septicemia. And when that happens, we're usually getting to the end of the string."

"You said you would let her go until ten o'clock," asked Stephanie.

"Right. That's decision time." He stood up and swayed for a moment from sheer tiredness. "And between you and me," he went on, "that is the time we'll know if she's going to make it or not."

"Should I call her mother? Or Evan?"

Mike thought for a moment. "No," he said. "She already knows that Evie's very sick, and there's no point adding to her worry now. And we can tell Evan when he shows up."

In the next several hours, the tension in the I.C.U. mounted. The nursing staff, all of whom knew Evie, somehow became aware that the moment of truth was approaching for her, and they redoubled their attentions. Stephanie put cold towels on Evie's forehead when her temperature went up, and talked quietly to her, holding her hand. When her temp was high, up around 103 degrees, Evie got restless and agitated, and seemed scared. Her eyes were wide open, and she'd talk fast; then she'd tire quickly and be quiet. Her breathing was rapid and shallow. When they drew her blood gases, and the results appeared on the unit's computer, Mike's already somber face showed that the news wasn't good. And the blood chemistries weren't any better. The amounts of urea and creatinine in her blood, waste materials that were normally cleared quickly by the kidneys, were rising slowly.

By nine o'clock, the atmosphere in the I.C.U. was tense, almost supercharged. Everybody who worked there was accustomed to serious illness and death, but to have one of their colleagues, particularly a young one whom they all knew and liked, in their charge and to feel unable to do anything to help her was almost more than most of them could take. Even the nurses and techs who weren't directly involved in her care felt the same way. Evie was one of *them*.

It happened thirty-eight minutes later. Everything in the unit was quiet. Many of the patients were asleep, and Evie too seemed to be asleep; her eyes were closed and her breathing was more regular. Stephanie had gone to fetch some lip salve and was heading back to Evie's bed. Mike was at the desk, talking quietly to the lab tech about an anomalous value on one of the chemistry reports.

"Oh, my God!"

Stephanie's voice, from Evie's bedside, was loud enough to make everyone jump.

Mike dropped the phone and was there in a few quick steps. For a moment he didn't see what the problem was. Then Stephanie, unable to speak, pointed at the plastic bag hanging off the side of the bed. It was almost full of clear, yellow, glorious urine. Evie's kidneys were functioning again.

"Well," said Mike, almost laughing with relief, and finding that Stephanie's hand was holding his in a firm grip, "I never thought I'd be so happy to see a plastic bag brimming with pee!"

Chapter 31

From that point, things moved very quickly. Within a half hour of Evie's kidneys starting to function, her temperature had come down to normal and she was sitting up in bed and drinking sips of water.

"God, my throat hurts," she told Mike in a hoarse voice. "When can we get that nasogastric tube out?"

"Maybe tomorrow," replied Mike, after putting his stethoscope to her belly and listening for a few moments. "You've got bowel sounds, which means your intestines are working again. Congratulations." He drew himself back up, and grinned tiredly at her.

"You look as pooped as I feel," said Evie. Her lips and mouth were so dry that she had trouble talking.

"Yeah." Even now he felt reluctant to leave her, although clearly she was on the mend. "I'm going home." He turned to Stephanie. "And you should too," he added.

"You're right," Stephanie agreed. She leaned forward and kissed Evie on the cheek. "I'll see you tomorrow, kid," she said.

Outside the I.C.U., Mike said, "Let's go somewhere

for a drink. I think this calls for some kind of celebration."

"Aren't you too tired? Shouldn't you just go home?"

"Yes, but we're going for a drink anyway. For one thing, I need to talk to you."

In a kind of foggy euphoria, they crossed the parking lot, and by the time they reached Mike's car, their arms were around each other's waists.

Mike drove down Elm Street, feeling as if something that had been delayed far too long was finally happening. He didn't look directly at Stephanie, but he was very conscious of her presence next to him. A hundred yards farther, he pulled into Aileen's Bar, a place he used to go to occasionally with his team, drove around the back, and found a parking space.

The only two good things about Aileen's were that it was near the hospital and didn't close until late. The place was dark, as usual, and there were only a couple of customers sitting at the bar. The bartender, washing glasses, looked up and nodded to Mike as they passed. Mike led the way to a small table near the far end of the room, and they sat down.

"I bet they don't have big electricity bills here," said Stephanie, peering at him through the gloom. "I can hardly see you."

"Just as well, probably, under the circumstances," replied Mike, rubbing his bristly chin. He went over to the bar to get their drinks, and she watched his broad back, thinking what a caring and wonderful doctor he'd been with Evie, and feeling a recurrent exasperation that he hadn't been as careful with her. Why not? Why had he been so unforgivably neglectful with her? She shook her head. It didn't make sense, and anyway she was too tired to think about it. But she knew that she was feeling something quite different about him, a kind of warmth and excitement that coursed through her when she looked at him . . . and that too was totally out of sync with the anger and dislike she'd felt for him until a few days ago.

Mike came back with two glasses and sat down. Miraculously his tiredness seemed to have evaporated, and aside from his three-day beard, he looked as alert and confident as the time she'd first stepped into his office. Stephanie felt the warmth surging through her again, and she leaned forward in her chair.

"That was just amazing, what happened to Evie," she said, hoping her voice sounded normal. "How did she get better so fast?"

Mike took a long swig from his glass. "It was a *crisis*, like what used to happen before antibiotics," he replied, very aware of Stephanie's physical presence, and trying to figure out what was going on between them. He forced himself to remember that she was his antagonist, with a lawsuit pending against him. "For instance, when a kid had lobar pneumonia, after about ten days the temperature would fall suddenly and the kid got better. Or else it didn't."

"But now there *are* antibiotics," said Stephanie,

talking mostly to keep her feelings down, "and Evie was on them. And it still happened."

"I don't know," confessed Mike. "The body does things we still don't understand. Something happened inside Evie that told her she wasn't ready to die yet." He took another long swig from his glass and put it down firmly. He sat back, and his jaw tightened. "There's something I need to talk to you about, Stephanie," he said, looking her straight in the eye. "It has to do with your . . . biopsy, and everything."

Stephanie leaned back, and her voice was suddenly guarded. "Go ahead."

"I didn't make a mistake with you," he said quietly. He told her about the sudden appearance of the second pathology report, how it had been inserted in her hospital chart, and about Tony's false explanation. "So when I operated on you, I was acting on the best information I had," he went on. "I still don't know how or why it happened. But it was *not* because of carelessness or lack of interest in the patient."

Stephanie felt blood coming into her cheeks and was glad it was dark.

"I've watched you for three days now," she said, "And I've seen how you are, how you work, how you interact with your patients. It made me mad that you hadn't taken care of me as well as you took care of your other patients."

Mike opened his mouth to interrupt, but she went on. "If I hadn't actually seen you in action, I might have thought you were lying to me about that pathology report." She paused. "Mike, I believe you." Almost against her will, her hand came across the small table, and he took it in his.

For a long moment nothing was said, and they just looked at each other, trying to figure out if what they were feeling was real.

"Okay . . ." Stephanie's words came out in a rush, ahead of her mind and her voice. "I did see a lawyer, a while back, you probably know that already, but I'm going to talk to him first thing tomorrow and tell him not to go ahead with it."

"I'm not sure you should do that just yet," said Mike. Stephanie's eyes were getting accustomed to the dark, and she could see the lines of anxiety in his face. "You see, there are some other things going on . . . I don't want to rock the boat right now."

"What other things?" She tightened the pressure on his hand.

"This is really a bit weird," he said, "but I was in the record room a few days ago and found that practically every biopsy that one of our surgeons does is followed by mastectomy."

"Dr. Spencer?"

Mike nodded. "I can't understand it. You know how well respected Dr. Spencer is . . . I don't even know if he's aware of what's happening, although I suppose he would have to be."

"Do you think that those cases are like mine? Do you think those pathologists can't tell a cancer from a benign tumor?"

Mike stared at her. "No . . . it's not that. They're very competent. But do you remember seeing those slides? I showed them to you on the monitor, but you didn't want to look at them. *They showed cancer cells,* just as they described in their report. I'm not a pathologist, but I know a malignant breast tumor when I see one, and I'm *certain* that's what it was."

Stephanie gently withdrew her hand, and Mike let it go.

They both thought about what he'd just said.

"And there are other things . . ." Mike felt relieved to be able to talk to her about this, and he outlined the other problems that had arisen with Radiology Associates and ConnPath.

Somewhere inside Stephanie's brain a small light went on—he was talking about things that reflected some of her own anxieties at work. *I don't know everything that goes on here,* Dr. Sammons had told her, *and quite frankly I don't want to.*

Then, as if he were pulling it all together for the first time, Mike told her about Pauline Minsky, how he'd gone to visit her husband Andy, and met Mrs. Newsome. "She's the widow of Dr. Newsome, who used to be head of the group," he explained. "He was killed in a plane crash a couple of years ago. Mrs. Newsome hired Pauline to find out what was happening in the group, and to figure out how the partners had all gotten rich so fast."

"And then *she* died. I mean Pauline." Stephanie sounded shocked; she was looking at him, and the light in her eyes gave them a glow that put Pauline out of his mind for a few seconds. Then he nodded, a strange feeling of apprehension beginning to take hold of him. At first he hadn't even considered that Pauline's death was anything more than a sad and unexpected misfortune, but now he wasn't so sure.

"It's very confusing," he said, smiling worriedly at her in the darkness. "Everything feels off balance—I don't know what's really happening here. I don't even know who I can trust and who I can't, and who's being truthful and who isn't. All I know is that something very strange is going on, and I have to find what it is."

Stephanie was silent for a moment. "You know that very blond, scary guy who works in your office?" she asked. "The office manager? The first time I came to see you, I went into his office by mistake. He was very polite, and showed me where you were. A few days ago I was in the elevator at work, and he got on. I saw him going into my boss's office— that's Carl Hartmann, the guy who owns the company. It was outside normal office hours, when there's usually not much traffic, and . . . well, he just looked as if he knew his way around, not like just a visitor. I don't know if that has anything to do with anything, but it just seemed a bit strange."

"Tony? Tony Danzig? You're sure it was him?"

"Sure. He's hard to miss, with that almost white hair and pale eyes." Stephanie gave a little shudder.

"Tony's a strange guy," he said. "He's supposed to be the office manager, but he's there only two or three days a week, and the other docs treat him with a lot more respect than I would have expected. It's more like deference than respect, actually, as if he's the one they have to answer to."

Stephanie reached over again and gently took Mike's hand. He leaned forward a little, and she did the same, until their faces were only a few inches apart.

"I'm feeling scared," she said. "It seems that Carl Hartmann was the one who really stopped my operation." Stephanie told him about her conversation with Jean Forrest and Ann Boyd, Carl's secretary, then explained the job she was doing for Carl. "He calls them Corporation One, Two, Three, and so on, and I'm sure Corporation One is Lovejoy Hospital," she said. Do you think the others could possibly be . . . ?" Her voice faded.

"Oh, Jesus," whispered Mike. "Of course! And they would all feed off each other, including Haiman Gold, who would finish up with all their malpractice cases. Why didn't I think of this before?"

"Right now it's just guesswork," Stephanie reminded him.

"You know, Stephanie," he said, after a long pause, "the most important thing that's come out of all of this"—he put both his hands out across the table, and she took them—"is *this*."

He stood up, and so did she, and he held her close to him, feeling her warmth, and caught up in a wave of emotion that threatened to sweep him away.

"It's getting late," he said, gently stroking her hair. "Stephanie, I'm taking you home with me."

Chapter 32

Tony Danzig pressed the down arrow on his keyboard until the name he wanted was highlighted, then he moved his mouse until it pointed at the *call* icon and pressed the left button. After a moment he picked up the phone just as Eric Tarvel, the pathologist, answered.

"Tarvel." The voice was curt.

"Ah yes, Dr. Tarvel, this is Tony Danzig from Dr. Newsome's office. First I'd like to thank you for handling the Minsky affair so efficiently. I was also wondering if anyone had shown any interest in the case, asked questions, requested copies of the autopsy report, anything like that."

"Questions? From outside agencies? No. Nothing at all. Dr. Li, from the medical examiner's office, stopped by and signed the papers for us, of course, but he didn't ask any questions."

"Anyone else? Any inquiries at all?"

"No. Dr. Richmond came down to the autopsy room to ask about the findings, but that wasn't surprising, I suppose. She was his secretary." Tarvel remembered his annoyance with Mike. "Of course, he had no business entering a restricted area, and we sent him packing."

Tony sat up straight. "Was he present during the autopsy?"

"No, of course not. We don't let visitors in for that kind of autopsy, and especially not for hers."

"What did you tell him?"

"Not much, basically what I put on the report. Just that the death certificate would read *Acute coronary arterial occlusion from atherosclerosis.*"

"I assume that's your language for a heart attack."

"Yes."

"Did he ask for a copy?"

"No, but I did tell him that if he had the proper authorization, he could obtain a copy of the report from the pathology office."

There was a pause, then Tony said, "Thank you, Dr. Tarvel."

He put down the phone. The record room business and now this told him he'd better keep a close eye on Richmond.

The next morning, Mike went to the hospital early and headed straight for the I.C.U. There he found that Evie's kidney function was satisfactory, her temperature was down to normal, and she was well enough to be transferred to a private room. Later, he came to visit her on the surgical floor. She had got out of bed and was sitting in a chair and watching television, although she was still weak and had lost a lot of weight. Mike chatted with her for a few min-

utes, then listened to her abdomen with his stethoscope. "You've got good bowel sounds," he told her.
"Good enough so we can take that tube out of your
stomach." He detached the tape that anchored the
tube to her nose and pulled slowly on the long plastic
drainage tube until it came out. She coughed and
spluttered, and her johnny came undone at the front,
exposing her breasts, but she was too busy coughing
and blowing her nose to cover them up.

"I tell you," she said, once she'd got her breath
back and retied the johnny strings, "being sick like
this doesn't leave you with a single shred of
modesty."

It hadn't occurred to Mike that modesty was something to take into consideration in the course of his
work, and she smiled at his male ignorance. "It's
important. Very." Evie cleared her throat, and
coughed again. "God, that hurts . . . yes, I'm not sure
that modesty's the right word, but it is important,
for women, anyway. When you're sick, you're vulnerable, and you hang on to how you look; you want
to be sure your makeup's okay, your hair, all that.
But when you're really sick, you just don't care. If
somebody sees your bare ass, so what? You don't
even think about it." She smiled wryly at him. "I
guess I'm just coming out of that situation." She
stared at him. "One of the girls told me what happened in the O.R.," she went on. "I wondered why
it was you and not Dr. Catlin who was taking care
of me in the I.C.U." She took his hand. "Thank you,"
she added simply.

"My pleasure," he said.

Evie let go his hand and sat back in the chair, exhausted. She grinned weakly up at him. "I have to tell you, Mike, you look like the cat who ate the canary. What happened?"

Mike's ears went pink. "I guess I'm happy you're better," he replied, but even he realized his explanation sounded rather lame.

"Yeah, right," she said. "You seemed to have made it up pretty well with Stephanie by the time you left last night."

"Right," said Mike, not getting drawn into a discussion along those lines. He straightened his white coat. "Well, I guess I'd better go find someone else to cure."

She was still grinning when the door closed behind him.

When Mike got back to the office, he noticed a different atmosphere about the place. Spencer was talking to the receptionist, and looked up and nodded at Mike. "Are you going to be in your office?"

"For about a half hour. Then I have to get back to the hospital."

"I'll stop by shortly. By the way . . ." Spencer's tone was neutral. "I'm glad to hear that your patient's doing so much better." He returned to his conversation with Imogene.

It wasn't anything really, but the approval was there. It was rare for surgeons to compliment each other, and Mike knew this was as much praise as he would get. He remembered his discussion with

Stephanie in Aileen's Bar the night before and
laughed to himself. He must have been crazy to think
that Spencer and his group could be involved in such
an elaborate scam. Then other memories of the night
took the upper hand, and he floated on air along the
corridor to his office.

Derek looked up as Mike walked past his office
and called after him. "Hey! What's the hurry?"

Mike came abruptly down to earth and walked
back.

"Come on in! Pull up a loose stool, and have a
seat." The light from the monitor shone on Derek's
face, and he pushed it around on its swivel. "I've
been hearing about Evie Gaskell," he went on after
Mike had sat down. "I guess you got her out of
deep trouble."

"She was lucky," said Mike, stretching out his legs.
"For a while I thought we were going to lose her."

Derek glanced at the door. "Rick Chalmers told me
what happened in the O.R. Terry came back with
some cock-and-bull story about you stealing his case,
but I believe Rick. He said Catlin simply didn't know
what to do." Derek surveyed Mike for a moment,
then leaned forward. "You're going to have to watch
out for Catlin," he said, his voice as serious as Mike
had ever heard it. "He'll do you in if he can."

Mike shrugged. "He's tried before."

Derek seemed about to say something more about
Catlin but changed his mind and went back to Evie.
"She's done good things for your reputation, my boy.
Devoted surgeon spends nights and days to save crit-

ically ill patient. Actually, the word is that you got her pregnant and she had an ectopic." He grinned at his little joke.

"Was that Terry's diagnosis?"

"No. It was mine. Listen . . ." Derek sat back in his chair. "While you were out there saving lives, the rest of us layabouts had a meeting—" He interrupted himself. "Have you spoken to Spencer today?"

"I saw him just now talking to Imogene."

"Well, at our meeting we decided to bring you fully on board, earlier than scheduled. Congratulations."

"Thanks." Mike grinned. He'd expected that the various problems he'd had would have slowed the process down rather than speed it up.

Derek moved in his chair, looking relaxed, but the look in his eyes wasn't at all relaxed. "But first we have to teach you some of the facts of life. This group is different from your average medical-surgical practice," he began. "For a start, let's be realistic. We're all in this strictly for the money." His voice was light-hearted, but his eyes didn't leave Mike. "Let me give you a for-instance. If a patient needs some treatment, or surgery, and there are two or three possible procedures or techniques available, we'll choose the one for which we get the most reimbursement from the insurance companies. That's the kind of thing I mean. We're very aware of such factors, and Tony has made up a reimbursement table to guide us in these decisions. Have you seen it?"

"No, I haven't." Mike wasn't surprised; most medical

practices did the same thing, and medical conferences abounded at which accountants and consultants taught doctors how to extract the most money out of Medicare and insurance plans. He had a feeling that there was more to what Derek was trying to tell him.

"And of course, that's just an example. This is a tough world, Mike, and people have to look out for themselves or they'll get trampled," went on Derek, speaking in a quiet, emphatic voice. "In our group, we're all smart, we're all ambitious, we all want to be rich." Derek took a deep breath. "We work very hard, and we're willing to do whatever it takes to reach our goals." His voice changed. "Which implies, of course, that we all have to share the same philosophy."

Mike waited. Derek seemed to be dancing around whatever he was trying to tell him and wasn't getting to the point.

"Spencer'll explain the rest of it to you," Derek said. "What I'm trying to say is that we're all willing to bend a few rules when we have to." He stood up. "And of course the payoff is a job that brings in seven figures every year."

Mike's eyebrows went up. "Sounds good to me," he said. "Seven figures . . . are you talking net or gross?"

Derek grinned. "Now you're talking our language," he said.

Mike went along to his office and sat down at his desk to think about his conversation with Derek. How many surgical cases would he have to do to justify a seven-figure salary? It seemed almost impossible. There had to be some other source of income—maybe they did outside consulting or some other work. Mike took a deep breath and exhaled slowly. All this continual harping on money was beginning to get on his nerves. Couldn't a doctor be successful *and* put patients' welfare first? he wondered, as Caleb Winter had always instilled into them.

The paperwork had piled up while he was at the hospital taking care of Evie, and he started to go through it. But he felt restless, and thoughts of Stephanie came flooding back into his mind. Finally he picked up the phone, called her office number, and they talked quietly for several minutes.

"Let me make dinner for you tonight," she said.

"Great. What time?"

"Whenever you're through. I'll be home by about six-thirty."

"Seven?"

"I can't wait."

Mike put the phone down just as Spencer walked in. He seemed in a hurry.

"Did you talk to Derek?" he asked Mike.

"Sure did."

"Good. I asked him to explain everything to you. Welcome aboard. Our group meeting is in a couple of days, and we'll make it official then." Spencer looked at his watch. "I'd love to talk some more with you right now, Mike," he said. "But I have a committee meeting starting in five minutes. I have to run.

Again, we're all delighted that you're now a full member."

After Spencer had gone, Mike sat back in his chair and smiled. Spencer certainly knew how to make people feel good. But Mike couldn't get rid of the nagging problems tucked away at the back of his mind: Pauline, Spencer's biopsies, Stephanie's near-catastrophe . . .

He picked up the phone and called Andy Minsky's home. Andy's sister, Annabelle, answered. "Could I come over to talk to Andy and you later this evening?" he asked her.

"Sure. You want to come for dinner?"

"I can't, but would nine o'clock be too late?"

"No problem, Dr. Richmond. See you then."

About five minutes later, George Rankin picked up the phone. "Mr. Hartmann? Rankin here. We've just recorded a couple of conversations from Dr. Richmond's office that you might like to review."

Carl closed the file he was reading. "I'll be right up." A minute later, puffing because he'd hurried up the stairs, Carl listened to the tape replay, and his mouth tightened with surprise and annoyance when he heard Mike's very personal conversation with Stephanie.

"That's your employee Stephanie Hopkins, sir," said Rankin, watching him. "Our equipment can decode the number that's been dialed, and we—"

Carl nodded irritably. "Yes, of course I know who it is, you idiot. She works for me. I know her voice."

After hearing Mike's second call to Andy Minsky, Carl sat down in a chair and stared at Rankin. "Why do you think he's calling Minsky? Why is he going to see him? The guy's a vegetable, right?"

Rankin didn't know. "He could just be sorry for the guy," he suggested. "Maybe just condolences, something like that."

"Yeah . . . maybe." Carl stood up and headed for the door. "All this doesn't prove anything," he said, pointing at the recording equipment. "But keep a closer eye on Richmond."

Carl took the elevator down, wondering if Stephanie was smart enough to go ahead with the suit, maybe split the take afterward with Richmond and live happily ever after. No, he thought, she's not that smart. If she's got a relationship going with Richmond, she'll call Haiman Gold and stop the lawsuit. And if she does that, Carl thought, I'll lose a bundle of money.

Chapter 33

Mike didn't have time to go home before leaving for Stephanie's, so he took a shower in the fully equipped bathroom attached to Spencer's office. It was large and luxurious, with its white ceramic tiles, gold-plated fittings, and thick white Turkish towels and robes. Spencer made it available to all the group members.

Mike hadn't got used to the idea of luxury yet, but he would . . . he scrubbed his skin hard with a washcloth, happy that his body felt as strong and as good as it did.

He'd be having dinner with Stephanie. He could feel himself tense with anticipation, and got dressed quickly. On the way, he stopped at a wine store for a bottle of Pouilly Fuissé.

Stephanie made a romantic little dinner for them, the table set with pale green linen napkins in silver rings, two candles in little crystal holders. She served homemade broccoli soup followed by a Cajun shrimp dish with rice which Mike found delicious—although he would probably have found anything she made delicious. After dinner, he told her that he had to go and talk with Andy Minsky, and explained why.

"Do you want to come?" he asked.

"I'm in this too now," she replied. "Yes, I'd like to come."

"Good. I'll call and tell them I'm bringing you."

When they arrived at the Minskys' home, Annabelle opened the door. Andy wasn't looking well. He was slumped in his chair, and his eyes were bloodshot and red.

"He hasn't been sleeping good," said Annabelle, seeing Mike's glance. "He really misses Pauline a lot, don't you, hon?"

Andy nodded. His eyes filled with tears and he looked away.

Annabelle kissed him on the top of his head. "We didn't have a real funeral," she said. "But we had a memorial service at the funeral home. Andy stayed there the whole time, and it really took it out of him," she said. "Pauline wanted to be cremated, and Andy wasn't too happy about that, but of course that was what we had to do."

Mike and Stephanie sat down on the chintz sofa.

"I'm sorry I couldn't get to the service," said Mike. "I couldn't get away."

Andy grunted something.

"He says now that they killed her," translated Annabelle, sounding embarrassed. "Of course it's just a hunch. There's no proof. The fact is, Andy, everything we *know* suggests that it was a natural death." She threw a glance at her brother as if to tell him not to make that kind of accusation, certainly not in front of a member of the very group he suspected.

"What about the lab tests?" asked Stephanie, turning to Mike. "Did they show anything that didn't fit?"

"No. I only got a quick look at her chart in the autopsy suite, but the ones I saw were about what you'd expect."

"How about the enzyme levels in her blood? Don't they go up with a heart attack?"

"Yes, muscle enzymes leak out of damaged heart cells into the circulation, but it can take several hours before they actually show up in the blood. In Pauline's case, there probably wasn't enough time."

Andy moved in his chair, anger and helplessness showing on his face. He mumbled something. Stephanie, watching, said, "Andy says he should never have allowed them to cremate her."

Mike looked at her in surprise.

"I spent a summer working with kids who had speech impediments," she explained. "Andy's easy." She smiled at him, and Andy managed to grin back, his eyes livening up for the first time that evening. "Andy, that's what Pauline wanted," she said. "You can't blame yourself for that."

"Let's change the topic, shall we?" asked Annabelle, coming back into the living room with a tray. "I'm sure there was something else that Dr. Richmond wanted to talk to us about."

"You're right," said Mike, carefully lifting an over-filled cup off the tray and sipping it. "I've been thinking about Dr. Newsome's plane crash and wondering if maybe it wasn't an accident after all.''

Again Andy said something that to Mike was unintelligible, and Stephanie translated. "When Mrs. Newsome first hired Pauline, Andy told them to find out about that accident . . ." Stephanie asked Andy to repeat the last part of what he'd said, and it took her several tries to get it right. ". . . so they sent for a transcript of the official National Transport Safety Board report. The cause of the crash was the main fuel valve . . . is that right, Andy? Okay, the valve had stuck, and the engine shut down while he was over forested country.''

"I'd still like to see that report," said Mike. "Who could I call about it? Do you have it?''

Andy shook his head irritably. "State.'' he said with surprising clarity.

"The state of Connecticut? They also investigate plane crashes?''

This time Andy nodded.

"I can find out who to talk to," Stephanie put in. "I have a friend who works up in Hartford at the capitol.''

Mike and Stephanie left soon after.

It was a clear, dry night, and the Aston-Martin purred along the highway back toward Stephanie's apartment building. Mike put a hand on her thigh, thinking how smooth and strong and utterly exciting it felt. After a few moments his hand slid gently upward, and he could feel her moving under his hand, and her breathing changed. Then as he approached the traffic lights at Park and Stevens, he had to change gears. He smiled sideways at her. "First time I ever wished this car had an automatic transmission," he said.

Back at the apartment, he helped her put the dishes in the dishwasher and she took a few minutes to tidy the kitchen and dining area. He watched her, admiring her shape and the way she moved, and although neither of them said anything, the excitement was palpable and rising like the mercury in a thermometer. And then, as if they were both participating in a kind of dream, she went over to him, took him by the hand, and led him into the bedroom.

Chapter 34

The next morning Stephanie drove her old Plymouth to work. All she could think about was Mike, the feel of his arms around her, the taste, the smell of him. Still in a contented daze, she left her car in the company parking lot and walked along Elm Street. She felt like skipping.

Since mail still came to her old office, she stopped by to check on it and to see how Jean Forrest was doing.

"How's your friend?" asked Jean, watching Stephanie with her big eyes.

"My friend?" Stephanie stared at Jean for a second. "Oh, Evie Gaskell. She's a lot better, thanks."

"Good. Mr. Hartmann's been here already, looking for you." Jean's voice dropped a little. "He didn't sound too happy. He wants you in his office as soon as you come in."

Carl seemed quite calm when Stephanie came in. "Good," he said. "I've gone over your accounting data for our companies, and it's actually very informative." He looked faintly surprised that a mere woman could do that kind of task efficiently.

"We aim to please," she murmured.

Carl gave her a penetrating look—Stephanie had forgotten that not much got past him unnoticed.

"Anyway, that's not what I called you about," he said. "How did you get along with Haiman Gold?"

"I saw him about a week ago," replied Stephanie carefully. When Mr. Hartmann looked at her like that, she felt like a deer in the beam of a searchlight. "He was very nice."

Mr. Hartmann didn't move; he was obviously not satisfied with her answer.

"He thought that I had a case," she went on quickly. "He told me he'd be doing some more investigation—*discoveries*, I think he called them—checking what I told him, I suppose."

"That's more or less what he told me," said Carl. "He thinks you have a *very* strong case, and he's looking forward to making a lot of money for you."

Stephanie's gaze wavered.

"I'm very glad you've decided to go ahead with it," Carl went on. "For one thing, you owe it to the other women who could have the same thing happen to them."

"Dr. Richmond took care of my best friend in the hospital," ventured Stephanie. "And he was really wonderful. If it hadn't been for him, I'm sure she would have died."

Carl pushed his chair back, and his fingers drummed on the desktop. "That may well be true," he said. "But your suit will put not only Dr. Richmond but also all the other surgeons who do this kind of surgery on notice to be more careful with their workups. Your lawsuit should save many women from undergoing mutilating operations they don't need." Carl stood up and came around the desk. His personality and presence were overwhelming, and Stephanie felt paralyzed. "I'll be following the case with great interest," he said, and now his voice had a peculiar insistence. "You're doing the right thing, Stephanie, and I'm quite sure you'll be successful."

When Stephanie left his office a few moments later, she walked down the corridor toward her own office, her mind in a whirl. Why was he taking such an interest in her lawsuit? And how did he know that she had decided not to go ahead with it? Because he *did* know—she was quite certain of it from the way he'd spoken to her. But the only other person she'd discussed it with was Mike. Suddenly she felt acutely uncomfortable, as if she'd found some stranger going through her private possessions. And now, faced with what was clearly an order from Carl to go ahead with her lawsuit, what was she to do?

During her coffee break, Stephanie called her friend Doreen in Hartford. She wasn't quite sure why, but she decided to make the call from one of the pay phones in the lobby. They chatted briefly, and then Stephanie asked her which government department investigated aircraft accidents.

Doreen thought it was a division of the Department of Transportation, but she wasn't sure. "I'll call you back," she said, and five minutes later, she did.

"It's called the Air Safety Unit," she said. "Actually, it's down to only about five people now, and they say the governor's thinking of disbanding it altogether."

"How can I get their report on an accident?"

"Just ask. It's public information. There's a form . . . actually, if you like, I can get a copy for you and send it. What accident was it?"

Stephanie gave her the few details she had, the pilot's name and the approximate date of the accident.

"Shouldn't be difficult," said Doreen. "We don't have that many. I'll put it in the mail for you."

About the same time next day, Doreen called Stephanie, and her voice was quite different. "What the hell are you up to, girl?" she asked. "I got that file, but there was nothing in it. I asked the head inspector or whatever they call him, and he said that all the reports had been sent to the NTSB in Washington." He also showed me a typed note clipped inside the folder. It said, *Report any inquiries to the governor's office.* The governor! Not just any old head of a department. Jesus, Stephanie . . . anyway, he promised not to mention that I'd asked about it, but you never know with those guys."

"Gee, Doreen, I hope I didn't get you into any trouble," said Stephanie.

"Forget it. But the name of the inspector who investigated the crash was typed on the outside of the file. Alvin P. Zimmerman. He's retired—that's all I can tell you."

"Thanks a bunch, Doreen." Stephanie scribbled the name on her notepad. "Give my regards to the governor."

"If I get fired, you can damn well get me a job in your insurance company."

"Do you think we should tell Mrs. Newsome?" Stephanie asked Mike later that evening. They were back at Andy Minsky's apartment, and she had just reported her conversation with Doreen.

"There's nothing to tell her right now," said Mike, and Andy nodded in agreement.

"Now we just have to find Alvin Zimmerman."

It turned out Alvin P. Zimmerman had been living in the same house for fifteen years. When they called, though, he was reluctant to say anything about his former employment. "I'm finished with that shit," he said. But after Annabelle told him that Andy was a P.I., and mentioned which case they were interested in, he became warily helpful. "I was wondering when somebody would start to ask about that crash," he said. "It's been on my mind for two years."

He agreed to meet with them at his home in Windsor, not far from Hartford, on Saturday morning.

They drove up in two cars in case Mike had to come back to the hospital, and found the house easily enough. It was a modest-sized house of 1930s vintage located in a pleasant part of town, with big trees and quiet shady streets. As they came through the front gate, a big plane came over, low enough for them to see the wheels, on its final approach for the nearby Bradley International Airport.

Alvin Zimmerman must have been watching out for them because the front door opened and he appeared as soon as they started to walk up the short path.

He was a small, round man, and had a shiny round forehead, thin but still dark hair, and bright, attentive dark eyes behind round glasses. He wore a hand-knitted beige woolen vest.

"Come on in," he said to them after they had introduced themselves and shaken hands. "Mildred's making some coffee." He led the way inside. It was dark in the hallway, but the living room was bright, with two big windows leading out to the back yard, which was blooming with zinnias and big, orange-petaled daisies. In the living room, every square inch of the walls and flat surfaces was taken up with photographs and various flying memorabilia, including a shiny chrome model of a Bell Huey Cobra helicopter in the place of honor on a cherrywood table set between the windows.

"Flew them in 'Nam," he replied tersely to Mike's inquiry. "Learned a lot about investigating plane crashes out there."

Once they were all settled, Mike asked Alvin about the crash that had killed Dr. Fred Newsome.

"I kept some notes," replied Alvin. "And I looked them over last night."

Andy pointed at him and grinned.

"He knows that I shouldn't have kept the notes,"

said Alvin, looking at Mike over his glasses. "The rules say that all notes have to be handed in when the official report is made."

"I tried to get that report," said Stephanie. "All I did was get one of my old friends in trouble." She told Alvin what had happened.

Alvin passed a hand over his head. "I'm not surprised," he said. "There's a lot of . . . well . . . okay, let me start at the beginning." He took the coffee mug his wife handed him, and took a noisy sip. "That Saturday, just over two years ago, our office got a call from the state police up in Winsted. A single-engine civilian plane had gone down in wooded country up in the northern part of the state. The pilot had made a mayday call, saying he'd lost all power and couldn't restart his engine. At the time, the weather was cloudy, with rain and some low-lying fog in the valleys. There was an eyewitness, a forestry worker, who heard the motor stop overhead. Then he saw the plane come out of the cloud and bank sharply, as if the pilot was looking for somewhere to land, but it's hilly, wooded country, part of a national forest. He lost sight of it for a few moments, and it must have spun in and hit the ground, because he saw and heard the crash a few seconds later, a mile or so away. The plane exploded on impact, and it took a few hours for the police to find the wreckage. We didn't get there until the next day, and even then we had to borrow a Humvee from the National Guard to get to the site."

Mike asked, "If he was looking for somewhere to

land, it doesn't sound as if he was committing suicide, does it?"

"Who said anything about suicide?" asked Alvin.

"His widow. He'd been very depressed, and she thought it was a possibility."

"No way. Or if that's what he had in mind, he changed it pretty damn quick, otherwise he wouldn't have made a mayday call. Anyway, when we got there, there wasn't much left, which in itself is unusual in a small plane crash. They don't go in as fast as the big jets, and they don't usually explode."

"But this one did?"

"It was more like a bomb than a plane," said Alvin. "And I saw something I'd never seen in all my experience with air crashes. About fifty feet away, there was a hand, a right hand, completely detached, grasping on to a branch, about six feet up. One of the state cops found it and threw up." Alvin's mouth twisted into a grin.

Stephanie made a face, and so did Annabelle. Mildred, Alvin's wife, looked up at the ceiling and sighed.

"How about the rest of the body?" asked Mike.

"Well, there wasn't much left, enough to identify him, but they needed his dental X-rays to do it," replied Alvin.

For the first time he seemed hesitant, and took a long swig from his coffee mug, which, Mike noted, had a colored picture of an P–51 Mustang on the side.

"From what the pilot said in his mayday call, and

from what the eyewitness told us, and he seemed reliable enough," Alvin went on, "there was probably nothing wrong with the control systems, and the problem lay with the engine, the electrical system, or, more likely, with the fuel supply. We were working with the wreckage, trying to gather up bits that would help us, and later that day the NTSB boys came along. They were led by a young kid"—Alvin's nose wrinkled with contempt—"fresh out of engineering school. Lehigh, he told me, and so he figured he knew everything."

Mike glanced over at Stephanie, who was listening with her head slightly to one side. She was wearing a gray dress and the hem came up above her knees. Mike forced his mind back to the crash.

"Anyway, they pretty well took over . . ."

"I always heard the NTSB investigators were pretty good," murmured Mike. "They usually seem to figure out what causes crashes."

"What's NTSB?" asked Stephanie.

"National Transportation Safety Board," replied Alvin. "Yes, they are good, but they're underfunded, understaffed, and a lot of times overextended. You probably don't remember, but in the week before this accident, there had been two commercial aircraft crashes, a Boeing 737 near Chicago and the other in Georgia, an old Lockheed Electra that hit an elementary school a mile from the end of the runway. It's that kind of situation they send their senior people to. For the little private plane crashes, well, unless it's somebody very important, they send out whoever's left. Anyway, we'd found a piece of a fuel line attached to a bent fuel selector valve, and this kid examined it and decided that the valve had stuck while in flight, starved the engine, which had cut out, and that was that. Tidy end of case." Alvin shrugged. "Actually, he wasn't being that stupid. There wasn't much else to go on, since most of the plane had been fragmented or burned or both."

"Is that what was in the official report?" Mike asked. "I remember Mrs. Newsome told us she got a copy."

"That was the NTSB report," corrected Alvin. "The State Air Safety Unit puts in its own reports for accidents within the state boundaries, or at least it did while I was there. Anyway, at this site one of my people found something on a rock about forty feet away from the impact. I happened to be near him, and he mentioned it so I came over to look. It was only a small blob of jellylike stuff, partially burned like everything else, and the guy was embarrassed that he'd even mentioned it, but I picked it up and showed it to the boy engineer. He barely glanced at it. 'That's just heat-congealed lubricating oil,' he said, and went back to examining his stuck valve."

Alvin held out his mug to his wife for a refill. "But that wasn't heat-congealed lubricating oil," he continued, in a tone of exasperated calm. "There's no such thing. But that was where my experience helped. I'd been in Vietnam, and flown hundreds of medevac missions, and I knew what that blob was. I'd smelled it on enough bodies . . . it was napalm."

Mike's mouth opened in disbelief. "You're saying a napalm bomb blew up in his plane?"

"No," said Alvin, after taking a sip from his refilled mug. "Not at all. What happened was that somebody turned his plane into a napalm bomb."

The silence in the room was electric.

Alvin put his mug down on the table. "It's very simple," he said. "Napalm is a combination of napthenic and palmitic acids together with aluminum hydroxide. If you add this to gasoline in the correct proportions, it makes a gel. So, for example, if you put it in a fuel tank, it'll turn the gasoline inside into a kind of jelly, and of course it won't pass through the fuel lines."

"But wouldn't Dr. Newsome have found that when he first started the engine?" asked Mike. "I don't see how he could even get down the runway if his fuel lines were clogged up with napalm gel."

"In this type of aircraft, there are two fuel tanks," explained Alvin. "One in the root of each wing. What probably happened is that the pilot started off in the normal way, using the main right tank, and, after flying for a while, changed over to the secondary tank, the left one. He would have done that to balance the aircraft, not because the main tank was empty. If the napalm had been added to the secondary tank, the gel would then be sucked into the fuel lines and block them. At that point he would lose all power and the plane would crash."

"You mentioned earlier that in this kind of crash, the plane doesn't usually explode." Annabelle, sitting next to Andy, seemed to be reading her brother's thoughts. Andy grinned appreciatively over at her.

Alvin seemed to ignore the question. "A strange thing happened, though," he said. "That blob of napalm—I put it in a container and sent it in with the report. Somehow it got lost."

A long, drawn-out sigh came from Andy.

"But like I told you," went on Alvin, "I'd had a funny feeling about this crash, so I didn't send in the entire blob. I kept a small sample, just in case. So when I heard the main specimen was lost, I got a friend who works in a forensic lab in Hartford to analyze what I'd kept. It was napalm, all right, but in addition he found traces of sodium nitrate and minute fragments of powered magnesium mixed up in it." Alvin looked around at them. "It was those additives that turned the Cessna into a bomb."

"So what do you think?" asked Stephanie, once they were back in the Aston-Martin and driving back to New Coventry. Mike was trying to fit what he'd just heard into all the other stuff he knew, and it was forming a rather scary picture.

"Right now the thing that bothers me is why was Alvin Zimmerman's report suppressed, and the NTSB one accepted?" said Mike. "And who suppressed it?"

"Do you think if Spencer was involved he would have enough clout to do that? Suppress the report?" she asked.

"I don't know, but I don't think so," Mike replied,

remembering that Spencer had operated on Florence, Governor DiGiovanni's wife. "But I don't see how that could happen at any level in the state government, do you?"

Stephanie smiled at him.

"Come on, Stephanie, even if your best buddy was the head of that department, you couldn't go up to him and say, 'Hey, I just blew somebody away in a plane, and I don't want any embarrassing disclosures, so just make the report disappear, okay?' "

"Well, somebody made it disappear. Unless it was the good people at the NTSB. Maybe they didn't like the idea of a state accident report that didn't agree with theirs."

"I suppose so." Mike shook his head. "But what I want to know is: why would anyone want to kill off Fred Newsome in the first place?"

Chapter 35

The next afternoon, just before five, Mike was summoned to a meeting of the group in the conference room. They had obviously been there for a while, and Tony was present also, separated from the others by an empty chair. On the table in front of him was a black box, about the size of a portable CD player, attached by a wire to something that looked like a microphone.

"Come in, Michael, come in," said Spencer, smiling affably. "I suppose your ears are burning. We've been talking about you."

As Mike came in, Derek, near the end of the table, pulled out a chair for him.

"Just one moment before you sit down, Dr. Richmond," said Tony. He pressed a button on the black box, and a red light went on. Then he pointed the wand at Mike. The machine made a high-pitched whistle, and after a second the light turned green.

"Thank you, Dr. Richmond." Tony's tone was neutral.

"What was that?" Mike asked him. "You think I'm carrying a bomb?"

"We don't allow any kind of recording apparatus at our meetings," replied Tony. "I was just checking."

Spencer didn't waste any time. "Mike, when you joined us we decided to give both you and the group a six-month probation period, during which we would see if we liked each other. Now, I'm not saying there haven't been problems." He paused, his hands on the table. "In fact, I'm sure you know that the unfortunate business with Miss Hopkins came close to bringing our relationship to an end. But we were able to put that particular fire out."

Mike listened carefully, but Spencer was smiling benignly at him. "Anyway, as I said, you've been doing great work otherwise. And so, Michael, in view of what we've seen, and I can tell you we've all been watching you carefully, we've unanimously decided to bring you on board as a full member as of today." Spencer paused for a second, watching Mike's face. "We're assuming, of course, that you're still interested."

Mike nodded, wondering what was coming.

"In that case, Michael, we all congratulate you on having joined the finest medical group in New Coventry."

The others clapped discreetly. They were all watching him, but with tense expressions that didn't quite seem to match the occasion.

Spencer's voice became conversational, almost confidential. "To be quite honest with you, Mike," he said, "one of the reasons we want to make you a full member is that we don't like having secrets in the group. They make us uncomfortable." He looked around the table at the others. "And as long as you weren't a full member, we necessarily had to keep certain business aspects of our operation from you."

Again there was a pause, as if Spencer were mentally checking on the progress of each phase of the conversation.

"Now, what we discuss at these meetings is confidential information, and I want to have your word of honor that you won't discuss what you hear with anyone, now or at any other time. We've all given our word to maintain this confidentiality. So, Michael, if you have any problem with that, now is the time to tell us."

"No problem."

"One of the benefits of having been around a long time is that we hear about everything that goes on," went on Spencer. "Isn't that right, gentlemen?" His gaze fixed unwaveringly on Mike. "Well, of course when I heard that you'd been doing a little research in the hospital records department, that bothered me. It bothered all of us, actually, but it was beneficial in that it showed us that we had a problem that urgently needed to be dealt with."

Derek, his arm draped along the back of the chair, lightly tapped Mike's shoulder in a friendly way, but Mike felt a sudden sweat on his brow and hoped it didn't show.

"So now that you're a full member, Michael, you won't have to try to find things out on your own.

We'll tell you whatever you need to know. Now, to go on to a more interesting topic, for a start, your annual income will rise by a factor of about four, assuming that your present work load will increase to match that of the rest of us . . ."

"What he's saying, Mike, is that you'll finally be able to get the brakes fixed on that old car of yours," said Derek, grinning, but Spencer's expression showed that his comment was out of place.

"Of course, a good part of that money will be placed in a separate escrow account to purchase shares in our corporation," went on Spencer. "But unlike with some other groups, you will be fully vested after you've been with the group for five years, after which time your entire salary will be yours to spend on car brakes . . . or whatever you wish." Spencer glanced reprovingly at Derek. "Most of our major investments are managed by a bank in the Channel Islands, for tax and privacy reasons," he went on. "Your escrow account will be handled in exactly the same way, and hopefully will increase as impressively as ours has."

"Tell him about the other stuff, Spencer," said Derek, with a touch of impatience.

"I was about to do that," said Spencer. "As you must already have figured, Mike, the amounts of money that we've been talking about are substantially more than the average member of a med-surg group could expect to make. And that is because of the way that we're organized."

Spencer took a deep breath. "We're part of a larger

organization that includes other professional groups," he went on, his voice carefully modulated. "These groups were selected for maximum benefit to all of us. We help them and they help us; for instance, as you have probably figured out already, we have a preferential arrangement with the Lovejoy Hospital. They send us patients and we help to keep their beds full." Spencer gripped the edge of the table; for the first time he seemed a little unsure of himself, but he went on. "And, of course, we have a relationship with the Radiology Associates downstairs, with ConnPath, and a group of attorneys who work in this town. Tony here is the one who coordinates us, and keeps us on the straight and narrow path. . . ."

". . . to the bank," said Tony. He didn't smile, and it occurred to Mike that perhaps he hadn't meant to be funny. His pale gaze was still fixed on Mike from the other side of the table, still unsmiling, assessing him, evaluating his responses. Suddenly Mike knew why he was there. Tony kept everybody in line; he was the enforcer. His job as office manager was secondary. Mike suddenly realized that it was already too late for him to get up, say, "No thanks, guys," and walk away. He felt the palms of his hands starting to sweat, and slid them down the sides of his thighs.

Spencer had finished, apparently, because Lou Gardner was now talking. "Now you're a full member, Mike, I have a case that I'd like you to operate on. She is a forty-five-year-old woman, Mary Culbertson, who has a positive barium enema, and a biopsy-proved cancer of the sigmoid colon. She's in the hospital right now. For the next forty-eight hours she'll be getting enemas to clean her out, and I took the liberty of scheduling her for you on Thursday. She'll be your first case."

There was a tight silence, and everybody watched Mike.

He pushed back his chair, just a little, and took his little black book from his pocket. "Mary Culbertson," he said, writing her name down. Then he looked up. "I'll be happy to take care of her."

Everybody stood up as if some strange rite of passage had been completed, and gathered around Mike to shake his hand and welcome him into the group.

A few minutes later, when everybody was leaving, Spencer put a hand on Mike's shoulder, and said quietly, "Michael, could you stick around for a moment after the others are gone?"

When only Spencer and Tony remained, Spencer said, "Michael, I didn't want to tell you this in front of everyone, but this morning I got a call from Raymond Avery at the Connecticut State Medical Society. Somehow they got wind of the Stephanie Hopkins case, and they're on the warpath. Ray told me that they're going to after your license."

Mike said nothing. He felt a tightness spreading across his chest. an old pal of mine," went on Spencer.

"Luckily and so I think we'll be able to take care cer easi did think you should know."

of it

"Thanks," said Mike. "I appreciate it."

"One more thing, Michael," said Spencer. "As you know, we all have malpractice suits against us, so we've had to develop a policy to deal with them. One of the key aspects of this policy is that we don't have any personal contact with the plaintiffs. We're very strict about that rule, aren't we, Tony?"

Tony was staring at Mike with his cold eyes, bouncing very slightly up and down on the balls of his feet, as if he were measuring up an opponent. "Yes, sir." he said slowly, not taking his eyes off Mike. "We certainly are."

Mike thought for a moment. "Spencer, I see your point. I'll take care of it."

"Good. I knew I could rely on your good sense. It'll work in your favor in the long run, you can be sure of that. Right, Tony?"

"Without question," replied Tony. He had a lot of very white teeth, and Mike had a disconcerting vision of them closing on his neck veins.

"Well, I'd better go and see my new patient," said Mike.

"Good luck with her on Thursday," replied Spencer, putting a friendly hand on Mike's arm.

After Mike left, Tony went to the door and closed it softly.

"So what do you think, Tony?" asked Spencer when he came back.

"I don't entirely trust him," replied Tony. "But his options are limited. He realizes that. But if he decides not to go along he'll lose everything He's not stupid, and this is what I think he'll do. He'll think the whole situation over tonight, find himself another girlfriend, operate on that woman on Thursday, and from then on, of course, he belongs to us."

"And if he doesn't?"

Tony smiled, and again he bounced gently up and down on the balls of his feet. "I almost hope he doesn't, Dr. Spencer."

Chapter 36

Mike left the conference room and went back to his office. He switched his computer on to review the history and test reports on Mary Culbertson. It was all there, X-rays and the biopsy report, including slides of the pathology specimen. It was a cancer, without question, an invasive tumor of moderate to high malignancy. He sat looking at the slides for several minutes, scrolling to examine every part of it. Then as he stared at a particular cluster of cancer cells in the top left-hand corner, examining their irregular black-stained nuclei, something stirred in his brain, a faint blip in his memory circuits. He'd seen that slide somewhere before . . . he sat back and thought. *Darla Finsten, the O.R. supervisor.* He'd seen her slides on Derek's computer. It took him a few moments to find her file, then he flashed the slides on the screen. They weren't quite identical but showed sections of what was clearly the same tumor. Mike nodded to himself. Now he understood how that part of the scam functioned. The pathologists could take hundreds of slides from a single tumor, then label them at will.

Mike turned off the computer, and a hard knot formed in his stomach. He had really fooled himself into thinking that he could work with this group, do an honest job, and not get involved in what they were doing.

He took the stairs down and walked over to the hospital. In the main corridor, he saw two men pushing a large trolley loaded with equipment. One of them glanced at him, and they recognized each other simultaneously.

"Zeke! How the hell are you, man?"

"Shit, if it isn't Mike Richmond!" Zeke, a heavily built, muscular black man, stopped the trolley and shook hands with Mike, then wiped his sweating face with his arm. "That sucker's heavy." He turned to his partner, standing by the trolley. "Hey, Bob, come and meet an old fellow worker, Mike Richmond. He used to install units with us when he was in med school."

"What are you guys doing?" He hadn't seen Zeke for ten years, and he hadn't changed much.

"We're putting in one of the new MRI scanners," replied Zeke. "Like the one you almost got killed with, except bigger and newer." Zeke told Bob about Mike's accident. "We thought he was a goner," he said. "Mike, show him your scar."

Mike grinned and stuck out his hand so that Bob could examine the back of his hand.

"Zeke, how long will you be around?"

"Couple of weeks. Right now we're putting in the

power supply and the generator. We'll bring the actual scanner in next week."

Mike arranged to meet them at Aileen's Bar for a drink the next evening, then headed up to the medical floor, where Mary Culbertson was located. At the nurses desk, he pulled the chart and read the clinical history. Mary was married, with two teenage children, didn't work outside the home, was quite healthy apart from some minor arthritis. She had first noted a little rectal bleeding a couple of months before. Copies of the test reports were pasted neatly in the chart.

Mike thought for a moment, replaced the chart, then asked the nurse to come with him. As they walked down the corridor, she asked how Evie Gaskell was doing. Evie was home already, he told her, and should be coming back to work in a week or so.

Mary Culbertson smiled at Mike when he came in. "I've been hearing all about you," she said, sitting up. She was wearing a lacy blue nightie with a little bow on the front, and reminded Mike a little of his mother. "Everybody says you're the nicest surgeon in the hospital," she said to him. "And Dr. Gardner says you're one of the best. I'm glad to meet you."

"I have to pay a lot to get people to say things like that," he replied, smiling back at her. He sat down on the edge of the bed. "So tell me what's been the matter with you," he said. "Dr. Gardner told me a bit about the problem, but I'd like to hear it from you."

"Straight from the old horse's mouth, is that what

you mean?'' She had plump little dimples in her cheeks when she smiled. She seemed so secure and comfortable, Mike could visualize her at home with her family. "Well, as I told Dr. Gardner, I've never had anything wrong with me except this darned arthritis . . ." She held up her hands, and Mike saw the swelling around her knuckles. "Anyway, aside from that, about a month ago I noticed that my bowel movements were dark, almost black sometimes. Then one day there was a little red color, and I got scared, thinking it looked like blood. I told Bob, that's my husband, and he said of course to get it checked. And so I did, and here I am, a whole lot of tests later."

Mike asked about her family history, about her diet, then asked, "By the way, Mary, do you take any medication?"

"Only for my arthritis," she said.

"And what do you take for that?"

"Aspirin. It bothers my stomach a little bit," she went on, "but it takes the pain out of my joints better than anything else I've tried."

Mike nodded. Aspirin could cause intestinal bleeding in otherwise normal people.

Mike examined Mary carefully, then did a rectal exam.

"I'm sure Dr. Gardner told you the surgery is scheduled for Thursday, Mary," he told her, pulling off the glove. "Your bowel has to be clean as a whistle for this kind of surgery; otherwise you can get a really serious infection."

On the clinical order form he checked Lou Gardner's prescription, a program of enemas and cathartics, to start that evening. It was just what he would have prescribed himself.

"Now, about the operation," he went on, sitting down on the side of the bed and taking out his notebook. "This is the large intestine," he said, drawing two curved, parallel lines, "and the tumor is . . . here. What we'll do is remove this section and join the two ends together. No very big deal," he went on, smiling at her. "Just a bit of plumbing."

He told her about what she could expect after the operation, about the tube in her stomach, how she could deal with the pain by self-injection, and how long it would take before she could eat again.

Then he went back to the desk and paged Lou Gardner. The phone rang a moment later. "Lou? I saw your Mrs. Culbertson, and I agree with your diagnosis," he said. "I agree that her bowel needs to be prepped, and agree with the enemas and cathartics you ordered for her, so we should be good and ready by Thursday."

"Great, Mike," replied Lou. "I'm sure everything will go well. And by the way, welcome to the group. It's good to have you on board."

"Thanks, Lou. My pleasure."

Mike walked back along the corridor, wondering how he could get out of operating on Mrs. Culbertson, when he saw Florence DiGiovanni, the governor's wife, going into a patient's room just ahead of him. She stopped and greeted him like an old friend.

Mike asked what she was doing in the hospital.

"I'm visiting a neighbor," she replied. "Dr. Spencer's operating on her tomorrow. She's a sweet woman, and very scared. Her name's Ursula Martin. Come in and meet her."

Mike followed her into the room. Ursula was in her early forties, delicate-looking, and quite obviously frightened to death.

Mike chatted with them briefly, trying to sound reassuring, but when he looked at Ursula's pale face, right then he made up his mind, and turned to Florence. "Mrs. DiGiovanni," he said, "could I talk to you outside for a moment?"

In the corridor, Mike faced her and blurted out, "Mrs. DiGiovanni, you cannot let Ursula be operated on tomorrow."

Florence stared at him, astonished. "And why ever not?"

Mike told her about Spencer's breast biopsies, and how most of these women finished up with a mastectomy, whether they had cancer or not.

"I just can't believe it," she said, shocked, when he'd finished. "Do you have proof?"

"Yes." Mike suddenly felt apprehensive, and unsure if he was doing the right thing, but he went on. "There are hospital documents that can be subpoenaed, and people who would testify if they had to."

A determined look came into Florence's face. "I'm going to tell Jack about this, and he can take it from this point," she said. "Please stay home tonight—Jack or one of his people will call you. If not, call me at this number . . ." She took a pen out of her purse and scribbled a number on a piece of paper, then turned quickly back to Ursula's room.

Later, back in his apartment, he picked up the phone and listened to the dial tone. It sounded normal. Then he dialed Stephanie's number. Still no clicks or anything to suggest that there was a tap on the line, but he wasn't taking any more chances.

"Stephanie?" His voice sounded a little strained. "Listen, Stephanie . . . there's something I need to tell you. No, not over the phone."

"Is something the matter?" she asked. He could hear the sudden concern in her voice. "You sound very strange."

"Well, yes, sort of," he said in the same tone. "Look, can I stop by for a few minutes?"

"Now?"

"Yes, if that's convenient."

"*Convenient?* Yes, Mike, it's convenient. But what—"

"I'll see you in ten minutes, then, okay?" He hung up before she could reply.

Ten minutes later, she opened the door for him, looking very attractive in a pretty white dress with diagonal blue stripes and buttons all the way down.

"You sounded weird, Mike," she said, closing the door behind him. "What was that phone call about?"

He kissed her, then they sat down on the sofa, and he told her about his meeting with Spencer and the group.

"First they made me a full member of the group," he said, "with an income so high the space shuttle wouldn't reach it. And then they set me up to do a cancer operation on a lady who just needs to stop taking aspirin."

"My God . . . Mike, all this is really frightening. How long do you think this has been going on? How many patients have been put through this?"

"A couple of years, anyway, and a few hundred patients, I would guess."

Stephanie shivered. "You know, I remember Dr. Spencer from when I worked in the I.C.U. He was so nice, and took such good care of his patients . . ." She stood up. "Mike, I think we should call the police."

Mike shook his head, remembering what Laura Newsome had said. "Spencer has a long reach, and so does Carl Hartmann. They'd hear about it within minutes, and we'd be in deeper trouble than ever."

"Then I'm going to call Evie to get her brother's number. You met him, remember?"

Mike nodded. "Evan. I remember him in the I.C.U. Quiet guy, didn't say much."

"Evie thinks he's a pain in the butt, but I like him okay. Anyway, he's some kind of agent with the FBI, and that's why I think we should talk to him."

Evie was home. "I'll have him call you," she told Stephanie. "I know he's home because I just talked to him." Evie was obviously burning with curiosity. "What's going on, Stephanie?"

"I'll tell you later. Ask him to call me *now*, okay?"

Less that a minute later, Evan called. "Couldn't this wait until tomorrow?" he asked, after Stephanie had outlined the problem.

"Evan, I'd really appreciate it if we could talk to

you tonight." She glanced at Mike, who was saying something to her. "We're going over to Mike's apartment," she went on. "Have you eaten? No, we haven't either. We'll pick up a pizza for the three of us on the way over."

When Evan arrived, still in his dark work suit and blue tie, Stephanie kissed him on the cheek. He shook hands with Mike. "Thanks for taking care of Evie," he said. "She thinks you walk on water."

"My pleasure. Evie's a great person." Mike said. "Would you like a beer?"

"Yes, thanks, I could use one." Evan's normally serious expression changed to a grin. "And that pizza sure smells good."

A few minutes later, they sat down around the coffee table, Mike and Stephanie on the sofa and Evan on the easy chair, the pizza between them in its open box.

"I put it in the oven to warm up," said Stephanie. "I hope it doesn't taste of cardboard."

"So what's up?" asked Evan, folding a slice of pizza lengthwise. He had the same blue eyes as Evie, but his expression was a lot tougher.

Mike cleared his throat. "Okay, let's start at the beginning . . ." He told Evan about Stephanie's near miss, the second pathology report, and how practically all Spencer's breast biopsies resulted in mastectomies. Evan seemed to have some difficulty following the clinical material, but he perked up when Mike told him about Pauline and how she'd died in a way that wasn't typical of a heart attack.

"Did they do an autopsy?"

"Yes. The report said that she'd died of a heart attack."

Evan stopped eating and stared at Mike. "Doesn't that answer your question?"

"No. The pathologists are a part of the group, and I think they falsified the report, although I can't prove it. And she was cremated," he added, "which doesn't help."

"What's the name of this pathologist?" he asked, but already he seemed to be losing interest.

"Eric Tarvel. His partner's name is Marilyn Fox."

Evan wrote the names down in his diary. "What else?"

Mike told him about Dr. Newsome's plane crash, and about their visit with Alvin Zimmerman, the state investigator, who told them about the napalm, and how his report had been suppressed.

Evan nodded, and thought for a moment. "Yeah. In this kind of case, Mike, a federal agency report would always take priority over a state one," he said. "This would be the governor's call, and I don't see him or any governor of any state, for that matter, challenging the NTSB. My guess is that nobody wanted that kind of confrontation, so the governor bagged his own guys' report. I heard they're disbanding that unit, anyway."

"Come on, Evan!" said Stephanie, alarmed at the way the discussion was going. "Somebody turned that plane into a bomb!"

"Stephanie, the NTSB has a rep as one of the best federal units around. They're better funded, better equipped and have better engineers than any of the state investigators. If the NTSB says it was a blocked fuel valve, or whatever, in the minds of most people that's what it was, and nothing some state investigator's going to say will make any difference. What's more, nobody's going to want to reopen the case.''

"I just thought of something,'' said Mike suddenly. "Coming back to Pauline. When a patient's brought in to the emergency room, they draw blood, some for the lab, but a tube also goes to the blood bank in case they ever need a transfusion. The blood bank doesn't belong to the lab, and Tarvel doesn't have any control over it. That tube could still be there, in their freezer, and if she was drugged or poisoned or anything, it would show up in the specimen.'' Mike stood up in his excitement.

"Could you get that tube? If it's there?'' Evan evidently didn't think this was much of a breakthrough.

"They wouldn't give it to me, but *you* could get it, I suppose.''

Evan made another note, then he stood up. "Okay, guys,'' he said. "I'll look into what you've told me, but quite honestly, unless something more definite comes up, I don't think it's going to go anywhere.''

Evan was leaving when the phone finally rang, but it wasn't the governor's office. The call was from a Dr. Raymond Avery, who, he said, was the secretary of the New Coventry Medical Society. "We'd like to talk to you about one of your cases, Dr. Richmond . . . let's see . . .'' Mike could hear the rustling of papers. "That would be on a Stephanie Hopkins. We've received information that this case was seriously mishandled, and that legal action has already been taken against you. We'd like to hear your side of the story, Dr. Richmond, if you could come to our offices on Oak Street tomorrow and tell us about it. That would be at ten o'clock tomorrow, Wednesday morning. Now, we have a long schedule, so please be there on time, and bring the patient's office chart, X-rays, lab reports and any other relevant material with you."

Mike thought about his schedule. There was nothing he couldn't postpone for a day. "Okay," he said slowly. "I'll be there."

"Good. Dr. Richmond, I want you to know that this may be your only opportunity to discuss this in an informal way with your peers. I strongly advise you not to miss it."

An hour earlier, Carl Hartmann, working late at the office, took a phone call from Hartford which left him breathless and coldly angry. He summoned Spencer, Tony, and George Rankin to an emergency meeting in his office. He also called Lou Gardner in. "We have a major problem," he said, "that concerns Dr. Richmond. I know you were against his joining the group, so you'd better come too."

"I'd like to bring Dr. Catlin in also," replied Lou quickly. "You remember he's Bruce Catlin's son, and he knows the score. He could be very helpful."

"Okay," replied Carl after a moment. "Just get yourselves over here as soon as possible."

The group assembled; first, Tony, who came in with George Rankin, then Spencer, looking scared and concerned, and finally Lou and Catlin.

"I've just had some very bad news," said Carl grimly. He told them about the governor's phone call. "It's now clear that Mike Richmond is trying to sabotage us. There's been no actual damage done so far, not that I know of, so what we have is a containment problem."

"I can't believe it," said Spencer in a bewildered tone. "We all talked to him this afternoon, brought him on board as a full partner, he got a huge raise . . ."

"You'd better believe it," snapped Carl. "Our problem now is what to do about it." He glanced at the group. "If it comes to the point of Richmond making allegations against us, our best defense at the present time is to destroy his credibility," he went on. He turned to Spencer. "First, you're going to call your friends at the Medical Society and get their investigation started into the Hopkins situation. Yes, tonight, as soon as we're through here. That'll be a start, and then . . ." He went on to detail his plan.

As soon as the meeting was over, Spencer made his phone call to Dr. Avery, and the group dispersed. Terry Catlin thought Carl wasn't going far enough and said as much to Lou.

"My dad always says go for the jugular," he told him once they were outside. Lou had noticed that Terry had a slight twitch in his left eye when he was excited, and it was twitching now. "He wouldn't waste time fooling with Richmond's career or credibility," Terry went on in a low, passionate voice. "He'd blow away a guy like him without mercy."

Chapter 37

The next morning, Mike woke late, and jumped out of bed when he remembered his ten o'clock appointment with Dr. Avery at the Medical Society. He called in to his office, but there were no messages for him, and he went to do rounds at the hospital. At nine-fifteen he stopped in the office to pick up a copy of Stephanie's chart. The only person he saw there was Derek, who gave him what seemed like a rather chilly hello.

He went back to his car and checked his watch. Oak Street, where the Medical Society had its offices, was on the other side of town, and the quickest way there was to get on I–95 and off at the Oak Street exit. Mike didn't notice a large gray Ford Crown Victoria leave the curb and follow him. In fact, he didn't notice it until several minutes later, when he turned onto the ramp leading up to I–95. The car came up behind him, and once they were on the interstate, switched on flashing red lights tucked away behind the radiator grill.

Mike pulled over, and the car stopped right behind him. In his rearview mirror Mike could see two cops in the car. The driver, in a state police uniform, got out of his vehicle in a leisurely way, and came up to the driver's side of Mike's car. "I'd like to see your license and registration, please, sir," he said with gritty politeness, watching Mike with an unfriendly eye.

"Did I do something wrong?" asked Mike.

"Your brake lights aren't working. License and registration, please, sir," repeated the cop.

Mike had the papers behind the sun visor. He reached up and handed them over. The driver went back to his car, to check his onboard computer, or so Mike assumed. He looked at his watch. Five minutes passed. Watching in his rearview mirror, nothing seemed to be happening. He turned the ignition key and pushed hard on the brake pedal while looking in the rearview mirror. He could see both brake lights reflected in the grille of the police car, and they went off when he took his foot off the brake. Then Mike got out of his car, and as soon as the door was closed, the driver came out again, fast. "Put your hands on the side of the car, sir, please, and spread your legs," he said in a clipped tone that dared Mike to resist.

Slowly, Mike did as he was told, wondering what was going on. The cop frisked him, didn't seem surprised that he found nothing, then said, "Sir, we'd like to take a look inside your car, please."

Mike knew that if he refused, as was his right, he'd have to go down to the state police headquarters, and it would all take a lot of time.

"Look, Officer," he said, "I'm a doctor at Lovejoy

Hospital, and I have to be at a meeting on Oak Street in twenty minutes. There's nothing in my car that could possibly interest you." Mike knew that cops usually took it easy on doctors, maybe because they so often worked with them in emergency rooms.

"Sir," he repeated, "we'd like to inspect your car, please."

Out of the corner of his eye, Mike saw the second cop, a big, grizzled, slow-moving man who looked to be in his fifties, clamber out of the car and stand by it, watching them.

"Go ahead," said Mike. "Then can I go?"

"Step away from the vehicle, please, sir. Five paces."

Mike moved back on the wide shoulder. The traffic was slow, and he could see the drivers staring at him as they passed.

The cop opened the door and reached into the back. After a few moments, he came out and signaled to his partner to join him. The second cop ambled over without even glancing at Mike.

They consulted for a moment, then the driver came over to Mike, holding in his hand several glassine bags containing white powder. He held them up. "We found these in the back of your vehicle, sir," he said. "Do they belong to you?"

"No, and I've never seen them before, as you very well know," replied Mike.

"Are you saying I put them there? Sir?" There was a barely controlled aggressiveness that made Mike narrow his eyes. He'd met people like that on the football field. They were dangerous opponents, always spoiling for a fight.

"I'm not saying that. You asked if they belonged to me, and I said no, they don't, and they weren't in my car five minutes ago."

The second cop came over to join them, leaving Mike's car door open. Mike could see the dark patches of sweat under the man's armpits.

"This man just offered me five hundred dollars to forget about this," said the first cop to his buddy, indicating the glassine bags. He turned back to Mike. "Would you please repeat that offer in front of Officer Pinelli?"

"I said nothing of the sort," said Mike. "And my brake lights are working. You have no right to stop me, and I'd like to see your identification, please." Mike had heard of several cases in the last year where people had been stopped on I–95 by robbers masquerading as police officers.

Slowly, keeping his eyes fixed on Mike's, the driver took his wallet from his pocket and gave Mike a glimpse of a metal badge inside it.

"I didn't have time to see it," said Mike, keeping his anger under tight control. He had been set up, both these men were in on it, and he was also going to be late for his meeting at the Medical Society. But it obviously wasn't a shakedown for money.

"We're arresting you for possession of a controlled substance," said the driver. Mike dimly heard the standard recitation of his Miranda rights. "Put your hands together behind you, sir." In total disbelief

Mike heard the second cop click the cuffs behind him. At this range he could smell the sour sweat on the man.

"This is crazy," said Mike, getting more and more furious, and now helpless with his hands cuffed behind him. "What about my car?" he asked as they walked him to the police cruiser.

"We'll call a tow truck for it," said the driver.

It wasn't easy getting into the back of their car with handcuffs, and the older cop put a hand on Mike's head as he backed in. A moment later they drove off, and Mike caught a glimpse of his beautiful Aston-Martin standing forlornly on the shoulder, the driver's door still open. He hoped that the tow-truck operator would treat it with care.

Fifteen minutes later, they arrived at the state police barracks in Bridgeport, just off I–95, and he was led in to the bleak receiving area where he was duly charged. Mike noted some tension between the cops who had brought him in and the desk sergeant.

"You guys again," said the sergeant, looking at them with unfriendly blue eyes. "What is it this time?"

"Possession," said the driver.

The sergeant shrugged. "Yeah," he said.

Mike spent the next hour being charged not only with being in possession of controlled substances, but also with attempting to bribe a police officer. Again he was told his rights, then taken down a corridor where a young woman fingerprinted him. He was told to take everything out of his pockets, and the contents were placed in a large brown bag and labeled. He was given a receipt for the bag and taken back to the holding cell.

When he was finally allowed to make a phone call, his first instinct was to call Stephanie, but instead he phoned Derek.

"I was supposed to be at the Medical Society offices at ten," he told him, after explaining what had happened. "Could you give them a call and explain that I couldn't make it?"

"I'll do that," said Derek in a strange voice. "Look, Mike, I shouldn't be telling you this, but what you need right now is a lawyer. Where are you?"

"The state police barracks, Troop G, down in Bridgeport. It's just off I–95."

"Okay. I'll call Del Visic, if I can reach him. He's good, and he'll have you out of there real soon."

Still shaken, but slightly reassured, Mike was escorted back to the holding area. Sure enough, within a few minutes, attorney Del Visic called, and spoke briefly to Mike.

"Don't tell them anything," said Del, in a voice that sounded as if it had said the same thing a thousand times. "Don't answer any questions, just your name, Social Security number, and your address. And don't volunteer any information, either. As soon as you're out of there, come to my office. It's at 1001 Elm Street, just opposite your building. Now let me talk to the desk sergeant."

Sure enough, ten minutes later, an officer told Mike that he was free on bail.

"Where can I pick up my car?" he asked as he retrieved the brown paper bag with his belongings.

"At the Acme towing garage on Warwick Street," the officer at the desk told him, without looking up. "You'll need your I.D., and there's a fifty-dollar towing fee. And here's your envelope with your possessions."

Feeling shaken, angry, but relieved, Mike reached into the envelope, pulled out some change, went to the row of public phones, dialed Stephanie's office number and asked her to pick him up. "As soon as you can," he said. "I'm at the Bridgeport police barracks. I'll explain everything when you get here."

He put the phone down and, on impulse, took the paper with Florence DiGiovanni's number out of his wallet and dialed it.

She answered, and he heard her sharp intake of breath. "Why are you calling me?" she asked in a brittle, hard tone.

"I didn't hear from the governor's office yesterday," he replied, surprised at the hostility in her voice. "I wondered—"

"I told Jack what you told me," she interrupted. "And he immediately made some inquiries. He found out that *you* are the one who's been doing unnecessary surgery, and that you're into other bad things too. I'm disgusted with you, and disgusted with myself for believing in you. Don't ever call me here again."

Chapter 38

Thirty-two minutes later, Stephanie turned into the visitors parking lot of the barracks, jumped out of the car, and ran into the gray concrete one-story building where Mike was waiting for her.

"What happened?" she asked, giving him a quick hug, then leaning back to look at him anxiously. "I've been trying to figure what you could have done . . ."

Mike said nothing, but took her arm firmly and steered her out the door. In the car, he said, "Let's go get a cup of coffee."

There was a Dunkin Donuts just down the street, but Mike wanted to go farther from the barracks, so they pulled in at a Friendly's a few blocks farther along.

Sitting at a table, Mike told Stephanie briefly what had happened.

"But why?" asked Stephanie, her eyes flashing. "This is America—we don't do that kind of stuff."

"Yeah, right." Mike grinned.

"Anyway, the sooner you see that attorney the better," Stephanie said.

"We're going there now."

Stephanie dropped him outside number 1001, across the street from Mike's office building, and went back to her own office, hoping her absence hadn't been noticed. Mike stood on the curb, watching Stephanie's car go around the corner, then glanced up at the tall building with red brick facing and dark windows before going in.

Del Visic was a cheerful, round man with a pink face. He wore a gray suit that looked too tight for him. His chilly, watchful eyes didn't match either his face or his friendly tone.

"Your bail was ten thousand dollars, Doctor," he told Mike. "The fee is ten percent, so that'll cost you one thousand to start with. And my rates are one hundred fifty dollars per hour, expenses additional, plus a five-thousand-dollar retainer. Visa and Master-Charge accepted. Now tell me what happened."

When Mike finished, Del leaned back, his eyes fixed on Mike. "You're quite sure those bags didn't belong to you?"

"Quite sure. They were planted. Those two cops put them there, in the back of the car. There's no doubt in my mind."

Del paused as if a thought had struck him, and he stared at Mike. "Do you happen to remember the names of the cops who stopped you?"

"Yes I do. The driver was Guercio, the other was Pinelli."

Del wrote the names down on a yellow pad in front of him. "I'll check . . ." He picked up the phone and made a call. The conversation was brief, and during it he stared even harder at Mike. "I got a couple names here," he said after listening for a while. "Guercio and Pinelli." Finally he put the receiver down very slowly.

He stood up, went to the window, looked out for a moment, then came back and sat down again. Mike felt that Del's eyes were going right through him.

"There's a small unit within the state police," Del started, picking his words carefully, "just a handful, maybe half a dozen. They're not officially a unit, but they don't draw regular duty and aren't ever reassigned. They do guard duty at the governor's mansion, they drive him around, do some security work. They're all handpicked, the governor knows each one of them from 'way back. They are also reputed to do certain special jobs for the governor. Well, officers Guercio and Pinelli just happen to be part of that elite group."

"I suppose I should feel honored," said Mike, thinking hard. "But I'm not. I'm just plain scared."

"Maybe they were just trying to tell you something," said Del, standing up. "Like mind your own business, something like that."

Mike shook his head but didn't say anything.

"Did they give you a piece of paper with the date of your hearing?"

Mike pulled a yellow sheet out of his inside pocket and handed it to him.

"Okay . . ." Del checked the date. "That gives us a little time. Meanwhile, I suggest you either don't drive around or else rent a car for the next week."

He stood up, smiling cheerfully, and stuck out his hand. "Doctor, it's been a pleasure. I'll be in touch later today or tomorrow. Pay Sally, please, at the desk."

Mike took a cab to the Acme Garage. His car looked just as it had when he'd left it. He paid the towing fee at the entrance booth, and was getting into the car when the mechanic leaned out the door and called out to him. "By the way, sir, you need to get your brake lights fixed. They're not working."

Chapter 39

After dropping Mike off at the attorney's office, Stephanie went back to work, and was walking along the corridor toward her office when Carl Hartmann's office door opened rather abruptly, and the blond man she now knew as Tony Danzig came out. As he strode past, grim-faced, he gave her a long, speculative look, and there was an aura of tense anger about him that felt like a cold wind as he passed.

Stephanie opened her door and went in, closing it behind her, and was tempted to lock it. She sat down, turned on her computer, put in the access number, and came up with a blank screen. She switched off, tried it again with the same result. With a growing feeling of apprehension, she sat back, wondering if all the computers were down, or if it was only hers. She picked up the phone to call Jean, but the phone was dead. Suddenly panicked, she almost ran to the door, expecting it to be locked, but it wasn't, and she went along the corridor to Ann Boyd's office.

"Ann, my computer's down, and my phone doesn't work." she said.

"Right." Ann's voice was clipped, and her normally friendly expression was now distant. "Mr. Hartmann asked me to tell you that he won't be needing your services anymore, and you are to return to utilization review for the present."

"For the present? What does that mean, Ann?"

Ann returned to her work and pretended that she hadn't heard her.

Stephanie went down the corridor, turned left at the end and down to the U.R. section, past the booths to Jean's office. Jean was on the phone and held up a warning hand when Stephanie started to come in. So Stephanie waited outside, wondering what had happened but certain that it had something to do with Mike and the events of the last few hours.

Finally, Jean put the phone down and stared at Stephanie for a moment before signing her to come in. "I've been told to give you a booth," she said, in a strange voice. "I guess you're coming back to work in U.R. . . ." She looked as if she wanted to ask questions, but didn't have the nerve. "There's no one in booth five, Stephanie, would that be all right for you?" she asked, her tone so apologetic that Stephanie smiled. "Sure, Jean. And no, I don't know what's happening, either."

But as she sat down in familiar old booth five, the booth she'd used before she was promoted to supervisor, she had a creepy feeling that this was only the beginning, that it was all building up to something worse, and that it wasn't going to end with her being merely demoted.

*   *   *

Mike felt the chilly atmosphere as soon as he stepped into the office. Imogene, the receptionist, stiffened when he came in, and didn't return his greeting. He walked through the big lobby where patients were waiting or being interviewed in the glass cubicles. He had the sense that all the staff members had seen him but were not acknowledging his presence. The doors to the doctors' private offices were closed, unusually, as was Tony's. There was no one in his outer office, but inside his own office the red light was blinking on the phone console. He had voice mail—that was something, a little comfort. Feeling utterly isolated, Mike pressed the appropriate buttons and heard Derek's voice, sharp and unfriendly. "Mike, this is Derek. I called the Medical Society at your request, and Dr. Avery said they will reschedule your appearance." There was a pause, and Mike thought it was the end of the message, but Derek's voice came back on. "Mike, I have nothing further to say to you, so please don't contact me."

Mike slowly put the phone down.

The door opened, and Spencer came in without knocking and stood in front of Mike's table. "We've had official notification of your arrest by the state police this morning, Mike," he said. "Under the circumstances, I've decided to reassign your patients to Terry Catlin until this matter is resolved. Meanwhile, you can stay in this office if you wish, but you will have no duties or responsibilities, and no access to the computer or other facilities. I might as well also tell you that your privileges at Lovejoy Hospital have been temporarily revoked as of this morning, pending the outcome of various inquiries.'' He stared at Mike with an expression that reflected his deep sense of anger and betrayal. ''I really had faith in you,'' he said, then turned and walked out.

Mike, feeling as if his entire life was crumbling around him, went out, passed Terry Catlin coming in, then took the elevator down to the garage level. His car was in its usual place, but when he came closer, Mike stopped dead in his tracks. Someone had sprayed the word *Asshole* in pink Day-Glo paint on the side of his beautiful, shiny green car.

Mike turned and went back to the elevator, back into the office. He strode across the foyer and along the corridor until he came to Terry Catlin's door and flung it open. Terry was on the phone, and put it down immediately. ''What the hell do you want?'' he asked Mike, jumping to his feet. He sounded aggressive enough, but the fear in his eyes gave him away. Mike took two steps forward. ''Let me see your hands.''

Catlin instantly put his hands behind him. ''Get out of here,'' he said, ''You've no business—''

Like a flash, Mike caught Catlin's right forearm and wrenched it around to the front. Sure enough, there were pink paint stains on two of his fingers. Pale with pain and fear, Catlin said, ''I'm calling the police . . .''

''I warned you not to fuck with me,'' said Mike.

With a quick move he yanked Catlin away from the desk and slammed him against the wall, hard enough to rattle his teeth. Taking his time, Mike smashed his right fist into the side of Catlin's face, jerking it around just in time for a left to the mouth. Mike felt something crunch under his fist, a tooth maybe. Catlin opened his bloody mouth and tried to scream, but couldn't. He slid to the floor, but Mike wasn't done. He picked the terrified Catlin up by the front of his white shirt and propped him up in the corner, preparing to beat him to a pulp. Then he smelled something and looked down to see a wet stain spreading over the front of Catlin's pants. Disgusted, Mike let go of the shirt, and Catlin slid down to the floor again. Mike turned and went into the adjacent examining room, where he washed his hands at the sink before walking out.

An hour later, Mike was home, wondering how to clean the paint off his car and trying to figure what he should do next.

Meanwhile, Catlin had picked himself off the floor, cleaned up in the bathroom, found a change of clothes, and now was in earnest discussion with Lou Gardner, Tony, and the security head, George Rankin.

Chapter 40

At five o'clock, Mike went down to meet his old work buddies at Aileen's Bar. Zeke and Bob arrived at the same time as he did.

"What's going on, Mike?" asked Zeke after they had sat down with a beer. "There's a lot of talk about you at the hospital."

Mike shrugged. "I guess I'm in sort of a tight spot right now, but it'll all work out. What are you guys doing?"

"Well, the transformer's in, and we tested it today. Boy, does that sucker use current. When we put it on full load, the lights dimmed and a bunch of interruptor alarms went off. Normally it runs at sixty percent of max, so it should be okay."

They discussed the technical aspects of the installation for a while, then talked about people in the company they both knew. The conversation had turned to football when Mike's pager went off. He didn't recognize the number in the window, but called it on his cellphone. It was a few minutes short of five-thirty. Stephanie answered—she'd paged him from a public phone booth at the corner of Elm and Vine.

"Mike, I'm sorry . . ." Stephanie sounded almost tearful. "I went out to my car and it has two flat tires. Can you pick me up?"

"*Two* flat tires? Sure, I'll see you in ten minutes."

Carl joined the group in the security area, and they were now gathered around the telephone monitoring equipment. Sam Scheiffer was leaning against the edge of the bench, playing with an icepick. After the click that denoted the end of Mike's call to Stephanie, Carl nodded to Catlin, who was standing with his back to the door, one hand covering his mouth.

"Good thinking, Doctor," said Carl. "I just hope the rest of it goes as well." Catlin had argued that it was time for definitive action, and after he outlined his plan and showed how there was no way that they could be implicated, even Carl was convinced.

Mike pulled up outside the fenced parking area reserved for the Hartmann employees and jumped out. Stephanie was waiting by her car, and Mike ducked under the barrier. He looked at the wheels. Both rear tires were completely flat, and he checked them visually for nails or sharp objects, then ran his hand around them. Nothing. The valves both had their plastic covers on, and he took them off. He'd seen wooden matchsticks jammed in the valves to let the air out, but these looked okay.

"The garage people said they'd fix the tires and put them back on," said Stephanie.

"Good. Let's go home. I'll bring you back in the morning."

When they'd driven back to his apartment, Mike cooked some pasta and made a sauce with a can of baby clams and salsa. It wasn't a particularly cheerful meal. There was a scary, electric tension in the air that neither of them could dispel. Mike had a feeling that Stephanie's car had been immobilized for a reason, and one of the reasons could be to bring them together. To turn them into a single target, he thought.

"I'm not going back there," said Stephanie after they'd put the dishes in the washer, "except to pick up my car. I don't think they would fire me, because I have a good record and I haven't done anything wrong . . ." "Anyway," she went on with forced cheerfulness, "there's always work for someone with my skills."

"I wish I could say the same," said Mike. "Maybe I can get myself a job in Namibia, or Zaire. I'm sure they need car mechanics there."

For some reason, they were both very aware of the telephone, sitting quietly on its hook between the kitchen and the living room. Neither of them was expecting a call, and it didn't ring. But there was something menacing about its very silence, and Mike felt as if they had been shut off from the rest of the world. Before they went to bed, Mike checked the locks and the windows with more than usual care. He picked up the phone, and felt slightly reassured when he heard the normal, banal dial tone.

It had been a warm evening, but it took Stephanie several minutes in Mike's arms before she stopped shivering.

Next morning, the alarm woke them at six, and by a quarter of seven they were both ready, more out of habit than necessity.

"Let's go somewhere for breakfast after we pick up your car," suggested Mike. "Today I could use a stack of pancakes a foot high." They decided to go to the IHOP on Sycamore, a hangout of the NCMC students. Then, Mike said, he'd go to the blood bank at Lovejoy and try to retrieve Pauline's blood sample, if there was one.

"Shouldn't you rent a car, like your lawyer said?" asked Stephanie. "You don't want to get picked up again, and your car sure stands out in the crowd."

"I'll do that as soon as we get back," he promised.

It wasn't quite light yet when they went down in the elevator to the garage. The place was silent, and their footsteps echoed on the concrete floor. Bare lightbulbs hanging from the low ceiling gave the place an eerie, cold glow.

Feeling unaccountably nervous, Stephanie took Mike's hand, and together they walked over to Mike's green Aston-Martin. He'd done a good job cleaning off the Day-Glo paint, but his mouth tightened as he glanced at the dulled finish on the door. Catlin would be waking up this morning with a sore mouth, at least, and Mike derived some comfort from that thought.

Mike opened the passenger door for Stephanie,

then checked the rear compartment: no glassine packages, nothing unusual. He walked around and climbed in. The motor started with the first push on the starter button, and he backed carefully out. Something in the steering gear scraped when he was on full lock, and he made a mental note to check it later.

As he approached the exit, he saw the security guard in the booth. She was on the midnight-to-eight shift, he thought, and must be looking forward to getting off in an hour or so. She raised the barrier and waved, and as they passed she shouted something, but he didn't hear. He stopped, wound the window down, and leaned out.

"What did you say, Emma?"

Emma poked her head out of the window. "I said they came to change your car battery, Dr. Richmond," she said. "The mechanics. They came around two this morning, in a little red van."

Mike stared at her for a moment, then opened the door and jumped out. He bent down to look under the front of the car, and saw a package wrapped in green plastic with silver duct tape attached to the steering box. He could even hear the ticking of a timing mechanism.

He leaped up. "Get out!" he yelled at Stephanie. He ran around and almost dragged her out of the car. "Run back into the garage!"

Emma was watching from her booth, openmouthed.

"Run!" he shouted at her. "There's a bomb under the car and it's going to go off . . . Get away, Emma!"

She came out of the door at the side of the booth, and Mike grabbed her arm and pushed her after Stephanie. At that moment, a blue-white flash lit up the entire garage, followed instantly by a deafening explosion accompanied by the sound of tearing metal and flying glass. Then the shock wave struck, and Mike was picked up from behind like a piece of straw, and flung headlong against a concrete pillar.

Chapter 41

"**H**e's dead."

"No, he isn't. Shut up and keep pumping." The older EMT shouted at the rookie and held the oxygen mask tightly over Mike's face. Thick smoke was still billowing through the garage, and with the help of a fireman they ran the stretcher up to the ambulance at the top of the ramp, the rookie still jolting on Mike's chest with the heels of both hands.

Waking up was a slow and painful process. The first thing Mike was aware of was the sounds of an I.C.U. around him, the distant hiss of a respirator, the muted voice of the paging system calling someone . . . He opened his eyes for a moment, and when the lights struck his retina it felt like shards of glass being pushed into his eyeballs.

"He's awake." It sounded like Stephanie's voice, but he wasn't sure, and he tried to raise himself up but couldn't.

"Hey, don't move," said a warning voice. It sounded distant and metallic, and he couldn't tell if it was male or female.

Mike half opened one eye, then the other. A white oval in his field of view slowly became Stephanie's face, but she was almost immediately replaced in his field of view by Evan Gaskell. Mike closed his eyes. All he knew was that he didn't want to hear or see him.

"Can you hear me?" asked Evan.

"Yes. You don't have to shout."

"Do you know where you are?"

Mike didn't feel the question was worth answering, so he didn't. Instead he mentally checked his legs and arms. Every part of him felt painful and stiff, as if he'd been scientifically clubbed by someone who knew where to find each individual muscle in his body.

"You're in Lovejoy Hospital. In intensive care."

Mike looked at him and tried to move, but both wrists and forearms were strapped to I.V. armboards and the most he could do was straighten out his fingers. Stephanie's hand was there, and he managed to grab it with his right hand. He thought he'd been sort of awake before opening his eyes, but he wasn't quite sure about anything.

"Why?" he asked. He licked his dry lips. The sound wasn't coming out of his mouth the way he wanted it to. "Why am I here?"

"There was an explosion," said Evan. "Do you remember anything about it?"

Mike thought. "No," he said.

Evan told him. Various events and recollections came back to Mike, like cars speeding past him on a racetrack, coming, there, gone, all in a flash. He lay back with his eyes closed while Evan spoke.

Mike managed to say, "Stephanie, are you all right?" but it took a huge effort just to get the words out.

"Sure. A few bruises, nothing much. Mike, you're squeezing too hard, you're hurting my hand. Just lie still. Everything's all right."

Struggling to sit up, Mike said, "We *have* to get Pauline's sample from the blood bank . . ." The effort was too much for him and he fell back, his eyes closed.

And then, in a kind of fog, he heard another voice. It sounded like Lou Gardner's. "He's okay now," he said. "We can move him out of here into a regular room. I've ordered a private duty nurse for him, and she should be here in a couple of hours. Her name's Riva Zorek, and she'll take good care of him." Lou's voice was at its kindliest. "And you must be exhausted, Miss Hopkins. I suggest that you go home now and get some rest." His voice became more insistent—it was an order, not a suggestion.

Mike let go Stephanie's hand, and he heard nothing more until he woke up again two hours later. He realized that he'd been moved. The bed felt different, and there were none of the usual I.C.U. sounds.

Stephanie was still there, but Evan was gone. His pager had gone off, Stephanie explained, and he'd left in a hurry without saying anything.

Mike's head was beginning to clear, and Stephanie reached out and held his hand again. With an effort he turned his head. Her face looked drawn and scared.

"What's the matter?" he asked.

Stephanie didn't answer, but took a folded newspaper out of her purse and handed it to him.

He stared at the type, but it was blurred. "I can't read it," he said.

Stephanie took it back. "It's this afternoon's *Register*," she said and started to read. *"Car bomb explodes in downtown New Coventry."* Her voice was unnaturally quiet, and Mike had to strain to hear what she was saying. *"Several people escaped with their lives this morning when a car bomb exploded at the entrance of a parking garage in downtown New Coventry, starting a fire that was brought under control by two units of the Fire Department. Three people were injured, two severely, and both were admitted to Lovejoy Hospital. Emma Lowther, forty-three, a guard employed by the Secure I-T corporation, was struck by flying glass, and a hospital spokeswoman stated that her condition was critical. Dr. Michael Richmond, who was driving the vehicle, a 1961 Aston-Martin, was also injured. A State Police official told the Register that Richmond had been arrested the day before and was out on bail on a charge of drug possession and attempted bribery of a State Police officer. The official said that preliminary investigations suggested that the car bombing was drug-related. A spokesman from the Connecticut State Medical Society said that Dr. Richmond was already under an unrelated investigation into alleged improper medical conduct, and the Society would deal with this new situation when more facts were available."*

Stephanie's voice faded completely, and they looked at each other.

"Jesus." Mike's voice was a hoarse whisper. "Those bastards . . ." Stephanie, you're sure you didn't get hurt?"

"No, I'm okay. They said I had a mild concussion and my ears are still buzzing. Otherwise, no problems."

"And Emma? The guard?"

"Dr. Gardner said she had a cut artery in her leg, but they fixed her up and she's doing well."

There was a long silence, and Mike could feel waves of anger and fear threatening to engulf him.

"Did you say there was a police guard?"

"They had one outside the I.C.U. while you were there, but he's gone now."

"What about Evan?"

"He left too. I'm not sure, but I have a feeling he won't be back."

"My car?"

For answer, Stephanie showed him the photo next to the article she'd read. "I'm sorry, Mike." The photo showed a mass of tangled wreckage that was barely recognizable as having once been a car.

Mike stared at the photo for a long time. When he spoke, his voice was quiet. "That was a close call," he said. Forgetting that he was tied down, he tried to reach for a plastic cup of water on the small table beside him. Stephanie picked it up and held it to his lips. He gulped it down thirstily.

"More?"

"Yes, please. What time is it?"

"A few minutes before twelve."

"At night?"

"Yes."

The door opened and a nurse came in. She checked Mike's vital signs, and made a notation on her clipboard. As she was leaving, she said, "Your private duty nurse, Ms. Zorek, called in a little while ago to say she's been delayed, but she'll be here in about an hour."

Like the foggy recollections of a nightmare, the memory of Lou's words struggled to come together. Private duty nurse . . . *Riva Zorek* . . . Where had he heard that name before?

"Try to get some sleep," said Stephanie. "I'll put the lights out."

"You too," said Mike. "Can you sleep there?"

"There's a recliner in the corner. I'll be fine."

Five minutes later, only the sound of regular breathing could be heard in the room. A night light at the side of the bed provided the only illumination. Everything was silent in the corridor outside, as if the entire hospital had fallen asleep.

Four floors below, the E.R. was in full activity. In the last few minutes, ambulances had brought in victims from a house fire over by the railroad station, while the staff were still trying to deal with the results of a major pileup on I–95. Terry Catlin, in his white coat, slipped in unnoticed through the E.R. doors.

"There he goes," said Sam Scheiffer, standing with George Rankin and Tony Danzig, watching the monitors from the Hartmann building three blocks away.

"That guy's a loose cannon," said Rankin, watching Catlin as he disappeared from the monitor field. "He's too personally involved, and too anxious to get rid of Richmond."

"Shut up, George," said Tony. "Carl's agreed with what he's doing. What's more, you could have been given that job, so shut your face and be thankful."

Catlin hurried along the main corridor to the elevator, one hand in the pocket of his white coat. Waiting at the elevator was Brian Folsom, the night blood bank tech, holding his equipment basket. Brian was a familiar figure around the hospital, instantly recognizable by his brightly colored striped jacket.

"Working late, Dr. Catlin?" said Brian as they waited together. Catlin's face was puffy and his right eye was almost closed. He kept his face turned away, and placed a hand over his mouth so Brian couldn't see the split lip. He said nothing, stared straight ahead, and just gave a contemptuous shrug. Brian, about the same age and size as Catlin, flushed and said no more until he got off at the third floor and headed down the corridor toward his lab.

Catlin went on up past Radiology to the fifth floor. Lou had told him the number of Mike's room. "We've pulled the police guard," he'd said, "and I told the Hopkins woman to go home. So he should be alone for about an hour until Riva gets there. And he's out of it—he won't even see you."

The lights were dimmed for the night on the fifth floor, and the elevator couldn't be seen from the nurses station. Not a soul stirred. Catlin, silent in his rubber-soled shoes, headed for the bathroom halfway along the corridor. The lights were bright in there, and it took him a few seconds to adjust. He went into one of the two booths, locked the door, and pulled a 20ml syringe and a full 20ml ampule from his pocket. He checked the label on the ampule. *Potassium Chloride, Intravenous solution. 3Meq/ml. Do not administer in undiluted form.* Catlin grinned, and it hurt his lip. When this stuff hits his heart, he thought, it'll wake him up and he'll fibrillate long enough to know he's dying. Taking the pink plastic cover off the needle, he stuck it through the central membrane on the ampule and filled the syringe. Then he replaced the cover and put everything back in his pocket.

A minute later, Stephanie became suddenly alert, wakened by the quiet turning of the door handle. There was something slow and surreptitious about it, and she thought her heart was going to stop. The door opened a crack, and she froze. A face appeared slowly in the doorway. Through her almost closed eyes she saw a damaged, scary face, and realized who it was.

He stayed there for almost a minute, watching, and Stephanie thought she was going to scream, but she just lay very still on her recliner, her eyes closed. What did he want?

Catlin, at first unnerved by Stephanie's presence, decided that they were both sound asleep, and anyway he would be in there for only a moment. There was just enough light for him to do what he'd come to do. He opened the door enough to slip in, reached up and turned the stopcock to shut off Mike's I.V. He took the syringe from his pocket, stuck the needle through the transparent tubing, and slowly injected the solution up into the filling chamber. He glanced quickly at the length of tubing—it would take about a minute before the potassium hit his heart, long enough for Catlin to get quietly away. He turned the stopcock on, opened the door, and whispered to Mike's sleeping form, "You're dead, asshole."

Chapter 42

The door closed softly behind Catlin, and after waiting one panic-stricken moment, Stephanie jumped up as silently as she could. Desperate with fear, she lunged for the I.V. tubing and pinched off the flow with one hand and shut off the stopcock with the other. Keeping one eye on the door, terrified that Catlin would come back, she waited for a moment before gently shaking Mike's shoulder. This time he woke up instantly, and she put a hand over his mouth to prevent him from saying anything. She leaned forward and told him in a quick whisper what had happened.

Mike sat up. "Take out the I.V." he told her. "I don't need it anyway."

Stephanie hesitated for a second, then decided this wasn't a good time to argue, so she took the tape off and pulled the needle out of his vein.

"We have to get out of here," he said, putting a finger on his I.V. site to prevent if from bleeding. "I remember who Riva Zorek is. She was the nurse who was with Pauline when she died," he said, then sat up, and groaned with the pain that hit him between the eyes. "Where are my clothes?"

Stephanie went to the closet. The clothes that Mike had been wearing were there, or what was left of them.

"What do we do if he comes back?" Stephanie was so frightened she could hardly speak.

"I'll kill him," replied Mike, and he meant it. She helped him put his clothes on, although they were dirty and torn from the explosion. Very carefully he stood up.

"Mike, what do we do now?"

Mike paused with his hand on the door handle. "They'll be back," he said. "And when they find we're not here, they'll come looking for us."

"Why don't we just go out? Leave the hospital? I could call a taxi . . ."

"The only door that's open at night is the E.R., and you can be sure they wouldn't let us out," said Mike. He was thinking hard. "The other thing is, we need to find Pauline's blood sample in the blood bank, if it's there. It's our only hope of proving that she was killed."

An idea struck him, his face hardened, and he grabbed Stephanie's hand. "We're going down to the X-ray department. It's one floor down, right below us, and it's one of the first places they'll come looking for us. If we're lucky, we'll have time to do what we need to do. Let's go."

Mike went out first, followed by Stephanie, who momentarily expected to hear a shout from the nurses station, but they made it unnoticed to the fire-escape stairwell and down one flight of stairs. Mike quietly opened the door into the central corridor of the Radiology department. Only a few lights glowed dimly, just enough illumination for Mike to find his way.

"We're looking for where they're putting the new MRI unit," he whispered, taking Stephanie's hand.

They found it at the far end of the corridor, without difficulty, because of the protective paper matting on the floor between it and the service elevator. The double doors of the room were jammed open with wooden wedges. The light inside was even dimmer than in the corridor, and Mike stood in the doorway, trying to figure out where things were. Most of the room was bare, and the floor was covered with the same paper matting. Zeke and Bob had obviously been working over at the far end of the room, where a big stainless steel cabinet about seven feet high was humming quietly.

"That's the transformer," said Mike. He looked at his watch. "We're going to need about fifteen minutes," he said. "If they get here before then, we're dead meat." He took a deep breath and switched on the room lights.

"What do you mean, he's gone?" The night nurse, a gray-haired, middle-aged woman looked up into Riva Zorek's square face, with its frame of short, straight black hair.

"Room 525," said Zorek. "Dr. Richmond. There's nobody in there."

"Of course there is. You must have gone into the wrong room."

"I did not." Zorek spoke quietly, but something in her eyes galvanized the night nurse, and she put her book facedown on the desk so as not to lose her place. She heaved herself out of her chair. "Okay," she said. "Let's go and see."

Mike opened the doors on the back of the transformer and peered inside. It was a lot bigger than the ones he'd helped install years before, and the refrigeration unit for the superconducting magnets was new. The *on-off-test* switches were on the right outside wall of the cabinet rather than inside, another technical improvement, but the overall design appeared to be the same. He looked around for what he needed—Zeke had told him that he'd completed the testing procedures, and for a moment Mike had a cold chill thinking he might have taken away the shielded wires. But there they were, paired red for positive and black for negative, neatly coiled up on a big spool on the opposite side of the room with all the other test equipment.

"What are you doing?" asked Stephanie. She was afraid that the lights would attract attention from a security guard on his rounds. "Mike I'm really scared . . . Let's just go down to the ground floor, find an exit and get out of here."

She was trembling, and Mike gave her a brief reassuring hug, although he himself was sweating and didn't know if he'd be able to get them out of this.

"Uncoil those wires for me, Stephanie," he said, pointing at the big spool. "And bring the ends with the alligator clips over here to the transformer."

While she was unrolling the spool, Mike went to the back of the cabinet and, with a big effort, lifted two of the shiny stainless steel doors off their hinges and took them, one at a time, to the doorway, and laid them on the floor, side by side, about an inch apart, just inside the room.

He looked at them for a second. From outside, and with the main lights out, they wouldn't be too noticeable . . . Maybe he should put a piece of the protective paper over them . . . No, that wouldn't work. He'd have to chance it the way they were. Mike found two narrow strips of wood and placed them lengthwise between the doors to keep them from touching.

Stephanie had unrolled the heavy double wires back to the main cabinet, and was breathing hard. "There are alligator clips on both ends," she said.

"Good. That makes life a lot easier." Mike silently thanked Zeke, went to pick up the other ends, and with Stephanie's help dragged the wires across the floor to the doorway. He looked at his watch. Jesus. He'd better hurry up. It took only a moment to fasten the insulated alligator clips to the vents of each steel door, but it took longer to run the wiring along the inside wall, out of sight of anyone in the doorway, back to the cabinet. With great care, and feeling his strength ebbing by the moment, he attached the alligator clips to the positive and negative terminals inside the cabinet, twisting the clips a couple of times to make the best possible metal-to-metal contact. Then he sat down, panting, too exhausted even to speak.

"So where could he have gone?" Tony was for once casually dressed in a dark turtleneck sweater, designer jeans, and Italian loafers, and he was visibly angry. Catlin had called for him and George Rankin when nurse Zorek reported that Mike had disappeared from his hospital bed.

"He's not here, not on this floor," said Catlin, his swollen face mottled with frustration and anger. "And we know he's still in the hospital. There's no way out except through the E.R., and we've got that covered. Up here, I've checked every closet and bathroom. He wouldn't have gone upstairs to the clinical floors because there are people everywhere. No, he's going to try to lie low until morning, and then somehow find his way out."

"What's on the floor below us?"

"Administrative offices, outpatient surgery, and Radiology. There are plenty of places he could hide down there."

"And below that?"

"More offices, physiotherapy, and the main hospital lab. It's all locked up except for the blood bank."

"Okay. I'll check the floor below us, and you go down to the blood-bank floor." He looked at Catlin with a slightly patronizing expression. "I assume you're properly equipped?"

"I have what I need up in my locker," replied Catlin.

They were standing by the elevator doors, which opened as Catlin was talking. Lou Gardner came out, obviously very upset. "What's happening?" he asked Tony. "Have you figured out where he went?"

"We're going to check out the two floors below us," said Tony. "He's skulking around in there someplace—don't worry, we'll find him." He put his foot out to prevent the elevator from closing, took a Glock automatic from his pocket, twisted a wide-bore silencer onto the muzzle, then stepped into the elevator. The doors closed silently behind him.

Lou turned to Catlin, his face grim. "Richmond could be heading for the blood bank," he said. "When he was in the I.C.U., he mumbled something about having to get Pauline Minsky's blood-bank sample."

"Good. I hope he's there." The intensity of Terry's fury startled Lou, and he took a quick step back when Catlin asked, "You want to come with me?"

"No way," replied Lou. "I'll just wait up here. Let me know what happens."

"Please, Mike, put the lights out." Stephanie was sitting next to Mike behind the big cabinet, and still shivering. "We'll be sitting ducks here."

"It's okay, Stephanie," replied Mike. With an effort he pulled himself to his feet. "We'll hear them coming. And it won't be long. You stay here and don't move from behind this cabinet, okay?"

He went over to the doorway, taking care not to step on the doors, and waited, listening. Everything outside was quiet, as if the hospital were in a heavy sleep.

A few minutes later, he tensed, hearing the faint hiss of the elevator doors as they opened at the other end of the corridor. The elevator closed, and then the silence fell again. Not knowing if anyone had got off, Mike waited a few more moments to give whoever it was time to get closer. Then he switched the main lights out and crept back to the side of the transformer. It left him partly exposed, but there was nothing he could do about it—he had to be able to reach the switches.

There was total silence for over a minute. Then they both heard the faintest sound of steps, but only for a moment. Stephanie felt a scream rising in her throat, and she could feel Mike tense next to her.

A black shadow appeared, outlined in the faint light from the doorway, and Stephanie, looking around the side of the transformer against Mike's specific instructions, bit the edge of her hand to control her panic.

"Mike?"

It was Tony's voice, soft, reasonable.

"Mike, I know you're in there. Come on out and let's talk this over."

Mike stayed frozen where he was, trying to control his breathing so it wouldn't be heard.

A pinpoint of light appeared from the doorway, and the pencil beam started to go slowly around the room. Mike tried to figure exactly where Tony was standing, but he couldn't be sure. The beam landed on the transformer and stopped there for a moment before going on.

The beam caught Mike a moment later, and everything happened at once. A bullet crashed into the transformer a foot away from Mike. Simultaneously he hit the On button on the side of the cabinet. A huge crackling flash lit up the doorway, outlining Tony. For a second he seemed illuminated, and Mike could see his mouth and eyes jammed open, his blond hair standing on end. A tetanic spasm hit all his muscles, and he made a wheezing, screaming noise. The gun and penlight went flying. He seemed to stand there, rigid, for an eternity before he collapsed on to the floor, the current still crackling through his body.

Shaking, Mike pressed the Off button. Stephanie was sitting on the floor, her eyes wide open, staring horrified at the body slumped across the doorway.

Mike left her and went over to the door and switched on the room lights. Tony was quite still, lying across the two metal doors, and a smell of burned flesh rose from his body. Mike walked over to help Stephanie to her feet.

"We have to put all of this back together," he said gently, indicating the steel doors and the wires. He didn't have the strength to pull Tony's body off the metal doors, so she had to help him, although she recoiled from even touching his stiff, dead arm. Mike detached the alligator clips from the doors and the terminals on the transformer, and Stephanie rewound the wire and rolled the spool back to its original position. The final task was to pick up the heavy doors and replace them on their hinges, but even with Stephanie's help, he barely managed to get them back up.

Then he slid to the floor and leaned his back against the softly vibrating transformer, his chest heaving. Stephanie sat on the floor too, looking anxiously at him.

"I'm okay," he said, seeing her expression. His face was grim. "I'm just disappointed it wasn't Catlin."

They rested there for about a minute, but it was clear that the sight of Tony's body was unnerving Stephanie, and she couldn't stop shaking.

"I can't help it," she said. "I keep thinking he's going to get up and kill us both."

"Okay, let's go," he said. "We have other work to do. Just help me to stand up."

They had to step over Tony's body to get out of the MRI room, and Stephanie could hardly bear to do it.

"We have to go to the blood bank for Pauline's sample now," said Mike, switching off the lights. "If we don't, it'll be gone in the morning, for sure. It may be gone now, for all we know."

Mike took Stephanie's hand. He knew he was in bad shape, and it hurt him to move or breathe, but that wasn't going to stop him now.

They stepped silently into the darkened corridor, wondering if the noise and lights had been noticed by the security guards, but all seemed quiet. Stephanie held onto his hand, and they opened the door into the stairwell. Mike could feel some of his strength returning as they walked slowly down the concrete stairs. The exit door on the blood-bank floor was heavy, and creaked when they pushed it open into the darkened corridor that led to the main lab and the blood bank. There was a light on at the far end of the corridor, to the right. The blood bank was manned twenty-four hours a day, and Mike knew that Brian Folsom, the night tech, would probably be there if he wasn't off delivering blood somewhere in the hospital. Mike knew Brian, and felt reasonably sure that he'd help them once he'd explained what he needed and why.

In total silence Mike and Stephanie walked along the corridor. Mike knew that nobody but the blood-bank staff ever came here at night, so they didn't have to worry about being seen, but there was something in the air he couldn't describe, and it made him feel nervous.

Mike stopped when the double doors to the blood bank came into view. They were open, and of course there was no one at the reception desk. Behind the desk Mike could see the lit interior of the lab, but the technicians' work area was out of his line of sight.

"Stay here," he said to Stephanie, just loud enough for her to hear. "I'll go in and talk to Brian."

Stephanie shook her head vigorously. "No way," she whispered back. "I'm coming with you."

Slowly they advanced through the open doors.

There was no sound, except for the humming of the big refrigerator units on the left wall of the lab, where the blood was stored. As they came into the lab, they heard the faint, scratchy, but somehow reassuring sound of music from a portable radio at the far end of the room. Mike walked cautiously forward, with Stephanie holding tightly onto his hand, past the row of staff lockers and the closed door that led to the main hospital lab, and started down between the two rows of benches toward the end of the lab.

Brian was at his desk, wearing his multicolored jacket. He was facing away from them, his head down on the desk as if he were taking a quick nap. Mike, still between two lab benches, stopped about fifteen feet from him.

Stephanie drew in her breath. "Oh, my God . . . Mike, is he all right?"

At that moment Brian moved slightly, and Mike nodded. "Yes, he's just sleeping," he said, walking forward. When he was a couple of paces away, he said quietly, so as not to startle him, "Hi, Brian."

There was a pause, then Brian straightened up and turned around. Only it wasn't Brian, it was Catlin, and on his bruised face he wore a snarl of such hatred that Mike stopped, his mouth open.

Catlin had a gun in his hand. "This is it, asshole," he said, and Mike saw his finger start to squeeze the trigger. Acting on reflex, Mike's hand shot out and swept a large glass reagent bottle off the bench and straight at Catlin. He just managed to get out of its way, but it smashed on the desk, splashing liquid all over him. He started to scream, and Mike grabbed Stephanie and dived back between the benches just as Catlin fired. He fired again as they reached the end of the bench, and Mike felt the wind of the bullet as it whistled past him and thudded into the wall. They crouched down, trying to figure out which way Catlin would come at them.

And he came, like a crazy man. He climbed on top of the bench and made his way toward them, knocking over centrifuges, glass equipment, everything in his path. He paused every few moments, still screaming, looking for them, knowing that they couldn't run down the aisle on either side without presenting an unmissable target. Mike listened, trying to figure a way of escape. Then his nose twitched with the heavy, corrosive odor from the spilled reagent.

"Oh, Jesus, that was sulfuric acid," he said to Stephanie. He peered over the top of the bench, and felt the hair on the back of his head crawl. Catlin was standing on the bench about five yards away— his clothes were smoking and his face was already blotchy and stained where the acid had splashed on it. But he saw Mike, and his shot came so close that Mike felt the tissues of his face being sucked out by the shock wave. Catlin started to stagger toward their end of the bench, scattering glassware and equipment in his path, shouting and screaming at the same time. Mike grabbed Stephanie, and they made a dive for the communicating door to the main lab, hoping it would be open. It was their only chance—there was nowhere else for them to go. The door was locked. In desperation Mike smashed against it with his body. At the same time the lights went on in the corridor outside, and they heard shouts and the sound of running feet. Trapped, with nowhere to go, they saw Catlin half jump, half fall off the bench and come around the corner after them. He looked terrifying. His left eye was already clouding, his face was unrecognizable, and the acid was eating holes in his clothes. Catlin stopped momentarily, still screaming, and turned as someone came around the corner into the lab. Mike and Stephanie heard two shots in quick succession, and then Catlin seemed to rise up in the air. He fell back with a thud onto the floor, the gun flying out of his hand.

Evan Gaskell appeared around the corner, gun in hand. A moment later the lab was full of police.

"We picked them all up," Evan told them, after making sure that Mike and Stephanie were unharmed. "Spencer, Hartmann, the lot. I'll tell you about it later."

Epilogue

At ten o'clock the next morning, Mike and Stephanie met with Evan Gaskell at the FBI headquarters building in downtown New Coventry.

"Sleep all right?" Evan grinned at Mike.

Mike nodded. "I still don't know what the hell happened yesterday," he said. "It feels like some kind of bad dream."

"Did you see this morning's paper?"

Mike shook his head.

"Well, a lot's happened. Right after your car explosion yesterday morning, I got a warrant to get Ms. Minsky's sample from the blood bank. It was still there, and I had somebody take it straight up to the federal lab in Hartford. We got the results back last evening." He grinned at Stephanie. "That's why I left in a hurry after Mike woke up. Ms. Minsky had enough insulin and nembutal in her blood to kill a horse." Evan was sounding very pleased with himself. "After that I went to see the pathologist guy, Tarvel, at his home. He lives with his partner, Marilyn Fox, and she bitched like hell about being wakened up. I leaned on Tarvel a bit, I guess. Anyway all of a sudden he starts to come out with the whole story, and the Fox woman jumps on him—I thought she was going to kill him."

"After that I had my guys pick up the others, Hartmann, Spencer, Rosenfeld, and the attorney, Haiman Gold, but they wouldn't say anything without their lawyers. We're offering Tarvel immunity in exchange for the whole story, so we should be able to wrap it up."

"What about Catlin? How did you happen to appear in the blood bank last night?"

"You probably won't remember this, but when you were waking up, you said, 'We *have* to get Pauline's blood-bank sample.' Well, Dr. Gardner had just come into the room, and when he heard that, he stopped dead in his tracks, just for a second. So after you disappeared from your room, I figured you would probably go down there, and they might come looking for you."

"What about Brian? The tech? How come Catlin was wearing his jacket?"

"We found him in the third-floor men's room. He'd been hit on the back of his head, presumably by Catlin, and was just beginning to wake up."

"And Tony Danzig?" Mike watched Evan's face carefully.

"Ah, yes, Tony. Apparently he was wandering around the Radiology department about that time and electrocuted himself. They're installing some new equipment there, and he was poking around the testing gear and must have touched some live

terminals. He had a gun, and fired it into a transformer." Evan shook his head. "The guy must have
been crazy."

"Did you ever talk to Alvin Zimmerman, the crash
investigator?" asked Mike, worried that something
might have happened to him.

"I didn't, but one of my colleagues did, yesterday.
It's very interesting—and seems to lead directly to
the very top in Hartford." Evan paused. "Which reminds me," he went on, "the D.A. wants to talk to
you." He passed a piece of paper to Mike. "Bob
Spaltz. This is his private phone number. Call him
this morning, okay?" He escorted them down to the
front door and shook hands with them.

"Thank you for everything, Evan," said Stephanie,
stretching up to kiss him on the cheek. "You really
are a star."

"It's been a pleasure," he said, smiling and looking
slightly embarrassed. Then he added, curiously,
"What are you guys going to do now?"

Mike and Stephanie looked at each other.

"First we're going over to see Emma Lowther in
the hospital," replied Mike. "Then we're taking off
for a week in Cancun. After that, who knows?"

Ⓓ SIGNET   Ⓔ ONYX

BREAKTHROUGH MEDICAL
THRILLERS

☐ **SPECIAL TREATMENT by Nancy Fisher.** After years of finishing in the basement, Morgan Hudson's baseball team has a shot at winning it all. Dr. Adam Salt wonders if some new, undetectable drug is the secret ingredient in the team's incredible performance. But when players suddenly succumb to bizarre, uncontrollable rages, and the reclusive owner of the organization's club is inexplicably murdered, Dr. Salt along with beautiful magazine reporter Robin Kennedy must track down a killer with a motive.
(188705—$5.99)

☐ **FATAL ANALYSIS by Jack Chase.** Washington psychiatrist Dr. Jason Andrews knows the secrets of his powerful political clients. And when an innovative new drug promises to help relieve them of damaging past psychological traumas, Jason becomes one of the miracle drug's most enthusiastic supporters ... until the Vice President of the United States is found dead by his own hand ... and until other high-ranking patients are resigning or dying.
(187644—$5.99)

☐ **MINDBEND by Robin Cook.** It seemed a happy coincidence that the Julian Clinic that was treating his pregnant wife was owned by the giant drug firm where Dr. Adam Schonberg had recently taken a high-paying job ... that is until Adam began to suspect the terrifying truth about this connection ... and about the hideous evil perpetrated on the wife he loved by the doctor she helplessly trusted.... "The author of *Coma* at his novel writing best!"—*Associated Press*   (141083—$6.99)

☐ **THE DOCTORS by Tyler Cortland.** Funded by Texas matriarch Emma Chandler's millions, Chandler Medical Center is as up-to-date as the latest medical advances. But fueled by human weakness, the ambition, greed and lust rampant within its walls are as old as sin....
(184076—$4.99)

Prices slightly higher in Canada

Buy them at your local bookstore or use this convenient coupon for ordering.

PENGUIN USA
P.O. Box 999 — Dept. #17109
Bergenfield, New Jersey 07621

Please send me the books I have checked above.
I am enclosing $_____ (please add $2.00 to cover postage and handling). Send check or money order (no cash or C.O.D.'s) or charge by Mastercard or VISA (with a $15.00 minimum). Prices and numbers are subject to change without notice.

Card #_____ Exp. Date _____
Signature_____
Name_____
Address_____
City _____ State _____ Zip Code _____

For faster service when ordering by credit card call **1-800-253-6476**

Allow a minimum of 4-6 weeks for delivery. This offer is subject to change without notice.

Ⓢ SIGNET   Ⓞ ONYX

THE BEST IN
MEDICAL THRILLERS

☐ **A CASE OF NEED by Michael Crichton, writing as Jeffery Hudson.** *New York Times* **Bestseller!** Only one doctor is willing to push his way through the mysterious maze of hidden medical data and shocking secrets to learn the truth about a young woman's death. This explosive medical thriller by the bestselling author of *Disclosure* and *Jurassic Park* is vintage Michael Crichton. **"Superb!"**—*Los Angeles Times* (183665—$6.99)

☐ **DEADLY COMPANY by Jodie Larsen.** A brilliant research scientist, a committed first-grade teacher, and a single father must join forces to save a group of children from the force of evil whose tendrils extend from corporate boardrooms to reap profits at any price . . . and people who will use everything from sex to murder to keep a secret that is worse than death. (407075—$5.99)

☐ **SIDE EFFECTS by Nancy Fisher.** Dr. Kate Martin is happy to join the team marketing the breakthrough drug Genelife which restores youthful looks and vitality with stunning speed. But when Kate suspects that the drug, which she herself is using, has horrifying side effects that obliterate more than the appearance of aging, she hazards her life to find the terrifying truth about this so-called gift of youth. (181301—$4.99)

☐ **VITAL PARTS by Nancy Fisher.** Stunning model Vivienne Laker had it all—fame, fortune, and ideal, super-rich lover, Charles Spencer. But when Charles gives her the medical promise of eternal health and unaging beauty, Vivienne's curiosity plunges her into a spiraling abyss of hideous discovery that places her in deadly jeopardy. (174984—$4.99)

*Prices slightly higher in Canada

Buy them at your local bookstore or use this convenient coupon for ordering.

PENGUIN USA
P.O. Box 999 — Dept. #17109
Bergenfield, New Jersey 07621

Please send me the books I have checked above.
I am enclosing $_____ (please add $2.00 to cover postage and handling). Send check or money order (no cash or C.O.D.'s) or charge by Mastercard or VISA (with a $15.00 minimum). Prices and numbers are subject to change without notice.

Card #_____ Exp. Date _____
Signature_____
Name_____
Address_____
City _____ State _____ Zip Code _____

For faster service when ordering by credit card call **1-800-253-6476**

Allow a minimum of 4-6 weeks for delivery. This offer is subject to change without notice.

Ⓥ SIGNET BOOKS　　　　　　　Ⓑ ONYX　　(0451)

THIS WON'T HURT A BIT . . .

☐ **DEADLY PRACTICE by Leonard S. Goldberg.** An open vein of terror is turning a prestigious city hospital into a dangerous place of secret sex, scandal . . . and serial murder.　　(179455—$4.99)

☐ **THE YEAR OF THE INTERN by Robin Cook.** Young Doctor Peters must make life-or-death decisions, assist contemptuous surgeons, cope with worried relatives, and pretend at all times to be what he has not yet become. This is the shocking and compelling novel about what happens to a young intern as he goes through the year that promises to make him into a doctor, and threatens to destroy him as a human being.　　(165551—$5.99)

☐ **DEADLY MEDICINE by Leonard S. Goldberg.** Their throats bore the teeth marks of the kiss of death bestowed before their lives were taken. But this depraved horror gave no hint of the evil that the beautiful forensic pathologist and the police detective would uncover in the labyrinth of unscrupulous medical ambition and raging human desire in a prestigious Los Angeles hospital.

(174399—$5.99)

Prices slightly higher in Canada　　　　　　　**F119X**

Buy them at your local bookstore or use this convenient coupon for ordering.

PENGUIN USA
P.O. Box 999 — Dept. #17109
Bergenfield, New Jersey 07621

Please send me the books I have checked above.
I am enclosing $_____ (please add $2.00 to cover postage and handling). Send check or money order (no cash or C.O.D.'s) or charge by Mastercard or VISA (with a $15.00 minimum). Prices and numbers are subject to change without notice.

Card #_____ Exp. Date _____
Signature_____
Name_____
Address_____
City _____ State _____ Zip Code _____

For faster service when ordering by credit card call **1-800-253-6476**

Allow a minimum of 4-6 weeks for delivery. This offer is subject to change without notice.

Ⓓ SIGNET   Ⓔ ONYX

MEDICAL MALEVOLENCE

☐ **DEADLY DIAGNOSIS by Martha Stearn.** Beautiful and brilliant Dr. Katherine Crane is a top investigator at the federal center for Disease Control in Atlanta. But now she is on a trail of terror that goes far beyond the medical textbooks.   (184289—$4.99)

☐ **CRITICAL CONDITION by Martha Stearn.** A giant hospital becomes a deadly arena for unspeakable medical evil, when staff members and patients suddenly come down with the same deadly disease. Will Drs. Dale Harper and Nina Yablonsky be able to uncover the horror?   (175859—$4.99)

☐ **DANGEROUS PRACTICES by Francis Roe.** Doctors and lawyers—in a scorching novel of passion and power, where their medical secrets and legal manipulations will keep you turning pages until its last shocking revelations.   (177908—$5.99)

*Prices slightly higher in Canada

Buy them at your local bookstore or use this convenient coupon for ordering.

PENGUIN USA
P.O. Box 999 — Dept. #17109
Bergenfield, New Jersey 07621

Please send me the books I have checked above.
I am enclosing $_____ (please add $2.00 to cover postage and handling). Send check or money order (no cash or C.O.D.'s) or charge by Mastercard or VISA (with a $15.00 minimum). Prices and numbers are subject to change without notice.

Card #_____ Exp. Date _____
Signature_____
Name_____
Address_____
City _____ State _____ Zip Code _____

For faster service when ordering by credit card call **1-800-253-6476**

Allow a minimum of 4-6 weeks for delivery. This offer is subject to change without notice.